The Red Days is immersive ... It has it all—thriller, love story, adventure, and Sci-Fi.

— MAGGIE GARRED

The Red Days valued integrity, honesty, and intelligence over the flashy and superficial.

— JEFF DUFFEY

Ascalon is an expert at weaving a timeless tale into a contemporary setting.

— CHRISTINE TORRE

Beautifully written. Engaging. ...left me pondering about the events and characters long after I finished reading it.

— VICKI EITEL

What a great read! It has familiar Sci-Fi elements, but with a plot that's fresh and intriguing.

— KAITY BOWERS

The Red Days is *The Hunger Games* plus aliens in an exciting mashup that keeps the reader guessing who the true villain is.

— JON COPSEY

Ascalon uses descriptive dialogue and well-developed characters to pull you into the story. This would make a fantastic movie-- think *Avatar* meets *The Notebook!*

— COLLEEN KLABON

This well-written debut novel by a brilliant young author, ... I highly recommend *The Red Days* for lovers of fantasy fiction who want more than fluff in their storyline.

— JANET MILLS

It's definitely a fresh storyline. Just the right balance of action, adventure and romance. Nothing cheesy. I am currently reading it a second time.

— ANNE TEAGARDEN

...a wonderfully diverse set of characters and plot lines.

— ROBERT LOVERIN

Ascalon has written an entertaining story featuring an endearing heroine and a motley crew of interesting characters.

— LACY BOWCOCK

What a wonderful surprise! I'm not normally a reader of dystopian novels, but this one pulled me in from page one.

— SUSAN FREEBURY

THE RED DAYS

Will Aliens Rule Us?

KATHERINE ASCALON

Publish Authority

The Red Days: Will Aliens Rule Us
KatherineAscalon.com

Cover design lead: Raeghan Rebstock
Editor: Janet Silburn

ISBN 978-1-954000-81-0 (Paperback)
ISBN 978-1-954000-82-7 (eBook)

First edition published 2021 by Kathryn Wyvern
Second edition published 2024 by Publish Authority,
300 Colonial Center Parkway, Suite 100
Roswell, GA USA
PublishAuthority.com

Printed in the United States of America

For my parents, without whom this book
would be merely a twinkle in the eye.

Many thanks to my soul-sister Brittany, who believed in me.

And to Him be the honor and glory
and praise forever and ever, amen.

For if you remain silent at this time, relief and deliverance for the Jews will arise from another place, but you and your father's family will perish. And who knows but that you have come to your royal position for such a time as this?

— ESTHER 4:14

CHAPTER ONE

First, the world turned upside down, and now her life. Callista blinked and almost let the letter slip from her hand, clutching it at the last moment. Was this a prank? She glanced around the PO box alcove and down the hall, making sure no one filmed her with their cell phone for a good laugh. But no one was there. Silence reigned, the only movement coming from the dust motes wafting through the drafts, catching a glint from the skylights. She read the letter from the beginning again, paying closer attention.

Miss Callista Tristan,

You are selected to be interviewed by Admiral Negev Xornalden, Supreme Commander of the Alamgirian fleet and ruler de facto of the planet Earth, as he searches for a suitable wife. Your travel expenses to New York City on the third of September are paid for, and appropriate clothing and adornments for your interview provided. Your plane ticket and directions to the hotel where you will stay are enclosed.

Safe travels,

Lieutenant Pat-farfth

Callista snorted, snapped the PO box door closed, locked it with a twist, jerked the key out, and stormed to the door with the rest of the mail clutched in her hand. Outside, she stopped short when a falling leaf nearly hit her in the face. She glanced up at the tree, its orange leaves waving gently in the cool breeze. The same tree dropped leaves on her every fall. It watched her come, her hand small in her father's, and watched her walk out again years later, sorting through condolence notes. It would probably watch her grow gray hair, too. She took a deep, controlled breath and gazed at her truck and her mom inside it.

Mom insisted on going with her on errands, even though she never got out of the truck. Callista once begged Mom to come with her, to get her out of the house for a while, but the truck was as far as she'd go, and the pointlessness of the concession now annoyed Callista more than anything. All Mom ever did was sit and knit, which she did now, refusing to see and acknowledge the outside world unless it was presented to her by her favorite news anchor.

"Anything interesting?" Mom asked without a glance as Callista slid into the driver's seat. Callista stared down at the letter in her hand, pursing her lips as she fingered the smooth texture of the paper before handing Mom the rest of the mail. Mom took the stack and flipped through the letters, tearing open some to glance at their contents as Callista started the engine and drove out of the parking lot.

"I'm going to New York," Callista said once they were out of town.

"What?"

"I'm going to New York."

Mom snorted. "Sure you are."

"I really am, Mom. Day after tomorrow."

"Yeah? Who's taking you? Boyfriend I don't know about?" Mom laughed.

"I'm going to see the Supreme Commander."

Mom looked at her, the smile gone from her face. "Why are you messing with me?"

"I'm not." Callista tossed the letter on Mom's knitting without taking her eyes off the road. "I've been summoned to meet him. It's the same wife-finding thing they talk about on the news. But they're paying for my flight and everything, so I'm going. I'm not passing up a free trip to New York." She flexed her fingers on the steering wheel, her initial disgust fading at the idea of getting out of town for a few days, even if she did have to suffer the company of their conquerors for a few hours.

Mom's face whitened, and she clutched her knitting needles, eyes glued to the letter in her lap without touching it. "This is my fault, isn't it?"

"No, it's not your fault—"

"It is because after your father ... passed ... , I needed you home, and all your friends moved away, and you never meet anybody to go out with because there's only old people at my church, and you have to stay and make sure I take my pills, and now you're running off with one of those, those heathens and I'll never see you again, and you'll finally come home one day to find my mummy with a half-done scarf and months of my shows unwatched on the DVR."

"Don't be ridiculous," Callista said, fighting to remain both calm and respectful. "You're not sick. Even if you miss a few days of your pills, it won't kill you."

"But what if I take two or three on the same day? Won't that kill me? You don't know what it was like, walking in to find my husband ... ," Mom choked on a sob and grasped at her T-shirt.

Callista sighed as she stopped at a stop light. She reached down and handed a water bottle to her mother, who took three gulps before carefully screwing the lid on and wiping her eyes gingerly, even though they were dry.

"I have no choice, Mom," Callista said softly. "It wasn't a request."

"You're not going," Mom said, her voice both firm and

wavering with emotion. "The sheriff missed *the* pistol when they came to confiscate your father's guns after the conquest."

"You know I'm a pacifist," Callista said. The light changed, and they continued on their way. "Besides, if you killed one of them when they came for me, we'd get put in prison or worse. All he wants is to meet me." She reached over to take Mom's hand without looking. "He might even find one he likes before he gets to me."

"That program has been going on for months," Mom pointed out, picking up the letter for a moment before dropping it again.

"Yes. And what happened to those girls he didn't pick, hmm? Nothing. I'll be fine, Mom."

Mom's hand tightened in Callista's, her tone at once frantic and defensive. "Have you talked to any of them? How do you know?"

Callista furrowed her brows. "I have to go."

"You're not thinking!" Mom grabbed Callista's arm. The wheel jerked, and Callista slammed on the brakes as they swerved into the tall grass, which *thwapped* against the truck. Mom gasped and let go, sitting ramrod straight with her hands tucked under herself as if the near accident wasn't her fault, and they came to a stop three feet from a sign warning of an impending curve.

Callista bit back a word only her father was supposed to use and took deep, controlled breaths to keep from yelling at her mother.

"I'm tired of the same old scenery, Mom. And it's only for a few days."

"Just because you're tired of the same old trees and buildings, you're dashing off to crime-ridden New York, of all places, at the drop of a hat? Why don't we go into town instead, maybe for a bite to eat? Don't you think New York is too far away?"

Callista sighed. "I'll be fine. I'm a big girl. I can take care of myself. Nothing's going to happen. I'll text you and send you some pictures if I get the chance to tour." She cranked the wheel and guided the truck back onto the road, proceeding at a much slower pace than before.

"I've said it before," Mom whispered after a few minutes. "You can't leave me. You watch. With my luck, as soon as you leave, something will happen."

"What, you'll blow your brains out like Dad?" Callista snapped and regretted it, guilt twisting her gut. "Why don't you call some of your church friends and ask them to come spend the day with you while I'm gone?" she blurted.

"I couldn't intrude like that."

"What are friends for, then?"

"Casseroles," Mom said. "When your husband's died."

Callista spared a glance at Mom. "I'm not going to die, not for a good long time."

"How can you know? Don't you know what kind of people live in big cities? Besides, airplanes are dangerous."

"And cars aren't?" Callista asked, sending Mom a sidelong glance.

"And who knows what those aliens will do? They don't have the same moral code as us."

"None of the other girls were hurt in any way," Callista said.

"The news doesn't always know everything," Mom said. "Besides, even if nothing's happened yet, that doesn't mean it won't. With all those girls in one place, there has to be some temptation. Some of them probably never came home, but you don't know about it because it's under wraps."

"Let go."

Mom stared over at Callista in confusion. "Of what?" she asked, holding up her empty hands.

"Of me. You need to let me go, Mom."

Mom pursed her lips and gazed out the window, staring glassy-eyed at the passing trees and occasional pasture. "I let your father go," she finally said when they turned into their long driveway.

"I'm not going to war," Callista said and pulled up under the carport. She turned the engine off and sat looking at Mom, who didn't meet her eyes.

"Your father wouldn't want you to... to bow to their whims. They've taken everything."

"They just took our guns," Callista said.

"And our liberty!" Mom said, finally looking at her daughter with anger in her eyes. "They are the government now. I went to sleep a free American and woke up the next morning to find America didn't exist anymore."

"I'm not arguing politics with you." Callista opened the door and stepped out. "The bottom line is I'm going, whether you like it or not. I have to—not for them, but for me. I'm tired of this old town and this old truck and this old house that smells of sorrow and depression. Dad made the choice he did because he felt trapped and couldn't take it anymore."

Mom burst into tears. "It, it's all my fault, that's what you're saying. It's my fault he's dead."

Callista sighed and looked up to heaven. "No, Mom, it's not your fault. You did everything you could for him. We both did. Nobody's at fault, okay? I just need to do this. To breathe different air, see different sights, and meet different people. Can't you see that? Let me take this chance to see a piece of the world beyond the front porch."

Mom dug her fingers through the yarn in her lap, glancing at the letter frequently and taking deep breaths.

"I promise I'll come back," Callista said.

"Call me."

"As much as I can."

Mom nodded then, a short, jerking movement, and that was all Callista needed to have peace.

"Fine," Callista said then. "I'm going to go ahead and start packing."

"But you're not leaving for another day," Mom snatched the letter and skimmed it again.

"I know, but it'll give me more time to remember what I

forgot." Callista grabbed the grocery bags out of the truck bed and skipped to the front door. A thrill filled her. Not only would she see New York City, which few people in her town could say, but she'd also get to see an Alamgirian up close and the Supreme Commander. No one in her town could boast that.

But another emotion came close on its heels—worry. Callista worried that maybe her mother was right and something would happen. She snorted to herself and shook her head. Nothing would happen.

Nothing would go wrong.

CHAPTER TWO

After Mom became immersed in *Jeopardy* that night, Callista quietly called the airline and asked if she could get an earlier flight. When she explained how she got the ticket, or rather who it came from, they were eager to comply, and she switched it for a red-eye that night. She feared Mom might try something drastic if given more time to stew on the matter. Or cause Callista to go mad with her nagging and guilting. But that didn't stop her from feeling guilty about going that night and leaving nothing but a note behind.

As she waited for her taxi, she searched the internet, looking for reports on the previous girls who had met the Supreme Commander. Most of the girls she could find posted on social media about the copious number of dresses and jewelry at their disposal and the fact that they were allowed to keep what they wore but said little of the Supreme Commander. One girl said she thought he was handsome. Another, that he was boring. A third said he wanted to play some game with her she didn't know, and the conversation was super awkward and stilted after that, and she did most of the talking. Callista sighed. Didn't sound so bad. She had told her mother right after all.

She slipped into Dad's study. They hadn't touched anything

since his passing, much less been in there, and a thick layer of dust lay over everything. She should have at least kept it clean. But she didn't have time now. The taxi would be there any minute, and she searched for one specific thing.

She rummaged through the drawers of the desk, brushing away pens, pencils, coins, recipes, to-do lists, and the occasional button before she found what she hunted for—her grandmother's rosary. She pulled it out of the pile with a sigh, holding it up to the dim moonlight from the window, the black beads absorbing the available light. Her grandmother had given it to her father when it became apparent he was having a hard time since returning home. She said it'd give his hands something to do and his mind something else to ruminate on. He'd worry the beads between his fingers for hours. Even though Callista kept telling herself she wanted this trip, she needed something comforting, too. She dropped it in her pocket as headlights swept the forest out the window and pushed all concern for her mother from her mind.

A few hours later, she stood in line at the airport to go through security, looking on Facebook for one of the women who was part of the last round of interviews, when the hubbub of voices around her suddenly became muted. She glanced up and around, and her breath caught when she spotted them.

Alamgirians. Two of them. Their eyes, bright red and violet, respectively, appeared to glow in the bright fluorescent light. They strolled by the queue, searching the faces of the people in line. The aliens wore black uniforms with vertical insignia badges running down their right breasts and tall black boots that shone to perfection. Callista couldn't help but run her gaze over the aliens, looking for any physical differences from humans, but the only ones she could easily spot were superficial. One had dark blue skin and scarlet eyes, while the other had a deep turquoise complexion and violet eyes. It was those eyes that hushed the crowd and caused feet to shuffle and shoulders to hunch.

She began to wonder if they were looking for her. Should she step under the stanchions and go talk to them? From the corner of her eye, she watched them with her head bowed, heart pounding.

They strolled casually a few rows over, gaze darting back and forth. One of the Alamgirians—or Alamies as the humans came to call them for simplicity—paused and touched his comrade's arm, and they both strode down the edge of the queue before ducking under several stanchions to wade deep into the snaking line. They weren't coming toward her. She let out her breath. They stopped, and each took hold of a man in a long, khaki trench coat and walked to the back of the line with him before leading the man away from the security checkpoint, each holding one of his arms. The man glanced back and forth between them, asking in a high voice what was going on, where were they taking him, what were they going to do.

Callista wanted to laugh at herself and dismiss the whole incident, but her tense shoulders wouldn't relax. After that display, she half expected to see a few more presiding over the security check, but she didn't see another one, even though she kept her eyes open.

A businessman sat next to her as she waited to board the plane.

"Man, did you see that? How those Alamies hauled that guy off?"

"Yes, I did," Callista said, taking in his suit and briefcase. "Does that happen often?"

"I've only seen it happen once before, but some people I know have seen it too. One said the guy they were taking into custody punched one of them in the face and ran away, but they didn't run after him. They walked calmly like they knew no matter how fast he ran or where he went, he wouldn't get away." The man shivered. "Creepy Martians, aren't they?"

Callista blinked. "Wait, they're from Mars?"

The man barked a laugh. "No, they came out of some wormhole or something."

"Oh," Callista said, feeling foolish. She remembered that from the news stories now.

"They came knocking, supposedly just wanting to colonize, then the shooting started, and now they're our overlords," the man said, heaving a sigh. "But I can't complain much. Business is good." With that, he took out his phone and paid her no more attention.

Callista gazed around at the other people in the waiting area. Now that she looked, no one seemed changed by the aliens' invasion. There were smiles and laughter. Some people slumped in their seats, trying to catch a few minutes of sleep. Others stared at their phones, oblivious to what was happening around them. She guessed it wasn't just her remote town that remained largely unaffected by the extraterrestrial takeover.

Touching down in New York City two hours later, she understood why it was called a concrete jungle. The glow from the sun, not yet peeking over the horizon, backlit the skyscrapers and cast a pale haze over the city, still producing its own light. Unlike her hometown, there was rarely a tree in sight except for the swath of Central Park, and the gray tones did nothing to lighten her mood. The crush of people and the labyrinth of the city that lay beyond made her almost wish someone, no matter what planet they hailed from, would meet her to take her where she needed to go. She took a deep breath and told herself she could do this; it wasn't that hard, and she would probably prefer this way regardless.

While Callista waited for her luggage, she noticed Mom had called seven times and sent her a dozen anxious texts. Rather than calling her back and listening to the angry rant, she sent an explanatory text:

> I know you're worried, but I came a day early so I can see more and I don't want to be rushed finding where I'm supposed to be. I did some research, and the girls who met him said it was no big deal. Please don't be too mad at me or do anything drastic. I love you. I'll be home soon.

Mom would probably cry when she read it. Fat, ugly tears that dribbled into her knitting. Maybe she'd throw the wad of yarn across the room in anger; maybe she wouldn't.

With a deep breath, Callista shoved down anxiety for her mom. One thing at a time—first, find the hotel. Second, find out where she needed to be and when. Third, get the interview over with, go home, and squeeze in some touring if she could. Simple. Nothing to worry about. Nothing was going to happen.

A TV over the baggage carousel showed the news: a group of people protesting the Alamy regime. The camera panned to take in the Alamy guards, who watched the humans with unwavering indifference that sent a chill through her stomach. It gratified her some people weren't taking their new masters' whims lying down, but she also feared what those masters might do if they became too annoyed. She quickly retrieved her bag and hurried out.

The cabby knew which hotel she needed, took her there promptly, and gave her a warm thanks when she tipped him generously. And why not? The Alamies were paying. Inside the hotel lobby, the receptionist was talking with an Alamy, who wore a rumpled black uniform and a matching wrinkled cap. The Alamy finished the conversation with a nod of his head and turned toward her. His soft violet eyes swept over her as he started to pass, and he stopped short and looked again.

"You are early," he said.

Callista stiffened. "I needed to escape before my mom found a chain to secure me to my bed with," she said.

The corner of his mouth twitched up in a smile for a moment before it turned down.

"I'm exaggerating," she said.

"Oh, I am glad."

"But I did come early because I didn't want to suffer the guilting and the demanding I not go."

"Ah, good. We do not desire to cause a family rift. Especially over this." He smiled at her, creating more lines on his elderly face, and took the handle of her suitcase. "Come, let us go to your room."

The man at the desk had her card ready when they walked up. He explained that if she showed it to the server at the restaurant within the hotel, she would eat on the house. The Alamy escorted her to her room, explaining on the way she could do as she pleased since she was early, and there would be an orientation that evening after everyone arrived.

After a nap, Callista was eating lunch in the hotel dining room when she met the same Alamy. He eased down into the chair next to her. Callista's spine straightened, her grip tightening on her fork. He took a moment to relax before speaking.

"Explain to me why your mother was so upset."

She searched his violet eyes for signs of danger but found only curiosity. She shrugged in response to his question. "I'm her only child. She worries about what will happen to me. The letter summoning me was brief." She casually dabbed at the corner of her mouth.

"Ah, forgive me; I speak better than I write. I am Lieutenant Pat-farfth," he said, holding out his hand.

"You seem to already know who I am," she said, quickly wiping her sweaty palm on the napkin in her lap before shaking his hand.

"Yes, I had a good feeling about you when I reviewed who was summoned this time."

She glanced around, but no one seemed to be paying them much attention. A glance here and there, but no one appeared to think anything of an alien in the hotel dining room.

"How are people chosen?" she said, asking the question that haunted her.

"A computer algorithm first, then I go through the suggestions and pick." He leaned back in his chair. "We try to get people from all over—a good variety—though I am afraid I myself may be a bit ... invested? Ah, 'biased,' yes."

"That is inevitable," she said, sipping her water. Her mouth was dry.

"Perhaps, but not unavoidable."

"What happens after the first interview?" she asked, worrying her cloth napkin in between her fingers.

He chuckled. "No one has been invited to stay after the first interview, so I cannot say since we have not addressed it yet. I fear my nephew does not, how do you say, have his heart in it."

It took her a moment to connect the dots. "Wait, your nephew is Admiral Negev Xor-nalden? The Supreme Commander?"

"Yes," he said, pausing to thank the waiter who filled his glass with water. "He gave me the honor of making me his personal aide when he first became a captain. I have been with him ever since. We are the only family we have left."

"No one else came with you to colonize?" Callista asked.

"We colonized out of necessity," Pat-farfth said, a slight frown tugging at his mouth. "Our fleet was on maneuvers at the edge of the solar system when our sun unexpectedly collapsed and became a supernova. We were lucky any of us escaped." He gazed out the window. "It is hard to lose everything so suddenly."

"My father took his own life. I know what it's like to lose family unexpectedly, but I have no idea what it's like to lose everything you've known at once," she said, trying to find some commonality.

"Ah, perhaps you are familiar with the ... the numbing. The moving through the motions without thinking, perhaps?"

"Yes, we too experience that, in loss," she said, taking a sip of her water. A bus pulled up in front of the hotel's main doors and released several women, who caught Pat-farfth's attention.

"Ah, I must go settle the others," he said, standing. "You are all on the same hall if you ever wish to speak to them," he said, sliding his chair back in.

"Thank you," she said, relieved he was departing. "Nice talking to you."

"And to you. Until we meet again." He inclined his head to her before shuffling over to the lobby.

She took a deep breath but continued to stare after him as he greeted the new arrivals. One woman had long blond hair, perfectly curled, and sported a short mini skirt and six-inch heels. Another girl wore a frumpy sweatshirt and pulled along a stained suitcase. A third huddled in her hijab and gazed about with wide eyes. Callista couldn't get a good look at the others.

She sighed and turned toward her meal, and she started to relax. She wasn't sure if she would be able to stomach food in the future—anxiety made her nauseous—and she guessed things would only get more uncomfortable from there.

After she finished eating, she did the quintessential tourist thing and went to see the Statue of Liberty. Hunched in her coat against the chilly September breeze that played with her hair, she gazed at the folds of the monument's clothes and the ornateness of its torch. She took a picture of herself with the statue in the background to send to her mother. As she paused to look at the photo, she could tell her smile was a bit forced. As much as she kept telling herself everything was fine, she didn't feel it in her heart. Even though Pat-farfth was nice enough, it didn't seem real or natural that she talked to an extraterrestrial. Maybe it was just their presence causing her unease. She didn't believe in women's intuition, so it must be nervousness making her heart pound and her stomach queasy whenever she thought about meeting the Supreme Commander. Everything would be fine.

CHAPTER THREE

The next day, Callista found a note under her door telling her to be in the hotel's ballroom by 10:00 a.m. for a briefing. She breakfasted with the other girls, around twenty in total, sitting stiffly alone or with their heads bent together, getting to know each other. She sat at a two-person table with the woman in the hijab she saw the day before.

"English," the woman said, holding up her thumb and forefinger to indicate a small amount.

Callista smiled and nodded and pointed to herself, saying her name before pointing to the other woman.

"Enaya," she answered, adding, "Palestine."

Callista raised her eyebrows and nodded.

Enaya's gaze wandered about the room. She filled her cheeks with air before letting it out with a huff. Callista noted the worry and loneliness in her eyes.

Callista laid a hand on Enaya's and decided to risk offending her, thinking the language barrier warranted the risk. "*Shalom.*" She put as much earnestness behind the word as she could.

Enaya smiled. "*Inshallah,*" she said, raising her eyes to heaven for a moment before looking back at Callista and giving her a sad smile. Callista nodded and repeated the phrase before turning her attention to her meal.

"I contacted one of the girls who was interviewed the last time around," Callista overheard a girl with springy, curly hair confiding to the rest of her table. "She said he just talked to her, though he offered to play some board game with her, but she didn't know how and was too nervous to let him teach her. She said she couldn't remember much of the details because she was so star-stunned."

Callista turned to ask more, but the girls moved on to wondering what the Supreme Commander looked like up close. As she listened, she realized she didn't have a firm idea of his appearance herself since she only saw him once briefly on TV, and the podium stood far away from the camera, obscuring his features. She wouldn't recognize him if he walked into the room at that moment.

They soon filtered into the ballroom and found it filled with tables and clothing racks of accessories and dresses. Some of the girls squealed in delight and ran to start looking through the satin gowns. Callista's gaze swept over the table littered with glittering jewelry and on to another of hair pieces as she absentmindedly followed Enaya to a table filled with scarves that she fingered appreciatively.

"Welcome, everyone," Pat-farfth's voice floated over the babble, causing a hush as heads turned toward him. He stood at the door with a young Alamgirian officer next to him who looked like he put too much starch in his uniform. "As you may have guessed, this is for you," he said, opening his arms to encompass the contents of the room. "Take what you would like to wear, and you may keep it as compensation for your time. Interviews will begin tomorrow morning at the same time as this. Please be back in this room dressed and ready."

Some of the girls squealed to each other and snatched some dresses off the hangers the moment he finished, dashing to the makeshift changing booths set against one wall while others calmly continued to peruse the racks. Callista noted one dark-toned woman, her frizzy black hair cut close to her head, who glanced out of the corner of her eye at Pat-farfth and the other officer more than the dresses. Callista followed her gaze. The young officer handed out pieces of paper to some of the women, who still seemed bewildered. He wove his way over to Enaya, and Callista spotted the flowing cursive of Arabic on the paper he handed her. She glanced at Enaya, whose face sagged with relief. Callista realized it must be a copy of the instructions Pat-farfth gave them orally. Enaya carefully folded the paper and stuck it in a pocket before turning to Callista with a strained smile. She snatched up a scarf, wrapped it around her head, and gave Callista a grin. Callista nodded in approval.

They moved to the dresses and began flipping through them once they found their sizes. Callista was staring long and hard at a green dress when Enaya said her name. She turned and found her holding up an orange-red dress with a sweetheart neckline for her to see. Callista nodded in approval and turned back to her contemplation.

"La la la!" Enaya said, taking Callista's arm and turning her before holding the dress up to Callista.

"For me?" Callista asked, placing a hand on her chest.

"You, you," Enaya said and shooed Callista off to the dressing stalls where girls were already admiring themselves in front of the mirrors placed in between the rooms.

Callista took a moment as she changed to remind herself everything would be fine when anxiety started to bubble up again. She wouldn't be chosen. She passed the woman with the long blond hair who had the figure of a supermodel whom she had glimpsed the day before. The woman seemed to know it—the way she posed in front of the mirror in her new dress and assessed how it accentuated and revealed—all her curves told Callista the woman knew her business.

But no matter what she told herself, her heart still thumped firmly in her chest as if it were running a marathon, and the butterflies in her stomach would unexpectedly take flight now and again despite her attempts to keep them calm.

She emerged to find Enaya coming toward her with a deep blue dress draped over her arm. She gasped when she beheld Callista and nodded her head energetically. Callista smiled and turned toward the mirror, sucking in a little breath of her own. She hadn't been much for red in general, but the orange-red hue of the dress didn't make her pale skin tone stand out too much and seemed to bring out the subtle red hues in her brown hair.

The girl she eavesdropped on earlier bounced up next to her, wearing a pink frilly dress.

"Looks like you found the one; you look great," the spunky girl said. "Simple but profound." She bounced off to her friends before Callista could reply.

"You do look good," said the dark-toned woman who had been studying the Alamies earlier. She admired herself in a mirror adjacent to Callista, wearing a glimmering black dress.

"So do you," Callista said, glancing at herself again.

"I wish it was a little less mermaid." The woman ran her hands over her hips and thighs where the fabric fit snugly before loosening up to cascade to the floor. "I don't like my movement constricted."

"Well, hopefully, we won't have to do any dancing," Callista said.

"Or running," the woman added, smoothing her frizzy black hair, and turning from the mirror. "I guess this will have to do."

Callista waited while Enaya tried on the blue dress and a yellow one before settling on the blue, and then they followed the migration over to the jewelry table. The Super Model tossed the jewelry around as if she were picking through fruit while the girl who had the stained suitcase stared at a diamond pendant in awe.

"Pick something already, and let us have a turn," Spunky said, her pink frilly dress bouncing as she tried to see over the tall woman's shoulder.

Super Model finally took the necklace with the most jewels on it and the long earrings to match before trying them on in front of the mirror, ignoring her.

Callista's gaze swept over the table once, but she didn't want anything. She was not one for jewelry. She was standing to the side to give the others space as she waited on Enaya when Pat-farfth startled her by touching her arm.

"You do not desire any jewelry?" he asked, his eyes crinkling in a smile.

"It's all a little too flashy for me," she said.

"You like simple," he said, to which she nodded.

"Callista!" Enaya called. Callista turned her attention to see her holding up a ball gilded in diamonds with a fine tassel of tiny chain links extending from the bottom. Callista nodded in approval of her choice when Pat-farfth touched her arm again.

"Wear this," he said, holding out a white gold ring with a simple design etched into it.

"That's all right, I don't need anything," she said.

"Please, take it. Wear it tomorrow."

Mischief glinted in his eye, though she couldn't be sure— perhaps it was only the way the light played on his violet eyes. She sighed and took the ring. "All right, I'll wear it." She slipped it on her right hand.

Pat-farfth nodded. "Good. If you are not invited to stay, return it to me," he said before walking off with his hands clasped behind his back, seemingly pleased with himself.

Callista glanced around the room and felt like she was at a prom, but there were no nervous teenage boys fiddling with their ties or trying to act suave to impress the ladies, just plenty of preening girls, though the woman she spoke to earlier in the black dress stood off to the side, scowling at the group.

She slipped over to one of the mirrors and took a picture of herself, and sent it to Mom. She wasn't sure if it would cause her more or less anxiety—more to see how she was dressed and wonder what would become of her, or less to see her daughter was well. As she expected, she received a flood of texts with questions. She calmly texted.

Callista: We were given the dresses for our interview the next day.

Mom: What kind of interview requires a woman to dress like she's going to a prom?

All she could come up with was that people wore their best when they visited royalty elsewhere, so why would it be different here, but the question lingered. What kind of "interview," indeed.

CHAPTER FOUR

The next day, the ballroom was empty except for a few chairs along the walls. Callista waited to the side with Enaya while most of the girls huddled in the center in their colorful gowns, twittering to each other nervously like anxious tropical birds.

She glanced over at the pair of armed Alamgirian guards standing next to the double doors which, presumably, led to where the interviews would be held. During her conversations the previous day with Pat-farfth, she observed the coloring of the Alamgirian eyes close-up. Around the iris, the eye was all one color, while the pupil was only a few shades darker. From a distance, it looked like the eye was a single color, giving her the creeps. She couldn't be sure if they were directly looking at her or not unless she stared hard. She couldn't be sure, but they seemed to even glow a bit, making it feel like they could see through her.

One of the guards kept his violet stare on the larger group of women while the guard with scarlet eyes gazed about the room, his glance sweeping over them, her, and the various entrances to the ballroom. She wasn't sure which disturbed her more—the guard who glanced over at her frequently or the one who stared at the group, his hands rubbing his pants nervously from time to time.

Enaya must have felt the goose flesh because she commented and began to rub Callista's arms energetically. Callista wasn't sure if her chill was from nervousness or because she was wearing a sleeveless dress in the fall. She contemplated taking her hair out of its bun for the warmth it would provide over her shoulders but thought better of it. She'd spent too long fighting the comb to hold it in place.

The doors at the end of the room opened with an audible click, and a hush quickly fell over the group. Pat-farfth shuffled through the door and graced them with a gentle smile. His violet eyes twinkled as he surveyed the room of twenty women before he hobbled forward. The officer with too much starch in his uniform trailed behind, looking bored.

"Who wishes to go first?" Pat-farfth asked.

An uncomfortable shuffle among the girls was the immediate response.

"I will," a confident voice cascaded over the crowd.

All eyes turned to Super Model, who strode forward in a dress as short as it could go on the top and bottom. She tossed some of her blond curls over her shoulder and flexed her red talons as if scenting her quarry. Callista smiled grimly, hoping Super Model would be chosen and the rest of them could go home, although she heard some of the other women whispering, wondering if Alamies had only one spouse at a time or multiple.

Enaya spotted someone in the crowd she seemed to know and joined her, leaving Callista alone.

Pat-farfth walked among the flock of women, pausing to chat and make pleasantries here and there, which were politely returned, and eventually made his way over to her.

"How do you do?" he inquired in his well-practiced phrase.

"I am well, you?" Callista replied, going through the motions.

"Oh yes," he answered, making her uncomfortable at the

unusual answer, and he turned to stand next to her and gaze with her upon the crowd. "Why do you stand alone?" he asked.

"The crowd and noise do not appeal to me," she answered.

He nodded in understanding. "Are you afraid?" he asked after a few minutes.

"Nervous, more. I dislike the idea of being under scrutiny. And, of course, terrified I will be chosen. But that's not likely to happen, is it?" She gave him a strained smile.

He looked back at her, brow furrowed. "You do not fear meeting the Supreme Commander, but you do fear he will choose you. Why?"

"It's the unknown, I suppose. And the fear I'll have to spend the rest of my life with a man I don't care for."

Pat-farfth shook his head. "If you do not like him, you need not stay. We would not force you into such a commitment."

"That's good to know," she said, scratching her chin. "But what if it does work out, but I can't handle being, what, empress? What if I'm an utter failure and embarrassment? You see, there's so much to worry about."

Pat-farfth chuckled and shook his head. "You need not be in the public eye if you do not wish to be. Negev himself tries to stay out of it as much as possible."

"I see what you mean. Only yesterday I realized I couldn't pick him out of a crowd if I had to. I've only seen him briefly on TV once."

Pat-farfth nodded.

"But why should I worry?" she continued. "The chances are slim he will like me in the least, aren't they?"

Pat-farfth shrugged with a smirk and a twinkle in his eye she didn't like.

The doors opened again, and Super Model stomped through, her face red and her sweeping glare practically shooting flames. As the young officer handed off responsibility for her to a guard at a different door who would escort her out, Pat-farfth called out, "Who will go next?"

Spunky bounced forward, her pink frills bobbing, and followed the young officer to the doors of destiny. She spun around to flash a beaming smile and shoot the women a salute before the doors shut her away from view. Her attempt at humor sent a hush over the group. Callista turned to see Pat-farfth staring at her.

"Do you know why I and others instigated this program?" he asked.

"Because there are too few of your own women?"

He smiled. "Partly, yes. But also, we are afraid if he does not start a family soon, he never will. We want him to be happy, not just a good leader. He does not necessarily need a co-leader; he needs family who will accept him for who he is and who will love and cherish him as only family can, even if the public comes to hate him. The loss of our families is deeply felt." He looked away. "I sometimes wonder if it would not be better if we were consumed by the sun with them."

"I'm afraid many of my people would agree with you there," she said grimly. She remembered the riots that occurred when the Alamies took control of the greater governments and left the more local ones in place. The miserable and even apologetic look of the police officers quelling—sometimes with considerable force —the riots of their own people, whom they secretly agreed with, was heartbreaking. It was probably the reason the Alamies kept to the largest cities—they were conquerors keeping to the fortresses, wary of the peasants who outnumbered them.

"Yes. We try to be benevolent and lenient rulers, but your people do not make it easy or what we would like it to be. Although it gratifies me that, on the local level, everyday life has changed little, as we hoped." He looked back over at her. "You are aware, conquest was not our original intention. We simply wanted to co-exist here together on the same planet—we did not have enough resources to go and find another—but your people would not listen and fired upon us. After that, there was nothing to do but fight. Most were beyond reason at that point on both sides."

Callista nodded. "Land is the finite commodity that will always be a source of strife, I fear."

"Indeed."

The doors opened, and Spunky came back through, less energetic than before but with an indifferent look stitched into her face as she passed the group and was escorted out the exit.

"Why do you lead them back through here and not a shorter way out after the interview?" Callista asked.

"So you can see there is nothing to fear, so you will not worry about what has become of them," Pat-farfth replied and stepped forward to call another. A girl with long brown hair stepped forward, raised her hand to signal him she volunteered to go next and was led away by the stiff officer.

"I believe he will like you, Miss Tristan," Pat-farfth said. "But as I said, there is nothing for you to worry about—he will not force you into anything."

He nodded to her and sauntered over to talk to the guard at the door to the street, and the wary woman in the black dress Callista had spoken to briefly the day before slipped up to her as she stood staring idly at the warped reflections in the brass chandeliers.

"What was he talking to you about?" she asked Callista in a low, slightly accusatory tone.

"Random things. Wanted to know why I stood alone, if I was afraid, and he talked about himself and the Admiral a bit."

"Learn anything good?"

Callista stared back into her catlike eyes. "Such as?"

"You know, anything about him or the Admiral we could use to our advantage. Something we haven't heard before."

Callista wondered who "we" included. "Well, they seem to be more than happy to leave local governments as they are. And family is pretty important to them. That Alamy Lieutenant is the Admiral's personal aide and his uncle."

"Really," the woman purred, turning to look at the person of interest predatorily out of the corner of her eye. "I'll have to pass that along."

"To whom?"

"People," the woman said, looking back at Callista with her nose up in the air a bit. "People who aren't happy with the way things are these days."

"Best not tell me anything more," Callista said and looked away. "Knowledge is dangerous."

"Amen to that sister. Amen to that."

The doors opened again about ten minutes later, and the woman in black stepped forward quickly, giving Pat-farfth a wave of acknowledgment before striding through the doors to see her enemy face-to-face. Callista wondered if she would try something drastic but guessed she wouldn't since she had taken the time to gather information.

She had time to essentially commit to memory the patterns on the blue and gold wallpaper, the matching carpet, and the maroon chairs scattered along the wall before the doors finally opened again for the woman in black—much longer than the other three before her. She gave a nod to Callista as she passed to leave. Callista studied her face as long as she could, noting a thoughtful but passive look, and was glad, for her sake, that she had not caused a scene during her interview.

Four more women went in for their interview, some longer than others, and each candidate left with a different expression on her face. The anticipation and dread began to weigh heavily on Callista, and she decided it was better to get her turn over and done with. She moved to a position closer to the doors. Her roving gaze happened to meet Pat-farfth's, who smiled and nodded his acknowledgment that she was next, to which she replied with a matching nod.

When the candidate before her emerged and went her own way, Callista took a deep breath and stepped to the doors to face her fears. The walls were a dark shade of green, and the light was dim, reminding her of a cave. She flexed her fingers, trying not to grip her skirt and wrinkle it. Hopefully, he wouldn't shake her hand—it was coated in sweat. She tried to wipe her palms on her arms awkwardly as she was led down the hall to a side room where the Admiral sat, waiting for her.

CHAPTER FIVE

Callista paused in the doorway, taking in as much as she could at a glance. She found herself in a windowless office with ochre walls and a mass-produced, modern art picture on one wall typical of hotels. There was a desk in the center and a bookcase on one side with a jumble of various binders, nick-nacks and pictures. One picture in particular caught her eye, and she noted the family in the photo were all humans. This was a borrowed office, then. Two goose-neck lamps stood in opposing corners, affording soft light to the room and casting a golden glow over the only occupant in the room and the chess set that gleamed on the desk before him.

Admiral Xor-nalden sat behind the desk, rubbing his temples. He swept a few strands of jet-black hair back into place as he looked up at her. His gaze arrested her fully. She did not realize until that moment his eyes were two different colors: one scarlet red, the other a bright violet. Callista thought the contrast against this royal blue skin tone to be rather stark and wondered how she had never noticed his eyes before.

Xor-nalden rested his elbows on the arms of the office chair and steepled his eight fingers beneath his chin. He allowed her to stare for a moment before gesturing toward the chair opposite him. She uneasily slipped into the chair and glanced down at the chess set. Though she had not seen many in her time, she could tell this one was exquisite, with finely carved black and white marble pieces and the board inlaid with marble as well, bordered by polished wood.

He gestured with a hand toward her side of the board.

"White goes first, so it is your move," he said in a neutral voice.

Anger and indignation filled her, and it was all she could do to maintain a straight face by biting the inside of her lip. He demanded her presence, to drop everything and come at such short notice merely to play chess with him? Was his appetite not satisfied by the other women who came in before her? He didn't even bother asking her what her name was or even introduce himself. Were all Alamgirians so rude? Were humans so beneath him?

An idea came over her at that moment, and without thinking through the possible consequences, she acted on it. She hunched forward and picked at her lower teeth, vacantly staring at the board with dull eyes.

Xor-nalden heaved a strained sigh and asked, "You do not know how to play either, do you?"

She gave him a glassy-eyed stare before nodding her head in silent confession.

As he explained the rules, she allowed herself to even drool a little at the corner of her mouth, get distracted by an itch on her skin, and appear not to listen to him for a moment, though in reality, she studied him.

Rather than the dress uniform she'd seen him wearing on television broadcasts, he wore the black uniform standard for the Alamgirian military. He appeared to be approximately her age, with a strong jawline and a certain amount of softness about the eyes, which were themselves sharp and clear, piercing almost. But he seemed tired—exhausted, even. His shoulders drooped, and he slouched sideways in his chair a bit. She caught him repeating an explanation of one of the pieces, but he didn't seem to notice.

"Do you understand?" he asked once he had gone over everything.

She gave him a bewildered look before both shrugging and nodding in affirmation. He sighed, shooting the Alamy officer lounging by the door a long-suffering look and gestured to her to begin.

She screwed up her face in exaggerated concentration, picking at her teeth for a while before moving the pawn in front of her king up two spaces. She jerked her hand back and reached for the pawn again before snatching her hand away as if she were uncertain of her move and had the urge to change it.

He calmly moved a pawn two spaces to meet hers head-on, and she yawned for a long moment into her hand before seeming to randomly move her bishop to a point where it stood two spaces from her line of pawns and across from his bishop on the same white square.

"Your hair appears to be falling out of its clasp," he said softly.

Her hand flew to her bun, her gaze darting up to find him staring at her. Her hair was indeed starting to fall out. She hurriedly redid it, not caring how it looked this time, so long as it stayed up.

Meanwhile, he moved his knight out from behind the backline toward the bishop she moved, so that it was across from it with only one square separating it. Callista sat forward and gaped.

"Do they all jump? Like checkers?" she asked.

"No, just those, and at the angle, remember? Two spaces in one direction, and then one at a right angle, or one space and two at a right angle. What is checkers?"

"It looks like this, but all the pieces are the same. And not so … complicated," Callista groaned, rubbing her forehead with both hands.

"Life is complicated, is it not?" the Admiral said, leaning the chair back with a creak.

"More people, more mess. Why can't everybody just get

along?" she murmured, staring at the board. It seemed he was going with a common defense using the knights, meaning he'd probably move his other knight out on his next move. Or, if she moved a pawn, he might move another of his pawns to meet it and stop hers in its tracks.

"Everyone has their own interests, and often do not consider others, or how their pursuits will affect others. Differing viewpoints, ideologies, prejudices and approaches also play into the complexity," the Admiral continued.

Callista didn't bother answering. She shivered, goosebumps covering her bare arms. If it got much colder in there, she might be able to see her breath.

"Are you cold?" he asked, making her start and look up. He sat watching her intently, two fingers propping up his cheek as he leaned on the armrest.

"Uh, yes," she replied.

"Would you say you are cold-natured, or would most humans find it unpleasantly cold in here? I have noticed most of the other women before you also seemed a bit discomforted with the temperature after a time."

She blinked at him twice. "Um, it's pretty cold."

"What temperature is pleasant for humans?"

"Uh, seventy-twoish?"

The Admiral furrowed his brows. "Celsius?"

"No—the other one."

The Admiral cocked an eyebrow at her. "The 'other one'?"

"Yeah, the 'F' one."

Now it was the Admiral's turn to blink at her in confusion. He gave a shake of his head and shifted his weight to the other arm rest. "It's your turn."

Callista jerked up straighter a bit and wildly looked around, feigning confusion and the pressure to move quickly. She snatched up the queen and moved it on a diagonal line to the edge of the board, intentionally knocking the piece into the rim encompassing the board before snatching her hand away and burying her hands in her lap.

She saw the corner of his mouth twitch in a smirk for a moment before moving his other knight out as she anticipated, putting her queen in danger. If she didn't move it next turn, he could capture it.

"We come from a planet that was very cold. Thus, our ideal temperature is significantly cooler than what I suspect most humans would be acclimatized to. I have tried to compromise, but perhaps we can adjust further."

Callista wasn't listening. She stared at the board. Her heart pounded in her chest, her eyes racing over the pieces, checking and double-checking. Unless there was some complex rule she was not aware of, he had just made a fatal mistake.

She snatched up the queen and swapped it with the pawn diagonally next to the king, a square protected by her bishop. The king couldn't remove the queen threatening him because of it, nor could any other piece come to its rescue.

"Checkmate," she said and stood up.

He abruptly straightened and leaned forward, eyes flickering over the board, his mouth slightly open in incredulity.

"You may have learned our game of chess," she said, touching the edge of the board, causing the white gold ring on her finger to catch the light and his eye, "but you have not yet learned the finer art of poker."

With that, she stepped through the door before he could react and walked quickly down the hall, with the stiff officer hurrying to catch up with her. She kept her eyes on the floor so she would not look at Pat-farfth and make him suspicious or give him a chance to signal he wanted to talk to her as she walked back through the ballroom.

She hurried out the street door and glanced up and down, gasping for air and space, only to find the claustrophobic street hemmed in by towering buildings that tried to block out the sky from view for as far as the eye could see. The street was fairly quiet, with only a handful of people passing by. A row of yellow taxis waited up and down the street to take the girls wherever they wanted after their interview, with parking meters watching over them like sentries. She spotted the wary woman in black leaning up against one of the taxis down and across the street, talking to the driver. She picked up her skirts and ran on the balls of her feet across and down the street toward her. The woman spotted her coming and straightened up, her black dress rippling.

"What happened?" she called as Callista approached.

"I beat him in four moves," Callista replied, slightly breathless. "And made a sassy comment before I ran."

The woman's eyes widened, and she yanked open the back door of the taxi. "Get in, now." Callista dove in, and the woman immediately followed her. "Jack, get us out of here, fast but casual."

What had she done? She couldn't help but remember the man in the airport being led away by those two Alamies. She envisioned her mother getting a call that her daughter was in jail without bond. She kicked herself for playing the moron and making a fool of the Supreme Commander of the Entire World.

She wrung her hands as they pulled out of the parallel parking space and sped down the street. Both women turned to look behind them. As they were about to turn the corner, they watched two guards burst out of the building and wildly look up and down the street, zeroing in on them. The woman cursed.

"Jack, you'll have to do some fancy driving. It won't be long before they follow us."

Jack swung the taxi through two alleyways and onto a busy main street. They soon hit a stoplight and pulled up next to another taxi of a different company that was green. Jack rolled down the window and waved at the driver.

"Sampson, we have an emergency. Follow me for a sec, will ya, and help a brother and two sisters out?"

An affirmatory reply was given that Callista couldn't make

out, and when the light turned green, Jack maneuvered the taxi into another alley.

"Get ready to jump out and get in the taxi behind us," the woman instructed Callista, gripping the door handle. Callista did the same and tensed for action.

Jack slowed once they were in the middle of the alley, and the woman jumped out of the car. Callista followed suit on the other side and ran to the taxi that pulled up as they moved. Callista jumped in the back as her new friend jumped in the passenger seat next to the driver.

"Head over toward Brooklyn Heights, Joralemon Street," she told him as he started out into the service street and turned in the opposite direction from the car they were in. "You have a jacket or anything she can borrow?"

He pointed toward the woman's feet, and she pulled out a rain jacket stuffed in the floorboard. She handed it back to Callista.

"That red dress of yours is easy to spot—put this over yourself so you won't be so eye-catching."

"Long time no see, sister," Sampson said to the woman. "What you girls running from?" he asked, glancing over at his passenger next to him, the whites of his eyes flashing in his dark-as-night face as he uneasily gripped the steering wheel, no doubt taking in their formal dresses.

"Who do you *think* we're running from dressed like this, man? This girl beat the Admiral at his own game, and I'm getting her the heck out of Dodge."

"How should I know? You coulda been runnin' from some gang boss—I don't know who all you run with these days to get what you want," he said defensively. "You trust her?"

"If she snitches, I'll shoot her." She spun around and said, "Get down low so—" but stopped short when she noted Callista already slumped down so low her shoulder blades almost touched the horizontal part of the seat with the jacket draped over her dress. She turned back around and kept her head on a swivel.

"What's your name, girl?" she asked after they rode in silence for a few minutes.

"Callista Tristan."

"Niki Nain. Nice to make your acquaintance."

"And yours. Thank you so much for helping me."

"I'd help anyone who gives the middle finger to the Alamies."

"It's not just that," Callista said, rubbing her eyes. "I acted the moron when I came in and saw chess was the game, and I let him explain the rules to me even though I knew how to play, so he'd underestimate me. Then I *had* to sass him to his face when I beat him."

"Day-umn, I like you a lot already, girl," Niki said as she continued to look about.

"It was a stupid thing to do," Callista said.

"Nah, girl's gotta do what a girl's gotta do, especially against aliens," Niki said.

On their way to Brooklyn, there were several Alamgirian ships flying overhead like black, shiny vultures searching out their meal, and Callista squeezed her eyes shut every time they passed over and prayed they wouldn't be spotted. They pulled up in front of a townhouse, and Nikki led Callista to the door. Callista gazed up at the red brick and the blackened windows as Niki fished her numerous keys out of her bra and inserted the key into the lock bolted to a massive steel plate in the center of the door. It swung open with a creak, and Niki slipped into the dim passageway with Callista right behind her. The interior was concrete with metal pipes and exposed electrical wiring on the walls. A door marked "Electrical Distribution Room" stood at the other end of the hall. This wasn't a real house at all, but a façade for something else.

"Come on," Niki said after she locked the door. "This will get us into the underground."

"The subways?" Callista asked, hoping the answer wasn't the sewers.

"Yup," Niki said, taking an emergency flashlight from a box on the wall. "Hope you're not afraid of the dark. Or rats."

CHAPTER SIX

Niki and Callista picked their way down the dim, dank tunnels lit every so often by blue lights and tried not to breathe too deeply of the stale air laced with the stench of mold and rat feces. They lifted the hems of their long skirts off the ground and watched their footing, careful not to twist an ankle on the rail ties and loose gravel nor electrocute themselves on the live third rail. Niki kept checking her watch and looking nervously over her shoulder, and when they came to an emergency exit, she ushered Callista through and waited behind the door for a subway to pass before they trekked along the rails again. Callista knew she'd have a number of blisters by the time they arrived, wherever they were going—if they ever got there. They'd walked for miles by now, and high heels were not meant for subway tunnels.

When they arrived at the station Niki searched for, they navigated the motion detectors in the tunnel before emerging into the light. A train had just left, and because it wasn't rush hour, only a few people were on the platform. Most people were on their phones, so they were able to slip onto the platform without anyone noticing. Niki sidled along the wall to a door with a bronze plaque inscribed "Knickerbocker Hotel." She fished out another key and unlocked the door, then put her weight against it to force it open.

They walked through the basement of the hotel until they came to a room housing two machines with pipes that disappeared into the wall. Niki pulled out a pad of paper and a pencil from beneath one of the machines and quickly scratched on it:

SOS KH E-VAC – N.

She snatched the paper off the pad, folded it twice, and stuffed it into a two-foot-long tube. She lifted a hatch on the second machine and laid the cylinder in firmly before closing it and pulling two levers. The machine roared to life, and a needle on a gauge quickly going up caught Callista's eye. When the needle reached the green, Niki pressed a button, and the machine made a sucking sound and a whoosh as the mail tube was sucked down the pipe. It was like the pneumatic system in banks that take checks and cash from cars to the tellers and back, though this one appeared to be quite antiquated and had a larger carrying capacity. Niki stared at her watch for some time before she shut the machine off and took a deep breath.

"Now what?" Callista asked.

"We wait. I've sent word we need extraction. If they deem it safe, they'll pick us up. If not so much, they'll send a message back through here with instructions of where to hole up for a while, and we start back through the subway tunnels, as dangerous as it is," Niki said.

She pulled a smartphone out of her bodice and began thumbing through it. "Looks like there's a charity luncheon going on upstairs right now," she said after a moment. "If we get caught down here, we'll have to pretend we were there and got bored. The entrance fee is five thousand dollars, so it's the big wigs. Rich girls getting into mischief won't seem unusual."

"I suppose so," Callista said, completely unsure.

Callista paced the room. She realized with a sinking feeling she would be stuck in New York for quite some time and sighed, disappointed. She had interviews lined up for her job preserving the fading Appalachian heritage, and Mom would feel abandoned and worry, if not have a complete breakdown. She envisioned Granny worrying her rosary as she listened to Mom's hysterical rants when she remembered she had the rosary Granny gifted her father. She touched its hiding place in her bodice and considered getting it out and worrying it like her father did, but thought better of it. She didn't know the words. The idea of trying to call Mom and let her know she wasn't coming home anytime soon crossed her mind, but she dismissed it. If the Alamies were upset that she skipped out, calling would lead them right to her. Better to wait until this all blew over and suffer Mom's tirade about not communicating with her than to call her from a jail cell.

She paced a circuit around the room a dozen times when they heard a sound farther down the hall and footsteps headed their way.

"Hide?" Callista whispered.

"No use, come here," Niki replied and moved to one of the machines. "Act interested."

Callista peered closely at the machine as Niki did.

"What do you suppose they were used for?" Niki asked in a smooth, cultured accent as the door quietly creaked open behind them.

"Summoning your limousine, of course!" an accented voice behind them called.

Callista turned to find a man of medium height, with slicked-back hair and a pencil-thin mustache, standing in the doorway. He was wearing a tuxedo, his crooked bowtie signaling haste. His brown eyes twinkled.

"That was fast," Niki said, walking over to him.

"Your message was in all capitals, *ma chérie*. It seemed urgent indeed."

"Well, it kinda is." Niki jerked her head in Callista's direction. "They're out looking for this one. Let's get to safety quick."

"Ah, so you are the source of the ruckus," the man said,

stepping around Niki and extending his hand to Callista, giving a slight bow and kissing her hand when she gave it to him. "Their ships were flying around like angry hornets, and I even saw some taxi drivers pulled over. But allow me to introduce myself. I am Loui Bordeaux, *Mademoiselle*, at your service. It is a pleasure to have you join us in our humble holes."

"Now is not the time to invite her to wine and cheese, Don Juan," Niki said and started out into the hall, pausing to tweak his bowtie straight before continuing past him.

Loui smiled and placed Callista's hand on his elbow. "There is always time for wine and cheese. *Mademoiselle*, if you please, your car is this way," he said with a twinkle in his eye.

They strolled down the hall and up a flight of stairs. Callista caught the strains of violins playing from a distant room and spotted a man in a tux going into a different room ahead of them before they came out into a side street where a limousine waited for them. Niki and Callista got in the back, and Loui took his place in the driver's seat, putting a driver's hat on.

"Where to, *Mademoiselle* The penthouse or a five-star restaurant of your choice? It's not too late—I'm sure they're still open for dinner."

Niki rolled her eyes at him in answer. He chuckled and started the car, and they cruised out into the traffic.

"Where *are* we going?" Callista asked after a few minutes.

"Back underground, where the Renegades live. We're the people who don't like being conquered and the people who want to stay out of their way. You never know, they might see a homeless person on the street and think, 'Let's probe him—no one will miss him.'"

"Have people been disappearing?" Callista asked.

"Not that we know of, but that doesn't mean they won't. Point is, we're the people who joined the homeless who know every inch of the city you don't see, and we're watching and waiting for an opportunity for round two. You're something of a person of political interest now—you'll fit right in."

Niki leaned back and finally relaxed a little before continuing. "Take the scum bag in the front seat, for example—"

"I resent that."

"He's a top-notch thief and a real patriot. So he's something of an asset for us in case we ever decide we need something stolen, and he's protected by us in case the Alamies ever get any hard-core ideas about criminal justice and start doing anything drastic."

"So it's a group of doomsday paranoiacs?" Callista muttered to herself.

That earned her a sideways glare from Niki. "These paranoiacs will make sure you don't get haremized, buried so deep no one will ever know you embarrassed the Admiral or worse. I mean, come on," she said, sitting back. "Aliens ruled the world before we could react, much less draw breath to protest. So we joined the Mole People and called a time-out so we could wrap our heads around what's happened, how we feel about it, and what we want to do about it."

"It was a true Blitzkrieg if there ever was one," Loui put in with a shake of his head. "Over before it truly began."

The sun set as Loui pulled up in front of City Hall and handed back two hats and long black coats. They walked quickly into the building, which was closing for the night. They tried not to make too much sound on the marble floor as they hurried to the decommissioned subway tunnel beneath it. Callista marveled at the vaulted arches and brass chandeliers hanging over the platform, supplementing the waning light from the skylight.

They jumped down to the track and walked into the tunnel for a few yards until Niki stopped before some graffiti. She groped around in the dim light until she found the brick on a specific part of the territorial tag, and it sank into the wall. A jagged door of bricks receded alongside it, and gears clacked with the hum of an electric motor in the darkness. Niki stepped in, taking a small flashlight from Loui, who ushered Callista in after her. Callista took a deep breath and stepped into the darkness—her new home.

CHAPTER SEVEN

The trio wound through several commercially made access passages to various infrastructures and crude tunnels hewn out of the earth and rock and propped up with broken bricks and scrap metal. The homemade tunnels smelled of stale moisture, and Callista's foot slipped on a slick rock in one of the newly dug passages, making her put her hand on the damp wall. Loui caught her elbow to steady her.

"We are below the water table. Everything that wasn't commercially constructed sweats. It's something we have to deal with," he said.

"Are there rats?" Callista had to ask.

"Yeah," Niki replied. "Not nearly as many as there used to be, though. When the population down here grew, we started eating the rats while we set up a steady food supply from up top—which is a lot harder than you would think, 'cause we gotta do it unseen —and the rats got the message. Now, only the most stupid ones venture in. I'm proud to say we put a pretty good dent in their population, though," she said with a grin back at Callista, the whites of her teeth glinting in the ambient light from the flashlight.

Callista shivered and shrugged deeper into her coat.

They came to what appeared to be an old rail-car storage hangar. There were three parallel tracks long enough to house six cars in a row, but only a hint of the former rails remained. Now, there was a cooking station in one corner, and several picnic-style tables radiated from there, while in the opposite corner, the walls were covered with maps and charts, and there was a huge, round table around which several people bent over or stood near with arms crossed. Phosphorescent lights hung from pipes and rafters, but only the space beneath them was well-lit, causing the ceiling to remain largely in shadow, giving it an endless feeling. There were several tunnels and doorways leading off the room, some of which appeared recently and roughly constructed.

Niki and Loui walked toward the round table, and Callista drifted after them, fingering her hat, aware the people at the picnic tables were watching them. Not only was she self-conscious because she was new, but also because her formal dress peeked out from beneath the long coat she had been given, contrasting sharply with their worn, faded, patched clothes.

One of the men who stood around the circular table whistled when they approached. "Dang Niki, looking mighty fine. You and your friends looking for some action or something?"

Niki sent the man a withering look that wiped the jocular look off his face.

A tall, brawny man with sandy blond hair that dipped to his crystal blue eyes stepped toward them. "Who's she, Niki?" he asked, never taking his eyes off Callista.

"This," Niki said as she straightened up and laid a hand on Callista's shoulder, pulling her forward, "is the woman who beat the Admiral at his own game and sassed his face. She's one of us now, big time."

"'Big time,'" the man repeated skeptically. "Beat him how?" His eyes narrowed as he continued to stare at Callista, a gaze she tried to return as steadily as she sent it.

"He tests the women he's interviewing's intellect with chess, and if you don't do good, you're out. That's all there is to it, as far as I can tell. I held my own, but he beat me soundly—chess is not my game, never played it much. But this girl here," she shook Callista's shoulder a bit, "this girl beat him in—what did you say, four moves? How do you like that?"

"What did you say to him?" the man asked Callista.

"I pretended to be a complete idiot who didn't know how to play, hoping he would underestimate me. Whether he did, and that's what led to his defeat, we may never know. Anyway, I told him while he may have learned chess, he hadn't yet learned the finer art of poker."

Loui laughed. "*Mon Dieu*, 'the finer art of poker,' *ah, ma chérie*, that was *magnifique*! My sincerest compliments!" He stepped forward and took her hand. "I thought you were something special the moment I saw you," he said, kissing her hand again.

The tall blond came up and gently pushed Loui aside. "Hawkney Andor," he said, and he put out a hand for Callista to shake. "You?"

"Callista Tristan," she said, firmly shaking Hawkney's hand and looking him in the eye. The distinct scent of Axe hair product wafted to her, and she noticed the faint impression of a pair of dog tags through his black shirt.

"Where are you from?" he said.

"Georgia, north of Atlanta."

"How long you been in New York?"

"A day before I was supposed to appear for the interview."

Hawkney hummed in response and seemed about to continue before another voice broke in.

"We will have to do a full background check on you and follow up on your story before we determine your status in this community, Miss Tristan."

Hawkney moved aside so she could see the speaker and vice versa. An elderly man with a cane sat at the other end of the table, wearing a rumpled gray suit and black tie. His watery blue eyes seemed to sift their way through her skin, making her want to shiver—especially when she observed the murmuring around her going silent when the man spoke.

"I was there!" Niki said in protest. "She came out of the building not long after I left, and they came busting out after her as we took off!"

"Or that's what they *want* you to conclude," the man said.

Niki opened her mouth, snapped it shut again, and sent a flickering glare toward Callista. Niki probably remembered Callista conversing with the Admiral's aide.

"She will remain under observation and in the brig—comfortably—until our investigation is complete," the man said with finality, and no one else questioned him. "Hawkney, you're first shift guarding her." He paused, and some sort of secret communiqué passed between them with a long look. "Niki, get her some proper clothes. Loui, take care of the car," he said, taking several one-hundred dollar bills out of his coat pocket and counting out five, moving them out of reach when Loui reached for them. "We have a good relationship with the company—don't spoil it by having sticky fingers," he warned.

"Of course not, *mon capitaine*," Loui said, plucking them from his hand and departing.

"Come on," Hawkney said, taking hold of Callista's arm and gently pulling her toward one of the doorways. They passed through a room that held electrical boxes and wiring and came into an abandoned subway tunnel lined with bunk beds three high with an assortment of plastic tubs and crates between them. An old woman fought a losing battle against the moisture with a mop, and a few children sat on the bottom of two bunks and took notes while a woman sitting on a trunk read to them.

Hawkney took out a ring of keys and unlocked a padlock on a door in the side of the tunnel, and ushered her in. She found herself in a water main access room with two twin beds and a table and chair.

"Have a seat," he said before firmly shutting the door behind him.

Callista sat on one of the beds, and Hawkney moved the chair from the table to sit in front of her. He leaned toward her a little, putting one hand on his knee with his elbow out at an odd angle. "Tell me about him."

She played with her fingers a moment. "I never noticed he is heterochromatic," she finally said, thinking of nothing better to say. "I have seen him before, giving speeches on TV, but I didn't realize one eye is red and one purple."

Hawkney didn't say anything and continued to stare at her.

"He ... seemed tired," she continued after a few moments. "Only a few people went before me, but he already leaned in his chair and just looked ... weary."

"What did he say to you?"

"He explained chess to me."

"What else?"

"There *wasn't* anything else!" she said, raising her voice and splaying her hands. "It's not like he detailed his grand plans to me. I was there to play chess with him—I don't know why chess, but that's what happened. Ask Niki!"

"*Relax*," he said, his demeanor unchanged. "Did you overhear anything?"

"The Admiral's aide talked to me because I acted like a loner. He said the Admiral would like me, which is why I got the hell out of Dodge while I could. He claimed the Admiral wouldn't force me into anything I didn't want to do, but come on, he's the Supreme Commander. I wasn't going to take my chances with someone no one could hold accountable."

"Why did he say the Admiral would like you?"

"I don't know. Maybe he thought my looks would appeal to him, or because I didn't melt in fear when he started talking to me."

"You must have a high opinion of yourself."

"It's because I *don't* that I wasn't about to be put in any position where I would have to face any of it," Callista countered, heaving a sigh, fighting back tears.

He cocked his head and gazed at her for a long moment. She squirmed under his stare.

"He also fed me some propaganda," she added hastily.

"Such as?"

"It's not their fault; we shot first; their planet was destroyed, so they can't help being here; they're trying to be nice rulers, that stuff."

"Yep, that's utter BS, except for the first shot part. I wouldn't know about their planet."

"I assumed so—I don't pay attention to politics and news much. I'm content with my own little world back home, talking to elderly people and writing down their stories and knowledge." She heaved another sigh as the dread she would not see home again for a very, very long time washed over her. "You ... you don't suppose your leader will let me go home and call it even, do you?"

"Not a chance. You've seen this place. Not to mention, if they are looking for you, they'll watch your home so they can snatch you up when you go back."

Callista's heart sank as her fears were echoed. She hung her head for a moment before jerking it up when a thought struck her. "You don't think they'd hurt my mother, do you?"

"Hurt? Probably not. Question and intimidate? Probably. I wouldn't worry too much, though, especially if they search the house and find no evidence you've been back." Callista wasn't sure if she should be relieved or not. The last thing she wanted was the Alamies pestering her mother. Better for her to worry and believe she was in their custody rather than at large.

"You can't call her either, ever," he continued. "They'd trace your call in an instant, find security cameras around where you made the call, and track you wherever you went, so don't ever think about it."

Callista hung her head, dismayed but also a little relieved.

"What else did the aide say?" he asked, leaning back in his chair and crossing his arms.

She puffed out her cheeks for a moment. "Uh, well, he talked about knowing the Admiral since he was a kid because they're related or something and how he was honored to be his aide. I'm guessing it's more of an honor than practical since the guy seemed a little decrepit and, well, elderly. Likes to talk about the past a lot —that sort of thing."

"Mm," was all he said before there was a rap at the door, and he stood and opened it.

Niki stood with a bundle of clothes in her arms. She wore camo pants with an open camo jacket, revealing a black tank top and a pair of dog tags. A red beret with three silver stars pinned on the side rested on her head. She handed the clothes to Hawkney without a word.

"You okay?" Hawkney asked her.

"Just a little keyed still, I guess. And pissed at everything, as usual."

He smiled. "We'll talk later."

Niki nodded in response and turned to go, Hawkney closing the door firmly behind her. He handed the clothes to Callista.

"Change," he commanded and moved the chair back over to the table, facing it in the opposite direction from Callista, and sat so his back was to her. She hesitated before setting the stack of clothes on the bed. She took off the coat and dropped the hat on top. Her heart sank when she reached up behind her for the dress's zipper. She couldn't reach it. She belatedly remembered Enaya had done it for her when she first put it on.

"I can't reach the zipper," she said glumly.

Hawkney rose without hesitation and stepped over to her. She turned and soon felt his warm fingers on her back. He deftly undid the hook on the dress and moved the zipper until it was over her lower back, then resumed his seat with his back to her.

She hurriedly took off the dress and pulled on the ragged jeans with the knees missing and a flannel shirt two sizes too big with patches on the elbows. She rolled up the red dress, scooped up the coat and hat, and plopped them on the table next to Hawkney, the sound and movement making him turn his head. He turned his chair so he faced the table and could see her.

"Anything else you want to tell me?" he asked, crossing his arms and looking up at her.

She blinked and stared into space, thinking for a few minutes. "The aide said the program wasn't the Admiral's idea but his and a few others'. He said they wanted him to be happy, and somehow, in their minds, that required marriage."

"That might explain why he wasn't enthused," Hawkney said, standing. "You hungry?"

"A little thirsty."

Hawkney nodded and stood. "Someone will bring you some water. We'll let you know once a decision has been made, but it will take some time, so get comfortable."

He scooped up the discarded clothes and left the room, closing the door with a clang that made her jump, and she turned to it as the padlock rattled on the other side. She gazed around at the dim room and the tangle of pipes casting shadows on the wall, illuminated by a single bulb. Had she leapt from the frying pan into the fire?

THE ONLY SOUND in the office was the tapping of Admiral Negev Xor-nalden's pen on the wide, dark oak desk as he gazed out over the city. His aide came in and sent him a kindly smile and turned to gently close the door behind him.

"Give me a good reason why I should not have you court-martialed and thrown in prison," Negev said testily in their native tongue.

"What have I done to incur your displeasure?" Pat-farfth asked meekly, seeming unperturbed.

"You stole from me. The ring. The woman wore my mother's ring."

"Yes."

"Why did you steal it and give it to her?" he asked, splaying his hands.

"Because she is the one for you."

"Oh, *really*. How in the constellations do you know that?"

"I know it in my heart," Pat-farfth said, laying a hand on his chest.

Negev snorted and leaned back in his chair. "Then *you* marry her. And why did you have to give her the ring? You know it is all I have of her ... of them ... ," he stopped when his voice caught, and he shifted his gaze down to where his hand gripped the chair's armrest, his knuckles white.

Pat-farfth slowly walked over to him and laid a hand on his shoulder. "It will come back to you. And with it, the woman who will bring you happiness, the happiness you deserve."

"What makes you think I have to be married to be happy? What makes you think I am not happy now?"

"Because you are not," Pat-farfth answered flatly, and Negev lowered his gaze to his hand again. "I see how this job sucks the life out of you," Pat-farfth said, taking a seat on the arm of Negev's chair. "I am your aide and your uncle. I see how the stress is turning a few of these hairs gray," he said, running his fingers through his nephew's thick black hair, in which a few silver hairs hid.

Negev leaned into the touch before suddenly burying his face into Pat-farfth's side, not caring if it was a childish thing to do. Negev heaved a shuddering sigh.

"Your mother would be immensely proud of you. They both would be," Pat-farfth said comfortingly.

"How proud will they be when my head ends up on a stake?" Negev straightened with a deep sigh and composed his features. "What of the search for the woman?" he asked, adopting his authoritative tone.

The intimate moment over, Pat-farfth stood and moved to the other side of the desk. "We are combing the city now. But if she does not show up by tomorrow, we both know where she has gone."

Negev rubbed his temples.

"Shall I prepare a search party to seek her out there?" Pat-farfth asked.

Negev stared out the window for a few moments. "No, not now. Let it all calm down a bit first. She will emerge eventually, and when she does, we will decide how to act."

Pat-farfth nodded. "As you wish. Do you have any instructions for me?"

"No, nothing now. Dismissed."

Pat-farfth nodded with a small smile on his face and left the office as Negev gazed after him. What would he do if his uncle truly became senile?

CHAPTER EIGHT

T hree days later, the leader of the Renegades came to see Callista. She was reduced to counting the rivets on the pipes and trying not to worry about what the Alamies said about her on the news or what they were doing to her family to try to learn of her whereabouts. She was glad to have some company to get her mind off it all, even if he did make her uncomfortable. Hawkney took up a post next to the door, leaning back against the jamb while his superior sat in the one chair and stared at Callista. She studied the wrinkles rippling out from around his eyes and the thinning white hair making a weak effort to cover his head. His long stare gave Callista a bad feeling.

"Your story checks out."

She let out a long breath.

"Our hackers found the security tape of your chess triumph. We also found the record of your plane ticket and footage of you in the hotel the day before with no suspicious Alamy contact—we could read your lips easily enough when you spoke to the aide in the dining room. The evidence suggests you are as you say." He leaned toward her as she started to breathe easier. "However, I am not wholly convinced."

Callista's stomach muscles tightened.

"One wrong move, any hint you work for *them*, and you will spend the rest of your life here and die in this room. Do you understand?"

Callista met and held his gaze. "Perfectly."

He continued to hold her gaze for a moment. "Good." He stood slowly, relying on his cane, and moved toward the door.

"What of my mother, my family? The Alamies aren't hurting them, are they?" she asked in desperation, leaning forward.

"As far as we can see, your family members only received a phone call. What the Alamies told them, we don't know," he answered before leaving without another word.

Hawkney straightened after his superior left the room, giving her a small smile.

"Who *is* he?" Callista asked.

"The boss, Herald McCaffrey. Used to work for the CIA. He knows his stuff; taught us how to move around unnoticed, how to set up this place and keep it unknown. We wouldn't be here without him."

"Well, that explains his distrustfulness," Callista murmured.

"We'll keep an eye on your family, don't worry." Hawkney gently laid his hand on her shoulder. "Come with me," he said with a soft smile, inclining his head toward the door before going through it himself. He led her back through the bunk hall and into the expansive room she had first come into, and they headed toward a group of people huddled around a table, staring down at something. When they moved closer, Callista caught the sound of her own voice and realized they were listening to a recording of her chess match with the Supreme Commander.

"You may have learned our game of chess," her voice said over the recording, "but you have not yet learned the finer art of poker."

The crowd erupted into "ooohs," and a few people clapped and laughed. Someone caught sight of Hawkney and Callista approaching.

"Hey! Here comes the sass-master herself!" and they turned.

Some came and shook Callista's hand; others slapped her on the back and congratulated her for her brilliance, overwhelming her.

"All right, all right, break it up," Niki called, pushing through the crowd. "Good to see you again, sister," she said, shaking Callista's hand. "I'm your 'big' in our little family here. I'm responsible for you, and you come to me for anything, okay?"

"Sure, glad to have you. Thanks."

Niki shrugged. "I like you, so it'll be fine."

"*Mademoiselle*, you were even more *magnifique* than I imagined." Loui burst through the crowd, reaching for her hand. "I am honored to have assisted in your grand escape," he continued with a sweeping bow and a kiss on her hand.

"Don't let him sweep you off your feet," Hawkney said with a soft snort. "Listen, I'm head of security. You see anything weird or suspicious, you come tell me. Okay?"

"Okay," Callista responded. Hawkney nodded and left the group.

"Allow me to give you the grand tour, won't you?" Loui asked with a pearly-white grin.

"Sure," Callista said, shooting Niki an uncertain look. Niki shrugged and nodded.

Loui walked Callista through the base, starting with the bunk rooms snaking their way out from the central room. They toured the near-empty storeroom—just a few crates stacked in a corner and a few extra fold-up chairs, some spare pieces of wood leaning against the wall, and a broken shopping cart in a corner. Next, Loui showed her the place for personal hygiene. The fixtures were makeshift, composed of anything from plastic buckets for the toilets to steel cans for shower heads. He showed her the mess hall —a corner of the main room—the "library" comprising two bookshelves, a few board games, some chairs, and a small, makeshift table. A corner of one of the bunk rooms hosted a few candles and a crucifix. Another room housed their few medical supplies and two cots. The tour ended in the communications room, where Hawkney and Niki loitered, looking at the screens.

This one starkly contrasted to the other rooms. It was stuffed with electronics, while there were scarcely any in the others.

"And this is the communications room, where we watch and listen for any Alamies sniffing around our access points or looking for one of our own."

Hawkney turned toward Callista. "This is Ali, Jose and T'Chamba, my security team." He indicated a skinny, turbaned man wedged in the corner, a man with short black hair and a goofy grin sitting at the desk who flashed her a victory sign, and a tall, dark-skinned man who nodded solemnly at her, his broad frame seeming to fill half the space. "The Alamies combed the city harder for you than I've ever seen them search before after their initial reaction didn't come up with anything," Hawkney continued. "They really must not want word to get out that you embarrassed the Admiral and that they lost you."

"I hope they didn't cause you any trouble," Callista commented.

"Nah, we laid low once we knew something was wrong... thought maybe Niki blew her cover, trying to find out what was really going on with that program." He received a glower from Niki. "Hey, it happens to the best of us, girl."

Niki rolled her eyes in response and turned her back on him.

"They could have realized we forged your invitation, and you weren't on their list—I half expected that to happen," Jose said, twiddling his thumbs.

"Anyway, it's no skin off our noses," Hawkney said. "Reports say they kinda radiated the search outward and are now keeping an eye out in the surrounding states, so we'll be back up to normal operations in a few more days once we're sure everything's calmed down."

"What kind of operations?" Callista asked hesitantly. "Is there anything I can do to help? I feel like I should do something for all the trouble I've caused you all."

"Oh, you'll be assigned a job soon enough," Hawkney said. "Those who work, eat. It's too dangerous for you to do any of the surface jobs—getting food mostly and other supplies—so we'll probably put you on something like cooking or cleaning, I dunno. Job management is not my department."

The others chatted a little longer, with Ali's worried questions countered by T'Chamba's soothing baritones and Jose's light banter before Callista and Niki left together and headed back to the main room.

"Wait here and get some chow," Niki said when they came to the kitchen corner. "I'm going to find Betty—she's the woman who makes this community run. She'll know what to do with you," she said before turning away to start her search.

Callista received some stew and sat down to begin eating when a voice intruded on her thoughts.

"I really liked your dress." An Asian girl sat at the next table and smiled shyly at her.

"Thank you," Callista said. "It was a little out of place down here, though, wasn't it?"

"It's pretty, though. Besides, it could be worse. One man got away from the Alamies in just his underwear—they came for him during the night after he stole a piece off one of their spaceships," she said and smiled, forming dimples in her cheeks. She stood and offered Callista her hand. "My name is Chu Changying, but everyone calls me Butterfly." She gave a little bow when Callista took her hand. Callista matched the bow and gave her own name.

"I heard what happened, how you stood up to the Admiral," Butterfly said, her eyes wide and shining as she sat next to Callista. "You were so brave. I would have fainted with fear."

"Well, you must be at least a little brave to live down here," Callista said.

"Oh, my reason is not so heroic," Butterfly said, inclining her head and fluttering her long lashes for a moment in hesitation. "I stole food from a vendor, and some Alamies standing nearby gave chase, but Hawkney grabbed me as I ran by and took me down here, and I've lived here ever since."

I 56 I

"How did Hawkney come to be down here?" Callista asked, crossing her arms.

"He started the community with McCaffrey and Niki, kinda out of spite for the Alamies. He and Niki were together in the United Nations Peacekeeper's company, and they were upset they didn't get to fight the Alamies and at least try to keep them from taking over without a fuss. And then they suffered the 'humiliation' of having their ranks taken away from them. Hawkney said it was like having an arm torn off. He and Niki didn't know what to do with themselves afterward—their livelihood was taken away. So, they started this underground community, taking in the people who wanted to get away from the alien government and protect those with no place to go. I think he sees himself as a kind of Robin Hood."

"I guess that makes Niki' Lady Marian' and Loui' Little John,'" Callista said, making Butterfly giggle. "So, do they fight the Alamies?" she asked.

"No, not really. We don't want to attract that kind of heat. We steal from them sometimes, food shipments mostly, or money occasionally. But always from what's going to the Alamies, never from our own people. We get a lot of donations too."

"I see."

A commotion at the other end of the hall interrupted them, and people started forming a line, which Butterfly guided Callista into right behind her.

"What's going on?"

"It's the water ration. It's hard to get clean water down here," Butterfly said.

Callista observed the people eagerly drink the small bottle of water granted to them and longingly watch their neighbors. "You have to get it from someone on the outside?" she asked.

"That's right. Sometimes, the providers have to miss a drop if they don't get a chance to smuggle it down. With all the heat from the search for you, we have to run on extra low rations for another day or two until it's safe."

Niki came along the line from the far end of the tunnel toward them with an elderly woman. Tall and thin with long white hair braided down her back, she wore a patchwork skirt and a worn button-down shirt with extra pockets sewn onto the front. She encouraged the people she passed, patting shoulders and tousling hair with her dark, bony, wrinkled fingers.

"Callista, Betty," Niki indicated when they reached Callista and Butterfly. "She'll show you what to do. I have a job of my own, so I'll see you around." Niki headed off into one of the tunnel entrances.

"Good to have you with us," Betty said, extending her hand, her voice quiet and kind. "What was your job?"

"I work as a historian. I gather stories and knowledge from elderly folks who remember a different time and help compile books of it," Callista said. "I volunteer at the Humane Society sometimes, too."

Betty smiled. "Well, I suppose you know how to clean as well as anyone."

"That's true," Callista recalled the hours cleaning cages.

"Well, part of our efforts down here is cleaning. I'm sure you've noticed it is quite damp underground. We must mop up the water daily to keep it from becoming a hazard. I'll put you on the cleaning team for now."

Callista nodded once. "Sounds good."

Betty moved on, and Callista gazed around. People clinked bottles of water and drank to each other's health, laughing and smiling, and a glimmer of hope rose in her heart for the first time. Rather than living like scared rabbits, these people found contentment. She straightened her back and nodded her head, determined to take whatever came and make the best of it.

CHAPTER NINE

Mozart's music played softly in the background of the luxury penthouse. The whole place seemed too soft and plushy to Negev compared to the austere ship's quarters he lived in for five years before reaching this planet. Here, the space felt overwhelming—not only did he have a separate bedroom and bathroom, but the main living quarters encompassed a spacious sitting area, a full kitchen, and a small bar against one wall. He was accustomed to walking into his quarters and being faced with his bunk on one side, his desk before him, and his bathroom on the other side, the rest of the wall space comprising storage. The extra space somehow made him insecure.

He stood at one of the floor-to-ceiling windows that gave him a sweeping vista of the city and could just make out where the horizon disappeared despite the urban jungle. The door softly closed behind him, and he turned his head slightly to catch the reflection of Pat-farfth in the glass.

"Nothing yet, sir." Pat-farfth came to stand next to him,

Negev heaved a heavy sigh at the news.

With a glance at him, Pat-farfth said, "She'll turn up. She's frightened of you, of what it would mean to be your spouse. Once she calms down, she'll move and try to go home. Then we'll have her, and you two can sit down and have a long chat, and she will no longer be afraid." He went silent for a moment before he asked, "You do not want to continue to interview more women, do you?"

"No." He never had, but his uncle and some of his other trusted advisers insisted on the scheme. This was as good an excuse as any to quit the proceedings he considered ridiculous. He didn't care what they may believe it implied his feelings were toward the woman.

"I thought not," Pat-farfth said. "She is a very nice woman, smart, and ... aware of certain realities. She would be good for you."

Negev rolled his eyes. "You were always more socially adept than I," Negev admitted. He turned his gaze away from the vista below him and let it fall on a painting hanging on the wall surrounded by protective glass. He could not shake the feeling the depicted woman's smug smile mocked him, scorning him with every decision he made like she knew something he didn't, something that would come back to bite him, and it irked him.

"Lieutenant, have that picture returned to the museum it was removed from when it was given to me."

"You do not like it?"

"I was told it is considered one of the greatest pieces of art, and I simply want it available to the public as before," he said, feeling a little guilty that he made excuses to his most trusted confidant.

"Certainly, sir," Pat-farfth said, looking back and forth between his superior and the Mona Lisa with a bemused smile on his face not unlike hers. "I will have it returned tomorrow."

"Thank you, my friend," Negev said softly and continued to gaze out the window.

Pat-farfth rubbed Negev's back. "We learn more about this place and these people every day, and I am sure this woman will be an immense help to you when she comes to see what is required of her."

Negev bowed his head. "I hope you are right, Uncle. It seems like everything I do makes a dozen more problems and unrest, and I do not want this woman to be caught up in any trouble on my account."

Pat-farfth's smile turned into a frown. "We both know little, if any, is your fault. It's all *his* doing," he said, his voice tinged with anger. "I don't trust Gren-del any more than I did the day you were promoted to Captain and came fully into his radar. He hated you then, and that hatred has only grown as you have climbed the ranks, I am sure. He is undoubtedly trying to destroy you."

"And do we have any hard proof of that?" Negev asked patiently.

"No, of course not. He's too clever and careful."

"Then we can do nothing." Negev suppressed a shudder.

Admiral Gren-del's recent declaration that the resources produced in his assigned corner of the world—encompassing Europe, the Middle East, and half of Russia—were to remain there was troubling, indeed. It was not necessarily indicative of clandestine or rebellious activity, but it was concerning nonetheless. None of the other admirals made such odd moves.

"Yes," Pat-farfth said glumly. "Nothing to do but watch our backs and be very, very careful." He brightened for a moment. "How about I dig up some information on the woman? Maybe it will take your mind off that monster, give you something less sinister to contemplate."

Negev secretly questioned whether the woman, if truly brilliant as Pat-farfth guessed she was, would not become a monster in her own right. Regardless, it was best to know one's adversary.

"Very well. Enjoy," he consented, teasing his uncle. "I still think you should marry her."

Pat-farfth rolled his eyes and shook his head with a smile before he left Negev to his thoughts. Negev remained at the window until the sun dipped out of sight, and the city became shrouded in darkness. He didn't stay long enough to see it fully come alive with lights.

CHAPTER TEN

Callista sat with the cleanup crew on break, sipping her water ration as she stroked her ribs. They protruded a little before, but now she wondered if they would soon stick out in desiccated fashion with the limited amount of food she ate and the unusual amount of physical labor, cleaning the tunnels and doing laundry in barrels, wringing them out by hand. Would her clear blue eyes lose their luster and sink into her skull, and her cheekbones make themselves all too clear? These days she dreamed most of sneaking to the surface and finding a public water fountain and gorging herself. There must be a better solution to their water problem.

She had asked Niki about it. No, they knew no one at the water company, and tapping a pipe was not only too dangerous, but they might notice the significant increase in outtake from the line and investigate for leaks.

She spotted Niki passing in the main room and called out to her. She veered toward Callista.

"'Sup?"

"What if we collected the rainwater coming from the rooftop gutter? It would be a lot cleaner than what comes off the streets."

"This is smog city, honey. Nothing out of the sky is clean."

"But it would be clean enough to wash clothes and clean floors with, don't you think?"

Niki tugged at a loose strand of hair at the back of her neck. "Yeah, I guess so. Guess we could find a good hole to store it in down here. Trouble would be getting it piped from the gutter drains into our own system and getting the materials to do it."

"Something has to be done. Rations are so thin we're all probably a little dehydrated."

Niki snorted. "Yeah, probably. Problem is, McCaffrey has the heart and soul of a bureaucrat—it'll take months for him to get off his hands and give his approval to something."

"I would think an issue like this has a little more urgency than whether a short-cut tunnel should be dug or not."

"You would think. But I've noticed it takes him a hot minute to commit to anything that wasn't his idea. Hawkney says he's thinking it through carefully, but I believe he likes being our messiah a little too much," Niki said.

Callista shrugged.

"Callista!" Butterfly called to her, running from one of the tunnels toward her. "Come quickly." Butterfly grabbed Callista's hand and tugged at it. She screwed the cap on her water bottle and hurried after Butterfly.

"What's wrong?" Callista asked as they wound through tunnels and into the street-level sewers.

"I found a cat! It's stuck down here and scared. You worked with rescue pets—you'll know what to do."

They soon found the cat, barely visible in the darkness due to its tortoise-shell coat. But its green eyes gleamed in the glow from the shaft of light that came from the sewer opening, and its white paws shone like pebbles in the shadows.

"Here baby, it's all right," Callista soothed, reaching out a hand toward the cat who clawed at her approach. She noted the mangy fur and lack of a collar. She continued to talk soothingly and held her hand out—not so close as to be threatening, but so it could catch her scent. After no improvement, she carefully poured the cap of her water bottle full of water and scooted it near the cat before backing away a little.

The cat watched her for some minutes before inching near the water and lapping it up. When it finished, Callista cautiously approached the cat again. It retreated back into the corner. She refilled the cap and repeated the process twice until the cat didn't withdraw to the corner. She stayed as the cat drank and held out her hand for it to sample.

The cat cautiously sniffed her hand and began to purr. Callista carefully petted its head before trying to pick it up. The cat stiffened when she reached under it but allowed her to pick it up, though its arms and toes were outstretched when its feet left the ground. She stroked it while she held it until it relaxed a little. With a sigh of relief, she glanced through the slit of the gutter at the wheels of the passing traffic.

"What should we do with it?" Butterfly asked, stroking the cat's head.

"Is there an animal shelter around here?"

"I don't think so. The only one I know of is across town. It'd take us a long time to get there," Butterfly said, looking down the sewer drain.

"Well," Callista said, glancing back out at the traffic. "It can't stay down here. Let's head that way and ask people if they want to adopt a cat as we go." She watched the cat daintily clean its paws. "It might be a bit feral, and I'm sure it needs some shots, but it's not mean."

"We're not supposed to go above ground," Butterfly said, squinting out at the traffic as she rubbed her arms and backed away from the light.

"Butterfly, when's the last time you've been out there?"

Butterfly chewed her lower lip for a minute. "Almost a year, I think."

Callista looked at her, saddened. "Come on, let's get out of here." She moved toward the manhole ladder.

"But Hawkney will be so mad, and Boss might throw us out!"

"They don't have to know. And besides, they're not looking for you, and they're not looking for me in the city anymore. We'll be fine." Callista gazed up at the manhole cover. "You'll have to lift that off. I have the cat."

Butterfly chewed her lip, glancing from Callista to the cover and back again. The notes of a trilling bird sounded over the noise of the traffic, and a breeze wafted down the drain mouth, bringing with it the scent of exhaust, wet leaves, food, perfume, and a hint of the nearby sea.

Butterfly heaved a sigh, climbed up the ladder, and cautiously lifted the cover. A pedestrian tripped on the rising cover and swore at her before moving on, causing Butterfly to duck back down before she slowly lifted it off again. She cautiously climbed out, searching the faces of the people passing on either side of them. Some afforded her curious glances before passing on; others didn't notice her. Callista climbed up behind her with the cat over her shoulder, clinging to her jacket for dear life.

"Anyone want a stray cat?" Callista called out good-naturedly to the passersby but received no more than a slight smile from a few. She pulled her beanie farther down over her forehead. "Ready to go?"

Butterfly stood, mouth slightly agape, staring at the pale blue sky.

Callista looked up and back at her. "Butterfly?"

Butterfly shook herself. "Right, right." She replaced the manhole cover and returned to Callista's side, taking her hand.

"Come on, let's go someplace less busy," Callista suggested.

NEGEV STARED at the stills taken by the traffic and security cameras. A woman with long brown hair wearing a jacket, ragged jeans, and a beanie pulled down tightly around her head held a mottled-brown cat. She was with a young girl of the Asian ethnicity, similarly dressed in worn clothing. He checked the analysis—100% match. He glanced over at the dossier on her. It didn't tell him much—her education, her places of employment, who her family was. Facts that told him little about who she was.

More photos popped up on the screen. He leaned closer to one of the new photos and zoomed in on the cat. Or rather, the hand that held the cat. His mother's ring was still on her finger. He leaned back with a sigh of relief. He had worried she would pawn it and he would never see it again.

Another photo popped up. They were in a residential section now. Townhouses with stucco and red or brown brick faces stood shoulder to shoulder, with steps down to the street, some with flowerpots on the steps, others with boxes at the windows, with pansies of white, purple, and yellow defying the cold. A few trees pushed up between the sidewalk and street, shedding their golden, orange, and brown leaves onto the unyielding surfaces that tried to shut out the prying roots.

They talked to an older woman who swept her stoop. A photo popped up of the woman petting the cat. Another with the woman splaying her hands and seeming to shake her head. Another of her pointing up to one of the windows and of her heading inside with a finger upheld, indicating she would return in a minute.

Negev rubbed his upper lip as the photos continued to come in. He slapped the desktop and looked up their location on the map, doing a quick calculation of where they came from and the general direction they headed in. He rose from his chair, snatched up his coat, and swept out of the office.

CHAPTER ELEVEN

S o far, they had no luck finding anyone to take the cat, and they were nearing the animal shelter. Callista was commenting on how the cat was falling asleep in her arms when Butterfly screeched to a halt, and Callista bumped into her, causing the cat to awaken and give an annoyed meow. Callista sent a glance at the frozen Butterfly before following her gaze—straight ahead in the direction they were going—and she, too, caught her breath.

An Alamgirian leaned against a lamp post, wearing a coat similar to a trench coat with the looks of a uniform beneath it. He smiled and inclined his head toward them.

"Just keep walking but keep your head down—don't make eye contact," Callista murmured before pushing Butterfly forward. Callista started talking about the questionable contents of hotdogs as they approached but couldn't resist glancing up at him again, and this time, her jaw dropped, and she stopped. Butterfly also stopped and looked back at Callista and the Alamy, eyes widening and spine stiffening, her hand subconsciously lifting slightly to point out his eyes.

"Go," Callista said, her gaze arrested by the heterochromatic eyes that stared at her, unwavering. "Just go."

Butterfly needed no more encouragement. She took off at a full run.

The cat meowed in protest as Callista squeezed it too hard. The Admiral stood from his repose against the lamppost and moved to stroke the cat's head.

"You need not be afraid," he said softly in a smooth voice that surprised her in its gentleness. "You have done nothing wrong—much."

"What do you want with me?" she asked in barely a whisper as he continued to stroke the purring cat.

"Only that which was stolen from me, and we need never see each other again." His piercing gaze met hers.

"W-what?"

"That ring," he responded, stroking it on her finger, making her snatch her hand back and look at it. "My aide stole it from me —it belonged to my mother." He cocked his head and continued to look at her. "It is not your fault, of course—how could you have known?"

Callista looked back up at him.

"Simply give it back to me," he said, "and there will be no more trouble. You needn't live underground if you do not wish to."

Callista caught her breath and stared at him a moment before she glanced back down at the ring and moved to pull it off before realizing she couldn't with the cat in her arms. Without much thought, she handed the cat to the Admiral, who graciously took it. Her fingers had swollen a bit since she first put the ring on, and she worked at it for a long moment before it came off her finger with a jerk. She glanced up to find Xor-nalden smiling at her with amusement as he stroked the cat's back. She moved to put it in his hand, but instead, he stretched out his smallest finger since he held the cat with both hands, and she slid it on.

"You search for a home for this ... what do you call them?"

"It's a cat," she responded.

"Cat. You search for someone to take it?"

"Yes, or take it to the Humane Society."

Admiral Xor-nalden gazed down at the purring cat, who appeared to be smiling in contentment to match the smile on his face. "I will take it," he said.

Callista straightened up. "It will need updated shots. It should have a full checkup, too. And you will need to find some toys so it won't tear up your furniture, and a litter box, and—"

"This thing you Humans have—the internet? I find it quite useful for any questions about anything to do with your people and this planet. It may be helpful in apprising me of such information, will it not?"

"Yes, yes, of course. I just ... ," She rubbed her arms and glanced down at the cat. "I used to volunteer at the Humane Society."

"I know," he said, smiling, giving her a cold feeling in her stomach. "Be careful, Callista Marie Tristan. The people you currently associate with are not considered to be the healthiest by your society. I would return to your home if I were you. Good day," he said, bowing his head to her before turning and walking away with the cat.

She stepped over to the light post and nearly collapsed against it, reminding herself to breathe as she studied his retreating back. She had no idea what to do.

After she caught her breath and calmed herself, she wandered in the direction Butterfly went when she noted one of the street signs said JORALEMON STREET and remembered Niki took her to the fake townhouse there. She found the façade and moved to sit on the front steps when the door jerked open, and Hawkney stood in the doorway.

"Get in here," he hissed and shoved her in the door and slammed it behind him. When she turned around to face him, he grabbed her by the throat and pinned her against the wall.

"What the *hell*. Do rules mean nothing to you? You think just because the heat started to die down the cameras weren't watching for you still? You think you're immune? That you can do whatever you want?"

Butterfly sobbed from somewhere down the hall.

"He *knows*," Callista gasped out, pulling at Hawkney's hand around her throat. "He already knew about the Renegades."

Hawkney's eyes widened, and he relaxed his grip on her, making Callista gasp.

"How? Did you tell him?" he demanded, leaning closer to her.

"No, he referenced it and said I should go home because he thinks you all aren't great people. All he wanted was the ring his aide gave to me. He said it belonged to his mother, and the aide stole it and gave it to me. He said he won't bother me again."

Hawkney stared at her for a few moments before closing his eyes and leaning his head back. "It was bugged. There was probably a tracker in the ring. That's how they knew. But now that he's taken it back, we can't prove it and extort it."

"But how would he know I would flee and come down here?" They were both silent for a moment. "Unless there's a tracker in all the jewelry, in which case if Niki took any, there should be some in there too, right?"

"I don't think she took any," he said.

Callista groaned in response. "Maybe he's right. Maybe I should go home. I've been nothing but trouble."

"Yes, you should," Hawkney concurred, crossing his arms. "We're going to go to the bus station tomorrow and get you a ticket back to Georgia."

"No, you're not," Loui intruded, making Callista and Hawkney turn their heads.

"Excuse me?" Hawkney said.

"She's a celebrity now. I've been watching the internet. She's not just famous, she's become a symbol. A symbol of defiance and the human spirit. We can not only use her for our cause; we *need her* for it."

Hawkney growled in his throat and glared at Callista, who innocently gazed back.

"But the Boss!" Butterfly wailed from farther down the hall. "He'll lock her away for sure."

"Yes, he would, which is why we're not going to tell him," Hawkney said resignedly, walking toward Butterfly. "So get ahold of yourself. I won't tell him you went out either, okay? Nobody needs to know."

"But now we know the Alamies are aware of us," Loui said. "Do we do nothing and continue blissfully ignorant or take action?"

"You're going to have to tell him, aren't you, so they'll understand?" Butterfly sniffed after a few moments.

Hawkney scratched at the scruff on his jawline in thought for a moment before heaving a sigh. "Yeah, I guess I'll have to. We will need to amp up security big time or move entirely to account for our blown cover."

"It shouldn't be hard to rig water and electrical booby traps and the like," Callista said.

"I don't want to hear another word out of you," he said, pointing an accusing finger. "You're going to keep quiet and do as you're told, or I really will throw you out." He whirled and started down the hall toward the subway access. "Come on, let's get out of here."

Butterfly hurried after him, and Callista followed, meeting Loui, who waited on her.

"A hollow threat if I ever heard one," he said, putting an arm around her and leading her down the hall. "You will be indispensable before long."

Callista secretly questioned whether she wanted to be.

CHAPTER TWELVE

H e said he wasn't infatuated, and he wasn't. A few days after he talked with her in the street, he stared at the photos of her, trying to figure out what attracted his thoughts to her. Once he could figure out what it was, he could test and dissect it and probably do away with it. It irked him to consider his uncle could be right about her and him. It irked him very much.

Negev sighed and minimized the photo album. He marveled at her decision to remain with the underground community rather than return home, but he had other matters, or people, to worry about, especially about *him*.

Pat-farfth opened the door and stood there, the blood drained from his face.

"What's wrong?" Negev asked, fear crawling up from his stomach onto his sternum.

"There has been an ... incident ... in Russia," Pat-farfth said, slowly turning around and closing the door.

The fear jumped into Negev's throat. That was part of Grendel's area of jurisdiction.

"How many?" he asked hoarsely.

Pat-farfth gave him a sorrowful look before wiping a hand down his face.

"Far, far too many."

IT HADN'T BEEN hard to convince the council that more security measures needed to be taken, but Callista guessed it wouldn't compare with the efforts they would need to make now.

They huddled around a small TV in the main room, staring vacantly at the screen in horror as news of what happened was solemnly reported, along with blurry photos quickly snapped by cellphones.

The short of it was this: during a peaceful protest against citywide wage cuts in St. Petersburg decreed by the Alamy regime, the Alamies became trigger-happy and started shooting. Hundreds were dead, and thousands had fled the city. People fled from the sound of gunfire in the footage, dropping protest signs and climbing over each other as they ran, a picture of absolute panic. Everyone looked to Admiral Xor-nalden for a statement on the tragedy, but all was quiet.

Callista scanned the crowd around the TV until she spotted Loui on the periphery and moved to stand beside him. He gave her a sad look and put an arm around her, and she hugged him back.

"What's going to happen now?" she asked quietly.

"That's for McCaffrey and the elders to decide."

They stood with the others for some minutes until Hawkney, who stood directly in front of the TV, turned and headed over to the war room table. The other elders followed suit, and the rest of the Renegades closed in their wake, jostling for a better vantage of the TV. Loui brushed Callista's arm and nodded for her to follow him toward the table. The two of them took up position on the outskirts of the group against the wall where they could hear without intruding.

"We have to do something," Hawkney said, opening the meeting. "This is the last straw—we can't stand by and do nothing anymore. This could be only the beginning—will they come for us next? What group of innocents will they murder without a care?"

"Let's take the fight to them." Niki nearly shouted. "Eye for an eye and tooth for a tooth. We have the head honcho right here in our city. We could easily organize a blitz and take the entire city within a matter of hours and hold the guy hostage—make him pay."

"His silence on the matter is incriminating," McCaffrey said, sitting to Hawkney's right.

Callista leaned over to Loui. "I don't believe he had anything to do with it."

"No?" he whispered back. "Why not?"

"He doesn't strike me as the type to incite mass murder. I think he has at least a few compassionate bones in his body."

"We can't afford a war," Betty said. "We have too many civilians. If we incite them, and if your little blitz doesn't work, they will burn us out of these tunnels, and what of the defenseless? How many more innocents will you sacrifice?"

"Collateral damage is inevitable in war," McCaffrey said, earning him an aghast look from Betty.

"Callista does not think Xor-nalden is responsible," Loui spoke up, making all eyes turn toward them, and Callista want to shrink into herself. "There are others of Xor-nalden's rank who are his equals in all but title. I know they divided the world among them to closely supervise humanity, and our district is under Xor-nalden's purview. We should learn who initiated the wage cuts and whether the guards were ordered to shoot or not, then we'll know who is responsible and plan our action accordingly."

"That could take weeks!" Niki protested. "We need to act *now* before people forget and move on. We can't let this go."

"Then we should do it without violence," Callista said, taking a steadying, deep breath and stepping closer to the table. "Did we learn nothing from Gandhi? From MLK? Hong Kong? Violence will get us nowhere—only demonstrations and peaceful protests. Make ourselves so annoying we cannot be ignored."

"Peaceful protests got the Russians nowhere either," Hawkney snapped.

"Then we take a different approach," Loui said, stepping up beside Callista at the table. "Let us rally the public's outrage, but not by marching in the streets. We can rig a mechanical printing press and print hundreds of posters and leaflets and litter the city with them, scattering our outrage without putting a target with it."

"I like this," Betty said. "This way, we will not endanger our people, especially if we scatter the propaganda at night."

"We can use social media too," Callista added. "Make ourselves heard without speaking a word out loud."

"All the easier to ignore," Hawkney said, crossing his arms.

"Callista is already a celebrity on the internet," Loui said, putting his hands on her shoulders. "Let us use that popularity to our advantage. Like the painting 'Liberty Leading the People,' let us have her hold the flag around which the people will rally and voice their outrage as one."

"Are you trying to spark the next French Revolution?" Hawkney mocked.

"The Revolution was no bloodier than the American one or any others—it was the bloodlust afterward that made it infamous," Loui said.

"I don't remember you getting put on the board of elders," Hawkney snapped. "Get lost."

Loui sniffed at him before putting an arm around Callista. "Come, *ma chérie*, let us leave these fools."

They headed toward the crowd, a few members of which broke away and surrounded them.

"What did they say?" Butterfly asked nervously.

"They agitate for war," Loui said, shaking his head. "I do not agree with it at all. I will not take part in such a foolish maneuver, especially when we do not have all the facts. What if the news agencies are making it out to be worse than it is? What if we shoot an innocent man? No, I will not fight until I know more. I will not be part of the kind of bloodlust my people experienced in their revolution."

"Xor-nalden is the ultimate leader," Ali said, his turban casting a shadow over his face from the above lights. "He is ultimately responsible."

"True, but he is not directly in charge of every region," Loui said.

"I've met him," Callista said, crossing her arms. "I saw evidence of compassion and concern, at least, for my welfare. I don't believe he would blatantly have ordered an execution of people who did no harm and had good reason to be angry."

"And it is not like it has never happened before," T'Chamba said in his deep voice. "Irate police officers have shot at crowds in the past. This crowd looked like one for the record books. Who's to say it wasn't just a panic shot that turned into a massacre, no orders given?"

"Exactly," Loui nodded.

"Callista, couldn't you talk to him?" Butterfly asked timidly. "You said he was concerned for your welfare—do you suppose he'd see you, and you could ask him to do something about it?"

"Ask him to do what? I'm sure he's already dealing with it—how can he not?"

"He has said nothing about it, and it's been almost twenty-four hours," Ali said. "Perhaps he is choosing to ignore it."

"Couldn't you at least talk to him so we know? So Hawkney and the others could know?" Butterfly persisted.

"And what if he does come, and Hawkney takes a shot at him? That'll be the end of that," Callista said with a wave of her hand.

"That will not be the way this time," T'Chamba said, crossing his arms. "I was in Andor's unit—I know where he's coming from. We've seen atrocities firsthand like this and couldn't do anything. I'll talk to him, cool him down."

"I still don't think talking to Xor-nalden is our best bet right now," Callista said.

"So we're just going to do nothing then?" asked a woman who joined the group. The whole crowd had turned their attention to them.

"Loui suggested we make flyers and posters and use them to protest. By covering the city with them, we do something without putting targets on our backs by marching through the streets, just in case the Alamies react badly to our speaking out," Callista said, rubbing her jawline.

"I know a guy at Pratt Industries over on Staten Island," another man said. "Sometimes a batch of paper will go wrong—I can see about getting some duds for free or close to nothin'."

"I know how to make ink out of charcoal," a woman said.

Callista gazed around at the excited faces and looked to Loui.

"The council could take weeks discussing what to do," he said. "If we're all in agreement, let us not hesitate for the sake of our brothers and sisters in Saint Petersburg."

She slowly nodded and looked back at the crowd. "Then let's do it."

CHAPTER THIRTEEN

It didn't take long for the elders to put the pieces together—only a day. Being largely ignored by the community, the unusual activity, and the stack of signs demanding justice—the clearest giveaway—alerted the elders something was up. And, of course, as the designated troublemaker, regardless of fact, Callista was yelled at first.

"This is your idea, isn't it?" Hackney said, storming over to her after he found their pile of signs. She held her mop tightly in front of her, the only thing between her and him.

"It's actually Loui's idea, technically," she began.

"But you persuaded them to do it without the council's blessing. You instigated this!"

"We all agreed; I didn't ask them to," Callista said, raising her voice a bit as her exasperation started getting the best of her. "Why do you think everything is my fault? Did you even stop to consider how it began, or did you just jump to conclusions?"

He sighed and ran his fingers through his hair.

"Look, I know you're under a lot of stress," she said. "But don't take it out on me, okay? Get yourself a stress ball or something."

The corner of Hawkney's mouth twitched into a smile, and

he stared back up at her for a moment before stepping toward her. "You're right," he said, laying his hands on her shoulders, making her stiffen, unsure what he was doing. "I shouldn't take it out on you. I'm sorry."

She nodded once. "Apology accepted. Everyone thought the council would take forever to decide what to do, and they wanted to do something to protest what has happened in the moment, so we started making signs—"

"I get it," he said and squeezed her shoulders a bit. "When will they be ready?"

"We'll have over a hundred by tonight," she responded, his hands still on her shoulders, making her uncomfortable. "We were going to spread them around in high-traffic places while it was dark."

"Sounds good," he said, rubbing the curves of her shoulders. "Listen, what you said, I mean, we've gotten off on the wrong foot, and, well, how about we have dinner together in the mess hall tonight? We can have a friendly chat and just ... kinda ... start over. You know what I mean?"

"Sure," she said, wishing he'd take his hands off now. "That sounds like a good idea."

"Great," he said, his gaze falling on his hands. He jerked them back, wiping his palms on his pants as he stepped farther away from her. "See you at, um, second dinner shift?"

"Sure."

"Sure. Okay. See you then," he said with an awkward wave before walking away.

Callista cocked an eyebrow at his retreating back and smirked at the awkwardness of the situation before she returned to mopping up the condensation and water leaking through the cracks.

ADMIRAL NEGEV XOR-NALDEN woke up with the headache he had gone to bed with. He had no idea what to do about the incident in Russia, and the problem pounded in his brain. He could not order Admiral Gren-del to rescind his decree outright —that would take an agreement from the whole council of Admirals, and it would not raise the dead. After seeing the report, he had called Gren-del to hear his side of the story.

It was as bad as he had feared. Gren-del told him of the massacre he ordered as though it were nothing to be concerned about. It made his blood boil. He despised the man. He ordered Gren-del to appear before him as soon as possible to answer directly for his actions, even though it would be no more than a useless, empty gesture. Gren-del said he would get back to Negev on when he could come. Negev knew it would not be for months, if ever.

He slowly sat up in bed and waited for his head to stop spinning before he slid onto the floor and started his morning routine, mentally preparing himself for whatever disasters the day held. He had begun to review his messages and agenda on his tablet when he walked into his main room and saw it, stopping short and almost dropping the device.

There, on the panorama window overlooking the east side of the city, glared the word JUSTICE across the whole pane in red handprints.

He slumped into a nearby chair as the memory of a nightmare roared back to him, a nightmare he had tried hard to forget. In it, their red sun on his home world sent tendrils of blood to the planet below, and his people raised their hands to the sky to stop the massacre, but they drowned in the sea of blood coming from the sky, their bloody hands the last part of them to disappear. That was how his brain fantasized the supernova that destroyed his life. And now, here they were again, the bloody handprints, to forestall the bloodshed they could not stop.

He sensed it was an omen. Even though he was technically the Supreme Commander, he possessed little power in reality. Before the destruction of his world, he was placed in charge, yes, but Admiral Gren-del, whom he replaced, would remain in a joint position with him for a period of five years as he adjusted to the new position and responsibility. Negev had risen through the ranks so fast, he was quite young for the position, so the Consortium thought he was not sufficiently experienced despite his proven brilliance and capability. Gren-del had undermined his plans and made him look incompetent ever since he became sole commander seven years ago. It was nothing new. Gren-del had taken advantage of him ever since he had sensed Negev would one day threaten his position even when Negev was merely a captain of a support ship.

Gren-del was an insensitive and cruel leader; his own men admitted to that. By giving him the biggest territory to govern, Negev had hoped his attentions would be so divided and spread out he would not have the leisure time to be cruel or attack him. It would appear he was wrong. He gazed at the handprints on the glass and asked aloud, "What do I do? Is there anything I can do? How do I stop him?" The hands did not reply.

He buried his face in his damp hands. That was how Pat-farfth found him. Negev sensed him standing in the doorway, taking in the message on the glass and his superior in a dejected posture. Finally, he went over and began rubbing Negev's back.

"What do I do?" Negev asked into his hands.

"Give them justice," Pat-farfth said.

"How do I do that against one as powerful as I?"

"You destroy him, once and for all."

"And how do I do that without destroying ourselves?"

"You are the genius, not I," Pat-farfth said with a hint of humor in his voice. "There are many ways you could be rid of him. But I know you are loathe to stoop to such levels, so you will have to find another way."

"Even if I were to have him killed, his men would rise up in vengeance," Negev said, raising his head to stare at the window.

"He has garnered a close band of loyalists since my unexpected promotion."

"Yes," Pat-farfth agreed. "So show this world why you are Supreme Commander! Defeat him at his own tactics or adopt new ones he cannot defend against."

"And keep up with all my other responsibilities in addition," Negev said. "I am not a politician. I am a child in comparison to Gren-del's ability to twist and use words to his own advantage, nor am I willing to resort to deceit and subterfuge. I am a warrior —point me in the direction of the enemy, and I will find a way to defeat him honorably or die trying. But now, some of our own people are the enemy."

"I have faith in your capabilities," Pat-farfth said.

"That makes one of us."

"Though I would suggest you analyze outside the sphere here. No, this is not a case of fleet against fleet, soldiers against soldiers on a battlefield. This is a game of politics on a much larger scale than just between our people. Use everything and anything to your advantage, whether it be the terrain, the people, or the law. Gren-del will not be defeated by a military assault—you must use your wit and all the resources at hand."

"Against a master of cunning and subterfuge." Negev sat back in his chair.

"I have faith in you," Pat-farfth repeated with a smile.

"Again, that's only one of us." Negev rubbed his temples.

"Then perhaps you need to make it more. Garner the faith of the people."

"That is even harder to do than to take Gren-del down."

"Then perhaps you need only one."

"Who?" Negev asked, looking up at his uncle.

"Look," Pat-farfth showed him an image on his tablet. "This was taken by a security camera, which takes a photograph every few seconds." The image showed a woman holding a sign saying "Justice for the Martyrs" in red on white with the rough sketch of a woman in a red dress carrying a flag. She looked pale as a ghost in the black and white photograph, with the light shining directly on her face while the area around her was shrouded in the night. She wore the same beanie and ragged jacket from when he met her to get his mother's ring back.

"Her?" he asked, taking the tablet. "How would she be any help to me?"

"She is a growing legend, and it would appear the community underground is attempting to capitalize on it." Pat-farfth pointed to the sign on the screen. "This is supposed to be a representation of her in the red dress she wore when she defeated you at chess."

Negev's lip twitched. "So if I gain her support, others who listen to her may also be more amicable to me?"

"Precisely."

"It is a small chance," Negev said, sitting back in his chair. "First, she fears me. Second, she has no reason to trust me—"

"She and her friends have spread signs protesting the massacre," Pat-farfth said, showing him images of signs propped up throughout the city. "If you respond positively to their protests, she may be more willing to listen to you."

Negev sighed. "If the situation was not so serious, I would suspect you of orchestrating this to get me to interact with her more, trying to make this match work."

Pat-farfth smiled and spread his hands. "I am doing nothing, Negev, I assure you. I am simply letting nature take its course now."

Negev snorted, and his gaze fell on the window again, his smile fading. Pat-farfth followed his gaze.

"Shall I hire a window washer?" he asked.

"Please," Negev responded softly.

Pat-farfth patted him on the shoulder and left, leaving him to contemplate and consider his options. Negev stared out the window, trying to peer through the fingers cleaving to it and ignore them, even though he suspected, although soon to be washed away, they would cling to his memory far longer.

CHAPTER FOURTEEN

Callista walked into the main room and found everyone congregated in the center, slapping backs and shaking hands, all laughing and talking at the same time. At the center of it stood Loui, a grin from ear to ear, head held high, and shoulders back.

"What is all this?" she asked the nearest person.

"Loui scaled the Admiral's skyscraper last night, the daredevil," the man said, shaking his head in admiration with a similar grin on his face. "He painted 'justice' on the outside his penthouse window."

"But not just that," Loui said, catching the conversation and walking up to Callista. "I did it in handprints, red ones. Suggestive, no? I thought I'd give him a good jolt to go along with our protests."

"Oh, I'm sure." Niki put her hands on her hips and glared at him. "You put this whole community at risk. Do you really believe he'll take this lying down? How idiotic can you be? They'll come looking for the person who did it. Please tell me you didn't use your bare hand." The jubilant faces started to fall, one by one.

"*Ma chérie,* do you not remember who I am? I am the great

Loui Bordeaux! I have committed a dozen crimes I have not been identified for. Of course, I wore gloves."

"They'll still look for the person responsible. They'll tear the city apart if they have to. And what if they find us? We barely have the means to protect the entire community, much less you."

"Niki is right," McCaffrey said from the periphery, where he leaned on his cane. "Your insolence will cost us, Loui. If not just in money, in lives."

"Money?" Callista asked softly, her voice carrying in the acoustic tunnels.

"Yes, money," McCaffrey said. "A few well-placed bribes to keep it quiet and the searches lackadaisical, money for supplies we will need and the means to defend ourselves. Our resolve to prepare a defense was a precaution before. Now it's a necessity."

"The council has made a decision?" Niki asked, rubbing her palms on her pants.

"We have," McCaffrey said, stepping further into the crowd. "We will make this place a deathtrap to any who dare enter unguided. However, the more money we fling around, the more we chance it being traced back to us, as well as our activities attracting attention, but we'll have to risk it. Loui will contact black-market arms dealers and get us enough hardware to arm everyone in this community. We will not seek out war, but we will be well prepared should it come to us."

Butterfly came running down the tunnel as he finished, and all heads turned.

"Where's the fire?" Niki asked.

"Come ... come see ... ," Butterfly said between gasps, pointing back down the tunnel. "Admiral ...TV."

McCaffrey raised an eyebrow and started down the tunnel, the others following him. People crowded around the TV, but they parted to let the leaders get a good look. The anchorman was talking, but he soon replayed the clip of Xor-nalden before a press conference.

"The news of the incident in Russia has greatly grieved me,"

Xor-nalden said. "I am personally investigating the events surrounding the tragedy and have summoned Admiral Gren-del, who oversees the continent and who reportedly ordered the wage cuts, to appear before me and explain himself. Until such retributive action can be taken, I order a day of remembrance to be held three days from now and will henceforth be held annually on the date the massacre occurred. In addition, I have ordered no such drastic action to be taken by any admiral henceforth, and I will work to have the wage cuts rescinded. I will announce what action will be taken against those responsible for this unacceptable calamity when it has been decided. Thank you."

Hawkney snorted. "Rescind the wage cuts. As if they're not still saving money because hundreds are dead."

"And like he's really going to do anything to anybody," Niki said. "He'll slap a few people on the wrists and call it even. It's just a fat lot of lip service."

"Better than nothing at all though, I suppose," Callista murmured.

"This is ridiculous," Niki said. "We need to take action now."

"Calm yourself, Niki," McCaffrey said in a warning voice. "Rash action will cost us lives and get us nowhere. *Don't* make me consider removing you from a leadership position."

"Yes, sir," Niki ground out, bowing her head while she chewed her lip, her dark eyes gleaming at him.

"As I said previously," McCaffrey said, "we need to train everyone for war. You, Niki, will begin training everyone how to use guns and the basics of hand-to-hand combat. Hackney and I will draw up plans to rig the tunnels and put in additional safety measures like escape hatches and air vents in case they decide to flood or gas us. I see little harm in the signs arbitrarily put out without the council's blessing. However, any physical action on anyone's part will not be tolerated—we cannot endanger the entire community in such a way. Does *everyone* understand?" he asked, looking around the room, letting his gaze linger especially on Niki, Loui, and Callista.

After receiving several nodding heads and a few "yeses," McCaffrey nodded once and left to go over to the war room table Hawkney was bent over, pencil in hand.

"Well," Loui said, turning toward Callista. "I suppose I should start getting back in touch with some old friends. Care to come with me, *ma chérie*? A pretty face can go a long way with some of these men." He waggled his eyebrows at her, making her giggle and agree to come along.

"You will need to put on a dress where we're going," Loui said, making a turn around her, looking her up and down. "Perhaps the red one—yes, that will fit with the locale. Do you know where the dress is?"

"No, but I bet Butterfly does since she's a seamstress. They might have repurposed it already, though."

"That would be a great pity," he said. "You were a vision in it. I will also dress and meet you back here, yes?"

She replied in the affirmative and searched for the dress she disliked so much, wondering where in the world Loui was taking her that would require something so nice.

It turned out Butterfly did still have the dress. Callista met Loui in the main hall, finding him in a bright blue button-down shirt under a navy blazer and dress pants, his hair slicked back and shining under the glare of the lights high above.

"*Ma chérie*, you are a vision, just as before," he said, arranging a few locks of her hair about her face before nodding with approval. "Shall we?"

They left the tunnels through the old, unused subway station under City Hall, and Callista marveled again at the ornateness of the station. Brass chandeliers hung from the ceiling in between the skylights, and the walls and arches above the tracks and along the walls were decorated with a warm cream and green tile.

"Now, be your beautiful, charming self, and let me do the talking," he said as they waited for a taxi on the curb.

"Where are we going?" she asked.

"A nightclub called Morticia's, where disreputable persons

with reputations like mine frequent for such company. Don't get into long conversations, but don't refuse a dance or two either. You're with me, but I do not have exclusive rights. Good to keep them hopeful, if you know what I mean. Makes them more willing to negotiate."

"So I'm eye candy to sweeten the deal?"

"Something like that—more likely I need you to put them at ease, make them feel empowered. I have faith in your capabilities."

"Your confidence in me is inspiring," she said with a hint of sarcasm as a taxi pulled up, and Loui opened the door for her, gallantly ushering her in before stepping in himself and giving the address to the driver.

Seeing a big, burly bouncer at the door of the club made her a little nervous, though it didn't surprise her. Loui hopped out and offered his hand to help her out before he walked her up to the suited bouncer without hesitation.

"Marcus! *Mon ami*! How are you?" Loui said as he approached the man.

A wide smile spread across the bouncer's face, and he held out his hand to shake Loui's. "Been a long time, Bordeaux. Good to see you."

"And you, my friend. Tell me, is Foxfire in the house tonight?"

"You know as well as I he never comes in the front door," Marcus said with a smirk. "And you know he sometimes stays here for days. You'll have to go see for yourself if he's in."

They shared a chuckle at the inside joke, and Loui gave Marcus a little slap on the arm as he slipped him a friendly token of his appreciation and moved to go inside. Marcus opened the door and gave Callista a courteous nod as they went by.

The dark room was dimly lit by blue and purple lights. The brightest spot was the stage where a jazz band played, their suits white and the lead singer's dress glittering silver from spaghetti straps to flared skirt. The bar stock was backlit with neon as were some of the plants scattered around the booths. The door they came through opened at the top of a sweeping staircase down onto the main floor, with a few balcony tables and booth seats to either side.

She gazed around in wonder and caught Loui looking at her with a smug smile.

"You have not been to such a place, have you?" he asked.

"No, I've never been to a nightclub."

"Well, this is one of the classiest modern clubs you will find and the most exclusive. No one can just walk in—you have to be invited by a member."

Loui seated her at a table near the dance floor and, after getting her order, went to the bar for the drinks. Her gaze followed him. The bartender was clearly another old friend. A grin split his face when he laid eyes on Loui, and they clasped hands over the bar and talked earnestly.

The chair next to her lurched and creaked. She turned to see a man in a white suit with gelled blond hair that fell sideways over his face. A neon handkerchief peeked from his front pocket, glowing green in the black light from the ceiling. Both the smell of alcohol wafting off him and the way he slouched to the side immediately told her he was drunk.

"Now, what jewel has Bordeaux brought to the club this time?" the man said slowly, as if being careful not to slur his words, and leaned forward to take her hand. She smiled graciously.

"I've seen you somewhere before," he said, cocking his head and narrowing his eyes at her. "Has he brought you here before?"

"No, this is my first time. It's an interesting place. I rather like it."

"It's very exclusive, you know," he said, straightening up. "I'm its greatest patron. I don't leave for days sometimes, and then only when Morty says I'm getting ripe and have to go home."

"Foxfire! *Mon ami.* Just the man I was looking for," Loui said, clinking his and Callista's drinks down on the table. "Charming my lady already, I see. You are exactly as I last saw you."

"You're looking well yourself, Loui old boy," Foxfire said,

shakily getting to his feet and shaking Loui's hand energetically. "How's business?"

"That is what I've come to discuss with you. I work as an intermediary for one who looks to buy some hardware—in bulk."

"*Really*," Foxfire said, sitting down very slowly, his eyes narrowing at Loui. "Well, to open negotiations, how about buying me a drink? Oh, and do introduce me to your escort."

Loui chuckled and signaled to the bartender, pointing at Foxfire. The bartender nodded knowingly and set to assembling a cocktail. "This, *mon ami*, is Liberty *von Menschen*, a dear friend of mine. She is new to the city, so I'm showing her the sights."

"You can call me Libby," she told Foxfire in a sultry voice with hooded eyes, gently laying a hand on his arm and giving him a smile like women do in the movies.

"A pleasure, Miss Libby," he said, lifting her hand from his arm and kissing it. "So, Loui. Does your boss have the deep pockets necessary to open negotiations with me?" he asked, cocking his head at Loui and continuing to hold her hand.

Loui laughed. "I can tell you he's extremely stingy, but his pockets are deep enough. And he's in a hurry, so you can probably make a few extra bucks off him."

"Oh, how I do enjoy working with you, Loui, old boy," Foxfire said, taking Callista's arm and trying to pull her closer to him, making her lean over awkwardly. Loui moved his foot and pushed the leg of her chair closer to Foxfire's, so she could be more comfortable. She smiled graciously at Foxfire, who was none the wiser, and settled up against him, making him grin all the more. "So ... ," he said, not taking his stare off her. "What exactly is he looking for?"

"A little bit of everything," Loui said, taking a sip of his drink. "A large quantity of handguns would be best, a few Uzis if you have them. He has several ex-Army people; a few nice pieces for them would undoubtedly make them happy. They could probably do with a few cases of explosives too, for what they have in mind if you have any in stock."

"Sounds like a pretty big operation," Foxfire said, narrowing his eyes and stroking Callista's arm.

"It is—the incident in Russia has the boss nervous. He wants to beef up security big time."

"Well, you've come to the right place for hardware, and I can get him a decent price," Foxfire said, turning his attention back to Loui. "I've come into possession of an awful lot of hardware since the de-militarization of the world's armed forces following the invasion. I'm not joking when I say I have three warehouses stocked to the rafters, but don't go spreading that around," he said, giving a wink to Callista, who smiled and nodded. "If you want, you can bring your boss and his military boys with him, and they can pick out what they want. The window shopping might encourage them to get a little more than they intended too," Foxfire said, smiling knowingly at Loui.

"Perfect," Loui said, raising his glass and clinking it with Foxfire's, which the waiter had just delivered. Loui brought the glass to his lips with a smile and took a long draw. He raised his gaze as he put down the glass, and the smile melted from his face. Callista turned to see four Alamgirians standing in the doorway at the top of the stairs. The black lights made their violet and scarlet eyes glow brilliantly. The atmosphere of the room tensed a dozen notches as the patrons nervously glanced at each other and moved uneasily. Some whispered, asking if this was some sort of raid.

Callista looked back and met Loui's worried gaze.

"They're here for you," she said.

CHAPTER FIFTEEN

F oxfire glanced back over his shoulder and quickly turned back to them as the Alamies walked down the staircase. He swore softly. "Guess I better get going," he said, swaying to his feet and kissing her hand again. "Forget me not, dearest. Catch you around, Loui," he said before staggering off. Others quickly downed their drinks and slapped down coins and bills before sidling off themselves. Loui remained stiffly in his chair.

Callista peeked back at Alamy, who now stood at the bar, and her heart sank when she espied both violet and purple gleaming brightly from the blacklights. It was Admiral Xor-nalden.

"Go," she said, rising from her seat. "I'll distract him."

"*Quoi?*" Loui said with a start. "*Ma chérie, non,*" he said, catching her wrist.

"Isn't this why you brought me here? To be a distraction? You're far more important to the Renegades than me, go," Callista said and pulled her arm away from Loui and picked up her drink. She sauntered over to where the Admiral leaned against the bar, surveying the room. "Well, look who it is," she said in a smooth voice. "Come to get away from it all too?"

"I rather hoped a respectable woman like you would not

associate with such disreputable people, though circumstances put you in their midst," Xor-nalden said, turning toward her. She belatedly realized he might be here for her and clutched her drink.

"And whose fault is that?" she said flirtatiously, trying to keep the tension out of her voice, and leaned toward him, bending her head so she gazed up at him at an angle. He gazed at her for a moment before he slipped the drink out of her fingers and placed it on the bar.

"Let us dance, shall we?" he said, taking her arm and leading her out onto the dance floor amid two other couples who nervously swayed. He pulled her against him, and they swayed to the soft jazz, Callista counting the seconds Loui had to get away, far away, from there. After a few moments, though, Xor-nalden looked down at her. "Now, you are either thoroughly drunk, which has made you fearless and flirtatious, or you are hiding something."

"What if I am?" she said softly, heart pounding as sweat broke out along her spine. She parted her lips and moved her face close to his, glancing at his lips for a long moment before looking back up into his glowing eyes.

The corner of his mouth raised in a smile. He tightened his grip around her waist, turned her so her back was to the audience, and kissed her hard. She blinked, surprised he took her suggestive hints, until she observed he wasn't looking at her but at the crowd. The soft bang of a door sounded behind her, and he abruptly ended the kiss and snapped orders to his men. She turned to see his men dash toward the kitchen and guessed Loui had stayed in the shadows next to the door to see what would happen. She sucked in her breath. Xor-nalden gently grabbed her by the chin to turn her head back toward him.

"What are you hiding, Callista Marie Tristan?" he asked softly, his gleaming eyes seeming to look for the cracks into her soul. She swallowed hard and stared back at him for a moment, thoughts in a jumbled whirl as he continued to hold her close and sway to the music.

"I think the lady doesn't appreciate your company," a voice said from the side, and they turned their heads to see Foxfire standing near them. "I think she'd like a new dance partner."

"Ah, but our conversation just became so interesting," Xor-nalden said, his arm tightening around her waist, making her move her hand from the top of his shoulder to the front, a vain gesture of pushing away.

"An interesting conversation she doesn't want to have," Foxfire said.

"I tolerate no incivility here, *your Majesty*," a woman's voice said from behind Callista. She turned to see a woman with long, black hair and thick, dark eyeshadow wearing a fitted white dress with long sleeves and a black-beaded necklace. "I don't care if you are the ruler of the world. This is a safe place. If you don't play by the rules, I will have to ask you to leave."

"Your boys aren't here to tell her boys differently, either," Foxfire said, smirking.

Xor-nalden glanced back and forth between them for a moment, his gaze traveling to Marcus and another burly man standing at the foot of the stairs and around the room at the patrons watching with grim faces. He gave the pair a smile.

"But of course, my apologies," he said, releasing Callista but keeping her hand, kissing it. "I do hope we meet again to continue our conversation, Miss Tristan, under better circumstances," he said, using her hand to cover his mouth so the whole room would not catch his words, holding her gaze for a long moment.

Foxfire squeezed in between them before she could answer, pulling her from the Admiral's grip and whisking her into a quick waltz away from him. She glanced back whenever she could and saw the woman in the white dress leave. Xor-nalden continued to watch her dance for a long moment before he picked up his coat, where he left it on a barstool, and departed the way he had come. Callista and Foxfire both exhaled when the door closed behind him.

"Thank you," Callista said after she breathed for a moment. "I thought you left."

"Went upstairs to tell Morticia she had a distinguished guest," Foxfire replied, nodding toward a private study with darkened windows adjacent to the balcony seating.

"But what of Loui?" Callista asked, looking back at him.

"Let's go see," he said, leading her back toward the kitchen.

They found Loui wearing an apron and a ragged baseball cap on backward with his arms elbow-deep in the sink full of dishes.

"Are they gone?" he asked, looking at them from the side.

"Xor-nalden is, don't know about his goons," Foxfire said. "Why didn't you go into the wine cellar?"

"No time. They were right on my heels."

"True, true. Morticia would have hung you herself if you exposed her secrets," Foxfire said with a grin. "Stay put—I'll take the lady up to Morticia's private study for a bit."

Loui nodded and went back to scrubbing dishes.

Foxfire led Callista back out to the main floor and up a set of tight winding stairs next to the kitchen door and into a room with tinted windows that overlooked the club. The woman in the white dress stood at the window, smoking a cigarette from a long holder.

"I don't appreciate having trouble—especially from the Alamies—in my club," she said without turning around.

"Sorry, Morty—"

"You *know* not to call me that, Leonard."

"Sorry, Lady Morticia. But do you know who this is who has graced your club?"

Morticia turned around. "Who?" she asked, taking a drag from the cigarette at the corner of her mouth and fixing her languid gaze on Callista.

"This is the woman who beat the Admiral at chess. You hear about that wife-finding enterprise he discontinued a few days or so ago? Well, she's the one who put an end to it and outplayed him, literally and figuratively. I remembered where I'd seen her before when he started dancing with her."

"Hmm," Morticia said, sauntering up to Callista, arms crossed, cigarette held up at an angle. "I do appreciate a capable woman who doesn't take the patriarchal society's whims lying down, especially not something so ridiculous as that 'program' of his. But I can't have such attention drawn to my establishment," she continued, tapping her cigarette holder over an ashtray on the coffee table. "Business has been especially good for my patrons since the new establishment, and I'm sure they'd like to not have it put in jeopardy."

"I understand," Callista said, meeting her gaze. "We'll leave once we're sure they're gone."

"Good," Morticia said. "And don't come to my establishment again—you or Bordeaux, as much as it pains me to say it," she said, a hint of wistful remorse coming into her voice. "Do tell him for me, won't you, Foxy dear? I might weaken if I have to myself."

"Of course, my lady," Foxfire said with a slight bow. "It will be my pleasure."

"I'm sure," she said, rolling her eyes for Callista's benefit before giving her a smile. "But in appreciation for your ... courage against the Admiral tonight and previously, your drinks are on the house."

"Why, Lady Morticia! Your generosity is—"

"Not *you*, you glutton," she said, sending Foxfire a disdainful look. "You still owe me over a thousand dollars in booze."

"Well, Loui has an employer who's looking to buy in bulk, so I'll have some cash flow here soon, and I promise yours will be the first bill I pay," he said, taking Morticia's hand and kissing it. "Come on, Lady Liberty," he said to Callista, winking. "Let's go have a drink to celebrate your escape."

She glanced back at Morticia as Foxfire led her toward the door, and she received a respectful nod from the matron, which she returned. Foxfire opened the door for her and led her back down into the night.

CHAPTER SIXTEEN

hat was that? Negev stormed into his penthouse, mentally kicking himself. He went there to try to befriend her, not antagonize her. He totally blew it.

Now, how would he talk with her again and get her to like him, or just be willing to listen? He flopped down on the bed, rubbing his hands over his face. Gren-del was scheduled for a visit four months from now, with the legitimate excuse that there was a lot of unrest in his territory he needed to oversee personally. Negev needed to figure out how to nail him to the wall without drawing the ire of Gren-del's loyalists before then, and get some support from the Humans should relations go south with Gren-del or his men, and pacify Humanity in the meantime for his apparent inaction on the outrage.

And now he worried if the woman he sought support from was, in fact, working against him. He rolled over onto his side with a groan and pulled a pillow into his arms so he could bury his head in it, curling his legs under him. Always more problems, so few solutions.

He turned over the events in his mind again. He was curious when she approached him so easily. Seeing the drink made him deduce she was tipsy. But the flirtatiousness was a red flag—she showed no such attraction before. The fact that he smelled no alcohol on her breath nor noted any lack of control in her movements on the dance floor, her stiffness when he put his hand on her back to dance, the way she did not look at him as they danced until he spoke, and the glint of fear he marked in her eyes told him all was not as she wanted it to appear.

Augustus, the cat, jumped up onto the bed with him, purring and rubbing against his back. Negev rolled onto his back and the cat climbed onto his chest, closing his eyes as Negev rubbed under his chin and around his face. The cat appeared to smile in pleasure. Negev smiled too. He needed to stop worrying about what he could not change and consider what he could.

There was a soft knock at the door, and Pat-farfth came in. Negev ignored him and continued to stroke the cat, hoping his uncle would catch the meaning of his silence.

"Did you find her?" Pat-farfth asked, sitting on the edge of the bed.

"Yes," Negev said flatly, still not looking at him.

"It did not go well?"

"No," Negev answered.

"What happened?" Pat-farfth prodded after he didn't elaborate.

"She was hiding something, shielding someone." He sighed, making the cat float up and down on his chest. "My soldier side took over, and I was a bit rough with her. I succeeded in intimidating and being generally ominous. We will have to find our support elsewhere."

"You believe you have no further chance with her?"

"I am sure she was up to something, making her one of the last people I wish to gather to my side—she would probably stab me in the back."

"Then from whom will you seek support?" Pat-farfth asked.

Negev was silent for a moment before answering. "Politicians, religious leaders—those who have the people's ear and trust." He slid the cat off his chest and rolled over to face his uncle.

"Organize a dinner so I might address them and talk with some of them individually in a more personal setting. Relationships earn trust better than press conferences."

"Agreed," Pat-farfth said. "I will make the arrangements—how about the first of December? That will give them time to plan. Put together a list of the persons you wish me to send invitations to," he said, rising. Negev nodded, stroking Augustus thoughtfully.

Pat-farfth moved to the door but stopped and turned back. "I do not believe you should give up on her yet," he said, opening the door. "You speak of relationships—you have one, whether you admit it or not, whether it is where you want it to be or not. You might need it one day. Pursue it a little longer." He bid his nephew goodnight and closed the door behind him.

Negev sighed through his nose and gazed out at the twinkling lights of the city. His mind wandered back to what he considered to be his greatest triumph—the conquest of Earth with minimal bloodshed. It was all so simple, so straightforward. There was no worrying about stepping on toes or division within his ranks. Just his forces and the objective.

He lay back on the bed and reviewed it in his mind again, willing the clinical logic of it to soothe him as he again walked through every development, every thought, every decision.

BY THE STARS, it was beautiful. They hovered above the planet, its blue seas giving way to green and tan land, all shrouded in pure white veils of clouds here and there, as though the modest planet were trying to cover its beauty from the foreign eyes that beheld it.

An angular satellite drifted across the viewport, snapping Negev out of the stupor. This planet was quite inhabited.

"Status?" Negev asked the first officer.

"Language analysis at eleven percent."

"So slow?" Negev asked, cocking an eyebrow at him.

"It seems multiple languages are used on this planet," the first officer responded, touching a monitor. "The computer is having to catalog the differences as it picks up the communications before it begins to decipher it."

Negev turned to glance out the opposite viewport. His armada, or what was left of it, was arranged in a defensive formation as they orbited the planet. His critical eye automatically began cataloging the visual damage to the various ships. Some of the more delicate arrays were melted from the intense heat as they fled the sudden supernova of their sun. Others had entire wings torn off or gashes along the sides from the hazardous trip through the wormhole. No Alamgirian ships had made such a long jump through a wormhole before. Using wormholes to travel to different parts of their solar system was still in the testing stages and had only been accomplished by a few science ships. They had never visited another star system, and the wild ride had taken its toll.

"They've noticed us," the sensors officer said, her voice placid. "Multiple satellites are rotating our way."

"About time," muttered the first officer.

Negev secretly had to agree. They'd been orbiting for almost a tenth of a day cycle.

"Sir, there's what appears to be a space station coming up over the horizon," the sensors officer said.

"Perhaps it was they who spotted us," the captain muttered, pulling up the display showing the station. Negev glanced over at it.

"Weapon capabilities?" he asked.

"Appears to be none," the sensors officer answered.

"Sir, I'm picking up a strong signal," the communications officer said. "I believe it's directed at us."

"Let's hear it," Negev said. They all listened quietly as a voice tensely spoke. "Analysis?" Negev asked once it finished.

"Still not enough to make anything coherent out of it," the first officer said.

The voice went silent, and Negev pursed his lips. "How much more time?" he asked.

"Still quite a ways, sir. The computer is having difficulty. Although I suppose that's to be expected—we've never encountered an alien race before."

Negev nodded. "Open a return channel," he said, stepping over the communications officer. "Let's see if I can buy the computer sometime."

"Open, sir," she whispered.

"This is Admiral Negev Xor-nalden of the Alamgirian fleet. Our apologies for surprising you," he began, consciously keeping his tone light. "Our own planet has just been destroyed, and we seek solace. Our ships are damaged, our stock of resources minimal. If we do not settle here, we will need resources to seek out another habitable planet. We do not desire any hostilities between us and hope—"

"Incoming!" shouted the sensors officer. "Warhead fired from the largest continent, time to impact eight micro-cycles!"

"Shields up!" Negev shouted, moving back to his command console. "All ships move to dispersed formation and prepare for counter meas—"

A ship flickered past the viewport, its engines rattling the bridge, hurtling toward the oncoming warhead, which, according to Negev's display, had just left the planet's atmosphere. Negev ground his jaw. He immediately recognized the capital ship. It was Admiral Gren-del's.

Negev watched as the ship fired at the oncoming missile, exploding it before hurtling on past and firing at the installation from which it came. It then performed a perfect bounce off the atmosphere and climbed back into space, resuming its place in formation.

Gren-del's voice ground from the speaker. "You're welcome, *sir*."

Negev had to consciously relax his jaw muscles and made no reply.

"Sir, they're preparing to fire other missiles, from multiple locations," the sensors officer reported.

Negev sucked in a deep breath, taking a look at the blissful planet below him. "Launch the sky-knives," he said, his voice steely. "Use the cover of night. Destroy all missile launching facilities, but nothing more."

"Heard, sir," the captain said, relaying the information.

"Xor-nalden," Gren-del said, "we need to destroy all the military installations and the cities—"

"Move *Place of Rest* to the fore," Negev cut in, ignoring Gren-del. He moved the ships on his schematic so the other ships could see his vision. "Attract the fire of the missiles. Stingers, use ion cannons to disrupt the satellites, but do not destroy, we may need them. All other ships, focus fire on incoming missiles with the mother ship."

A squad of sky-knives zipped by toward the planet. Their skeletal frames looked like four knives in a rectangular array with a pod joining them where the pilots sat. With a ripple, they engaged their cloaking mirrors and seemed to vanish from sight. They peeled toward the dark side of the planet, where the cover of darkness would help hide them. Negev glanced down and saw Admiral Tert-chon had laid out their attack pattern, crisscrossing the planet from north to south to keep the ships in darkness as they eliminated their targets. He nodded, pleased.

"Sir, we're receiving another communication from the planet," the communications officer called.

"Analysis?" Negev asked, not bothering to listen to the gibberish again. The first officer stared at the screen for a long moment.

"They seem to be threatening destruction," he said flatly.

Negev gave a small snort, noting that they were easily eliminating the ballistic missiles before they reached half the distance to the mothership. He watched for a moment before a cold thought touched him. He spun to the sensors officer.

"Scan the moon again. We are certain there are no installations there?"

"Let's just destroy the whole thing to be sure," Gren-del's voice suggested.

"A waste of time and resources," Tert-chon muttered back, clearly focused on something else in his ship.

"Nothing there, sir, just a bit of debris," the sensors officer responded.

"Let the moon be," Negev said firmly. "Stay in formation." He smiled grimly. "This will be over soon."

AND IT HAD BEEN. But had he done the right thing? Should he have waited longer to attack and tried to talk first? Negev sighed, and Augustus rubbed his head against him. What was done was done. There was no changing it now.

After his space fighters had circumnavigated the globe and eliminated their targets, he sued for peace, threatening another round of destruction. By then, their computer had gathered enough communication activity to decipher it and make a legible message possible. The smallest, least prepared countries quickly capitulated when they regarded the casual way their neighbors' military installations were dealt with, and when the trickle began, it soon became a flood, with the largest countries stubbornly hanging on a few more hours to assess their capabilities before they reluctantly submitted for peace.

He pursed his lips. If Gren-del were in charge, there would have been no attempt at peace outright, and he would have wrought an apocalypse upon the world, careless of civilian or Human life in general, and been content to sit upon a throne of ashes and bones and remake the world in his own image from the rubble.

He groaned and rolled onto his side to look out at the

oblivious glitter of the city. If he didn't find a way to subvert Gren-del, that outcome may still come to pass.

CHAPTER SEVENTEEN

Foxfire put Loui and Callista in a cab in the wee hours of the morning. They rode for some time in silence before Callista spoke.

"I don't think he was there for you," she said softly to him. "He was there for me. He didn't react with surprise or anything when I approached him. He knew I was there."

Loui sighed in reply.

Callista stared out the window, dark alleys flashing by like morose thoughts. "What's going to happen now?"

"Now, we lay low for a while," he said softly. "Foxfire won't want to do any business with us until the heat cools down. Then he'll take me, probably Hawkney and Niki along for a ride, blindfolded, to wherever he has his stock, and then we make a deal."

"Do the Renegades have enough money for something like this?"

Loui gave a soft snort. "No, but we have a hacker. He can make money magically appear in our account out of nowhere. It's like counterfeit without the printing presses, and Foxfire won't care either way."

She nodded.

"Did he hurt you?" he asked after a moment, and Callista didn't like his tone of voice.

"No," she said coolly. "Foxfire and Morticia pulled me out of the sticky situation."

"Good," he said, relaxing back. "When I saw him kiss you like that, I feared he would take you with him against your will, and my instinct was to run and get help. Luckily, I recovered quickly enough when I heard him order his men after me."

"He did it to make you react so he could find who I was with. Clever, really."

"*Oui.* But the question remains: what did he want with you?"

Callista sighed and gazed out the window, recalling that the last time she met Xor-nalden, he said they need never see each other again. She also remembered Foxfire saying Xor-nalden shut down the wife-finding program after she beat him at chess. Did she just show how ridiculous it was, or was there something else, another reason? What if the ring wasn't his mother's but merely an excuse to talk to her? What if he decided she was a threat?

Then another thought struck her—what if he didn't truly care about the cat but took it to make himself look good and garner her trust. Her stomach turned with worry, and she forcibly flung the thoughts and questions away.

"I have no idea," she finally replied.

CALLISTA'S DAYS had settled into a nice routine over the last month. Get up, eat, mop, eat, scrub, eat, sort through the dumpster divers' findings, sleep. Simple. Callista liked simple. Simple didn't leave much margin for error and getting in trouble.

She started getting the distinct feeling Hawkney liked her. He kept hanging around where she worked, claiming to do survey work for the new defenses, though he took his sweet time and talked to her a lot. And, of course, he happened to be surveying the section the cleaning team worked on half the time. The conversations were awkward, too, like when they dined together a few days earlier. They usually followed the lines of a greeting, asking after health, how things went inside and outside the settlement, and that was about it. They couldn't even talk about the weather, since it changed little underground.

She didn't care, though—she was not interested in him. Maybe she was prejudiced after his initial distrust, but somehow, he just wasn't her type. He was nice enough, but he just wasn't right for her—she couldn't place why. Hence, she did nothing to help his conversation efforts.

She finished up mopping the condensation off a ceiling, pausing to wipe her brow and survey her work when an appreciative whistle echoed down the tunnel.

"My, my, you look just as fine with a mop as you do in a red dress, Lady Liberty," Foxfire called, his voice echoing down the tunnel.

"Foxfire!" Callista said in surprise. "What are you doing here?"

"I've come looking for the rumored Atlantis, and it would appear I have found it, along with a mermaid," he said, putting his arm around her and giving her a quick peck on the cheek.

"Well, it looks like they need to hurry up with those perimeter defenses, if a Kraken like you can swim in here so easily," she said.

He laughed. "Indeed, and that is why I have come. I'm looking for either Loui or his employer to get the deal we talked about underway. My tab at Morticia's only gets larger."

"I can help you find him," she said, leaning her mop against the wall. "Come with me."

Foxfire entertained Callista with descriptions of a fantastic new wine Morticia's started carrying and a mixed drink he invented one night in a drunken epiphany until they came to the center and nearly collided with Hawkney coming around the corner. He took one glance at Foxfire in his blue-gray suit and snatched his pastel purple tie, pulling it up so it constricted around Foxfire's throat.

"Who. Is. This." Hawkney asked Callista, his face in Foxfire's, never breaking his gaze.

"A friend of Loui's. He has the supplies we need, came looking for Loui to follow up on the proposed deal."

"Indeed," Foxfire said tightly, plucking at his tie. "You must be one of the military men Loui mentioned. What can I get for you? A Scar, perhaps? Or are you more the M-5 type? Or perhaps you'd like to go Russian with a PK?"

Hawkney narrowed his eyes but slowly relinquished his grip, making Foxfire gasp a little and a grin spread over his face.

"Come with me," Hawkney said begrudgingly and led Foxfire over to where McCaffrey sat at the war room table, looking over their plans. Callista watched them for a moment before going in search of Loui.

She found him with a few others, turning Christmas ball ornaments which had started appearing on shelves into smoke bombs, carefully ladling the ingredients inside, and quickly sealing the top as smoke began to wisp out.

"Foxfire is here," she told Loui casually. He nearly dropped the ornament he just finished sealing.

"*Quoi*? Here? How did he know how to get down here?"

"I don't know," she said with a shrug. "He said there were rumors about us, so he came looking."

"Eager to close the big deal we talked of, no doubt. Morticia must be pressing him for her money. It is unlike him to wait such a short time after an incident like the one four weeks ago."

"He did mention her too," she said with a smile, one Loui matched.

"I suppose I should go and make sure he does not blow it—he can be quite annoying and rub people the wrong way."

"No, really?" Callista said with a smile, and they headed back to the main hall.

They found Foxfire exhibiting his wares via photos he passed around to Hawkney, Niki, and McCaffrey, singing the praises, virtues, and conditions.

"Trying to skip the consultant's fee, *mon ami*?" Loui called out to Foxfire.

"You know I wouldn't do such a thing to a friend like you," Foxfire said, stepping over to Loui and shaking his hand. "But you have heat on you brother—I didn't want this deal to fall through, so I took matters into my own hands. Even if it meant slogging through sewers for hours. I hope I never have to do that again to chase down a deal."

"No, you prefer to do it in the comfort of Morticia's with a drink in your hand and a woman on your arm," Loui mocked, gently punching Foxfire in the shoulder.

"You know me all too well," Foxfire said, turning back to the table. "Well friends, anything catch your eye?"

"Indeed," McCaffrey said, laying down the photos. "I'm worried about the prices, though."

Callista tuned out the conversation when she spotted Butterfly running toward her.

"I found this stuck in the fence in front of our access on Joralemon Street," Butterfly said, handing Callista a paper rose with a pipe cleaner stem. Butterfly pointed to a petal, and on closer inspection, Callista spotted writing on it.

She carefully unwrapped the rose and flattened out the paper on one of the picnic benches.

MY APOLOGIES FOR THE OTHER NIGHT,
I'M AFRAID I GAVE YOU QUITE A FRIGHT.
I ONLY WANTED TO MEET WITH YOU
TO SEE WHAT, TOGETHER, WE COULD DO.
ALL IS NOT AS IT SEEMS,
THERE ARE MANY UNDERLYING SCHEMES
AGAINST MYSELF AND HUMANITY
THREATENING OUR SERENITY.
HELP ME FIGHT AGAINST THIS EVIL;
ALL TO YOU I WILL REVEAL.

COME TO THE BANQUET THE FIRST OF DECEMBER.
THERE WILL BE NO DANGER,
I FULLY GUARANTEE YOUR SAFETY.
I HOPE YOU TAKE THIS OPPORTUNITY.

SINCERELY,
N. X

Callista cocked an eyebrow. Butterfly looked back and forth between her face and the paper, in a position where she couldn't read its contents.

"What?" she asked, hopping from one foot to the other and glancing between Callista and the note.

"Well," Callista began. "It's not a bad poem, but it's definitely not great either."

Butterfly gasped. "Do you have a secret admirer?" she asked in a breathless whisper, clasping her hands together under her chin.

Callista snorted. "Hardly. Xor-nalden wants me to come to some party so he can talk with me and apologize. Or so he claims."

"Are you gonna go?"

"Probably not," Callista said, dropping the poem.

Butterfly snatched it up, her eyes darting across the page. "But shouldn't you go to find out what the evil is?" she asked desperately.

"It's too vague—it's probably just something to make me come."

"But it's a poem! With a rhyme scheme. He can't be too specific."

"It's not safe, Butterfly. He said we would meet again, and it sounded ominous. He suspects me of something underhanded. This is his attempt to make the meeting happen and probably arrest me."

"But—"

"No buts. Throw it away," Callista said, walking off. She had mopping to do.

CHAPTER EIGHTEEN

Callista was folding clothes the next day when Niki came up to her and held the crumpled poem up in front of her face.

"I know," Callista said, turning back to the clothes. "I told Butterfly to throw it away."

"You should go," Niki said.

Callista gazed at her, raising her eyebrows. "Are you out of your mind, Niki? This is obviously a trap."

"Or it's our in. We need to step it up. All the hogwash the Admiral said on TV is just that—BS. There's been no justice for the martyrs. We need to put more pressure on him."

"And get ourselves arrested? Even if they aren't going to arrest us the moment we set foot in there, if we try to do anything disruptive, they definitely will arrest us."

"That's why we should go in force—there'll be too many to arrest."

"So they start shooting instead, and we're Saint Petersburg all over again," Callista said, smoothing out a shirt she just folded.

"Oh, it'll take some planning, but we can pull it off. Foxfire talked about it yesterday—all sorts of leaders from around the world will be there. If we protest there, they'll also see us and maybe start putting pressure on Xor-nalden too."

"It's too dangerous," Callista said, reaching for a shirt at the bottom of the basket. "McCaffrey would never allow it."

Niki snatched the shirt out of her hands. "Callista! We are ghosts calling for revenge right now! Unseen, ephemeral ghosts. We need to make Xor-nalden feel the cold fingers of this ghost."

"So he can paint a target on us and call in the Ghostbusters. Great idea, Niki. The only outcome I still see in this is where we end up the next round of martyrs."

"You have no imagination, no faith," Niki said, throwing the shirt back at her. "I'm telling you we could be in and out of there with no more than a few tasered guards and keep our identities hidden, so he'd be none the wiser."

"You do know he knows about us, right? We'd be his first suspects, regardless."

"That's what all these defenses are for," Niki said with a grin.

Callista threw down the shirt. "You have a death wish, don't you?" she said, her voice rising. "Those defenses are pinches compared to what the Alamies have—they won't stop them for long, if at all. Do you not remember how they conquered the planet in a day? You want to goad them into coming down here so you get the fight you so desperately want. You're sick, Niki."

"I'm a *patriot*, what are you?" Niki snapped back.

"*Sane*, to start with. And unselfish enough to see this is not just about me or you. it concerns a lot of defenseless people. Whatever happened to the soldier's creed to protect the innocent?"

Niki made a scoffing noise and stomped away. Callista breathed a restricted sigh of relief, glad that was over and done with—crisis averted.

IT WASN'T. Somehow, Niki managed to persuade Hawkney, of all people, to her cause.

"You can't be serious," Callista said when he broached the subject to her a week later.

"It's not as risky as you may think," Hawkney said. "You go in, per your invitation. If they arrest you, our mission becomes a rescue op. If they don't, you're our insider to let us in. We demonstrate; you look innocent and unconnected, we leave, you talk to the Big Cheese and find out what he wants, all the while being oh-so unconnected to us. That'll make it look like a lot of people are not only upset about it but willing to act out against it."

"And if he doesn't believe me? He didn't believe me the last time I tried to fake him out. I fooled him into thinking I was a moron the first time we met—he's not going to be fooled again."

"Well, what did you learn about the art of lying when you failed last time at the club?" Hawkney asked a bit acidly.

"Oh, I don't know—that I'm terrible at it?" Callista said in a matching tone with a layer of sarcasm.

"Then get good. We're doing this."

"McCaffrey will not allow it."

"He won't be told."

"And if I tell him?"

"I'll tell him you're trying to contact your boss and rat us out," Hawkney said, his voice lowering in volume. "He'll love that. He'll lock you away so deep and throw away the key so no one will ever hear from you again."

Callista wondered now if his special efforts to hang around her and talk to her were because he liked her, as she originally presumed, or if he was really spying on her. Her uncertainty made her unwilling to call his bluff, so she stayed silent. Hawkney smirked, seeming to take it as a victory.

"Here's the plan," Hawkney started, but Niki grabbed his shoulder.

"Better she doesn't know, just in case," Niki said, and Hawkney nodded.

"Good idea. But regardless," he said, fixing Callista with an intense stare. "You will do exactly what I tell you, how I tell you to do it, when I tell you to do it. One slip up from you, and this could go to hell in a handbasket, and it will be all *your* fault. Clear?"

Callista swallowed and nodded once.

"Good," Hawkney said with another smirk he shared with Niki. "We'll be talking to you later."

Callista gazed after them as they left, their heads bent toward each other in conversation, and sighed. How had she managed to end up in the middle of such a huge mess?

THE DAY of the banquet came, and Callista felt sick—sicker than she had in the last month, seeing the others prepare their costumes and protest paraphernalia. Loui let her out of the limo two blocks from the banquet building. She wriggled in Niki's fitted black dress with its long black sleeves and a completely open back except for two crisscrossed straps across her shoulder blades, trying to get the wrinkles out and hide where it ill-fit her in places before putting on the long, black London Fog coat to protect against the December chill.

Loui handed her black clutch out the window to her, complete with lipstick, pepper spray, a lock pick he taught her to use, just in case, and a recording device in the lining.

"You will be fantastic, *ma chérie*. Just be your charming self as you were the other night at Morticia's, and you'll be fine."

"But that didn't work, Loui, and I feel like I'm going to be sick. This is a horrible idea," she confided, tucking a strand of hair behind her ear and touching all around for anything out of place in her French bun.

"I meant when you were charming Foxfire. And you won't be

sick, *Mademoiselle*, this is all a dream. It's not really happening. If something goes wrong, you will either be the heroine or simply wake up. Nothing to worry about," he told her with a wink.

"Yeah, right," she answered, not having it for a moment. She started down the sidewalk, her high heels clicking on the pavement. She wondered if she clicked them together and repeated "there's no place like home," she would magically wake up at her home in Atlanta and smile at the sunshine pouring through the window, glad it was all a dream, and quite a few degrees warmer.

If only.

She looked up from the pavement and saw him. He stood at the door, shaking hands with the other guests as they came in, looking sharp in his black dress uniform underneath the open trench-like coat. His Admiral's rank insignia on his breast glittered in the setting sun when he turned just right. The last guest in line walked in, and for a moment, he stood alone. He gazed up at the sky and the sunset spreading reds and purples across the horizon and heaved a heavy sigh.

Did he, too, wish he could be home again? But that was far more impossible than her fantasy. She took a deep breath, shook the tension out of her muscles, and slowly walked up the steps toward him from the side, pitying the king without a home.

CHAPTER NINETEEN

Callista's heels clicked on the stone steps, and Admiral Xor-nalden turned his head and looked her way, a soft smile spreading across his face. He held his hand out to her, and she stepped up to him and took it.

"Thank you for coming," he said, giving her hand a soft squeeze.

"Why am I here?" she asked, curious herself and knowing Hawkney and his other accomplices where listening to everything.

"The same as everyone else," he said, putting her hand on his arm and leading her inside. "To hear the true state of the government. If you wish, we may talk more afterward, though it will be a long night; I am sure everyone will have many questions. I am happy to make time for you, though."

Callista drew breath to ask why her, specifically, but Pat-farfth came up to them, smiling.

"You make a beautiful couple," he said. Xor-nalden narrowed his eyes and pursed his lips at his aide but made no rebuttal.

"Would you mind seeing the lady to her seat, Lieutenant?" he asked icily. Callista wondered at the subtext.

"It would be my pleasure," Pat-farfth said, extending his arm to Callista and leading her to a table at the edge of the ballroom halfway to where the podium was. This room was different from the one at the hotel where she first met Xor-nalden, with marble-tiled floors, fluted columns and skylights, making the whole space feel airy. She found herself seated with a news talk show host, the Pope and his translator, and two Asian persons she couldn't place.

Xor-nalden didn't eat after the appetizer was served. He moved from table to table, staying and talking with the people there for a few minutes before moving on to the next. She waited until they were well into the soup course to excuse herself and use the ladies' room. She instead slipped to the nearest side exit, and opened it, checking to make sure no alarm would sound if she did so.

Hawkney appeared a moment after she opened it, dressed in a white suit, white gloves, a white Bahama hat with a red band, and a white, emotionless mask on.

"A guard at the front, one at every other column," she said. "Not many cameras, lots of people."

"Xor-nalden?" Hawkney asked.

"Moving around the tables," she said.

He nodded and slipped a piece of cardboard in the door to prevent it from locking, and she sauntered back to her seat.

She resumed her seat and glanced nervously around the room. It wasn't long before she spotted people in white come up behind the guards and simultaneously clamp chloroform-soaked handkerchiefs over their mouths. A woman spotted one of them and opened her mouth to scream, but stopped when the man in white held up a finger to his masked lips and gave her the okay sign. The woman swallowed hard and looked about the room.

Callista glanced around too and noted the guards were now out of sight. A moment later a shout of "Justice" came from all around the room. People in white came from the shadows behind the columns with their hands raised in the air, dripping with scarlet paint.

They wove among the tables and columns quickly, leaving red

handprints on tablecloths, chairs, and columns, shouting for justice every five seconds.

"*Spravedlivost*—justice!" a woman's voice called separate from the rest.

Callista turned her head to see Niki, wearing Callista's red dress and a white mask, carrying a flag featuring a coiled rattlesnake above the words "Don't Tread on Me" on a yellow background: the Gadsden Flag, used as a warning before and since the American Revolutionary War.

"*Spravedlivost*—justice! Justice for the martyrs of Saint Petersburg!" She called, coming to a stop in the middle of the room near where Xor-nalden sat at a table, watching them coolly. "You!" She pointed a gloved hand at him. "You claimed you would dispense justice for the slain. You have done nothing. Their blood still cries out from the Earth for justice! Will you continue to sit and do nothing and give us more lies and excuses?"

"It is because of the dead I have gathered everyone here today," Xor-nalden said in a firm, loud voice for all to hear, rising to stand before Niki. "My world was ruled by a council—we have adopted a similar technique here on your world. I cannot make direct action against Admiral Gren-del, the man responsible for the massacre in Saint Petersburg until I have enough evidence to convict him before the council of other admirals. I was originally sole authority over the navy, but now that we are a fascist oligarchy, my position has weakened.

"This is why I have called you all together, to ask for your support," he said, looking around the room. "Gren-del is a cruel tyrant and should no longer be allowed to hold sway over anything, but I cannot bring him down alone without risking a civil war none of us wants—the collateral damage would be staggering. I need your help and your support in this."

Niki laughed, harsh and humorless. "You wish us to be your pawns to throw to the slaughter while you and your own remain high and dry."

"On the contrary," he replied, keeping his voice even and

patient. "My worst fear is there will be more massacres like the one in Saint Petersburg. My greatest goal in the war between us was to end the conflict quickly and with as few casualties as possible. I do not want you to fight and die for me, I want you to stay out of the way. Gren-del has hated me for years and done everything in his power to orchestrate my downfall. If it comes to war between us, and it probably will, I want you to listen to me when I tell you to flee this or that city. He knows how much I care for you and will slaughter you like insects without a qualm just to unsettle me. If you wish to fight against such evil by my side, I will certainly not refuse you, but honestly," he said, his arms spreading to the sides, "I do not know what else to do. If anyone can perceive a way where no one dies and we are rid of that monster in an *honorable* fashion, I am open to suggestions."

"I don't believe you. Not for a second," Niki replied.

"Of course, *you* do not," Xor-nalden replied, his eyes narrowing. "*You* are a soldier. One who did not get to fight against the invaders of your home. Your energy and hatred were never expended, and now you look for any and every excuse to pick a fight to expend it. I do not blame you. Any of you," he said, looking around at the other protesters. "But I would ask you to leave your finer grievances with me until after we have dealt with this much larger threat to us all."

He smiled at Niki and gestured toward the flag. "What is the American Revolutionary War mantra? 'United we stand, divided we fall'? That, too, applies here. Either we descend into chaos, both of us fighting on two fronts with Gren-del coming out on top, ruling the world in a reign of terror, or we work together, for the moment, and—"

"Words, words, words," Niki interrupted. "All I hear are words."

Xor-nalden gave her an icy smile. "And what comes out of your mouth?"

"Why you insufferable ... ," Niki lowered the flag toward Xor-nalden like a spear but was grabbed on the shoulder from behind by someone Callista guessed was Hawkney. He gave a hand signal and the other protesters began filing away. Niki struggled to get out of his grasp, but he pulled her away.

"The pen is mightier than the sword," Xor-nalden called after them, gaining confidence. "I suggest you examine your own motives and values before you begin calling me out on mine. You are upset over spilled blood and fear the spilling of more, but your own actions will do just that. How hypocritical," he said, sitting down again as Niki and Hawkney disappeared after the rest.

Quiet persisted for a long moment in the dining hall, and then everyone began talking at once. Xor-nalden jumped up and rushed over to the nearest column, where a guard slumped. He checked the guard's vitals and spoke rapidly into his communication wristband.

Callista took a deep, measured breath and sipped at her water. Now she would have to wait and see if Xor-nalden connected her with the protest or not and whether he would arrest her for collusion or let her walk.

CHAPTER TWENTY

I f you're tired enough, if you wait long enough and become bored enough, anything can become comfortable enough to sleep on. Callista fell asleep sitting in her chair sideways as she waited while half of the attendees of the banquet talked to Admiral Xor-nalden. He shook her awake and smiled at her as she slowly remembered what, where, who, how, and when.

"It is three in the morning," he said softly as she rubbed her eyes. "Shall I get you a room in this hotel or take you home?"

She hesitated, not relishing the idea of tromping in high heels and a long, formal dress through sewers that would be alive with rats and who knew what else. Her face must have reflected her unpleasant thoughts. Xor-nalden chuckled.

"A room here it is, then," he said, his eyes twinkling as he stood up from a crouch next to her. He walked across the room and spoke briefly to his aide, who nodded and departed. Xor-nalden returned to her, where she sat rubbing her eyes and held out his hand to help her up. She took it, and he led her to the elevator, where Pat-farfth met them and handed him a card key. They rode up the elevator in silence, Callista too tired to care or try to get anything useful out of him. He led her to her room, opened the door for her, and followed her inside.

"Is it to your liking?" he asked as she wandered in.

She gave a little laugh in response and ran her hand over the comforter of the real bed. He caught her meaning and smiled. She turned away from him, laying her coat on a chair, and he stepped over to her and gently touched her bare back.

"Are you all right, truly, living down there?" he asked when she turned.

"It's damp, but we make do."

"There is no reason for you to live down there," he said, taking her hands in his. "With the others, I assumed they were so upset with the new order they separated themselves from it in a sort of protest, but with you, it is different, correct?"

She sighed, weighing her words. "Part of the problem is no one knows what you'll do, how you'll react," she began, looking him in the eyes. "If you were a true dictator, like Gren-del, my beating you at chess might have warranted my execution."

He cocked an eyebrow at her supposition, but the grim set of his mouth told her she wasn't far from the truth with her supposition of Gren-del's cruelty.

"Running, hiding was a precaution in case you did feel that way," she continued.

"And now?" he asked.

She shrugged. "I guess I care about them too much to leave now." She dismissed the memory of Hawkney threatening to bury her if she didn't do what he wanted.

He cocked his head to the side, gazing at her for a moment. "Do you know why I played chess with those women?" he asked after a moment. "Because beauty is not as important to me as intellect. I want someone who can converse with me intelligently."

"Then why didn't you just talk with them?"

"Nerves," he answered. "Nervousness and fear cause one to choke on their words and say whatever comes to mind first, while if they conversed with a close friend, the conversation could be meaningful rather than flippant. By eliminating speech, by forcing them to strategize and take their time, I could not only determine their basic level of intellect but also gauge their reaction to me in general. If they could not stand my presence, we were clearly incompatible, etcetera."

"So where do I rank in all that?" she asked with a smile.

"At the top," he said, running his thumbs over the backs of her hands. "I fear I blundered a bit that evening at the nightclub, for which I apologize. I would like to get to know you better. Please do not be afraid of me."

"I don't think I am now—much," she said with a little smile. Xor-nalden smiled, too.

"It is late," he said, letting go of her hands. "Thank you, again, for coming. Sleep well. We will talk more tomorrow."

He left, leaving the card key on a table and gently shut the door after himself. She stood in the silent room, unsure what to think or do, but determined not to worry about it. She would take full advantage of the glorious king-sized bed and let tomorrow worry about itself.

THE NEXT MORNING, Callista went down to the lobby. She returned her key and started to walk out the front doors when she spotted Xor-nalden at a table in the dining area, staring at a data pad. She hesitated. She could slip out without being noticed and tell the others she never got a chance to speak with him. He sipped at his cup and heaved a tired sigh. She took a deep breath of her own and squared her shoulders, deciding to be brave and take her chances. Even though he seemed not to suspect her of collusion with the protesters last night, that didn't mean he hadn't put the pieces together by the morning.

He looked up at her approach, smiling. Callista imagined how she must look to him—about the same as the night before, but with her dress now a bit rumpled and her hair down around her shoulders. He stood and pulled out the chair next to him.

"Good morning," he said in his soft, smooth voice that always sent warmth up her spine. "Did you sleep well?"

"Best in a long while," she said, taking the seat. A waiter came up and asked her if she would like some coffee, which she declined, opting for water instead.

"Probably a wise choice," he said after the waiter left. "Your coffee is highly addictive." He held up his cup. "I find I cannot function without it anymore."

"You are hardly alone in that," she said with a smile.

He leaned back in his chair, taking a sip of his coffee. "What do you believe I should do about the protesters last night?" he asked, surprising her.

"Do? What do you mean?" she said, casually laying her clutch on the table.

"If you were in my place, what would you do about the incident?"

She chewed her lower lip for a moment. "Better security, I suppose."

"You would make no answer to their demands?"

"Did you not already do that, in a way? You held dialogue with them, and said you were already doing something about it, but nothing has come of your efforts yet."

"But if I appear to do nothing in addition, they may return with the same demands and perhaps resort to violence to make their demands more forceful."

She rubbed her fingers together for a moment. "Perhaps you should publish updates on the investigation. That way they can see the progress and see the truth as it unfolds. Fewer secrets are better than more."

He nodded slowly for a moment. "I find your advice agreeable. It shall be done." He set his cup down on the table.

"Are you going to arrest the protesters?" she asked, unable to contain her curiosity.

"No. What will that gain me? Yes, they have committed crimes by assaulting my soldiers if nothing else. But to arrest them would launch them into the public eye and affections. The media would spin it as a group of people arrested for exercising their right to free speech. It would only exacerbate my efforts to forge an understanding between us."

"So how do I figure into all this?" she asked when the waiter brought two plates with an assortment of breakfast foods.

"Whether you like it or not, you have become a recognizable symbol," he said, picking up his fork. "Did you notice how the spokeswoman wore your dress? Your publicized victory over me in chess and walking out has made you synonymous with pushing back against the regime. If you support my efforts for peace, people may be more willing to at least hear me out. It is the same with the Pope or the Dalai Lama, for instance."

"But people don't listen to me," she said. "I mop floors all day, whereas people actively seek the Pope for guidance."

He gazed at her over the rim of his coffee cup, taking another sip, his eyes twinkling at her. "You underestimate the power of social media and affection. And perhaps they do not listen because you have not spoken."

She remembered the night everyone looked to her and Loui to make protest signs and flyers. Was there a little something in what Xor-nalden said?

"Take a close look at the state of affairs in your little world down there," he said and reached for the salt. "Your leaders are a former CIA agent and some soldiers. The people respect them for who they were and what they did before the new regime. But now here you are, someone who has done something, something they admire, and that makes their current leaders appear inadequate. Perhaps that is why those in power have you mopping floors."

She stopped chewing and stared at him a long moment, cold filling her stomach as it sank in that he knew *exactly* what happened beneath the streets. She swallowed her food, which suddenly seemed thick in her mouth, and said hoarsely, "How do you know all that?"

He took a quick sip of his coffee and glanced at her. "We have monitored McCaffrey for some time—all former government agents. He has proven to be one of the more interesting."

Callista squeezed her eyes shut for a moment before forcing herself to take another bite. All illusions of safety and secrecy were thrown out the window. What would Hawkney and the others do and think when they listened to the recording and realized Xor-nalden essentially knew everything about them? She stared down at her plate. She couldn't take another bite, even though she had eaten only half of it. She set down her fork and wiped her mouth before looking at him again. "If you no longer require my presence, I should get going. Those tunnels aren't going to mop themselves," she said, forcing calm into her voice.

Xor-nalden's mouth curved in a smile. "Last I checked, your French friend slept in a car down the street," he said, wiping his own mouth. "Shall we order him a cup of coffee to go?" He signaled the waiter without waiting for a reply. He stood and moved Callista's chair for her, and they only waited a moment before the waiter came with the cup of coffee. Xor-nalden took it and offered her his arm, and he led her down the street.

They found Loui slumped against the door inside the car he dropped Callista off in. Xor-nalden rapped on the window, making Loui jump and grab the steering wheel. He looked around, and shock spread over his face to see not only Callista but Xor-nalden with her. Xor-nalden signaled for him to roll down the window and handed Loui the coffee cup.

"Here you are, Monsieur Bordeaux," Xor-nalden said. "Make sure you are fully awake before you drive the lady home. And you, Miss Tristan," he said, turning to her and clasping her hand. "If you ever wish to speak with me, my door is always open to you. Have a good day." He squeezed her hand gently before releasing it and walking back down the street toward the hotel.

Callista's gaze followed him for a moment before she turned to Loui. "Why are you here?" she asked.

"I could not just leave you," he said defensively. "What if you escaped in the middle of the night? What if he tried something naughty, and you needed a savior?"

She sighed in response and walked around the car to get in the passenger seat. Loui took a long drag of the coffee as she settled into her seat, put her elbow on the window sill and stared moodily out the window, her head resting on her fingers.

"Well," he said after a long moment. "How did it go?"

"He knows, Loui."

"That you are a compatriot?"

"About us. *Everything* about us. He's been watching McCaffrey from the beginning. He probably knows where in the tunnels we are, how many, what our capabilities are. We are not nearly as secret as we supposed, or secure for that matter."

He sat silent for a moment, staring through the windshield before he spoke again. "You think we have a mole?"

"That, or far more likely, they have some wicked good tech which allows them to do crazy surveillance," she said, rubbing her upper lip.

Loui grunted in response.

They sat in silence for a moment more until Loui slowly started the car and drove away. She wanted him to say something, anything, but what was there to say? It was what it was; there was nothing for it but to deal with it in the best way they knew how.

CHAPTER TWENTY-ONE

They told Hawkney and Niki first. Callista gave them the whole rundown of what Xor-nalden said, even though they'd probably listen to the recording later. Hawkney sat there, his face like stone, staring into space. Callista began to wonder if he was a ticking time bomb until he heaved a sigh and rubbed his face, leaving his head buried in his hands.

"Why are we even here then?" he finally asked. "What's the point? They know everything—we can't hide. We're just harming ourselves by doing so."

"But it's forged community," Callista said, trying to think positively. "I suppose we're making a statement by not settling for the Alamy regime and living apart."

"But once the Alamies get tired of us, they know exactly where we are and will wipe us out in a heartbeat," he said.

"We could go deeper," Niki said. "I'm sure our Sand Hog friends wouldn't mind finding some corners for us down there."

"Too hazardous," Hawkney said with a shake of his head. "It's far damper and we could get the bends if we have to scoot fast,"

Loui snapped his fingers. "That's it—Callista, *ma chérie* you are a genius!"

"What?" Hawkney asked grumpily.

"We are a living protest, a statement—like a sit-in or a monk on a pole. We must make ourselves known to the public, let them see how we do not put up with the Alamies—we would rather live in sewers. This way, if the Alamies do make a move against us, the people will take notice and will have another reason to be outraged. We will be fuel to the fire."

"And then we'll have the second American Revolution," Niki said jubilantly.

"Only you'll be dead," Callista said.

"I can still watch from the clouds," Niki said.

"Enough," Hawkney said firmly, leaning back in his chair. "We need to decide what to do about McCaffrey before anything else. If they somehow have a bead on him, we may have to expel him. I definitely believe he should be removed from office, at the least, in case he's become predictable."

"Agreed," Niki said. "I've thought it's time for new leadership for quite a while now."

"You just never liked him," Hawkney said.

"He always gave me an eerie feeling. Like I'm being watched in a bad way." Niki rubbed her arms.

"Do you think," Loui began cautiously, "that he works for *them*?"

Hawkney snorted in response. "If he does, why would Xornalden tell Callista?"

"Perhaps to make us question him as we are now," Callista said. "Make us suspicious, perhaps even remove a perfectly good leader."

"I'm not saying he should be totally removed from a leadership position," Hawkney amended. "I'm saying maybe he shouldn't be calling the shots anymore, just in case."

"We all agree on that, *mon capitaine*," Loui said. "The problem is getting the council to agree and McCaffrey to go along quietly."

"Who would be the new leader?" Callista asked.

Hawkney shrugged. "That's up to the council's vote. Could

be one of them, could be someone else. We haven't thought about it much, honestly. But if we disband, is there really any point?" he said, splaying his hands. "We gotta tell them the Alamies know everything. Our whole community is built around virtual invisibility, and now we know we never were."

"We'll have to tell them like it is and let them decide what to do," Niki said, standing and stretching her back. "Come on, there's no sense in waiting around. Let's get to it." She started toward the main room.

Loui followed her, and Callista started to when Hawkney laid a hand on her shoulder.

"What will you do if they decide to disband?" he asked her.

She shrugged. "Not sure." She could go back home, but she wasn't sure it was safe to do so, despite what Xor-nalden said.

"Well, if you want," Hawkney began, scratching nervously at the back of his head. "My brother has a farm out in Iowa. You could come with me."

Callista cocked an eyebrow and worked to keep her face neutral despite the surprise.

"We could hang out there for a while," he said, "until we figure out what we want to do now."

She gave him a small smile. "That's nice of you, Hawkney, thanks."

"So you'll come?" he asked, looking hopeful.

"I don't know. I'm going to wait and see what happens before I make any plans." Callista turned to follow the others down the tunnel. Best not to make promises.

———

THEY SPENT hours discussing the pros and cons of the community, secrecy or not. In the end, some stayed, others left. Those who decided to remain turned to the subject of McCaffrey. It wasn't exactly a landslide vote, and there was much hot debate, especially from McCaffrey, but the council voted him out of office.

"You shoulda seen his face," Niki told Callista at dinner as she lifted a forkful of spaghetti toward her face. "Black thunderclouds, threatening to rain down lightning on everyone. His face even turned a little purple when they nominated Hackney to be the new leader, and after the unanimous vote, he left the room in a huff. I won't be surprised if he stays in that dark mood for months, if not indefinitely."

"Does he just not like the idea of having a former subordinate be his new commanding officer?" Callista asked.

"Who knows. I don't really care," Niki said with a shrug of her shoulders. "I'm just happy he's out and Hawkney's in, and we're going to get some things done around here."

"How many people are leaving?" Callista asked and spooned in another bite of overcooked spaghetti.

"A lot of the older folk and the people with kids, which I thoroughly approve of—the dankness down here does them no favors," Niki said. "And some others who came down here, forfeiting family and jobs and stuff, which they would much rather have back now that they know it's no secret they're down here—or any probes up there."

"Don't have to pay taxes or anything, though," Callista said, smiling.

"Don't have to beg, though, either," Niki pointed out.

Hawkney joined them, and Niki slapped him on the back when he sat next to her.

"Congrats, Cap! Or should I call you General since your promotion?"

Hawkney rolled his eyes. "Very funny, Niki."

"What's our first move, boss?" Niki said with a grin.

Hawkney didn't say anything, taking a bite. "Loui might be right," he said after a moment of chewing. "We need to become a thorn in Xor-nalden's side, one the people can see and get behind.

Instead of the invisible community, we need to become the visible one everyone knows about."

"So we need some publicity," Callista said.

"Right. And you'll be a big part of that," he said, pointing his fork at her.

"Me? What do you mean?"

"You're the great chess champion," he said, taking another bite. "I thought we could ask a TV network or two to come down here and interview some of us, with you as the main attraction."

"To what end?" Callista asked. "What's the point in making a big deal out of me?"

"You're recognizable," Niki said. "You've done what a lot of people want to do every time they get mad at the Alamies. You're also relatable—and pitiful. Nice southern belle, forced to come up to the big, cold city and now lives in a sewer because of the aliens. What a sad story."

Callista sat and stared at Niki. She didn't like where this was going. They were making her into a sob story—one the Renegades could spin to their advantage. She stared down at her food. She didn't know what to do. Protesting would do little good. She began to consider going home again, especially since she was fairly certain Xor-nalden didn't care what she did.

Butterfly came up and wrapped her arms around Callista, squeezing the air out of her. "Boss-man is out, boss-man is out," she sang. "And Hawkney is in! Hal-le-lu-jah!"

"Amen!" Niki approved, making Butterfly giggle.

"Callista, I want you to go to the network tomorrow and talk to them about the TV spot," Hawkney said. "They'll recognize you—they'll know it's the real thing."

Callista stared at Butterfly and remembered how little she'd been on the surface in a long time. "Can I take Butterfly with me?"

Butterfly's eyes widened, and she gazed expectantly at Hackney.

"Sure, why not," he said with a shrug. "There's no point in secrecy anymore."

Callista smiled down at Butterfly and gave her a squeeze. At least the trip would not be only a pain. Maybe they could go to the park, too, and enjoy themselves without fear.

After she finished her dinner break, Callista was on her way back to where she left off making beds, when she ran into McCaffrey, who met her with a glare.

"This is all your doing," he accused.

"What is?" she asked, even though she had a pretty good idea what he was getting at. She edged away from him, hands twisting behind her back.

"Deposing me," he said, taking another step forward to close the opening gap. "I know you're a spy for them, and you're trying to destabilize us. Why else would he contact you and set up a time for you both to meet privately and take care of you so well? I will catch you red-handed. Justice will be served."

Before Callista could make any reply, he stomped off, his cane banging on the floor. She eyed him for a moment, shrugged, trying to work the tension out of her back, and continued about her business. She wasn't going to let McCaffrey add to her anxiety. But it took some time for her breathing to get back to normal.

CHAPTER TWENTY-TWO

Callista had had no idea. When she introduced herself to the receptionist at the network, the woman's eyes widened, and she immediately ushered Callista and Butterfly into a waiting area. It wasn't twenty seconds after the women left that a dozen people flooded into the room, jostling to shake Callista's hand and tell her how magnificent she was, what an inspiration she was, how much people looked up to her. She suddenly found a camera staring at her, a microphone thrust in her face, and questions hurled at her.

"Stop, stop, *stop!*" Callista yelled, first putting her hands over her ears then raising them in the air. "I came," she started as they quieted down. "To ask you to come see where I live, the people I live with."

"We call ourselves the Renegades," Butterfly piped in, saving Callista. "We choose to live underground in the sewers rather than under the Alamy regime. Come see how we live and interview us! You can interview Callista then, too. She'll be in the dress people will recognize—don't you suppose that would be better?"

"How soon can you have a team ready?" Callista asked, rubbing her eye. "Our leader said three days from now would be the earliest we could do—"

"That'll be fine," someone said. "Where do we meet you to get down there?"

Butterfly gave them the location where Hawkney would meet them. Callista turned to go when the same person spoke again.

"Miss Tristan! Stay for a quick interview, just a few questions!" and again, the mics were thrust in her direction.

"No, you'll have hours for that later," Callista said firmly. "I haven't prepared for it yet, and I don't want to make a fool of myself." She started to push through the crowd. "Prepare your questions for later."

She and Butterfly finally made it onto the street and quickly walked away. It wasn't long before they observed a camera crew tailing them.

"We should lose them," Callista said, glancing over her shoulder.

"Duck in a manhole?" Butterfly suggested.

"That'd take too long," Callista said. Glancing around for inspiration, she caught sight of Morticia's Nightclub. Marcus came out the door, broom in hand, and swept the sidewalk of trash and a few stray leaves. Callista grabbed Butterfly's hand and quickly darted across the traffic to the other side. He smiled at their approach, recognizing her.

"Marcus, do you mind if we pass through the place and go out the back? We have a tail to shake," Callista said, jerking her head to the side.

Marcus caught sight of the camera crew trying to keep her in sight between the passing cars while looking for an opportunity to cross. He smiled and opened the door for them, and they darted inside.

The lights were up, unlike when she had come there with Loui, making the place look like any normal restaurant. As she hurried down the stairs to the main floor with Butterfly in tow, she spotted Foxfire slumped at one of the tables, sound asleep. She would have let him be but had an idea and veered toward him.

"Foxfire," she said, shaking him with no results. "Foxfire!" Still nothing. "Leonard!" she said after a moment's hesitation while shaking him. He snorted and sat up blearily, looking around.

"What do you want?" he mumbled.

"Foxfire, do you have a car?"

"Lots," he said, lifting his head and letting it fall back down to his chest with a jerk.

"Well, do you have one here?"

"Yus," he said with the same motion of his head.

"Can I borrow it?"

He looked sideways up at her, causing him to fall sideways, but she caught him and righted him. "Anythin' fo' you, doll," he said and began to fish around in his pockets. He finally pulled out a chain lanyard looped around his belt that the key ring was on. He pulled it until a combination padlock came into view and slowly twisted in the combination. He stopped halfway through, blinking, and spun the dial and started again, going more slowly. It finally clicked open, and he unthreaded the chain through the keys, dropping them on the floor.

"Thanks," Callista said, picking them up. "I'll have Loui bring them back to you," she said before grabbing Butterfly's hand again and making their way toward the kitchen as Foxfire slumped back down on the table.

"You won't get far if you go out the back," Morticia's voice came down to them from above, making Callista pause, her hand on the swinging door of the kitchen. "That camera crew will probably pick you up again. Wouldn't want them to see you driving around in an expensive car either—it'd ruin your image. Wait for me." She strode along the balcony and down the stairs to them. "Come with me."

She led Callista and Butterfly down into the basement and into an alcove. She took a meat skewer that hung on the whitewashed brick wall and inserted it into one of the many tiny holes in the wall. She soon replaced it and, bracing her shoulder against the wall, began to push. When they perceived she made no progress, Callista and Butterfly came to her aid, and Callista grunted in surprise at the weight of the door. She soon understood why when it proved to be six inches of solid brick, not including the locking mechanism on the back. She gaped in surprise to find they were in a large, well-stocked wine cellar. Some of the bottles were covered in thick layers of dust, while others appeared to be brand new. Morticia led them to another secret door set in one of the lattices holding some of the wines, which proved much easier to open.

"Follow this tunnel, take the second right, and it'll pop up in the parking garage Foxfire uses three blocks down."

Callista glanced at Morticia, impressed, and thanked her heartily. She and Butterfly cautiously went down the poured concrete passage, dimly lit by infrequent red lights, filled with dim alcoves for people to ambush from. They soon found the correct passage leading off the main one and followed a ladder up to a fake utility manhole cover in the corner of the parking garage. They started going through each floor of the garage, clicking the keys to find Foxfire's car.

"Are we sure it's even in this deck?" Butterfly asked.

"Morticia said it would be, and Foxfire seems to be a creature of habit," Callista said as they walked up the ramp to the second-to-last level. She clicked the button again, and this time, they heard an answering beep. They hurried around the corner, and she clicked it again. The sound echoed through the concrete structure; the lights flickered yellow.

Both Callista and Butterfly sucked in a breath. Callista hit the button again, to be sure, even though there was only one other car on the level, and the car again flickered and beeped.

It was a lime-green Ferrari.

Callista knew she shouldn't be surprised—Foxfire was loaded, after all, but it sickened her. She was terrified she'd scratch it, or Foxfire would wake up and find his keys gone and not remember who he gave them to.

"Come on, let's go," she said, shoving away her worries, and quickly got into the driver's seat. Butterfly snapped her jaw shut, shook her head, and jumped in, too, excited. They both took a deep breath as they fastened their seatbelts—it still had the new car smell.

Callista made a mental plan as they drove out of the parking deck. She would drive to the Knickerbocker Hotel and leave the car in the parking lot. The place was swanky enough it wouldn't be too out of place. She would use the pneumatic tubes in the basement to send a message to the Renegades as Niki did the first time Callista met her, and Loui would come and take the Ferrari back while she drove the car he had. Simple.

She smiled to herself when some people stared at the car, grateful the windows were dark-tinted. If only Xor-nalden could see her now—what would he think?

As she waited for the camera crews to arrive, Callista tried yet again to smooth down the wrinkles in her red dress to no avail. It would take an iron to get them out—an iron they didn't have. The last few days, they had furiously cleaned the tunnels they inhabited. Even the bricks and concrete shone. One of the artists created a patriotic mural on one of the walls in the main room out of charcoal and the remnants in a paint can he found in a dumpster.

They decided Hawkney would meet the camera crew, decked in his old Army uniform, complete with his beret and sidearm. Niki too wore her uniform and would meet them at the edge of the encampment. The idea was they would slowly add and remove people as the camera crew went to give them a chance to talk to one person at a time.

Callista waited with Butterfly at the end of the converted curved subway tunnel that led into the bunk room. They sat on chests which stored extra clothes and tried to concentrate on mending some of them.

"How long do you suppose until they'll get here?" Butterfly asked into the silence. Most of the other people were in the great room, awaiting their guests eagerly.

"Depends on how long they talk to Hawkney and if he thinks to walk and talk or not," Callista said.

"But how long until they get to us?"

"If you want to join the others, by all means, go ahead."

"But I want to stay with you. I don't want you to have to sit here by yourself."

"Then stay."

Butterfly stared at Callista for a long moment. "You're not excited about this at all, are you?"

"No."

"Why not?"

"Because they're turning me into something I'm not," Callista said, calmly pulling her thread through. "I'm made out as someone who does not like the Alamies, demonstrated by my victory over the Admiral in a game when this is not the case at all."

"So you do like them?"

"There are good ones and bad ones, as with any group of people."

"But you did beat him in chess."

"The object of the game is to win. I simply used a few more resources than most may think to."

"But you ran away," Butterfly said, fingering her thimble.

"I panicked. Wouldn't you?"

"Oh, I guess so."

Callista smiled and folded the newly mended shirt and reached for another.

"So you're afraid of the Alamies then?" Butterfly asked after a moment.

"I feared Xor-nalden would make me his wife right there or arrest me for impudence."

"You really suppose he would have done that because you beat him at chess?"

"Now I know he would not have, but at the time I did not know him from Adam. All I knew was that he was extremely powerful, and power can make an individual touchy."

"So why are you sitting here in the red dress if you're not what everyone thinks you are?" Butterfly asked as she dipped her needle through the cloth.

"It would appear, one way or another, war is inevitable," Callista said, repositioning the fabric on her lap. "If nothing else, it could force humanity to put aside our differences and old hatreds. A common enemy unites old foes."

"So you do want people to hate the Alamies?"

"I don't want anyone to hate anyone. I want them to unite against the right foe, and right now it sounds like that is Gren-del, not Xor-nalden. I fear he'll get caught up in the wave of animosity though, even if humanity starts with Gren-del. We tend to stereotype."

"So what will you tell them when they interview you?" Butterfly asked.

"I'm going to stress Gren-del is the real enemy, and I'll make Xor-nalden out to be little more than an impotent puppet, which was my impression during the banquet the other day. That'll encourage people to largely disregard him, at least as an enemy, and be more inclined to focus on Gren-del instead."

Butterfly and Callista continued to work in silence for another hour or so until Niki stomped down the tunnel toward them, soaked to the skin.

"What happened?" Callista asked in alarm. "Did a water main break?"

"No," Niki said, seething. She flung open a trunk and rummaged around for clean clothes. "An Alamy hosed me."

"Hosed you?" Callista said. "Start from the beginning, Niki."

"I was showing off our defenses to the camera crew," Niki began as she stripped off her outer shirt and wrung it out on the floor, making Callista groan inwardly. "I threw one of the Christmas ball smoke grenades at the wall and the place filled with smoke; it was funny to see them gasp and the look of surprise on their faces. We were under a manhole, so I climbed up and opened it so the place would vent. We went down the tunnel and showed them some other stuff and then came back the same way, 'cause the smoke just about cleared out by then.

"Well, as we're coming up to the manhole a pair of legs swing down into the hole, and there's an Alamy sitting on the edge of it. I look at him, he looks at me, he smiles and squirts me with the firehose in his hands and laughs his head off to see me scramble and sputter, and those cameras watching the whole thing right behind me!"

Callista couldn't help but laugh, which earned her a glare from Niki who scrambled into dry clothes.

"What's so funny?" Niki demanded.

"They thought there was a fire down here, clearly," Callista said, wiping at the corner of her eye. "He realized it was your doing and squirted you for fun—let me guess, he was young, wasn't he? It's such a young man thing to do."

"Young or no, if he was down on my level I would'a shivved him then and there, but he pulled his legs out and replaced the cover before I could get my footing back."

"That's good—wouldn't want you to start a war over a practical joke."

"There was nothing practical or joking about it." Niki demanded, jerking a dry jacket on.

"Niki, if that had been Hawkney, would you have reacted the same way, honestly?"

"I'd'a shivved him too."

"No, you wouldn't have. Slapped him, maybe," Callista said with a smile, continuing to sew. "You need to let it go."

"Let it go? *Let it go?*" Niki said, no calmer than before.

"Yes, let it go. You need to pick your battles carefully."

"Who are you, Sun Tzu?" Niki said before turning and stomping back down the tunnel.

Callista chuckled. "Like I said, Butterfly. There's good ones and bad ones in every group."

CHAPTER TWENTY-THREE

Callista didn't care if there were chores to do. After a two-hour interview the day before with the news crew, she was exhausted and took a personal day. It was like she'd taken the hardest test of her life—the interviewer constantly tried to get her to make a strong statement condemning the Alamgirians and/or their government. She kept replaying the whole thing in her mind, paranoid she said something she would regret, but as far as she could remember, she always turned the conversation back to the fact Gren-del was the threat, the one they should blame for St. Petersburg.

She rolled onto her stomach and buried her head deeper in her pillow, deciding she should stop thinking about it and risk going insane. Footsteps came near, but she thought nothing of it until they stopped next to her cot.

"Callista?" Hawkney whispered.

She took a long moment to decide whether to ignore him or not. The blanket tugged when he perched precariously on the edge of her cot, and she started when he laid his hands on her shoulders and started rubbing.

"Ca-lli-sta," he said softly in a sing-song voice. "Rise and shine, sleepy head. The TV special is on in an hour, and we're setting up a watch party."

"I'm not coming," she said into her pillow.

"Why not?" he asked, his hands ceasing to seek out the knots in her shoulders.

"The whole thing gives me anxiety," she said, moving her head so he could hear her better. "And I hate seeing myself on film. I sound so weird."

"Not to me, you don't."

"That's because you don't hear it from inside your own head normally," she said, burying her face back in the pillow.

He rubbed her shoulders in silence for a moment and soon gave a sigh. "All right," he said softly, running his fingers through her tangled hair and brushing it away from her neck before leaning over and kissing it gently.

Callista tensed but didn't react.

Hawkney hesitated before he stood and walked away. She heaved a shaky sigh once she was sure he was gone and tried to coax her now-tense muscles to relax. Hawkney seemed to be falling into the same trap everyone else did—seeing her as something she wasn't. She wanted to find a dark hole, curl up in it, and stay there where no one could find or bother her. No more questions about what she thought in the moment she defeated Xor-nalden at chess, or what message she wanted to give the people, or what did she *really* think of Alamgirians? Now she understood why her father bought a house in the middle of nowhere after receiving his medal of honor so he could change his address and phone number and disappear. Unwanted publicity, especially about something you were not proud of, was a nightmare.

She groaned and put her pillow on top of her head, trying to muffle the voices in her mind. Yet again she considered going home, but the worry over putting Mom in danger flooded in right behind it. She dreaded meeting people on the street and being recognized and swarmed. Unlike her father, she didn't have the benefit of growing a beard to hide in plain sight. And what if she ran into Xor-nalden again on the way? Was this his idea of her speaking up? Did she do enough to shift the blame onto Grendel? Would he resent and even hate her for calling him an impotent puppet? Her stomach turned at the thought—what was she thinking? What would he think? She thought he would *probably* choose to ignore it and let it go, but what if he didn't?

Taking a slow breath, she tried to force out her anxiety as she exhaled. As a mental exercise and to distract herself, she tried to picture every nook and cranny of her grandmother's house she had not been inside for years. She ran her fingers through her tangled hair and rolled onto her side.

She yearned for the simple life her grandmother had led: married to the love of her life after high school—how she envied such certainty so soon—quietly raised children, worked at the church, nursed her deranged mother until she ate mothballs and passed on.

She sighed. Her grandmother's life maybe wasn't as simple as she initially imagined it, but at least she didn't have to deal with extraterrestrials.

As she rolled over, she tried to tell herself it didn't matter what Xor-nalden thought of her. All she could do was follow her conscience and do her best, for that was the best she could do.

A FEW DAYS after the TV spot, Callista needed some space from the denizens of the underground, at least for a little while. The overall atmosphere worried her. There was a hint of pride in it, due to their TV special going over well, plus a sense of renewed defiance that troubled her because it was deeply colored with fearlessness.

She decided the Joralemon Street façade needed cleaning on

the inside, whether it did or not. It took her a while to weave her way over there and a few hours to clean the inside from top to bottom. When she finished, she opened the front door and threw her dirty mop water out into the bushes. She started to go back inside when a flicker of red caught her eye. Pausing in the doorway, she spotted a rose stuck in the fence. She set her bucket down in the doorway and walked down to investigate.

It was a silk rose, limp from the morning's dew, but as she gazed at it, she spied a note tucked deep inside, spared from the elements. She took it back inside, closing and locking the door before moving to the single light in the hall to read the note, steeling herself.

> MY DEAR, YOU WERE MAGNIFICENT, TRULY.
> YOU HANDLED THE WHOLE THING QUITE COOLLY.
> ALL THAT IS LEFT IS FOR US TO DISCUSS
> HOW BEST TO UNITE OUR CAUSES
> INTO ONE UNIFIED FORCE, AND THUS,
> I AWAIT THE NEXT TIME WE SHALL MEET
> WHEREVER YOU BELIEVE IS DISCRETE.
>
> YOURS,
> N. X

Callista took a slow, measured breath, dread filling her stomach. Xor-nalden still had the impression she had more influence underground than she did. She folded the note and stuck it in her breast pocket and fingered the rose in thought. She wasn't going to try to meet him. At least not yet. The time wasn't right, even if she did have enough influence to persuade the people to work with Xor-nalden rather than against him. They were getting fired up to fight any and every Alamy. They hadn't fully realized Gren-del was the true enemy, at least for the moment.

Or was Xor-nalden playing the same trick she pulled on him?

Was he bluffing? Playing the puppet to remove or deflect animosity onto someone he wanted to get rid of?

She threw the rose into the bucket with all her might. Loui said Gren-del was indeed a monster, but was Xor-nalden truly much better? There had not been any massacres like in Russia, but that didn't mean there wouldn't be. She remembered the man she witnessed led away by two Alamies in the Atlanta airport, looking bewildered and terrified.

She slumped onto the floor and leaned her head back against the concrete wall. She hated politics with a passion. It made her sick—she was terrible at divining a lie. How did she know Xor-nalden wasn't trying to manipulate her? Filling her head with ideas of her self-importance and the extent of her power, which she was still fairly certain was non-existent. She closed her eyes. All she could do was pray for Jesus to take the wheel and give her wisdom and discernment, though she'd need enough to rival Solomon to cope with her situation.

The inner door leading to the subway grated open, the sound making Callista nearly jump out of her skin. Hawkney came in and shut the door behind him.

"There you are. I wondered where you slunk off to."

"You nearly scared the ghost out of me," she said, her hand still over her heart as she took deep breaths.

"Sorry," he said, dropping down beside her. He reached back and put his arm around her shoulders. She remained sitting upright instead of leaning into him and looked away, making the whole thing awkward. "You're mad," he said after a moment. "Out with it—what's wrong?"

She rubbed her arms for a moment. "I feel powerless. Here I called Xor-nalden a puppet, when I myself feel like little more than a pawn everyone tries to move around."

"You're not a pawn—you can do whatever you want."

"Can I though? What if I said no to the interview, hmm? You would have made me do it anyway, because I'm your golden girl."

"That's not true," he said patiently.

"Isn't it though? What *would* you have done?"

"The same as we did, just without you."

"How would you have gotten them down there in the first place?"

"Our unusualness. We don't need you *that* badly, Callista. You're simply a weapon in our arsenal we're making use of instead of letting you lie."

"Now you're objectifying me, which proves my point," she said, looking away from him.

"A soldier's metaphor," he said, scooting closer to her so his side touched hers, making the scent of Axe waft over to her and tickle her sinuses.

"Well, what are we going to do now?" she asked, leaning away from him.

"In two weeks, we're supposed to pick out a few pieces and give Foxfire a place to deliver the rest of our order," he said, leaning away a little, picking up on her movement. "Why don't you come? Get out of the tunnels for a while? And it will be amusing to see if he remembers you borrowing his car or not."

"That will be interesting to see," she agreed with a little smile. "You don't suppose he'll be mad, though?"

"Somehow, I don't think so. It seems like something that would happen to him a lot, and maybe the girl wouldn't come back with the car most of the time."

Callista giggled. "True."

"So it's a date then?" he asked.

"Where do I meet you and Loui?" she asked, ignoring his choice of words.

"Main hall. Then we go over to Morticia's, where we're supposed to meet Foxfire out front. He has some special car with tinted windows or something so we can't see where his place is. Supposed to take all day."

"Sounds like it."

"I don't suppose you'd be willing to wear the dress—"

"I hate that dress. Don't even," she said, standing and brushing her pants off out of habit, and he stood with her. Together, they packed up her cleaning supplies and returned to the labyrinth.

CHAPTER TWENTY-FOUR

egev stared down at the report on his desk, his head in his hands. He felt sick. He took slow, measured breaths and tried to calm his racing heart and his queasy stomach. The report came from one of his loyalists in Gren-del's territory. It informed him that Gren-del had banned religion in his territory, citing religion as an impetus for unrest, and ordered the destruction of religious sites and iconography.

He forced himself to look at the map of the world outlining each admiral's territory. His fears were confirmed: Gren-del's territory included Jerusalem, Mecca, Medina, and Rome, and other places of religious significance or with renowned religious sites. He cursed under his breath. He had wanted to give Gren-del the continent of Australia and the surrounding islands, but protocol demanded the more influential regions be given to the most senior admirals, who were more logically up to the task. The other admirals had insisted on it, clinging to every shred of the way their world operated. And, of course, some were far more loyal to Gren-del than to him.

He sighed and steepled his forefingers over his mouth in thought. He now saw the wage cut and subsequent massacre were an experiment to see how outraged the people at large would be, whether they would express their displeasure violently, and if he would be stupid enough to overreact in a similar manner. Now Gren-del pushed it much, much further.

He wondered with a twitch of his mouth if Gren-del claimed the decree came not from him, but from Negev. What if he did the same thing in his territory as Negev did in his—point a blaming finger elsewhere. He did not doubt it.

He took a slow, deep breath and reached for his notepad, fingering his pen. He did not know why he felt the urge to reach out to her, to ask for her help. What could she do? Even if she did tell the media this was not his doing, he doubted they would listen.

And what could he do? He had already set a date for convening the council of admirals to discuss Gren-del's previous actions. He supposed he could add this to the list. He smiled humorlessly. The list might become lengthy by the time they convened—*if* they convened. Suddenly the idea of simply "removing" the problem seemed like not a bad idea.

He sighed through his nose and gripped his pen harder. No— he would not be one of *those* rulers. Not only would the sin be on his conscience, it would also haunt his rule and cast a shadow over everything he did.

He took a deep breath and began writing out the note. Maybe she would have some ideas or be an oracle and reassure him of his doom.

"You got mail," Niki said to Callista, who sat in her bunk reading a book, and held out a crude white paper flower to her. A note clearly stuck out of the petals.

"Where did you find it this time?" Callista asked, taking it from her.

"That old Alamy you said is Big Man's aide walked along,

knocking on manhole covers with his cane, and waited to see if anyone answered. Figured I should see what he wanted. Pulled this out of his lapel and gave it to me, said it was for you."

"I'm surprised you were so cordial about it, and didn't knife him on sight," Callista said as she took the folded note out of the center of the flower and read it, frowning.

"Hey, they know about us. No use pretending they don't. Besides, at least he knocked first. So what's the note about?" Niki asked, leaning over to look. Callista handed it to her.

"'You have surely heard the terrible news by now,'" Niki read aloud. "'I am at a loss at what to do—I feel my options dwindling. Please meet me in Central Park today. Perhaps talking with someone familiar with Humanity will give me some insight in how to proceed,'" Niki finished, ignoring the signature "N.X."

"Why do you suppose there's a bishop chess piece drawn on there?" Callista asked. "If he drew a pawn, I suppose it'd reflect how he's feeling, but a bishop?"

"Maybe you're thinking about it too hard. Maybe it's his favorite piece?" Niki said.

Callista caught sight of Loui coming toward them, his footsteps echoing off the brick walls. Niki stuffed the note in her breast pocket. Callista slid the flower under her blanket.

"Have you heard?" Loui said. They stared at him expectantly. "Gren-del has banned religion in Europe and his portion of the Middle East."

Callista glanced at Niki, realizing what Xor-nalden wanted to talk about and saw in Niki's eyes that she had put the pieces together too. They held each other's gaze for a moment, and Niki gave her a slight nod. Callista sighed and nodded, too, swinging her legs out from under her warm blanket and pulling on her hiking boots that were one size too big.

"Where are you going?" Loui asked.

"I need some air," Callista said. "Think I'll go take a walk in Central Park."

"I'll come with you," Niki said, and Callista nodded.

"Mmm, be careful, *oui*?" Loui said. "Who knows what riots will happen now."

"Sure," Callista said, standing and pulling her thin camo jacket more tightly around her. "Lead the way, Niki. You know these tunnels better than I."

CHAPTER TWENTY-FIVE

"I guess he'll find us," Niki said, looking over the map of Central Park.

"But it's so big," Callista said, hugging her jacket around her and kicking herself for the eighth time for not borrowing something much heavier. The temperature was no higher than the twenties, and it was snowing to boot. Her thin canvas jacket and her jeans riddled with unintentional rips did her no favors.

"Well, we know they have good surveillance, so that's probably the deal," Niki said.

Callista sighed, her breath making a cloud in the air, unconvinced. She pulled the note out of Niki's pocket and looked at it again. It almost surprised her it wasn't in a poem this time. Almost, since she could see the situation didn't warrant taking the time to figure one out. She assumed he had written poetically before to disguise the notes if they were ever found by someone else, although this time, he had it delivered.

But it seemed unlike him to be vague about a meeting place, especially because he was a military man. She fingered the crude drawing of the chess piece and glanced back up at the map, her gaze landing on a pavilion toward the center, and she caught her breath.

"Niki, there's a chess house!" she said, pointing.

"Yeah, so?" Niki said, continuing to survey the goings on around them.

"So maybe that's why he drew a chess piece. It makes perfect sense, and he probably drew a bishop to help allude to what he was referencing in the news. Let's go there in case I'm right—like you said, if he will pick us up, it won't matter where we are."

"Sure, okay," Niki said, ripping her gaze from a hurrying businessman with his collar up. "Let's go."

The park was decked out for Christmas. Tree trunks were wrapped in lights, and light nets were draped over bushes, red bows adorned the lampposts and swans outlined in lights sat upon a frozen pond. Snow had fallen for some time, blanketing everything in white, giving the whole place a hush. There were few people out, and Callista surmised people didn't feel like being out and merry with the news their favorite holiday might be cut short and never return.

The Chess and Checkers house was an octagonal building surrounded by awnings which shaded cement tables inlaid with checkered boards. The tables and chairs were mostly covered with snow, and the hibernating vines on the lattices also sported their own coats. Two old men had dusted off one table and a pair of chairs and quietly played checkers, each so bundled up only their eyes showed.

Callista and Niki walked around the building and soon spotted him. Xor-nalden sat at a table, his scarf tied tightly around his neck, fingering a chess piece in his lap, his head bowed.

"I'll wait here," Niki said softly when they spotted him. "You go talk to him." Niki took out a vape pipe and wandered away.

Callista took a deep breath to calm her nerves as Niki dusted off a bench and sat down nearby. Callista noted Xor-nalden had thoughtfully dusted off the chair opposite him and laid out the chess pieces retrieved from the building. He glanced up as her boots crunched through the snow. A sad smile spread across his face, and he stood to greet her.

"Thank you for coming," he said, reaching for her hand.

She nodded jerkily, trying not to shiver, and stuck her hand out from the relative warmth of her armpit. His eyes darted down to her slightly blue hand at her icy touch, and he whipped off his trench coat and placed it around her shoulders before she could protest.

"Th-thanks," she said, slipping her arms into the sleeves. His lingering body heat made the coat gloriously warm.

"Are you warm enough in the tunnels?" he asked, concern written on his face.

"Y-yes, mostly. I, I just didn't think ... everything so fast," she said, waving her hand around her head.

He nodded his understanding, and they both sat at the chessboard. He leaned an elbow against the table, his head cupped in his hand, and stared blankly at the checkered board.

She glanced from him to the table for a minute before quietly saying, "It's your move."

He started, his eyes glanced around the board before he hurriedly moved a piece. She moved one of her own in response.

"What did you want to talk about?" she asked quietly.

"I do not know what to do," he said, moving one of his pieces. "I feel hopelessly trapped."

"Because you can't stop Gren-del without consent from the other admirals?" she asked, shifting a pawn.

"Yes. The bureaucracy is too slow." He stared vacantly at the chessboard.

"Well, you're the supreme ruler, and this is not your home world. Adapt. Take matters into your own hands. If people see it is for the better, which it obviously will be, they won't begrudge you in the long run."

"But then I will be in danger of becoming a dictator."

"So call it 'emergency powers' or something. Look," she said, leaning forward. "Make it public you rescind Gren-del's decree and do it quickly."

"But I technically do not have the power to do so because it affects only his territory."

"Doesn't matter. It's a technicality—people will see you do not approve of it, and that Gren-del ignores you, jurisdiction or no. That will help you look better in this crisis."

"But this is only the beginning," he said, looking up at her. "First Saint Petersburg, now this. He is prodding, hoping I will make a mistake that will allow him to overthrow me."

Callista sat back. "Then war is inevitable, isn't it?"

He took a deep breath, exhaled, and ran a hand over his face. "Yes, I suppose it is."

"Then make this your rallying cry. If you wait, it will be about you trying to save your skin. If you draw the line now, it's about preserving the people's freedom, something Humanity values greatly, especially religious freedoms. You will have a much greater ally in Humanity that way than if it's about infighting, in which case we would sit back and watch you both destroy each other before making any move of our own."

"Yes," he said, crossing his arms. "Yes, I suppose you are right. I just fear the collateral damage."

He stared vacantly at the board. Callista tapped her heel nervously. She looked around at the other chess players and Niki, who released a cloud of water vapor into the air, watching it float away and disappear before taking another drag. Callista looked back at Xor-nalden, who maintained the same posture. Had she said enough? Had she said the right things? She took a slow, controlled breath to steady her nerves and surveyed the chessboard again.

"I shall do as you say," he said quickly, making her start. He sat up straighter and smoothed his uniform. "I will start with talk, while I prepare my offensive, and learn who my allies are in the other admirals. That way Humanity will see I am not complacent and will not be so surprised when I declare war on Gren-del." A glow seemed to come into his eyes, and a slight smile spread across his mouth. "Gren-del is supposed to come and answer to me about Saint Petersburg," he said, moving a chess piece. "Perhaps I can make my move then and thus avoid a major offensive."

"That sounds like a good idea," she said, moving her queen. She clenched and unclenched her fingers in her lap. He might not be the only one making a move if Gren-del came to New York. She bit the inside of her lip.

Xor-nalden gazed through the latticework above them in thought. "The question is whether I can have everything ready by the time he gets here. If he bothers to keep his appointment, which I doubt, he would be here within a week or two."

"That I cannot answer," she said, and he turned his head and smiled at her.

"Your assistance has been invaluable. You have helped me think straight and find a course of action—thank you," he said, standing. "But I do not want to keep you. Will you speak for me if asked?"

"Of course," she said, also standing, resolve hardening in her heart. "For better or worse, I've put my eggs in your basket. Whether they hatch or are crushed, we shall see," she said, shrugging off his coat.

"Keep it," he said, holding his palm toward her. "This would be a pleasant day on my planet. I am accustomed to the cold."

Callista raised her eyebrows and hesitantly pulled it back on.

"My sun was sickly, remember? But it had been so for such a long time, people forgot what it was like to see it healthy," he said with a grim smile. "Hence, the shock of its demise."

She nodded. "You realize if they want to do another protest, like the one at the banquet, I won't be able to stop them. I have no real power—I'm just a figurehead."

"I understand." He held out his hand to her. "Until we meet again, then, and the best of luck to you."

"And to you," she said, accepting his handshake.

He nodded again and strode away into the winter landscape.

She watched him go for a moment before walking over to Niki, who was keeping watch out of the corner of her eye.

"Well, how'd it go?" Niki asked.

"There's going to be war between Xor-nalden and Gren-del if he can't take him out quickly." Callista took a deep breath, fighting against the pressure in her chest.

Niki grinned at her. "Good."

CHAPTER TWENTY-SIX

"You're falling into his sympathy trap," McCaffrey snapped at Callista at the council meeting where she relayed her conversation with Xor-nalden. She ground her teeth, wanting to snap back at him, but she knew it would only make things worse. Everyone was on edge now that they knew an Alamgirian civil war was imminent.

"We're going to have to choose one devil, and at this point, I'd much rather have Mr. X," Betty replied, sitting back with her arms crossed.

"Agreed. For now," Hawkney said before turning away to pace.

"You told him about Foxfire, didn't you?" McCaffrey said. "You told him about our capabilities, our resources, our—"

"Oh, shut up," Niki snapped. "I was there the whole time. They talked about Gren-del, not us. And I, for one, think she did good, getting us all this intel, so keep your paranoia and suspicion to yourself."

McCaffrey continued to glare at Callista, grinding his teeth but holding his tongue, and the conversation moved on.

Callista was relieved when she was able to leave the camp to go meet Foxfire a week later. The oppressive atmosphere of worry and McCaffrey's open distrust, whenever they crossed paths, was wearing on her soul.

They found Foxfire wearing a vibrant blue suit with a turquoise handkerchief in his breast pocket, his hair slicked back as usual, with the afternoon sun glinting off it. He smiled as the trio—Hawkney, Loui, and Callista—walked down the sidewalk toward where he waited, leaning against a limousine in front of Morticia's.

"Merry Christmas!" he said, greeting Hawkney with a handshake, Loui with a hug and a slap on the back. He reached for Callista's hand.

"How did you enjoy my Ferrari the other day, Miss Liberty?" he asked with a wink and a kiss on her hand.

"It rides well, but I could never own one. I was racked with paranoia every moment I sat in it."

"Well, it helps to be rich," Foxfire said and opened the door of the limousine. "*Entrez*, my friends. Let us go for a drive."

"Thanks, Santa," Hawkney said, laying a hand on the roof. "Quite the sled you have here. How many reindeer under the hood?"

Callista smiled and got in first and noted Hawkney was right about Foxfire keeping the location of his warehouse a secret—the windows were blacked out. Hawkney got in and took a seat next to her while Loui and Foxfire took up residence opposite them. Foxfire doled out drinks and offered hors d'oeuvres.

"I saw your interview on the TV the other day, my dear—in fact, I watched it twice," Foxfire said as he poured himself a glass of champagne. "You've missed your true calling—you should be a politician. You handled those interviewers admirably, all things considered, and you continually tried to bring the conversation back to your points. Very well done. I drink to your success." He raised his glass to her and drained half of it.

"Thank you, but I hope I never have to do it again. The stress probably took five years off my life," she said with a humorless smile.

"You don't believe in yourself enough," Hawkney said, sipping his mixed drink.

"I agree," Loui said, setting down his champagne. "Have a little more faith in yourself, my friend."

Callista rolled her eyes but didn't press the subject.

"So how long are we going to drive around in circles?" Hawkney asked after a moment of silence.

"For as long as it takes us to get tired of each other's company," Foxfire said with a grin. "So, to answer your question—probably the wee hours of the morning."

Hawkney groaned and knocked back a larger gulp of his whiskey.

"I see how it is," Callista said, eyeing Hawkney. "You're trying to get us good and liquored up so we'll give you more money, is it?"

Foxfire laughed. "Close, my dear. It's so if you try to keep tabs on where we are in the city, you'll lose track as the spirits take hold. And it will help us to have a jolly good time—after all, it is Christmas day!" he said, pouring himself more champagne and refilling Loui's glass. "Are you sure you do not want any, my dear?" he asked, leaning the bottle toward her.

"Perhaps a bit later," Callista said.

"Very well then," he said, replacing the bottle in the ice. "What's next for you all, then? Surely you're going to follow up your great success."

"Indeed," Hawkney said, putting his glass down in a cup holder. "We're considering something of a protest in Central Park, especially with what's going on across the pond."

"It's more of a patriotic rally," Loui amended.

"True. The point is to build unity and patriotic fervor rather than raise hell. That way, the Alamies can't get as mad at us."

Callista was surprised but not shocked. She'd heard nothing of this. It must be what he and his military friends were discussing quietly in corners since news of the impending war.

"We're going to set up a stage," Hawkney continued. "And

play patriotic music to get the people pumped up, give some speeches, that sort of stuff. Keep us in the public's eye, and put pressure on Xor-nalden by showing him we're not lying down— we could mobilize the people at any moment—so he'll hurry up and do what we want, or else."

"Sounds like a good idea," Foxfire said and popped a grape into his mouth. "But what if this ends up like Saint Petersburg?"

"That, my friend, is why we will wait for your delivery before we hold our rally," Loui said. "Unlike Saint Petersburg, we will have our own security. We will not be sheep to the slaughter."

Callista pursed her lips, trying to decide whether to stay out of it or not. "This sounds like a bad idea," she said at last, deciding to demur. "Like you're expecting it to go bad."

"Not at all," Loui said. "You've met with Xor-nalden. You say he is not as bad as Gren-del; he would rather talk than shoot. We are banking on your judgment but are prepared for the worst, nonetheless."

"But if we are seen with guns, wouldn't that suggest we are not conducting a peaceful rally but trying to start a mob?" she asked.

"They would be concealed, naturally," Hawkney said.

She wanted to ask whether she would be required to attend but feared she already knew the answer and didn't want to have an argument in front of Foxfire.

"I'll have that drink now, Foxfire," she said instead, and he smiled in appreciation.

"As much as you want, darling. As much as you want."

Loui changed the subject to talk about old times, and he and Foxfire regaled the group with stories of their escapades until they arrived at Foxfire's warehouse a few hours later. Callista followed them around as Foxfire showed off his wares, everything from machine guns, pistols, explosives, to even a few small warheads, but she soon became both bored and sickened and excused herself to go back to the car.

She found the driver asleep at the wheel, the cap pulled over his eyes and snoring softly. She couldn't blame him; it had to be at least two in the morning. She started to quietly get into the back when a wad in the chain link fence on the other side of the car caught her eye. She peered at it in the dim light coming from the warehouse and moved around to the other side of the car to investigate.

It was a black silk rose. The sight of it turned her stomach. She untangled the stem with shaking fingers and took it inside the car. There was indeed a piece of paper inside the folds of the petals. She slowly pulled it out and unfolded it before holding it so the tiny light in the car would illuminate it.

YOUR CURRENT ACTIONS ARE QUITE CONCERNING. THE MAN, COLLOQUIALLY KNOWN AS FOXFIRE, HAS A VAST SUM OF WEAPONS THAT COULD DO AN ENORMOUS AMOUNT OF HARM. I ASSUME YOU AND YOURS HAVE ACQUIRED SOME OF THEM. IF I FIND ANYTHING ELSE PORTENDING AN OUTBREAK OF VIOLENCE, I WILL BE FORCED TO ACT FOR THE SAFETY OF THE GREATER PUBLIC.

IF THE INTENT IS TO ASSIST ME IN MY OVERTHROW OF GREN-DEL, WE NEED TO COORDINATE. I CANNOT HAVE YOUR COMPATRIOTS IN MY LINE OF FIRE. PLEASE COME AND SPEAK TO ME—I DO NOT WANT TO PUT A WEDGE BETWEEN US.

YOURS,
N. X.

Men's voices came toward the car, and she quickly wadded up the note, stuffed it in her pocket, and opened the car door on the opposite side of the men to throw the rose on the ground. She grabbed her champagne glass and downed the rest of its contents before replacing it and turning a smile toward them. Loui jumped in as Foxfire opened the limousine's trunk, and Hawkney deposited a hard case into it.

"I wondered where you disappeared to. Did we bore you to death?" Loui asked.

"I'm tired of listening to what is essentially a foreign language," she said, giving him a brilliant smile.

Loui paused in the midst of lifting his own glass to his lips and narrowed his eyes slightly at her for a moment.

Hawkney and Foxfire laughed as they, too, got in. Hawkney slid in next to Callista and gave her a peck on the cheek, making her jump.

"Ah, it's a good day to be alive!" he said, and Callista caught the scent of alcohol on his breath. "If I wasn't smarter, I'd be on Niki's side—I almost want them to come at us now."

"Good God, Hawkney," Callista said softly.

"What? We'll be practically a fortress now. They'll have hell to pay if they come after us."

"Can we go home now? I don't feel well," she said.

"Too much to drink? You don't look it," Foxfire said and sipped at his glass.

"I'm just tired—it's been a long day."

"Indeed. A long one but a good one," Hawkney said, raising his glass. "To business and a bright future!"

"*Prosit!*" Foxfire said and clinked Hawkney and Loui's glasses and downed the contents.

After driving in circles two hours, Foxfire let them out a few blocks away from Morticia's, and they started walking toward their access point of choice, passing by darkened houses. They were silent for a while, but Callista could not remain so.

"How come this is the first time I've heard about this protest?" she finally asked.

"What do you mean?" Hawkney asked. "It's not like you're on the board or anything. Why are you used to everyone coming to you with the scuttlebutt?"

"But this is huge," she said. "This concerns the whole community—it's a huge risk."

"It'll be fine. We're going to have all we need to protect ourselves by tomorrow. Besides, you said it yourself—Xornalden's an impotent puppet. What's he going to do?"

"To begin with, he could arrest us," she answered, pausing to look back and forth before crossing the street. "Disturbing the peace, possession of illegal firearms—"

"Let him try."

Callista stopped short and whirled on Hawkney. "Do you hear yourself right now?"

"I just remembered, I have to make a short detour, but I'll take that, *mon ami*," Loui said, taking the hard case from Hawkney. Now, with a case in each hand, he stepped around them and beat a hasty retreat into a side alley.

"Loui, don't—"

"Do you have a problem, Callista? Do you doubt my leadership?" Hawkney asked, stepping toward her, making her step back so she stood almost against the wall of a house.

"Hawkney, you're drunk—"

"Oh, so now I'm crazy?"

"You're making rash statements and promises when you're not in your right mind," Callista said. She took another step back in response to Hawkney's forward movement and found her back up against the wall.

"What are you saying?" he said as he leaned toward her, the alcohol on his breath washing over her face.

"You're full of liquid courage that will get people killed. And I'm dismayed you would forget your training and prime directive to protect your own first and foremost to go ahead with something this dangerous."

"You think I'm not courageous?" he asked, and in the dim light, Callista caught a hint of crazy in his eyes, and a quiver of fear ran through her guts. "You think I don't have a—"

"I don't doubt your salt at all, Hawkney. All I'm saying is I worry about you."

He cocked his head to the side and took a long glance at her lips. "Yeah?" he said softly, looking into her eyes.

"Yeah," she said flatly. "I don't want you doing something unnecessary that'll get you and others killed. I don't think the time is right for a protest—rally—whatever it is. Not with Grendel's decree making people already hot. It's too big of a leap from 'hey, here we are,' to making ourselves out to unionize the greater public and make it look like we're a force to be reckoned with."

"But we are a force to be reckoned with."

"One that doesn't want an all-out war."

"But that's always been the endgame," he said.

Callista stared at him for a long moment.

"McCaffrey and I? We're just waiting for the time to be ripe," Hawkney said. "We never surrendered. If this Gren-del person is such a threat that Xor-nalden's getting so desperate he's reaching out to the Pope, they'll weaken each other in a civil war soon enough, and that will be our time to strike."

"Then why make ourselves known now?"

"To distract him from Gren-del. He stops staring at Gren-del for just a moment to glance at us, and that'll be all the time Gren-del will need to make his move."

"Hawkney," she said, looking at him aghast. "Gren-del *is* death. If he comes down on this city, he will burn it and everyone in it. We're just cannon fodder to him. He will mow through anyone in his path. Xor-nalden actually cares."

"No, he doesn't. He's using you, Callista. He's trying to use you to slow us down, make us hesitate, or give it up entirely, but I won't let you. Maybe McCaffrey is right. Maybe you are his stoolie. But I don't want to believe that. Make me not believe that," he said, leaning in for a kiss.

"You touch me, and I scream," she said through clenched teeth. A car door slammed behind Hawkney.

"Miss, are you all right?" an accented voice said as a flashlight shone on their legs.

It was an extraterrestrial accent.

Hawkney slowly turned around, and as he did, she could see beyond him and caught sight of the glowing red eyes of an Alamy.

"Nothing to see here, *sir*," Hawkney ground out.

The Alamy held his gaze for a moment before slowly circling them so he had a better view of Callista. "Are you all right, miss?" he repeated the question.

"Yes," Callista squeaked unconvincingly, making Hawkney look back at her with a cold glare. He shifted his weight away from her.

"I take you home, miss, yes?" the Alamy said after a moment. Callista stared back at him, feeling Hawkney's gaze never leave her. She glanced back at the SUV and spotted another pair of glowing violet eyes watching them from the driver's seat. She looked back at Hawkney.

"Actually, you should take *him* home," she said, edging around Hawkney. "He's had too much to drink tonight. It's making him think he's a lot bigger than he is, if you know what I mean."

"Certainly," the Alamy said with amusement in his voice. "Come on, big boy," he said, waving his flashlight pointed toward the ground. "Let us take a little ride, you cool your head off, shrink back to right size."

Callista could feel the heat of Hawkney's glare at her as he slowly, reluctantly moved toward the car. She stayed where she was as he slowly got in the back, and they drove off. She stood there a few minutes more, steadying her breathing. Though the city never fully slept, plenty of it did, and she closed her eyes, feeling the quiet slumber of the city. She took a deep breath and silently prayed the relative peace it enjoyed would not be disturbed in the nights to come, though she knew, in her heart, this was not to be.

CHAPTER TWENTY-SEVEN

Callista sat on the edge of her bunk, fingering Xornalden's warning note. What did he mean by "take action"? Would he lock them all up if he thought the guns were meant for him?

She quickly folded the note and slid it under her pillow when she heard footsteps approach, then glanced up to see Betty, who gazed down at her with a smile and sat next to her. She wore a homemade dress and her waist-length, braided gray hair framed her dark, wrinkled face which had lost none of its quiet beauty.

"Betty, why did you come to live down here?"

"Well, maybe I've seen too many alien movies," she said, leaning over toward Callista for a moment in a confidential manner. "I feared they might start killing people or taking them for experiments or laying eggs in them or something, so I fled with a bunch of people. Most realized the egg thing wasn't going to happen and returned to their homes after a few weeks. I stayed because there were plenty of scared people still here who didn't know how to take care of themselves when everything wasn't automated or done for them. And when most of those people left, I stayed for the same reason you're still here."

"What's that?

"Family," she said, looking at Callista. "You and I? We've come to care about the people down here. Our nurturing instinct wants to take care of them. And maybe the way they grip freedom with everything they have strikes a chord in us, and we don't want to be told what to do by outsiders any more than they do, whether we'll admit it or not."

"I guess you're right," Callista said, looking at the note in her hands folded into a wad.

"The heart is a strong organ and sometimes has a mind of its own," Betty said.

Callista glanced up, cocking her eyebrow.

"You wanna chat about what happened last night?" Betty asked.

"What do you mean?" Callista asked.

"I know a man who's had trouble with his woman when I see one. Hawkney's been storming around here like he's wrestling with a devil. What happened between you two?"

"Okay, first," Callista said, holding up a finger, "I am most certainly not his woman, and I sincerely hope he's coming to realize that. Second, I told him his new plan will get fire and brimstone rained down on our heads."

"What you talking about?"

"This rally he and Loui are planning, to whip up the people and give Xor-nalden the middle finger. I'm apparently the only person who didn't know about it."

"Well, I haven't heard about it, and I ain't happy either," Betty said, crossing her arms in a huff. "He puts us up there; he's painting us as threats—not just a peaceful community that doesn't want any part of the aliens' reign."

"Exactly," Callista said, throwing up her hands and letting them fall back on her lap with a slap. "And now, with the guns we have that they intend to pack with them, it just makes the whole thing look worse."

"Oh no, he didn't."

"Oh yes, he did, or will."

"That's it—the last straw," Betty said, standing up. "I'm having a private talk with the council members. It's time we got the military folks out and us peaceful people in before they get us all killed. If they want to go off on their own and cause trouble, that's their God-given right, but they are not dragging these innocent, defenseless people with them. Not on my watch."

"Preach," Callista said, standing also. "If there's anything I can do to help, please let me know."

"Well, there is, but you're not going to like it, and you'll have to play it just right."

"What's that?"

"Make up with Hawkney."

Callista gave Betty a look.

"I know, I know, you don't want to encourage him, but he's a ticking time bomb, honey. Smooth his feelings over a little and get him to calm down so he won't lash out in anger, 'cause then we might have real reason to be sorry."

Callista puffed her cheeks out for a moment.

"A tall order, I know," Betty said, "but I have faith in your powers of persuasion." With a smile, she walked away.

Callista sighed, closed her eyes for a moment to gather herself, and went to find Hawkney.

It took her a while, but she found him in a dead-end tunnel she'd never been in before. There were mechanical parts littering the floor, and what appeared to be the skeleton of a car in the middle. Hawkney crouched on the ground, trying to tighten something with a wrench. As she paused, he jumped up and threw the wrench against the wall with a roar, making her flinch. He started pacing around angrily and caught sight of her in the dim light.

"What did the wrench ever do to you?" she asked weakly with an attempt at a smile.

Hawkney looked away and kept pacing.

"Hawkney," she began, but he seemed to ignore her, finding something else for his hands to do. "Walk a mile in my shoes for a minute." She took a step closer to him. "A drunk man who is taller and a whole lot stronger than me pins me against a wall in the middle of the night with no one around and moves awfully close, and his lips even closer. And he's talking eagerly about violence to boot."

He slammed down the wrench he held and turned to her. "I would never hurt you, you know that!"

"No, Hawkney, I don't! I don't know you from Adam. Not really."

He snorted and started pacing again.

"You kiss me when I don't want to be kissed, and when you touch me, I don't know what you're going to do. Are you just massaging my shoulders, or is that your excuse—the place you start from?"

He whirled on her and started to put his hands on her shoulders but stopped when she jerked away. He slowly lowered his arms to his sides. "I swear on my life I would *never* do anything to hurt you, *never* do anything you didn't want me to do."

"That's all well and fine," she said, tears coming to her eyes. "But I just don't trust you yet. Not like that. I don't *know* you, and all this talk about war and fighting scares me. It's not the answer, Hawkney."

His jaw moved, and he turned away again.

"Do you want me? Do you ... *love* me? Prove it. Find another way. Having the means to protect ourselves is all well and good, but if we flaunt the weapons, Xor-nalden will assume we'll use them, and it'll be a domino effect and we'll end up with body counts."

"You don't know that," Hawkney said, turning to her again.

"Yes, I do," she said. "Because if they come to arrest any one of us, your soldiers will not go quietly, and there *will* be blood. Do you want to finish this?" she asked, pointing toward the car bones. "Do you want your kids to drive it? Then find another way."

Hawkney stared at her, a gleam in his eyes, saying nothing.

"Something worth having you have to work for," she continued. "You can't get a lover with a single kiss; you can't get freedom with a single fight. It takes time, years. You're responsible for the lives of everyone down here, and if you start a war, you're responsible for everyone who dies too. If you can't bear that then give the job to someone who can."

"Now you think I'm weak again," he said, turning away slowly.

"No, I think you're a man. You're—you're Batman, not Superman."

He looked back over his shoulder after a moment with a slight smile on his face. "Batman, huh?"

"Well, you do live in a cave."

He gave a soft snort in appreciation. "All right ... Cat Woman. I'll think about it."

She smiled at him for a long moment before she turned and left. Hopefully, she'd changed his mind, and there would be no rally.

NEGEV SKIMMED the new report on Gren-del. Evidence of law-breaking? Yes. Circumstantial at best? Yes.

He walked into his office, still staring at the report, when he caught sight of papers on his chair out of the corner of his eye. He glanced down, regarding papers scattered over the floor around his desk. He looked up for the feline suspect and spotted him crouched in front of the window, his tail twitching as if he had nothing to do with the fact that the papers were no longer stacked neatly on his desk. This was the third time this week.

"Augustus, I know this is your doing, but why you get any pleasure from it, I do not know. You have plenty of toys to play with."

Augustus gazed back at him innocently for a moment before coming over and rubbing against his leg.

"Do not try to pretend like it did not happen," he said, reaching down and stroking the cat's head. "I know it was you, and you cannot convince me otherwise. You are as bad as Gren-del —all innocent and flattering but with malice in your heart."

The cat looked up at him quizzically.

"No, I apologize; you are not malicious," he said, moving the papers off his chair onto the desk before sitting back in it. "One of these days I will catch you in the act, and we will see what you have to say for yourself."

The cat suddenly stiffened and stared at the door, and a few moments later, Negev heard someone walk past.

"Hmm. No, you will not get caught that way, will you? Your hearing is too good." He reached down to lightly brush the hair ends on the cat's ear, making it twitch. "I will have to catch you some other way, perhaps with a video camera." He smiled to himself at the idea of seeing the cat scatter his papers on film when the smile froze and his eyes widened.

That was it.

He tried to catch Gren-del in the act, but that was entirely the wrong approach. Gren-del knew there was no evidence against him, and his self-confidence and bravado might make him willing to talk about that fact and admit to what he did because Negev possessed no way of proving it before a council.

Unless he had Gren-del's own testimony.

Negev smiled to himself and leaned back in his chair, stroking the cat's head. Gren-del was coming to "answer" for the tragedy in Russia. If he interviewed him alone, Gren-del would likely be unable to resist throwing in Negev's face how powerless he was to stop him from doing as he pleased, and Negev could use it to convict Gren-del before the council. However, Gren-del would undoubtedly have a detection device on him to guard against any listening device.

He frowned and glanced back down at the cat. But what if,

instead of trying to come up with some new undetectable technology, he retrograded? A young protégé told him about a spy museum in this nation's former capital, which displayed vintage spy equipment. Perhaps he should visit to get some ideas.

He took a slow, nervous breath and gazed out the window, repeating to himself that he could, in fact, do this.

CHAPTER TWENTY-EIGHT

Apparently, after Callista talked to Hawkney, Hawkney talked to Niki and/or McCaffrey, and all her hard work flushed down the tubes. The rally was on.

The idea was to make it the Fourth of July in January. Everyone was supposed to wear only red, white, and blue—which, for Callista, meant wearing her red dress, unfortunately. Flags were stuck around the rallying place while the stage was set up. Others passed out and posted flyers announcing the rally later that afternoon. Niki procured fireworks, making Callista all the more nervous. She hoped the Alamies knew about fireworks and didn't get spooked.

She sighed as she picked up a potholder, and removed the smoothed brick from the stovetop, wrapped it carefully in a rag so it wouldn't tear at the dress, and started ironing.

Hawkney came up to her, wearing a white suit with a navy button-down shirt, a red scarf, and a white hat with a red hatband. He held the mask he wore at the last protest in his hand. She said nothing at his approach but continued to iron her dress.

"I know you're mad at me—again—but I've thought this through—in a sober state of mind—and I'm sure this is the right thing to do."

"You're the boss," she said softly and continued to iron.

"Look, it's like a form of checkmate," he said, perching on the side of the table where she worked. "Celebrities have power because so many people pay attention to their opinions. We need to threaten the power of the Alamy government by having the general masses in our pocket, who will riot in an instant at our encouragement. If they don't do what we say, they'll have a mob on their hands and citywide unrest. If they kill us, they make us martyrs, and we're an even bigger problem. Martyrs become a rallying cry. They have songs sung about them and their likenesses tattooed on people's arms," he said, gesticulating more as he became increasingly animated. "We need to be feared because of the sway we hold over the people rather than any military strength we might have. So, the only way to get out of the problem from the Alamy's perspective would be to discredit us, set us up for some terrible thing and make a stink about it, attack our character, etcetera, which takes time and is not wholly effective."

"The fact we live in tunnels and some of our members have criminal records should do the trick," she said quietly.

"Okay, first, Loui doesn't have a criminal record in any police files—he's never been caught," Hawkney said, standing and moving to her side. "Second, the people already know why we live down here, thanks to the TV spot—it's because we don't want to live under their rule."

"I just have a really bad feeling about this," she said and laid aside her brick iron.

"Trust me, it'll be fine. Nothing is going to happen."

"But what if Xor-nalden takes it the wrong way?"

"It's a risk, but any reaction is better than no reaction."

"I—I'm scared, Hawkney," she said, turning toward him. "I don't want to be up on stage—please, can't I stay here?"

Hawkney chewed on his lower lip in thought. "Okay, you don't have to stay up there the whole time, just for a minute. Then you can wander around if you want. But I need you there, Callista. You're our Lady Liberty," he said with a smile.

Callista stared down at her shoes.

Hawkney awkwardly squeezed her shoulder in encouragement before stepping away. "Get dressed. We leave in ten minutes," he said and walked away. Callista sighed and jerked the dress off the table.

***

CALLISTA WONDERED YET AGAIN why they couldn't have waited to have the Fourth of July in July. She clutched Xornalden's coat around herself, feeling like she was turning into a red and blue popsicle as the wind bit through her clothes and gnawed at her skin despite the coat's warmth. She began to worry she might lose her nose and toes to frostbite.

Some people were already there as the last preparations were made. They set up their lawn chairs in a row near the stage, staking their claim early. She couldn't help but notice as people began streaming onto the meadow, the dead and frozen atmosphere winter imposed on the park was supplanted by a new kind of life. The density of the people became thick—almost standing room only. But though she strained her ears, she heard not one word of complaint. Instead, she heard laughter, jovial greetings, offers to help and move a little so someone could see. She saw people sharing extra jackets and scarves, water, and food. Perfect strangers gave each other hugs for warmth. Even though the music had not yet begun, she sensed something had already been accomplished. Maybe Hawkney was right—maybe the people just needed a reason to reconnect with each other, see each other, and gain such a comradery with their neighbors that they would do anything to help each other, come what may.

A loud pop from the speakers made everyone jump and laugh at their tension, and Hawkney tapped the microphone.

"Goooooood afternoon, ladies and gentlemen!" Hawkney said through his patriotic mask, making sure his hat rested firmly on his head. "One quick thing before we begin," he held up an air horn. "If I at any time blow this," he did it once to demonstrate, and the piercing shriek rang over the crowd, "this means the Alamies are taking us a little too seriously, and everyone should scatter, but be careful not to trample each other—safety first—okay?"

He held out the mic toward the crowd to catch their returned "okay."

"Before we play some of our favorite tunes, I'd like to read you all something, would you mind?" The crowd affirmed him with shouts and a round of applause. "Don't applaud me, I haven't started yet!" he joked and unfolded a piece of paper from his white blazer.

"This is a speech given off the cuff by one Patrick Henry to the Second Virginia Revolutionary Convention on March 23, 1775." A few people who recognized the speech cheered Hawkney on. He started out evenly in a clear voice and had the crowd's full attention as he read the speech.

"'Our petitions have been slighted; our remonstrances have produced additional violence and insult; our supplications have been disregarded; and we have been spurned, with contempt, from the foot of the throne. In vain, after these things, may we indulge the fond hope of peace and reconciliation. There is no longer any room for hope.'"

Callista gazed around the crowd as he continued, using inflections and pauses as if he were Patrick Henry himself. She could see a growing light in the eyes of the people, and as she listened to the words over 200 years old, she admitted Patrick Henry was indeed an excellent orator and a passionate one.

"I repeat it, sir, we must fight! An appeal to arms and to the God of Hosts is all that is left us! They tell us, sir, that we are weak, unable to cope with so formidable an adversary. But when shall we be stronger? Will it be the next week or the next year?"

She looked around again, but fearfully this time. These were fighting words. She could see the people getting agitated already—she heard cries of "amen!" and "preach it!" plus the approving whistle here and there, giving her a sense of dread. She knew this was a bad idea—that they would take it too far too fast and end up with a violent mob. And after Hawkney—or Patrick Henry—brought God into the mix, she wondered if it could get any worse.

"There is no retreat but in submission and slavery! Our chains are forged! Their clanking may be heard on the plains of Boston! The war is inevitable, and let it come! I repeat it, sir, let it come!

"It is in vain, sir, to extenuate the matter. Gentlemen may cry, 'Peace! Peace!' but there is no peace. The war is actually begun! The next gale that sweeps from the north will bring to our ears the clash of resounding arms! Our brethren are already in the field! Why stand we here idle? What is it that gentlemen wish? What would they have? Is life so dear, or peace so sweet, as to be purchased at the price of chains and slavery? Forbid it, Almighty God! I know not what course others may take, but as for me, give me liberty or give me death!"

Hawkney screamed into the mic at the end of the speech, and the people responded with resounding shouts. The music started with a bang, and hundreds if not a few thousand voices joined in to the music, making a deafening sound Callista feared would be heard all the way to the Admiral's building and not go unnoticed.

They began playing peppy songs and moved on to the tear-jerkers before going back up with the passionate ones again. Callista had a headache from the noise and dearly wished for the umpteenth time she had brought earplugs. She was shocked from her waiting stupor when Loui grabbed her by the upper arm and dragged her toward the stage. Up the stage they went, and Niki followed with two yellow Gadsden flags. Loui took one from her after he dragged Callista to the center of the stage, and he and Niki waved the flags with gusto. Hawkney snatched the American flag from center-back stage and shoved it into Callista's fumbling arms. He grabbed her wrist and raised it high in the air like she had won a prize fight.

"Ladies and gentlemen, I give you Lady Liberty, who will lead these people to liberty or death!" The crowd went wild, throwing up their arms and their hats in celebration. Callista's stomach turned. She stepped back when Hawkney let go and used his hands to hype up the crowd. She tried to stay calm as she placed the flag back in its stand, crouched at the back of the stage, and carefully jumped off it to the ground.

Gasping for air, she moved behind the stage where a line of trees stood. The cold sent knives into her lungs and only intensified her headache. She stood in the bushes, her hands on her knees as she bent over, gasping. Tears fell from her eyes with little smacking sounds on the dead leaves as she perceived that her own chains had been forged for some time, and she could only now hear them clinking. Leaves crunched behind her and she stood up abruptly, making her tears cling to her cheeks. A hand landed gently on her shoulder as she turned.

"Are you well?" a man said, his voice muffled through a scarf wrapped about his face. Large sunglasses covered the top half of his face with the hood of his jacket pulled down to them. Callista wished she had dressed so snugly. She couldn't feel her fingers well, and she couldn't feel her feet at all.

"Yes. I, I guess I'm getting overwhelmed with the noise and, and, everything," she stuttered, shivering uncontrollably, and pulled Xor-nalden's coat around her more snugly. She couldn't figure out the clasp on short notice and settled for clutching it around her.

"I completely understand," he said and stepped closer to her. "Allow me," he said and began deftly fastening the coat. She gawked, fascinated, as what appeared complicated was, in reality, so easy. "Being the leader of a people is one of the hardest, most terrifying jobs. You have the lives and fates of so many in your hands."

182

Callista only sniffed in response as he wrapped one arm around her and rubbed her arms for warmth. She was too upset to try to straighten him out about her status in the community, the full extent of which she had only just understood, and tried to stop crying and keep her nose from running. Then, it occurred to her that she had heard his voice before. She stared back at his face for a few seconds before noticing blue skin peeping out from where his scarf didn't meet his glasses on the sides of his face. She sucked her breath in and tried to bolt from Xor-nalden's grasp. He was here—they were here. She had to tell Hawkney, to warn them all before he made arrests—

"Miss Tristan, please," he said, and managed to grasp her wrist as she tried to wriggle away. She used a self-defense technique and quickly twisted her wrist and pulled at the same time, causing him to lose his grasp. He tried to make another grab for her, but she kicked him in the shin with all her might, surprising him and causing him to lose his footing on the slick leaves and fall to a knee. She almost lost her footing, too, on the damp leaves, but she still managed to run back into the crowd, never looking back. There was no time to lose.

She darted and wove through the thick mesh of the crowd back to the stage steps and stumbled up them, tripping on her dress and sometimes missing the steps entirely. The comb holding her hair fell out, and her long brown hair now splayed across her shoulders and face wildly as she finally reached the top of the steps. She shrieked Hawkney's name as loud as she could, but the music and the crowd were so loud he didn't hear her. She lunged toward him and snatched the air horn from the back of his pocket, grasping his shoulder with splayed fingers for support. He glanced over at her, lowering the mic a little from his mouth, but she still blew the horn in the general direction of his face which coincided with the microphone.

The already loud horn amplified five times louder, and it was as though the trumpet of God wailed over the park with the expected result—the sea parted. Not forming a causeway but creating a hole in the center that grew larger. Callista stood stunned for a moment, watching the people with fascination until Hawkney grabbed her wrist and dragged her down the steps. They were soon in the thick of the crowd, and Hawkney lost his grasp. He turned when he lost her, and as the crowd separated them, he called her name, and she tried to weave her way back over to him. She glanced over her shoulder, looking for Niki or Loui when she wasn't getting any closer to Hawkney, and sighted three Alamgirians in plain clothes climb to the top of the stage.

When she turned to look for Hawkney again, she tripped, and someone stepped on her ankle. Despite the noise, she imagined she heard the crack. She cried out, and pain spiked through her leg as she fell, subsequently getting kicked in the head by someone else. Other kicks landed from the fleeing people, and she couldn't think straight as her ears rang from the blow to her head. Before she knew it, everyone was gone.

Someone touched her arm, and she groggily looked to find Xor-nalden crouched next to her, his scarf pulled down and his sunglasses on his head, his violet and scarlet eyes staring intently into hers. He spoke but sounded far away as if he were talking from behind glass.

He appeared to figure this out as she did and bit his lower lip for a moment. He reached out and cupped her chin, gently moving her head so he could see the cut on the side of her head she hadn't realized was there. He pulled out a handkerchief, pressed on it on the wound, and moved her hand to hold it there. He gazed down at her ankle, and she followed his gaze to see her foot twisted at an unnatural angle. She gave a cross between a strangled cry and a moan and moved her hand from her head to her mouth in horror, letting the handkerchief fall. He picked it up and replaced it on her head and moved her hand back to it.

He slung her other arm around his neck, slid his arms under her back and knees, and slowly picked her up. The movement caused her ankle to shift, and she cried out in pain and arched her back before burying her face in his shoulder. The pain made everything even blurrier and more incomprehensible than before, and she couldn't concentrate on anything else.

CHAPTER TWENTY-NINE

She woke to the smell of acrid cleanliness and a clacking sound. She started to open her eyes and regretted it, grunting as she squeezed her eyes shut and tried to move her sluggish hands to her eyes to shield them. The clacking noise ceased. There was a creak to her right, and footsteps moved around to the foot of her bed. When they stopped, the lights dimmed, and she could open her eyes.

Xor-nalden stood next to the door, his hand on the light switch.

"The doctor said you might be sensitive to light and sound," he said softly as he moved back to her right, where there was another bed littered with papers and a computer. He leaned over and typed another moment before moving to her bedside, sitting on the edge, and taking her hand. "How do you feel?"

Callista didn't reply. She nervously eyed the room. Like many other hospital rooms, it had two beds, medical monitors, a chair against the wall, a TV hanging from the ceiling, and a faded abstract on the wall near the window. She soon perceived her right foot looked bigger than her left under the sheet.

"They said it was something of a nasty break," he said, gently moving the sheet so she could see her foot. It was heavily bandaged, with only her now-purple toes peeking out of it. "You will have to stay here for a few days and then stay in a wheelchair for another week or so before you can go to crutches. If you like, though, I can take you to my medical facility, and I know they could shorten the healing time significantly."

She bit her lip as she stared at her purple toes a moment longer until he gently covered them.

"How do you feel?" he asked again. He waited patiently when she still didn't answer and avoided his gaze.

"I didn't want to go," she finally said. Out of the corner of her eye, she saw him cock his head. She continued, "I thought it was a horrible idea, and people would get hurt, and of course, it had to be me."

"Then why did you not call it off?" he asked quietly.

She looked at him sharply. "Contrary to your impressions and what Hawkney would have everyone believe, I have absolutely no power. I told him I didn't want to go, and he essentially said 'too bad.' I tried to talk him out of it, and it did squat. I'm just another lemming, caught up in the herd and rushing over the edge with the rest of them."

Though she continued to stare at the abstract hanging across from the foot of her bed, she sensed him continuing to stare at her as he played with her fingers, entwining his with hers.

"I am sorry," he said softly after a long moment. "I believed you were at least an ambassador between us."

"Nope," she said flatly. "I'm just a pawn. A messenger at best."

He sighed and gazed down at their fingers. "I cannot help but believe this is somehow my fault, then."

"How can that possibly be, unless you count the fact you invaded us, etcetera."

His mouth twitched in a smile before quickly fading. "I do not know—perhaps because of the silly wife-finding program."

"That's still going a ways back."

"Consequences tend to have a domino effect."

"True."

He gave her a rueful smile and looked back down at her hands. Now, it was her turn to stare at him for a long moment.

"What are you going to do with me?" she asked softly.

He took a deep breath. "That is the question I have asked myself ever since you were in my arms," he said, turning his gaze to her. "Your people's acquisition of weapons troubles me. I cannot afford to fight two wars right now. My forces have confiscated everything in the warehouse you visited, but there was evidence a great number of items were recently removed, which I assume is what your people acquired. Do you know where those armaments are?"

"No," Callista said. "No one tells me anything. I found out about the rally late in the planning process. I didn't even know the hardware had been delivered yet."

Xor-nalden frowned and glanced away.

"What will you do?" she asked.

He looked back at her. "I do not know yet."

A female Alamgirian voice outside the door spoke emphatically, and Hawkney appeared in the doorway, dressed in camo pants and a brown leather jacket, glaring in at her. Xor-nalden said something in Alamgirian, and the woman at the door let him pass. Hawkney quickly moved to her side opposite Xor-nalden, keeping him in view.

"Are you all right?" he asked in an almost menacing tone, grasping her hand and only sending her face a glance before returning his gaze to Xor-nalden.

"I'm as good as I can be," she answered.

"I will let you two talk," Xor-nalden said. He turned and gathered up the papers scattered across the adjacent bed and closed the tablet against the detachable keyboard. He turned back to Callista, the papers and tablet clutched to his chest. "If you need—"

She lunged and grabbed his sleeve. "Don't go," she said, her voice quavering. Xor-nalden hesitated, and they locked gazes, and she put as much pleading and fear into her eyes as she could. He glanced between her and Hawkney a few times before slowly laying the papers back down on the bed as if he meant to stay.

"Callista," Hawkney said softly, and she looked back to see sadness in his eyes.

"There is a guard at the door," Xor-nalden said, his gaze lingering on Hawkney before moving to Callista. "If you need anything, call her."

She gave a slight shake of her head and continued to send the same message with her eyes. Xor-nalden cocked his head and sent a sidelong glance toward the door. Callista followed his line of sight and spotted the security camera above the door.

"I will be back. I am going to check on the other patients who were trampled," Xor-nalden said gently. He squeezed her hand and left, pausing in the doorway to give Hawkney a warning look.

"Seriously, you all right?" Hawkney said, turning to Callista. "Did he question you? Did he—"

"Hawkney, the papers," Callista said, looking at the stack Xor-nalden left on the bed.

"Watch the door," Hawkney said and hurried around her bed to the other one, slipping a tiny camera out of his pocket. He snatched a surgical glove from a box on the table next to her and slid it on his left hand and began photographing the papers without studying them.

She dutifully stared at the door until the clicking of the camera stopped, and she looked back to see him straighten the papers and put them back exactly as they were.

"What are they about?" she asked softly.

"They're in Alamy," he said, taking off the glove and throwing it in the trash. "We have a translation sheet somewhere, though. We'll translate them. Now come on, let's go."

"I can't. My ankle's broken."

"I'll carry you. Let's go," he said, pulling on her arm.

"No!" she said loudly, and squeezed her eyes shut and covered her ears against the loud noise she made. At a squeak of rubber she opened her eyes. The guard stood in the doorway. Leaning against the door jamb, she crossed her arms and stared.

"I have a concussion, Hawkney," Callista said. "And bruises all over. I'm not going anywhere."

Hawkney let go of her arm. He glanced back at the guard. "I guess I can't stay with you, then," and the guard shook her head in the negative. He sighed, letting his head hang down as he leaned against the short rail on her bed, rocking back and forth in thought. Callista didn't relax.

Finally, he looked up and put his arms around her, burying his face in her hair. He breathed in deeply as he held her and let out a shaky breath. He glanced up at the guard after a moment. "Would you mind giving us a minute?" he asked softly, and she grudgingly moved back to her position outside the door. Hawkney let go and fished a flip phone out of his pocket, pressing it into Callista's hand.

"Niki's number is the first one in there," he said. "If anything happens, he pressures you in any way, you call, okay? You don't even have to talk about it. Just keep it under the sheets and hit the button the minute you think he'll detain you indefinitely or *anything*, okay?"

Callista nodded and slid the phone under the sheets. Hawkney sighed, seeming unsatisfied, and leaned on the rail again, biting his lower lip as he stared at her.

"Go get those pages translated," she said. "They could be invaluable."

He continued to chew on his lip and stare at her for a moment before standing up and nodding. "I'll come back tomorrow, or someone will." He slowly walked toward the door, stopping to look back. "Take care of yourself," he said softly and left.

She heaved a sigh of relief and leaned her head back, closing her eyes. What did those pages contain? If Hawkney left the building with the camera, it meant Xor-nalden wanted them to see their contents. If they were classified, whoever manned the security camera would have him stopped.

Footsteps stopped next to her bed, but she didn't bother opening her eyes.

"Shall I continue to keep you company, or would you like to be alone?" Xor-nalden asked her.

"What's on those pages you wanted him to see?" she asked, eyes closed. She sensed his smile.

"Everything I have so far on Gren-del, as immaterial as it may be," he said, the adjacent bed creaking as he sat down. "They are not convinced I am doing anything? Well, now they have everything, too. If I told them myself, they would be far less likely to believe me than if they 'stole' the information for themselves."

"True," she said softly.

"I am rather gratified you caught that," he said admiringly. "So. Shall I stay or depart?"

"Whatever," she said, barely above a whisper.

"How do you feel?" he asked after a moment of digesting her answer.

"My ankle hurts," she said, the throbbing beginning to take over her consciousness.

"Ah. The doctor said you should take two of these."

She opened her eyes when the bed creaked to see him unscrewing the lid off a bottle on the large nightstand between the beds. He laid the pills on the table and poured water into a glass from a pitcher. He held it out to her, and she started to struggle to sit up.

"Wait," he said gently and set the glass back on the table. He reached his arms around her in a loose embrace and gently helped her to sit up, and he hurriedly propped the pillows up behind her. As she relaxed into them, he handed her the pills and the glass and returned the glass to the table after she drained it.

"My question still remains." He placed his hands on the rail and leaned on it as Hawkney had.

She gazed down at his hands, saying nothing, an old scratch

on one of his fingers arresting her attention. After a moment, she slowly moved her hand to stroke his fingers. He unfurled them, and they began playing with each other's fingers again, weaving them in and out, feeling the texture. She didn't want him to leave, for some reason she couldn't quite place. His presence calmed her, especially after Hawkney's upsetting visit.

He heaved a heavy sigh, making her look up at him.

"What's the matter?" she asked softly.

"I wish there was more ... rest," he said.

"As opposed to unrest, you mean?"

"Yes. Did I not say it right?"

"You did, but because a word can have different connotations and meanings, it can be confusing."

"I have become *very* well aware of that while learning your language," he said, smiling.

"Well, as my grandmother used to say, 'Do the best you can, because that's the best you can do.'"

He cocked his head, continuing to gaze at their intertwined fingers. "I like that," he said. "It is rather comforting, though sobering at the same time, if your best is not enough."

"That's the beauty of it," she said. "If your best is not enough, there's no point in worrying about it because there's nothing more you could have done to make the outcome different, because you did your best."

"But what if you did not know if, in fact, you did your best?" he asked, looking up at her. "For example, what if I forcefully sought you out at some point after our first meeting or sent you home? You would not have a broken ankle and a concussion now."

"But you would also have robbed me of my choice to stay or go as I pleased," she said, squeezing his fingers gently. "Then we never would have gotten to know each other better."

"But I would not have believed you were more than you were and placed you in an uncomfortable position."

"Everyone makes mistakes, Admiral. Even you."

Xor-nalden looked up at her. "I don't like the way that sounds coming from you."

"That you make mistakes?"

"No," he said, the corner of his mouth twitching in a smile. "'Admiral.'" He took her hand in his and raised it to his chest, gently massaging her palm. "Call me by my given name, please?"

"Negev?" she asked uncertainly after searching her memory for a moment.

"Yes. We have been through enough to warrant a first name basis."

"If you say so. You're the man in charge."

"Well, I do say so, and so it shall be."

She closed her eyes with a contented smile, and he gently squeezed her hand.

"Sleep, my friend," he said quietly. He gently placed her hand back on the bed and helped her to lie down again before returning to his work on the adjacent bed.

As she drifted off to sleep, she hoped the papers Hawkney took photos of would convince them of what she already knew— Negev Xor-nalden was not the enemy.

CHAPTER THIRTY

She was just making sure she got every bit of the banana pudding off her spoon when Negev walked in to find her with said spoon completely in her mouth. It made an embarrassing sucking noise when she pulled it out abruptly at his entrance.

"How do you feel today?" he asked.

"My head's much better, and as long as I keep the drugs in me, my ankle's not too bad either. It annoys me, though, because I'm scared to move in the least," she said, setting the spoon down on her tray.

"The injury can be quickly cured if you would like to utilize our medical facilities," he said, stepping over to her bedside.

"You mean you can heal my ankle a lot faster than normal?"

"Correct."

"What's the catch?"

"Catch?" he asked, cocking his head.

"Catch," she said, crossing her arms. "There's no such thing as a free lunch. I either have to repay you in some way, or there's going to be some physical toll on my body you're not telling me about because you feel guilty and want me to get better faster."

"Ah, I see what you mean. Yes, you need to be given

intravenous supplements to assist in the regrowth so it does not decimate other parts of your body, and you will be greatly fatigued for a few days. Most sleep through it."

"And what do you want in return for the favor?"

"Nothing."

"Really? Why?"

"It is an investment in our friendship," he said with a smile, holding out his hand invitingly.

Callista gazed at him a moment before she nodded her head once. "All right," she said, not taking his hand. "Find me some clothes and I'll go."

"It is a deal," he said with a smile and left on his quest.

Callista waited a moment, chewing on her lip before she slid the phone out from under the sheets and texted Niki that she agreed to be taken to an Alamy medical facility and she'd text them the location when she could.

Negev returned with some gym shorts, a few sizes too large, and a sleeveless muscle shirt. "These were in a donations bin—I thought these shorts would be best, because they are big enough to fit over your cast but have a drawstring so you can still wear them."

"Good thinking," Callista said and accepted the offering.

"Thank you," he said, standing there.

"Mind giving me a minute to put these on?" she asked after an awkward moment.

"You do not need help?"

"I'll holler if I need help," she assured him, making herself busy by laying out the clothes. He nodded quickly and slipped out of the room in a hurry, and she caught a hint of a blush on his face, turning his cheeks a shade closer to purple, making her smile.

After she slipped the clothes on, she swung her legs over the side and marveled again at how much bigger her wounded foot was compared to her uninjured one. "You can come back now," she called out, and Negev appeared in the doorway. "We're going to need a wheelchair," she said.

"That will not be necessary," he said, coming over to her.

"No? Crutches?"

"No," he said and slipped an arm under her knees and another under her shoulders, picking her up as if she weighed no more than a child.

"My, aren't you strong," she said in a sarcastic, flat tone, making the corner of his mouth curve up in appreciation. He dismissed the guard at the door on their way out and headed toward the elevator.

"Push the button for the roof," he said when they were inside.

She reached down and pressed it.

"I take it we're riding out in style?"

Negev smiled and gazed at her slyly.

The doors opened, and they walked out onto the landing pad. Callista caught her breath. She'd never seen an Alamgirian spaceship up close before, only blurry photos she hadn't been interested in. The Alamies were careful to keep Humans away from them.

The sleek black ship was made of material that shone like glass. Its sharp, streamlined angles made it look dangerous and meant for speed. A stepstool led up to the tinted canopy which quietly slid opened at a touch of Negev's finger on a sensor. Negev walked up the steps and swung his legs over to stand on the pilot's seat and carefully crouched to deposit her in the co-pilot's seat. She couldn't suppress a shiver once he let go and looked around, trying to memorize every detail.

She settled in as Negev situated himself in his own seat and pressed a button for the canopy to close and start the engines to warm up with a deep hum. He reached over and showed her how to strap in and made sure she was secured before he strapped in himself and grasped the controls, gently taking the ship off into the air. He pressed another button, and she observed the ship was now cloaked when the black wing in her field of view outside the canopy appeared to disappear, leaving only a faint ripple in the skyline.

"Do you mind if we take a short detour? I want to show you something," he asked.

"I don't mind. What do you want to show me, the Statue of Liberty?"

He smiled in appreciation of the irony. "No. Something far better," he said and lifted the ship straight up into the sky. She sucked in and held her breath. She felt herself being pressed into the chair for a moment, but the pressure soon eased, though their speed did not. She wondered at the technology that could negate the gravitational force equivalent on their bodies despite their high acceleration.

The blue sky darkened, and more and more stars appeared until they filled the view. Negev rolled the ship abruptly, making the whole star scape whirl and the earth flash by. Callista gasped and grabbed the side of the ship with one hand and made a grab with the other, finding his arm and hanging on for dear life and to her lunch. He chuckled and leveled out the ship so stars filled the view of the starship's canopy. She stared at the Milky Way—a soft yellow glow, a cluster of billions of stars that faded out at the edges.

"Beautiful, do you think?" he said after a long moment.

"Yes," Callista breathed. Each star pulsed rainbows, the pattern like a silent song. "'When I consider your heavens, the work of your fingers,'" she began softly, a passage from the Psalms coming to mind. "'The moon and the stars, which you have set in place, what is mankind that you are mindful of them, human beings that you care for them?'"

Negev stared at her for a long time. He pulled her clenched hand from his arm and slid it into his hand. She tore her gaze from the hypnotic view and glanced down at their clasped hands.

"Why did you bring me out here?" she asked quietly.

"Do I have to have a reason?"

"No one does anything for no reason," she said, looking up at him. "You now know I have no weight with my people, yet you're still trying to gain my trust and favors. Why?"

"Do you remember I did not approve of the wife-finding program?" he asked, laying his head back and looking up at the stars.

"Yes."

"Well, though I hate to admit it ... , it does not mean it did not work."

The seconds ticked by as he let her soak his words in. He looked back over at her, and their eyes locked for a long moment. She bit the inside of her lip and looked away first. He grasped her hand a little tighter and turned so he faced her a bit more.

"Your strategic value does not matter to me. I do not care if you are popular or not, if you have power or influence or not. You have intrinsic value—who you are—to me, which is what I ... love."

Callista stared down at her restless hand in her lap. Did he noticed her other hand had gotten sweaty in his, or that her face turned a bit pinker? He loosened his grip on her hand without letting go and shifted so he sat straight in the seat again.

"I do not expect you to have any feelings about me. We are different species, after all. Nor do you need fear I will force you into anything," he said, looking over at her and giving her a look, undoubtedly remembering the first time they met.

"I am surrounded by secrets and false smiles day in and day out," he continued. "I am sick of them. What I want, Callista, is someone I can be completely honest and open with. Think of it as an adviser. You are wise. You could be indispensable to me and your people and do them much good just by being there for me to talk to."

She rested her head back. He let go of her hand to make an adjustment to the ship and also rested back, letting her absorb everything he said. Callista tried to look at the situation from the outside and soon realized something.

"You have offered me two avenues to immense power," she said, looking over at him. "Is this a case of 'keep your friends close, and your enemies closer?'"

He furrowed his brows, staring into space. "An interesting concept," he finally said. "I shall have to consider it in depth... . But you are certainly the friend in this case. Regardless of the reality, you are viewed as someone with influence in the public's mind. That makes you a target to someone, well, like me. It is Gren-del who worries me, though. He makes me want to keep you close to keep you safe, yes."

"I doubt my star status extends to Europe. Why would he care?"

"Because he will eventually want to take the whole world for himself. And when he does, you will become his problem."

"But to get over to America, he'll have to take you out, and if I'm closer to you, he's more likely to get us both at once," she pointed out.

They were both silent for a moment.

"True," he said. "You see? You are wise."

"Or I just have an excellent self-preservation instinct."

"That is a form of wisdom. One we both need the most right now." He glanced back over at her. "No need to decide now. Just ... consider it."

He fired up the engines, and it surprised her they headed toward the moon. They skirted low over the craters and soon were over the far side of the moon, currently veiled in night. She tried to pierce the blackness and see something, but the darkness was total, so she turned her head to see where they were going and caught her breath. It was like looking at a city at night, only it was a mountain.

"That is our capital ship," he said after a moment. "In translation, its name means 'Place of Rest.'"

She continued to marvel at its enormity as they approached and landed inside a spacious hangar, and Negev powered down the ship.

"Do you think," he said, unclasping his harness, "you can manage to sit on the edge of the ship so I can come and lift you down from behind?" He pressed the release on the canopy.

"I think so," she said, putting her good foot up next to her on the seat. Pushing up with her arms and leg, she stood on the seat, and did a little hop so her back was to the edge of the ship. Negev scrambled out, slid down to the floor, and hurried around to the other side. The transfer went off without a hitch, and she settled in his arms again.

He started with her toward one of the doors and was met by a high-ranking Alamgirian officer, or at least Callista guessed he was —he wore a lot of chest bling like Negev did. He greeted Negev in their tongue and commented about Callista, gesturing toward her with a smile. Callista glanced up at Negev to see his blue cheeks darkening in a blush as he gave a firm negative comment, which the officer laughed off. Negev noticed her watching him, and he rolled his eyes, making her smile as she leaned her head against his shoulder.

Callista got the impression the Alamgirians on the ship were assigned to it because they could not speak an Earth language, a supposition built on the fact Negev translated for them.

"When the procedure has been underway for about half an hour, you will become exhausted, and it is all right to go to sleep," Negev translated for the doctor. "If you are comfortable here by yourself, I am going to check on the ship while you sleep."

"Okay," Callista said with a nod.

"You are certain?"

"Yes," Callista said, not looking at him but watching the doctors prepare the supplements and the machine that would increase her rate of healing.

"Very well. Until you wake up, then," he said and hesitantly left the medical bay. The doctors gazed after him and chattered among themselves with grins and chuckles.

True to their word, about half an hour after they started, Callista started dropping off to sleep, her last thoughts mulling over whether her friends would ever believe she had gone to the far side of the moon and been on an enormous spaceship.

CHAPTER THIRTY-ONE

Admiral Negev Xor-nalden of the Alamgirian fleet, Supreme Ruler of Earth, felt one foot tall. It was how he always felt in Admiral Gren-del's presence. Like a young child who got into an enormous amount of trouble and was brought before the father to answer for his iniquity, he wished the floor would break open beneath him, and gravity would whisk him out of sight. It did not help that he got the urgent call from his aide, of Gren-del's arrival while he was on *Place of Rest* with Callista and had to hurry back in a flurry. He was still trying to keep his breathing calm and steady. He did not want to betray his anxiety or his earlier hurry to get to the meeting room before Gren-del did, to set everything up.

He now sat across from Gren-del at the long table, attempting to evenly match the man's one-eyed stare as always. Negev didn't know how the man lost his eye, and frankly, he sometimes questioned if the eyepatch was really meant for intimidation. The one eye he could see was a deep red, which always brought blood to mind and lacked the bright luster of most Alamgirians' eyes, red or otherwise. His skin tone was a few shades darker than Negev's, and a scar ran across his right cheekbone, starting at the right side of his upper lip and disappearing at a point almost parallel with his eye. Negev always thought he looked like a crook.

"I did not come here so you could try to stare into my soul," Gren-del said in their language, breaking the silence in his over-quiet voice that sent chills down many a spine. His comment struck Negev as ironic—he imagined Gren-del tried to do the same to him.

"No, you did not," Negev said in a similarly quiet, even voice. "I summoned you here so I could be certain you understand you and your men are not to kill another Human without due process of the law, whether they have ignored your decrees or not." He skipped the discussion of whether Gren-del was responsible for the massacre in St. Petersburg or not—they both knew he was. Gren-del was smart enough not to admit to anything outright, and any direct questions on Negev's part would cause him to shut down.

Gren-del gave a crooked smirk and sat back further into the chair. "What do you care?"

As he suspected, Gren-del did not bother denying the indirect accusation.

"Everyone on this planet is my responsibility," Negev said. "I cannot have them killed for no reason. I will also have the council rescind your pointless ban of religions."

"We are their conquerors. What reason do we need?" Gren-del said, his eye half closing.

"Just because we are conquerors does not mean we need to be tyrants. A tyrannical rule like yours breeds unrest and suffering, and we cannot have that."

"Again, I ask, why do you care?" Gren-del asked, cocking his head to the side and studying Negev. "They are livestock. Insects. Whether they live or die is no concern to us."

"Say how you truly feel," Negev said sarcastically, borrowing from a Human phrase.

Gren-del narrowed his eye at him. "Ah, now I see. You have grown fond of them. I hoped this rumor of your searching for a

Human wife was just that. Despicable. If you are truly in need of female services, I am sure one of our own would be willing to oblige you."

"If we are to survive into the next generation we must mix. There are too few females of our own. We would be outnumbered at sixty million to one in the course of fifty years."

"All the more reason to cull them now. Weaken their numbers, so they are too concerned with rebuilding their lives and keeping the remains of their family close to bother us. But why am I telling you this?" Gren-del scoffed and gazed out the window. "It is the same advice I urged you to take when we considered our options from afar."

"And I will continue to disregard it. I worked too hard to come up with a plan to take this planet with the fewest casualties possible. I will not have you destroy it with your flippant regard for life."

"And what will you do if I disregard you?" Gren-del asked, leaning forward a bit, his gaze boring into Negev's. "The old hierarchy, the old balance of power, is gone. You do not want a war? Stay out of my way, or we will certainly have a civil war."

"And what if I arrest you here and now for treason?" Negev asked.

Gren-del grinned. "You know what will happen," he said, standing up. "You better find a Human female who will take you soon, Little Negev, and seal your pact by marriage. You will need all the allies you can get soon. Very soon." Gren-del strode to the conference room door and opened it, pausing to look back at Negev. "Do not bother contacting me again unless it is to give me your command. I will ignore anything you or the council want me to do—I shake you off and leave you to rot among the Humans." With that, he left the room, closing the door a little too hard behind him.

Negev leaned back and let out the breath he didn't realize he held and closed his eyes. It was as he feared. Gren-del now officially ignored his commands with no one to stop him. Now he worried about how many of the admirals would rally around Gren-del.

Pat-farfth came in and looked at him expectantly. Negev pushed back his chair and slid the recording device out from under the table, and carefully detached the wire connected to a flower in the centerpiece above the recorder in which nestled a microphone. He hit the rewind button so the film would move back to the first wheel and hit the play button on the vintage recording device, and Gren-del's voice came through, loud and clear.

Pat-farfth gazed at him with a smile that quickly faded when he caught Negev's worried one. "What is wrong?" he asked. "Did you not get what you wanted?"

"No, Gren-del showed himself to be the monster he is," Negev conceded. "But he has also broken away. There is war on the horizon and approaching fast. Alert the troops. I suspect he will cause unrest while he is here. Then he can watch the 'wailing beasts' eat me and get the satisfaction of seeing those I seek to protect do his dirty work for him."

Pat-farfth nodded once. "I shall assign two to guard you at all times, and I shall assign a detail to watch Gren-del and his men while he is here."

"No need to assign them to me. As I said, I am fairly certain he will goad the Humans into doing it for him, and even if he did move against me himself, it would take an army to protect me, and I will not live in constant fear."

"As you wish," Pat-farfth said, moving toward the door.

"Be careful, uncle."

"You as well," Pat-farfth said, leaving the room, gently shutting the door behind him.

CHAPTER THIRTY-TWO

Callista questioned for a long, hard moment if what transpired the day before was a dream or not. She woke up gazing at the same abstract painting she had stared at for hours and realized she was in the same Earth-side hospital room she had been in before. A sniff made her look over to see the Alamgirian who formerly guarded her door sitting casually on the other bed, scrolling through the holographic popup from her wrist communicator. Callista rustled the covers as she stretched, and the Alamgirian glanced over at her.

"He could not stay. You healed, can go, if like."

Callista glanced down at her ankle. There was no more cast, only a wrapping, and it appeared only slightly swollen with a hint of a bruise left.

"Be careful with it, do not try too hard," the woman cautioned.

"Okay," Callista said, sitting up and swinging her legs over the side. "I can go?"

"Yes. Want ride?"

Callista accepted and was dropped off in front of the Joralemon Street façade. She waited until the white SUV turned the corner before she fished the key out of its hiding place, let herself in, and wove her way down into the subway system. Instead of taking the circuitous route Niki had used the first time, she chose the far more direct route Hawkney taught her.

She was on the outskirts of the settlement, trying to figure out her story as she carefully limped down the unused section of subway tunnel, running her fingers along the wall. The lights were turned off in that section, with only a faint glow coming from farther down the tunnel where the settlement started in earnest. This section was almost pitch dark, and the last thing she needed was to twist her bad ankle.

She smiled to herself, thinking about what their reaction would be if she told them about the mountain-sized spaceship on the far side of the moon and that she'd been there, when a movement of shadow caught her eye. She turned her head but suddenly found a hand clamped over her mouth and cold steel at her throat. She barely had time to gasp when the knife stung into the side of her neck. Callista grabbed for the hand holding the knife and jerked her leg back as hard as she could, hitting her target—her attacker's crotch.

He sucked in his breath, and she twisted sideways out of his grasp, though the knife slit a trail in her neck as she did so. She screamed with all her might and raced down the tunnel toward the light, jabs of pain shooting up her weak ankle. She heard a muffled curse behind her and instinctually ducked, expecting another attack, and the knife flew over her head. She screamed again and tripped but struggled on and almost reached the light when there was something like a banshee's screech behind her, and she was knocked down by a searing pain in her left shoulder. She face-planted in the gravel, her hands skidding over it, and thought she was done for, hearing the crunch of running feet behind her.

She glanced over her shoulder to see the figure coming up to her and moving his weapon to point at her when a blur of movement tackled the assailant with a howl. The two rolled in the gravel for a minute, grunts and muffled thuds marking punches in the dim light until she glimpsed a flash of a knife, and the assassin yelled in pain. After a few more red-tinted flashes, he fell silent and still. Niki rose from her straddled position on top of him after making sure he was dead and staggered over to Callista as more running feet came from the light.

"You okay, sister?" she asked Callista hoarsely.

Callista reached up and felt wet heat leaking from her neck. "No," she whispered. Gravel cascaded as Hawkney slid to a stop on his knees beside her.

"Callista! Are you all right? Where have you been? What happened?"

Callista's elbows buckled when she tried to push herself up from the gravel as pain and dizziness began to take hold.

"Neck ... help ... ," she murmured.

Hawkney whipped out a small flashlight and shone it in her face. He moved her bloodied hand to see the wound and dropped a few curses. He started yelling orders—the key word she caught was "cauterize"—and scooped her limp body up and ran down the tunnel with her, making her head bounce around, only adding to the dizziness and pain.

Callista was quickly pulled out of her semi-conscious state when a searing heat pressed into her neck. She yelled and tried to struggle, but there were three hands holding down her head and others holding down the rest of her. Finally, it stopped but the spinning of the room didn't, and the smell of her own burning flesh wasn't helping.

"Callista, what's your blood type?" Hawkney asked for the third time, giving her a little shake.

"... O ... ," She finally managed to squeak out.

"Positive?"

Callista could barely keep her eyes open, much less register the question.

"Get the tube; we'll have to risk it," Hawkney said, but she didn't register the meaning. "Give me that alcohol. We need to clean the one on her back and get it bandaged up. Find some aloe or salve for the burns, too."

Something cold touched the inside of her elbow, and she felt a pinch a moment later. She took a few deep breaths, trying to hold on to consciousness, and watched the blood race through a tube from Hawkney's arm into hers.

"You're going to be okay, Callista," Hawkney said softly, tucking a strand of her hair behind her ear.

She gazed at him blankly for a long moment and, when her gaze wandered, noticed McCaffrey standing at a distance behind Hawkney, frowning down at her. She winced when someone began cleaning her neck, and she screwed up her face in pain.

"Let's try to keep your mind off it," Hawkney said, stroking her hair. "Where have you been the last two days?"

"You ... you wouldn't believe me ... if I told you," Callista struggled out.

"Try me."

"Spaceship."

"You were on a spaceship?"

"Yeah."

"Why?"

"Heal ankle."

Hawkney glanced down and moved her leg off the injured one to get a better look.

"Wow ... that's... really something," Hawkney said, scratching at his stubble.

"That's enough blood," Niki said and reached for the tube, but Hawkney tried to fend her off with a hand.

"No, I'm fine, just a little—"

"You're pale as a ghost. If she needs more, I'll give her some," Niki said and detached the tube from them both.

"Niki," Callista said softly. "Thank you."

"Course," Niki said, shrugging it off. "Woulda done it for anyone."

"But who ... ," Callista began, touching the bandage Betty secured around her neck.

"It was an Alamy," Niki said grimly.

"What?" Callista asked, surprised.

"Yeah," Hawkney said, frowning. "Clearly, they think you're getting too—"

"Clearly, this is a setup," McCaffrey butted in, stepping forward. "She's gone to have a little chat with her master, and he's fixed her up nice and pretty and sent her back like a good little girl with an escort to make it look like she's done nothing of the sort and put her back in our good graces—make her even appear a hero."

"By almost killing her?" Hawkney said incredulously, looking over his shoulder at McCaffrey.

"The wound was not deep enough to make her expire in a matter of minutes," McCaffrey pointed out. "If he wanted to kill her with that shot, he would have used a blunt-force weapon instead of an energy one. It's obvious."

"Oh, go seed dissent someplace else, you old blunderbuss," Betty scolded and shooed him with her hands. "Go! Get out of here with your negative waves and let the poor girl rest."

McCaffrey left with a scowl, but not before shaking his finger in warning.

"How stubborn and pig-headed can he get?" Niki asked. "If all that were true, the Alamy wouldn't have worn a mask, and he would've run instead of getting himself killed."

"Agreed," Hawkney said, nodding his head. "That's clearly a load of baloney."

"So what're we going to do about this, boss?" Niki asked.

A wicked smile crept across Hawkney's face after a moment, sending a chill into Callista's stomach. "Oh, I have an idea," Hawkney said in a too-calm voice. "Everything all right here, Betty?"

"Sure, but eat something first to get your blood sugar up,"

Betty said, tying off the bandage on Callista's shoulder. "We'll get her cleaned up and put to bed so she can start healing."

Hawkney nodded once before leaning over to give Callista a quick kiss on her forehead, making her flinch in surprise. He didn't notice and strode away with Niki, their heads bent together, plotting.

Callista peered at them over the hill of her body until they were out of sight. What were they planning now? Hopefully, nothing violent. More violence was the last thing they needed right now.

CHAPTER THIRTY-THREE

Callista fell asleep not long after they left and slept soundly until early the next morning when the pain medications wore off. Her entire upper back seemed like a single wound, and she didn't dare move her head, as that would stretch and pull at the scab on her neck. Butterfly came by later that morning and sat on the edge of her bunk.

"How are you feeling?" she asked softly.

"Pain," Callista muttered.

"Should I go get you some meds?" Butterfly asked.

"No, I'm tired of being drugged up."

"Can't you at least take a few to take the edge off?"

"It'd take a lot to do even that with what we have."

"Are you sure you don't want any?"

"Yes."

"Can't I do anything for you?" Butterfly practically begged.

Callista gave a little snort. "Keep Hawkney away from me."

"I'll... try," Butterfly said. Callista gave her a tight-lipped smile before Butterfly dejectedly left her.

Callista drifted in and out of a pain-filled stupor for some time and eventually observed the tunnels were too quiet. She lay there, listening, until the quiet started to unnerve her. She staggered out of bed and started to look for people but found no one. She began to wonder if she had fallen asleep and was having a nightmare when she finally spied one of the elders hurrying by through a cross section, and Callista called out to her. The woman's eyes widened when she discerned how bad Callista looked and hurried to her side. As she approached, Callista noted the large pack on the woman's back and asked what was going on.

"You have not heard?" the woman asked, the lines on her face looking strained. "Hawkney and some of the others have gone insane and horribly endangered the community. The council decided we are moving everyone to the woods far outside of the city immediately. The last batch leaves soon. You should come and leave those fools to their fate."

"When did you start evacuating?" Callista asked hoarsely.

"Since Hawkney and his soldier friends kidnapped the Admiral and brought him down here this morning."

Callista stared at her in stunned silence, ice filling her entire body. "Where?" she asked, barely above a whisper.

"You shouldn't go, they're mad," she said, grasping Callista's arm and pulling her down the tunnel. "We have to go, they'll come looking for him any moment, and I doubt they'll leave anything, or anyone, standing in their way. We have to go now."

"No," Callista said, stopping despite her tugging. "Show me where."

She gazed at Callista for a long moment before silently nodding and led Callista in the direction where Hawkney's workshop was. A sense of dread filled Callista, making her feel sick.

As they approached the curve in the tunnel that led to the abrupt dead-end where Hawkney kept his car-in-progress, they heard a sound like meat being punched, and Callista's stomach tied itself in a knot when she realized what the sound was. The councilwoman tried to pull Callista away when she perceived the look on Callista's face, but Callista shook herself free and continued around the corner.

She distinguished Hawkney's back first. A floodlight stood beside him, shining down on Negev, who sat in front of the car frame, his arms stretched out across it and zip-tied to the frame. If she didn't know it was him, Callista wouldn't have recognized him. His entire face was swollen with multiple cuts and bruises, and his black uniform torn in many places. Niki stood to the side with a gleam in her eyes, rubbing her fingers together and rapidly chewing gum. Loui lounged in the shadows behind Negev, smoking. Hawkney adjusted the brass knuckles on his hands and raised his arm to hit Negev again when Callista spoke.

"Stop," she said in as loud a voice as she could manage, which wasn't much. Hawkney whirled to see her hunched over with the woman standing behind her, keeping a steadying hand on Callista's good shoulder.

"Callista, are you all right? Do you feel any better? What's the mat—"

"Get out," she said in a low, hoarse voice.

"Callista, you shouldn't be h—"

"Get. Out."

"Callista," Hawkney's voice changed from one of concern to one of authority as he stepped up to her. "I know what I'm doing. This is the quickest way—"

Callista hit him in the face. It barely even made him flinch.

"I told you she worked for *him*," McCaffrey said, stepping out of the shadows. "We should have gotten rid of her from the beginning."

"Oh, come on," Niki said. "Why would he have his own agent killed?"

"Because we were on to her," McCaffrey said. "He needed to take care of her, so she couldn't talk."

"I think," Negev spoke up from the ground, his voice barely above a whisper, his head still hanging, "that *you* work for *him*. How long has Gren-del paid you? Since the beginning?" he asked, letting his head loll to the side so his scarlet and violet eyes could peer up at McCaffrey. "Your kind thrives on chaos, always informed so you can ride out the mayhem on top. It makes sense you would make a deal; that you would help him destroy me so he can initiate the culling he has already begun. It makes perfect sense."

"Culling?" Hawkney asked, moving back toward Negev. "What are you talking about?"

"Saint Petersburg was only the preview, the banning of religion merely an excuse, from what I gather," Negev said, his gaze shifting to Hawkney, his head still resting on his outstretched arm. "But do not take it from me, take it from Gren-del himself. I made a secret recording of our discussion only yesterday where he stated his disgust of Humanity and his intentions to take over the world for himself and wipe out a large percentage of Humanity to make you more manageable."

"Obviously, a fake conversation," McCaffrey said.

"Let Sergeant Andor listen to it and be the judge," Negev said quietly, continuing to hold Hawkney's gaze.

"I believe him," Loui said after a long moment of silence, letting out a cloud of smoke from the corner.

"Why?" Hawkney said, looking up at him.

"Because of what those papers said. Of what I myself have heard of Gren-del from my friends in Europe. Because I do not believe Callista is an Alamy agent, and I trust her judgment of character."

McCaffrey scoffed. "You have no proof of any of that," he said.

"And you do?" Loui challenged.

"Is this man, this *alien*, not the one who conquered our planet? Who is ultimately in charge of the whole world and thus ultimately responsible?"

"Gren-del is no longer under my command. He broke away," Negev said quietly.

"Where is the tape?" Callista butted in.

"My office," Negev said. "I used some of your old recording

technology so Gren-del would not detect it. I was going to convert it later that day for larger distribution, but I was ... detained."

"Go get it, Hawkney," Callista said. "We can't make a good decision until we have all the facts and evidence available."

"And we need to leave here *now*," the councilwoman said, laying a hand on Callista's shoulder. "The Alamies have undoubtedly noticed his disappearance by now and will come looking."

"Agreed," Loui said, straightening from where he leaned against the wall.

"What do we do with him?" Niki asked, pointing with her chin at Negev.

"Leave him. They'll find him eventually. It was a mistake to take him in the first place," McCaffrey said, moving toward the tunnel entrance, his cane tapping on the floor.

"Can I never do anything right?" Hawkney exploded at McCaffrey, flinging his arms out to the sides.

"No, you can't," McCaffrey said, turning to him. "You're a born follower, not a leader. The sooner you realize that and give me back the reins, the better off we'll be," he said, and continued down the tunnel.

Hawkney stood looking after him, face red and fists clenched. He turned back toward Negev, a fire in his eyes, and Callista grabbed Hawkney's arm, thinking he might take out his anger and frustration on their helpless victim.

"Hawkney, the tape," Callista reminded him. "You have to hurry before they come down here and find him, so you can get in and out of his office while they're looking elsewhere."

Hawkney growled in his throat before signaling to Niki, Loui, and the other two soldiers who leaned against the back wall, and they all filed out past Callista and the council woman.

"Come on," the woman said, tugging at Callista's arm.

"No. I'm not leaving him."

"But they said—"

"You think I care, after all they've done?" Callista asked, looking back at her.

She stared at Callista for a long moment before biting her lower lip and nodding once. "Be careful," she said and hurried away herself.

Callista waited until she rounded the curve of the tunnel and looked back at Negev. His head still lay on his arm, eyes half-closed, some of the light seeming to have faded from his eyes, making a thrill of fear go through Callista's gut. She stumbled forward, the movement aggravating the pain in her shoulder and making a dull pain throb in her ankle. She clutched her shoulder, fell to her knees next to him, and tried to pry at the zip ties securing his wrists to the frame. He moved his head a little as she staggered to her feet and began frantically looking through the tools scattered about for something sharp to cut the bonds with.

As she searched, the emotion of the whole thing hit her, and she couldn't stop herself from bursting into tears. She finally found some wire cutters through the fog of her tears and stumbled over to him again. She cut one tie and stepped around him to the other, kneeling to get the right angle. She straightened up after it was cut and wiped at her eyes and was a little surprised Negev gently put his now free hand around her waist and pulled her toward him. She allowed herself to be pulled into his lap and let him wipe her face with his hand, content to sit there and be miserable. He gently touched the bandage around her neck.

"What happened?" he asked softly.

"An Alamy assassin tried to kill me," she mumbled. She stared at her hands for a long moment but peered up at him out of the corner of her eye when he made no reply.

His eyes now blazed with fury. "Is that so? That explains much," he said in a quiet, icy tone, making her eyes widen a little at him and her lips part in surprise. His eyes suddenly softened when he perceived her reaction. He put his arms around her and held her close. She nestled her face into his neck and continued her efforts to try to stop crying. He rocked her for a long moment.

"This is all my fault, isn't it?" Callista finally said.

"How could that be?" he asked, reaching up to gingerly touch his violet eye, which swelled in earnest now.

"I didn't try hard enough to make them see what I see—that you're a good, caring person," she said, her sentence punctuated by a hiccup.

"Even if you had, I do not believe it would have made any difference to those whose hearts and minds are made up," he said, rubbing her back. "Besides, you have clearly won over Mr. Boudreaux, at least."

Callista sniffed, not consoled.

"Look at me," he said, and she struggled into a sitting position to better see him. "I forgive you of any guilt you may or may not have. There, better?"

Callista gazed at his face, which looked like a boxer's who just went the distance and marveled he took the time to be concerned for her rather than himself. She looked down when her tears started up afresh.

"I don't deserve that—you're too good to me," she mumbled.

"No, you deserve far better. And for that, I ask you to forgive me," he said, tilting her head up. "You deserve peace and prosperity and a proper place to live without fear. I have been unable to give that to you and others, for which I am truly sorry."

"But you can't help it, there are so many other things, and, and ... ," Callista lost her train of thought when she caught a smile spread across his lips which became crooked when it caused his split lip to crack open again, and she discerned the point he was trying to make. She gazed up into eyes filled with a soft, gentle affection, and she had the urge to kiss him.

"Too bad my lip is broken and bleeding," he said softly, mischief filtering into his glinting eyes. Callista smiled at him, and they sat looking at each other for a long moment before she settled against his shoulder again.

"Do you really believe McCaffrey works for Gren-del?" she asked after some minutes of silence.

"I doubt it—Gren-del would not stoop so low to work with any Human—I simply wanted to sow dissent and suspicion to divert their attention from me and to help discount his claims against you."

"Oh," Callista said. "But what are we going to do now?"

Their attention was caught by a beam of light from a flashlight moving along the tunnel wall, coming from beyond the curve, interrupting them briefly.

"First, we get out of here and heal," Negev said, gently pushing Callista off his lap and helping her to stand before she did the same for him. "Then, we figure out how to survive Gren-del."

"Survive?" Callista asked. "Don't you mean figure out how to stop him?"

Three Alamies rounded the corner and spotted them, breaking into a jog, and one spoke into his wrist communicator.

Negev linked his arm with Callista's, and they walked to meet the Alamy soldiers. "Gren-del is a monster; there is no stopping him. There will be war. It is inevitable at this point. Our only hope is to survive before we can defeat him."

Callista nodded silently, her disappointment slowly drowned out by a new sense of dread. The worst was yet to come.

CHAPTER THIRTY-FOUR

Negev wondered if the muscles in Callista's face were getting tired from being screwed up in pain, but when the Alamgirian medic put the final piece of tape on her new shoulder bandage, her face relaxed. Her wounds were already healing exemplarily well because some of the fluids from healing her ankle injury were still in her system. The medic suggested injecting some of the medicine into his face, the idea of which horrified him and must have showed because when he balked at the idea, Callista's face changed to an amused expression before it contorted in pain again. Instead, he settled for rubbing some of it on the wounds.

Pat-farfth stood to the side, rubbing his arms and staring worriedly at him.

"I am fine, Uncle," he said in their own tongue.

"No, you are not."

"Yes, I am. Really."

"But for how long?" Pat-farfth asked, rubbing his arms with renewed vigor. "He seeks your death, I know."

"Yes, he does."

"How can you be so calm?" Pat-farfth asked, starting to throw his hands up and instead flapping them helplessly around his body. "We should gather those who are loyal and leave, find another planet—take the mother ship with us. That will teach him."

"What good will that do us? It could take generations to find another habitable one. And we would be leaving the Humans to certain destruction."

"But Gren-del has no honor, no scruples. And, and the Humans stole the tape you made! They will never fight for us."

"I told them to take it," Negev said calmly.

"Why?"

"Because this is clearly part of Gren-del's plan, and I wanted it to get into the Humans' hands as fast as possible rather than into his."

"But it is in our speech—they will not be able to understand it. The only way to get it translated properly is with our machines."

Negev gently licked the edge of his lip in thought. "So it is," he said and looked back at Callista, who had been looking back and forth between them. "Do you know where your friends are now?" he asked her in English.

"In the woods, beyond the city," she said with a shrug. "Don't know anything more."

Negev stroked his chin in thought. He caught the eye of a soldier who observed him attentively and nodded slightly to him. The soldier nodded back and left the room.

"What are you going to do?" Callista asked warily, watching the soldier leave.

"Your people will need the tape translated. I am going to help them do it." He winced when the doctor touched some more solution to a nasty cut over his right eyebrow.

"You're lucky they didn't put bamboo under your fingernails," Callista said with a smile. "You wouldn't be able to touch anything for weeks."

"It was suggested, but they had no bamboo—whatever that is.

They also seemed to prefer the idea of doing something a little more physical."

"Figures," Callista said, looking away.

"Did I not say your friends were not the best of company?" Negev said after a long moment, unable to resist the urge.

"Yes. More than you know, sometimes. But at heart, they're still good people," Callista said, looking back at him.

"I am glad to hear it because I will need their help far more than I would like to," he said, resigned.

A soldier burst into the medical room. "Gren-del is here," he said breathlessly in Alamgirian. Negev observed Callista's face change. Though she did not understand the language—the name was clearly all she needed.

"He cannot know you are here," Negev told her sharply. "You need to leave, now, before he sees you." He turned his gaze to Pat-farfth as Callista slid off the table. "Take care of her," he said, his tone saying much more.

CALLISTA'S GUTS twisted at the subtext of Negev's tone. Pat-farfth nodded once, took Callista by the hand, and hurried out the door. They jogged past the elevator to the stairwell and hurried down in single file until they heard footsteps ringing on the stairs below them. Pat-farfth glanced over the railing briefly before continuing to a landing, where he grabbed Callista by the waist.

"Pretend, be flirty." He nudged her into the corner and leaned against the wall close to her so he shielded her from view, placing his hands on her hips. He gave her a grin before beginning to chuckle. Callista caught on and placed her hands over her cheeks, pretending she was embarrassed, giggling and bowing her head toward him. She caught sight of the boots responsible for the footsteps a few seconds later. A sharp command sounded in the

Alamgirian language, and Pat-farfth whirled around and stood at attention, careful to keep himself between her and the speaker.

Callista pulled her hair over her cheek and chewed on the ends. She snuck a glance over Pat-farfth's shoulder at the speaker. The man wore an eyepatch, and his blood-red eye glared at Pat-farfth. She ducked her head back down again and stayed close to Pat-farfth and the wall, out of sight as much as possible. A tension-filled exchange passed between the two, and finally, Pat-farfth turned to her and said in English, "You can see yourself out," giving her a wink the others couldn't see. Callista quickly wove in between the two men and the three guards, keeping her head down and murmuring, "Excuse me, pardon me."

Continuing down the stairs to the ground floor, she opened the door to find several Alamgirian guards standing about the door, each carrying a heavy-duty weapon. They stared at her. She gave them flirty looks and suggestive smiles as she slowly walked by them, swaying her hips and passing close by some. After sauntering a few yards away, she glanced slyly over her shoulder and noted they still watched, some shifting their weight and looking uncomfortable.

Callista didn't breathe easy until she put two blocks between them, and only then did she pick up her pace and start rubbing her arms. Once again, she was out in the cold, unprepared. She hurried to the first café she came across and asked to use the phone inside. The hostess let her borrow her cell phone. She Googled the phone number for Morticia's Nightclub and waited breathlessly for three rings until an employee picked up the phone.

"Hello, is Foxfire there? Is he drunk? Tell him it's an emergency." The woman on the other end of the line said she'd check and Callista waited a long moment before there was a clatter at the other end of the line and Foxfire asked who it was.

"It's Callista," she answered. "Are you drunk? Can you come pick me up? We evacuated the tunnels, and I don't know where the others went."

"Sit tight doll, I'll come get you," Foxfire assured her, and after she gave him her location, he hung up. She breathed a sigh of relief for herself, but her worry for Negev remained at an all-time high.

GREN-DEL CAME into the medical room and grinned at the sight of Negev's mutilated face. "My, you are quite a piece of art," he said, stepping up to him, his arms clasped behind his back. "How I would love to hang you on my wall."

Negev narrowed his eyes at him. "You said you were leaving me to my fate," he said, trying to move his lips as little as possible to prevent them from cracking open again.

"Oh, I am. But, since I will not be coming back to this part of the world for some time, I am taking the opportunity to conduct some business. And I am sincerely glad I did since I now get to see you start to feel the consequences of your past decisions," he said with a grin.

"I am delighted you are amused," Negev said, keeping a straight face.

"Oh no, it saddens me to contemplate the great, all-wise, never-erring, Celestial-elect Prime Minister Nun-setten seeing his prized admiral sink so low and destroy himself, though it be viewed through the fog of the Abyss."

It rankled Negev to imagine the kind, warm-hearted Prime Minister—who had always believed in him, always been available for advice and council, and who was like a second father to him—should have ended up in the Abyss, tearing apart other souls in a ravenous frenzy. Negev was certain he resided in the Celestial Realm, contentedly creating new souls, using a piece of himself in each new creation until he was no more, but still living on in other, new lives. But he made no reply to the jab.

"What? The sharp-witted one has no reply?" Gren-del chuckled to himself.

"I just thought of your disappointment when you go to the Abyss yourself and find he is not there," Negev said. "He blocked you at every turn in life while you could do nothing, and he will not be there for you to destroy and get your revenge."

Gren-del's lip twitched, and he stepped closer to Negev. "What makes you believe I have not found the secret to immortality on this planet?" he asked in a low voice.

"Logic," Negev said.

"How is that?"

"If you are immortal, your body would be in a constant state of regeneration. If your body regenerated, you wouldn't have the scar or the lack of an eye," Negev said while he mentally calculated how far Callista should have gone by now.

"Oh-so clever," Gren-del said, straightening up. "But you do not know everything, child, and as usual, you assume too much."

"Do I incorrectly assume you did not command an assassination attempt on a Human woman yesterday? Do I incorrectly assume you are not, in fact, intending to leave but look for my downfall within the next few days?" Negev said, cocking his head at his enemy.

Gren-del held his gaze emotionlessly for a moment before letting a thin smile spread across his lips. "I assume we shall see," he said and turned and left.

Negev let out the breath he held, glad Gren-del did not try to arrest him then and there, and thankful his men, who were concerned for his health and had remained by his side, were still at hand when Gren-del came and outnumbered Gren-del's loyal soldiers. It gratified him to see them glare after Gren-del when he left, hatred and disgust in their eyes. It assured him he was not in the wrong.

Pat-farfth slid in the door.

"Well?" Negev asked, concern for Callista flooding back.

"I watched from the window. She got past the guards fine. She is a clever girl."

Negev took a deep, measured breath and let it out slowly, trying to grab hold of his emotions and put them in their proper place. He had work to do.

CHAPTER THIRTY-FIVE

Callista suspected Foxfire didn't own a car that wasn't expensive. He pulled up in a vintage Rolls-Royce, so shiny and clean, it could have been brand new. She hopped in, and Foxfire eased the car into the traffic.

"Dang, woman. Someone did you dirty."

"I was nearly assassinated."

"Ouch. How much was he paying you?"

"Foxfire!" Callista said, aghast. "I am not that kind of woman. Not in the least."

Foxfire laughed. "Sorry, doll. Where to?"

"I don't know," Callista said, propping her elbow on the windowsill and resting her chin in her hand. "I don't know where the others went, and I don't have anywhere to go."

"You can come to Morticia's. If Loui's as smart as I remember him to be, though with my frequent drunkenness, my memory is a little dubious, he'll think to come looking for you there."

"But Morticia said I shouldn't come back."

"Just because you're not that kind of girl doesn't mean we can't pretend you are. If I have a woman in one of the private rooms, nobody bothers me. She doesn't need to know."

"How do I know you won't try to make me that kind of woman while we're hoping Loui will come along?"

Foxfire glanced over at her with a hurt expression. "My lady, though most certainly a scoundrel, I am also a man of honor. I will do nothing you are not amiable to."

"I will hold you to that."

"As you should."

Callista gazed out the window, brooding in silence at the city scape rolling by.

"You're worried about them?" Foxfire said. "Don't be. Loui and Hawkney, and even that firecracker Niki have good heads on their shoulders—they'll keep them there."

"I'm more worried about Negev," Callista said, biting her lip when she perceived her verbal error.

"Negev? You mean Xor-nalden?"

"Yes. Gren-del is indirectly trying to get him killed too, and it looks like Gren-del's getting ready for a coup. Then we'll all be in really hot water."

"You're on a first name basis now?" Foxfire asked.

"It's a lot less of a mouthful than Xor-nalden."

"By one syllable."

Callista couldn't help but smile, trying to hide the reaction carefully with the hand that lazed around her face. Foxfire glanced over and spotted it anyway and gave her a backhanded slap on the leg.

"You're in love with him, aren't you."

"What? Don't be absurd," Callista protested.

"Hey, I'm not judging one's personal preferences."

"Don't condescend."

"But seriously, you are, aren't you?"

Callista continued looking out the window, feeling him glance at her when he could from the ever-seething traffic pattern. The fact she couldn't stop smiling and indeed, her grin only widening as she considered it told her a lot—besides the giddy feeling in her gut.

"Yes, maybe a little."

Foxfire laughed in glee and slapped the steering wheel. "Magnificent! When's the wedding?"

Now it was Callista's turn to give his leg a backhanded slap. "Oh, shut up you, I said just a little, not enough to commit." She settled back in her former position against the window. "Besides, we're about to be plunged into war. Now is not the time for love."

"On the contrary, it is the best time. You're reminded every day of the fleetingness of life and what little time you have to show the person you care about just how much you care about them and live life to the fullest. The time could not be riper. All is fair in love and war."

"It's the war part I'm most concerned about. I sincerely doubt Gren-del will observe the Geneva Convention."

"Well, because we have such a rule book, we certainly know how to fight dirty if we have to," Foxfire said, scratching his chin. "I wonder if we could figure out which diseases the Alamies have vaccinated against and which ones they haven't. For instance— and I'd have to do some research—if people are still vaccinated for smallpox even though it's rare for anyone to get it now, we could germ-bomb Alamy installations with minor risk to ourselves. I wonder if they vaccinate for the new strains of flu or chicken pox … ," Foxfire trailed off, lost in thought.

"Just don't bomb them with HIV or Ebola or anything, okay?"

"No, of course not, that's much too dangerous," Foxfire said, snapping out of his devious ruminations.

"Let's hope we don't have to resort to that at all," Callista said. "If we can take down Gren-del before he even gets started, we could avoid an enormous number of casualties on both sides."

"True, true. Now, I don't know if you're *this* kind of girl or not, but I do know a guy who could do the kind of job you may need done … ," Foxfire trailed off, looking over at her with his head tilted.

Callista bit her lip. "I don't know," she said after a moment. "I don't think I'm the one to even make that kind of call."

"Well, I'll shoot him a line and see if he's even interested in the job. Maybe get a price."

"I sincerely doubt it could be anything we could ever hope to afford," Callista said.

"Oh, I wouldn't be too sure," Foxfire said, pulling up to the back door of Morticia's. "He's Russian." Foxfire shot her a grim smile and stepped out of the car, letting that fact set in while he walked around the front and opened the door for her.

NEGEV CORRECTLY GUESSED which rooftop the Renegades would pick to survey the territory. He sat on the roof while the sun began to disappear behind the forest of steel towers, and when the Renegades arrived, nothing was left but a smear of red on the sky. He sat in the gravel with his back against the stairwell housing and was surprised they did not notice him, even though he wore his black uniform and had briefly closed his eyes. But they were professional soldiers. He expected better.

"What do you think, Loui?" Hawkney Andor asked Loui Bordeaux after he stared at the objective through a pair of binoculars for some minutes. It was a government building housing rooms full of translation computers and network servers. Even though Negev and others knew the English well, it was still faster for them to use their own tongue, and if the dispatch was directed to a different country, they would need it in the local language anyway. The building itself looked like a glass box only fifteen stories high, making it look squat compared to the surrounding sleek skyscrapers.

"We should be able to secure the zip line on the corner as I thought, thereby avoiding the security cameras at the bottom and not attract the attention of the patrolling guards on the ground floor," Bordeaux answered. "There is a rooftop access. I should be able to hack the key card lock, but in case I can't, I have my glass-cutting tools."

"What of the translation device? We know where it is?" A tall, muscular, dark-skinned man asked with a thick South African accent.

"No, so we'll have to split up and find it," Andor said. "There shouldn't be anyone in the building, but that doesn't mean there might not be janitors, so be cautious."

"Do we even know what it looks like?" a man in a turban asked. "Is it different from the other computers? We may have to turn them all on. And what if it's in Alamy?"

"We'll figure it out when we get there," Andor said. "But let's worry about that later. Loui, if you tamper with the card reader, you sure you won't set off any alarms?"

Negev had heard enough. "Sixth floor," he said, and they whirled around and pointed their machine guns at him. Niki Nain cursed, and her hands shook for a moment as she recognized him.

"And this might do the trick," he continued, slowly reaching up and drawing out a key card from his breast pocket and extending it toward them. "The computer you look for is on the east side," he said when Andor walked up, and snatched the card, and peered at it in the dim light. "I can show you, if you like."

"Why the hell would you help us?" Nain demanded. "We just beat the—"

"A war will start between myself and Gren-del any day now," Negev said. "That will mean casualties, an enormous number of them Human, and neither of us wants that."

"So you want us to take him down for you," Andor said.

"I want you to help me, yes," Negev said, slowly standing up. "What is it you say? 'The enemy of my enemy is my friend?' Please, I beg you to see me that way, at least for now."

Andor glanced back at the others. Bordeaux gave him a nod,

so did the turbaned man after a moment's hesitation, and the tall South African a moment later, clearly with reservations. Nain chewed her lip and stared at Negev.

"All right," Andor said, turning back to Negev. "We'll bring you along. But one wrong move, and I'll shoot you myself."

Negev couldn't keep the corner of his mouth from twitching in amusement. "Very well," he said, moving through the group while they hesitantly lowered their weapons. "I am curious to see what a 'zip line' entails." Bracing his hands against the wall at the edge of the roof, he gazed down at the city beneath them.

"I hope you're not afraid of heights," Andor said.

Negev turned to see Andor pull what looked like a harpoon gun out of a black bag.

"Here, T'Chamba, screw this into the concrete," he said, handing the South African a thick metal ring with a screw on the end.

Negev watched in fascination while they shot the line a hundred yards onto the edge of the target building and secured the line, making sure it had enough tension. By the time they were ready he could barely see the line in the darkness now that the sun's glow had dissipated.

"I go first," Bordeaux said, attaching the zip to the line, squeezing the catch to make sure that it worked and he could slow himself when he reached the other side.

"No, let me—" Andor started.

"No, *mon ami*, this is my plan, my equipment. If it fails, it should be me on the pavement."

Andor took a deep breath and nodded once. Bordeaux sat on the wall and swung his legs over, taking a moment to sling a bag over his shoulder before dropping into the darkness. The zip sang on the line as he slid toward the other building. They stared in breathless anticipation. Bordeaux reached the other side and successfully climbed onto the roof, giving them a wave after he checked the integrity of the anchor on the other side.

"Ali, you're next," Andor said, putting his hand on the turbaned man's shoulder. The man whispered *"inshallah"* before dropping into the darkness. T'Chamba went next, and then there were only the three of them.

"We only have two more zips, so you and Niki will have to go together," Andor said.

"Why me?" Nain complained.

"Because he looks lighter than I am, and you're the lightest of us all," he said firmly.

Nain sighed in unhappy resignation and attached the zip.

"Or I could walk over there and meet you inside," Negev suggested. "It may be difficult for me to persuade Gren-del's men to let me pass, but I *do* outrank them. If Gren-del has not given them specific orders to disobey me, they must comply."

"I like that idea," Nain said eagerly.

"I'm not letting him out of my sight. He stays with us. Besides, Gren-del's men might follow him throughout the building," Andor replied.

Nain grunted, scowling.

"Then let us continue," Negev said.

He sat on the roof next to Nain and wrapped his arm around her. She entwined a leg around his and put both her feet on top of his foot, wrapped both arms around his chest and clasped her hands over top of his shoulder.

"You will have to put out a hand to stop us," Negev commented, settling his grip on the handle.

"I know," she said in a tone stating she was no idiot, and they dropped into the darkness.

The yank on Negev's shoulder made him gasp, and he could not readily get another breath because the whipping wind tried to suck the air out of his lungs. He started tightening his grip on the clasp to slow them down once they were halfway across, and they came smoothly up to the building. Nain put out a hand to forestall a collision, but they still bumped into the building with some force. A dark hand reached down and grasped Nain's, and she quickly disentangled herself as T'Chamba hauled her onto the roof. Ali held his hand out for Negev and helped him do the same.

As Andor started his descent, Bordeaux already stood at the door to the stairwell, trying Negev's key card, which opened the door, naturally, and he peeked inside. They stalked down the stairwell to the sixth floor, and Negev led them to one of the computers that handled English translations. He had ordered a machine to read the film into the computer earlier and it sat there, waiting.

"You knew," Andor said after he divined what the converter was.

"Knew what?" Negev asked casually.

"You got this machine and had it ready here for when we came to convert the tape?"

"Of course I acquired it. Why would I record the evidence on a medium I could not convert?" he answered, glancing at Andor with a raised eyebrow and turned his attention back to the computer. Andor bit his lip, and the tension eased out of his body. Negev slowly let out the breath he too held, relieved he averted a crisis of trust.

"It is ready," Negev said after a moment. "Put the film in."

Andor produced the tape from a pocket on his vest, placed it in the machine, and set it to turning. Negev sat back in his chair while the tape digitized and ran through the translation software that created a script of the audio.

"Callista freed you, didn't she?" Andor said, seeing the conversion would take time.

"Yes." Negev kept his gaze on the screen.

"Why?"

"Why?" Negev repeated, pretending he did not understand the question.

"Why would she do that?"

Negev looked over at him and met his eyes. "Because she has

compassion. And she does not judge someone based on the color of their skin."

Andor held his gaze, and Negev thought for a moment Andor didn't believe his explanation.

"She likes you, doesn't she?" he finally said.

"We have developed something of a friendship, I suppose," Negev said, looking back at the screen.

"That's not what I meant."

"Then please abandon the English mode of speaking in metaphors and contranyms and be specific and clear," Negev said a bit testily and glanced back at Andor.

"Is she in love with you?" Andor said flatly, and they stared at each other for a moment, Negev frantically trying to think of how to answer him.

"I can *only* hope," he finally said softly, and Andor leaned back in the office chair he perched on, crossing his arms and continuing to stare at Negev.

The tape clicked to the end, making them break their staring contest, and the computer gave a happy chime a moment later. Negev calmly removed the tape and handed it back to Andor. Then he took a thumb drive out of a box on the desk, inserted it into the computer, and transferred the audio file and the translated transcription onto it. He stood and removed the thumb drive and handed it to Andor, who rose to take it.

"There it is," Negev said, unable to keep a hint of relief out of his voice. "I leave its dissemination to your discretion. You are undoubtedly far more knowledgeable of your people's social media. I just pray you do it quickly. Our time runs short."

"You mean *your* time runs short," Nain said from where she had slunk up behind him. Negev glanced back at her.

"Far more than you know, I fear," he said softly, and for the first time, the threat of his own death hit him, and he hung his head a bit. A quake of fear ran through him for Callista, and he looked up quickly and grabbed Andor by the shoulders, making

Nain and the other soldiers tighten their grips on their weapons and raise them a little.

"Take care of her, get her out of here, out of this, if you can," Negev asked him desperately. "She does not deserve this ... she, she is not meant for it."

"Well," Andor said as if he were speaking to an idiot. "How can I get her out of here if you have her and won't tell me where she is?"

Negev's jaw slacked, and the blood drained from his face. He felt like the air had been sucked out of his lungs. His fingers turned cold, and his knees threatened to forget their place and buckle out from beneath him.

"I thought she was with you," he said, barely above a whisper. His heart sank when he saw Andor's pupils shrink to insignificance and his spine become ramrod straight.

"I thought she was with *you*," he said, starting out equally soft but hardening into anger.

"She was, but Gren-del came, and, and my uncle helped her slip out. He said she escaped cleanly, but what if she did not, what if Gren-del recognized her and ordered his men go after her and, and—" Negev collapsed against the desk gasping for air. Andor turned and paced back and forth the short length of the space between the desks in the aisle, chewing on his lower lip.

"Foxfire," Bordeaux suddenly said. "She would've called Foxfire. She's probably at Morticia's now."

"You believe so?" Negev asked, air fleeing from him at the suggestion she was safe.

"We'll go there now," Andor said, grabbing Negev's arm and yanking him to his feet.

The bang of a door slamming open inside the nearby stairwell caught their attention, and they paused. Bordeaux cursed in French, pulled a tool out, and threw it to T'Chamba.

"Break a window," he said, and producing a thin line from his bag and started securing it around a support pillar. T'Chamba hurried to the nearest window and slammed the tool into the glass, causing a spiderweb of cracks to form on impact.

"I will stall them," Negev said and started to move toward the stairwell, but Andor's grip on his arm tightened.

"You're not going anywhere. You're staying with us."

T'Chamba hit the window again, and another spiderweb of cracks formed. Nain and Ali moved backward toward the window, their weapons held at the ready, pointing toward the stairwell.

"Your priority is the recording and Callista," Negev said, gripping Andor's wrist. "If they come for you, my appearance will be distracting. If it is as I fear, and it is Gren-del come for my head, you *must* flee now—you are your people's only hope."

T'Chamba hit the window a third time and the window sagged, more cracks forming.

"Trust me," Negev said softly.

Andor bit his lip and let go. "Good luck," he said, and the window shattered with the fourth blow. Bordeaux dove over the side the instant the glass finished falling, with Ali right behind him, sliding down the line. Andor turned and ran to the window with Nain by his side. Negev turned and ran to the stairwell.

He opened the door and quickly stepped inside to find Gren-del moving onto the landing. He pushed through his moment's hesitation, firmly shut the door behind him, and leaned back against it, meeting the man's one-eyed stare. "Looking for something, Admiral?" Negev asked casually but with distrust.

Gren-del smiled and took two slow, casual steps so he stood directly in front of Negev, making Negev want to press against the door to get as far away from him as possible. "Yes," Gren-del said softly, almost gently. "You." In a movement so quick Negev did not have time to blink, Gren-del's hand flew up to grasp Negev around the throat and squeezed. Negev instinctively gripped the hand crushing his windpipe.

"Negev Xor-nalden, you are under arrest for high treason," Gren-del said smoothly with a grin. He pulled Negev away from the door toward himself. "I look forward to meting out the punishment for high treason, personally," he said, his face right in Negev's gasping one, his breath smelling far too sweet.

Negev blinked hard as spots started to cover his eyes and kicked Gren-del in the shin while continuing to claw at the hand around his throat. Gren-del slammed Negev's head backward into the door and then bodily slammed him to the floor, making all go black.

CHAPTER THIRTY-SIX

Callista took another sip of her drink as Morticia laughed, her head thrown back while laying a hand on Foxfire's shoulder.

They had hidden in the curtained back table not fifteen minutes before Morticia had flung open the curtain, making Foxfire almost spill his drink on himself. She appeared nearly the same as before, with a long-sleeved, form-fitting dress that reached to the floor, but this time, it was a deep royal blue, and she wore a string of bright yellow beads and golden hoops in her ears. She gave Callista a long look, seeming to note the bandage around her neck and the one peeking out from under her shirt. Morticia stepped in, snapped the curtains closed behind her, and sat down next to Foxfire, taking his drink from him and sipping it before handing it back.

"Foxy dear, you're going to get yourself in trouble one day," she said now, hours later, sipping her drink. They had done everything from flirt to reminisce and back again. "But we've gone on long enough," she said, setting down her drink. "Poor Callista still looks miserable. We should address the elephant in the room."

Callista set down her own drink, preparing herself for a reprimand.

"Darling, I had no idea you were in such a ... hazardous relationship," Morticia said, looking at Callista with pity in her dark eyes. "I would encourage you to leave permanently, but I understand if you don't want to. Many women in your situation feel that way."

"In ... my situation?" Callista asked cautiously.

"My point is my doors are always open if you need to get away from him. He can't hurt you here."

Foxfire chuckled into his drink. "You think she's having 'issues' with that Hawkney fellow I told you about?"

Morticia gazed at him and raised an eyebrow.

"An Alamy tried to kill her, Morty. One who's against Xor-nalden. As for Callista's romantic entanglements, Xor-nalden is the one she's thoroughly in love with."

"It's not like that," Callista said.

"We should try to get the gang back together," Foxfire said, putting down his own drink. "I have a bead on where the Alamies moved my merch. We'll have all the hardware we'd need. Just need back the experts I know and love."

"I sincerely doubt you could get them to come back if you could even find them," Morticia said.

"Hey, it'd be worth the try. Besides, they'd have a vested interest in it—Xor-nalden is a whole lot more lenient with our folks than Gren-del is, from what I hear."

Suddenly, the curtains snapped open, making Callista jump again. Loui stood in the gap this time.

"Loui! We were just talking about getting the band back together—"

"*C'est fini*," Loui said, his voice dry and scratchy.

"Finished? What is finished? What has happened?" Morticia said, placing her hands on the table and standing up. Hawkney and Niki walked up behind Loui, their faces grim.

"Gren-del just took out Xor-nalden," Hawkney said, his eyes quickly moving to Callista, looking relieved when he spied her. "Xor-nalden helped us get evidence to prove Gren-del is a threat, and he stalled them so we could get away with the evidence. We saw them carrying him out, none too gently. Blood was all over his forehead."

Callista closed her eyes. She clasped her hands together and squeezed until her knuckles were white. It suddenly hurt to breathe, as if she inhaled icy air, but she tried to take deep breaths anyway.

"I'm sorry, Callista. Honestly," Hawkney's voice wafted into her consciousness. She became aware he sat down next to her and put his arm around her. "I didn't know you two had a ... thing ... going."

"Are you sure ... he's dead?" Callista asked, trying to make herself suck in air.

"If he isn't now, he will be shortly," Niki said. She restlessly scanned the room and its patrons, fire darting from her eyes.

"We need to help him. We ... he ... ," Callista struggled.

"Callista, I promised him I'd take care of you," Hawkney said. "I'm going to do just that. Even if it kills me."

Callista gave a strangled cry and quickly covered her mouth as she squeezed her eyes shut in vain against the tide of tears. Hawkney pulled her close, held her head on his shoulder, and patted her back awkwardly, trying to be comforting. Again, the conviction that this was all her fault overwhelmed her.

"None of this is your fault, Callista," Morticia broke into her thoughts. "This coup would have happened with or without you. I'm afraid we're little more than pawns."

"Then let us change that," Loui said, turning his head back to the group from where he stared off into space. "If Xor-nalden is alive, we need to be a distraction. Let us make Gren-del regret he ever set foot on this continent, much less this planet."

"Yes," Niki said jubilantly. "We need to distribute the recording *now*. We need to put Callista in the dress and send a message to the people. Rally them now, before Gren-del has time to solidify his claim to power."

"Agreed," Hawkney said. "Callista, you up for it?"

Callista pulled away and sat up straight, wiping at her eyes. She remembered the way Negev looked at his aide when Gren-del came, the way he said, "take care of her." The way their eyes had met for a brief moment when Pat-farfth took her hand. His eyes were full of longing and sadness. Perhaps he knew it was the last time they'd ever see each other.

She remembered his gentle tease when they were in the tunnel that if his lips were not split, he would have kissed her. Now more than ever, she wished he did, anyway, so she would have something solid to remember and hold on to.

"Oh yes," Callista said in a controlled, soft voice full of subtle menace. "I am more than up for it."

OUT OF THE OVEN, *into the fire. No, that was not it. Out of the pot, into the fire? That did not sound right, either. How did the Human phrase go?* Negev hissed through clenched teeth when the spiked electricity surged through his body again. *It has some kind of alliteration to, does it not? With the 'f,' in fire, perhaps? What cooking utensil starts with an 'f'?* He could have sworn the next surge was even harder than the last, though it probably was not. Still, he could not stop from letting a groan escape this time or letting more of his weight hinge on his wrists, suspended by a chain from the ceiling. *Fridge, no. Freezer, no, no, those did not make sense. Fork? ... no.* Negev could not stop a few tears from escaping with the next surge. *Fry pan. Frying pan? Out of the frying pan, into the fire? Is that it?* This time, he could not stop a yell when every nerve in his body was lit on fire and pierced over every square molecule.

And suddenly, it stopped. Negev gasped for air, grateful for the respite to try to again compose himself and block out the pain. But that was the thing about electricity. It lights every nerve and goes through the brain itself. It is impossible to block out. Terrified instinct takes over and ignores cool logic and training.

The door clicked unlocked, and Gren-del's men walked in with heavy footfalls. One of them reached up and made certain his wrists were still secure, while another checked that the electrodes were still firmly attached despite his sweat.

"I wonder," Negev said softly. "What he has promised you."

"Our rightful place over the Humans," said the one who checked his wrists. He had deep turquoise skin and violet eyes. "You would degrade us to their level. Gren-del will show them who is their master and make them do what we want."

"Just because they have not achieved the level of space flight we have, you assume they are beneath us?" Negev asked. "They have made significant progress beyond us in other areas."

"Such as their ability to share video of hairy animals on multiple platforms? What use is that?" asked the one, who had a forest green skin tone and red eyes, as he checked the electrodes.

"I simply wish to point out if you desire respect and honor, this is not the way," Negev said, trying to steer the conversation away from the Human's social media—it would soon be used to start a revolution. "That is gained by benevolence and good deeds, not fear and oppression. You deserve better than doing Gren-del's dirty work to gain an impoverished and burned planet. You know what kind of a man he is. No one deserves him."

Gren-del came in right then.

"Why, I am hurt," Gren-del said, theatrically placing his hand on his right breast over his heart. "You do not believe we deserve each other? And after all the work I will put into you?" Here, he slid his fingernail down the side of Negev's cheek, continuing down his chest to the waistband of his underwear, the only clothes to his name.

"You will be the most magnificent picture of pain when I am through with you. What shall I call him, my masterpiece, once I reduce him to nothing but bones and blood?" he asked his henchmen, turning his head toward them but keeping his gaze on his prisoner.

"Comeuppance of the Opposition?" Red Eyes suggested.

"Bland," said Violet Eyes. "And awkward. How about 'Dying of the Weakest?' You know how they have this 'Survival of the Fittest' theory?"

"Brilliant," Gren-del said, snapping his fingers in the man's direction. "I like it. We will go with that: 'Dying of the Weakest.'"

"How long will it take, Admiral?" Red Eyes asked.

"Only until Gren-del is deposed or killed," Negev said before Gren-del could answer. Gren-del punched him in the jaw.

"Oh, it will take quite some time," Gren-del half hissed. "I have dreamed about this for years—I want to savor it. Besides, the last time your loyalists checked, you were recovering from the unthinkable capture and the atrocious torture you underwent at the hands of Humans. It will take you months to recover if you do not finally succumb to your wounds, which I fear you will."

"Shall we continue with the spiked electricity or go on to something else, Admiral?" Violet Eyes asked.

"We will keep to that for now. I am busy, and I want to do the rest personally." He turned back to Negev. "I will see you soon, darling," Gren-del whispered in Negev's face. "Maybe I will even have your girlfriend for you, so you can watch her die, slowly, before I finish with you. Maybe I will even take everything she has in front of you, even though I do not have a taste for such carnal pleasures, just to spite you. Would you like that?"

Negev held his gaze steady even though his fists and jaw clenched and his stomach turned over. Gren-del backed away a step or two, holding his gaze, before turning to go, leaving the room colder than when he entered. Negev silently pleaded to the Celestial Realm that Callista was far, far away.

"He does not scream enough," Red Eyes said. "Let us go learn how to increase it."

"We must be careful, though—it is already high, and we do not want him to die. Gren-del would have our deaths," Violet Eyes said.

"True. But a little more will not hurt much."

CHAPTER THIRTY-SEVEN

Callista took a deep breath and once more smoothed her hair, paranoid a single hair might be out of place. Butterfly darted over to her and brushed at a perceived fleck on Callista's orange-red dress. Callista sat behind Morticia's desk in her private office above the club. Large and stained dark brown, the desk was empty of everything but her notes. A huge picture of Cleopatra hung on the wall behind her, flanked by sconce lights, giving a soft ambiance. Hawkney looked through the camera at her, making sure everything lined up.

"Are you ready?" he asked.

Callista took a deep breath and nodded.

"Remember, we can do multiple takes," Hawkney said. "Just relax and tell them like it is."

"Here," Butterfly said, pulling up a chair next to the camera. "You're talking to me."

"All right; ready, set, action," Hawkney said. Callista stared at the camera for a moment, its eye gaping at her, and then she remembered to close her mouth. Butterfly smiled and gave her a little wave, and Callista blinked hard and stared at her.

"Yesterday," she started, her voice sounding scratchy. She bent her head and cleared her throat, reminding herself all this could be edited out. "Yesterday, our only ally and advocate in the Alamgirian government, Admiral Negev Xor-nalden, was ... removed ... , by Admiral Gren-del. We have eyewitness accounts suggesting Gren-del assassinated him, but his death is unconfirmed." Her voice began to falter. She closed her eyes and took a deep breath to calm herself.

"Admiral Xor-nalden sought to obtain proof Gren-del meant to enact a worldwide genocide, not unlike the one in Saint Petersburg, Russia, and continued when Gren-del outlawed religion in his region of influence, knowing this was but another pretext to further his agenda of slaughter. Perhaps this is why Xor-nalden was eliminated. He decried Gren-del's actions vehemently and searched for a means to bring him to justice. The fact that Gren-del saw fit to remove Xor-nalden indicates Gren-del is indeed a real threat. We are certain his goal is world domination and destruction."

She took another deep breath. "Therefore, my brothers and sisters all over the world, we must band together immediately for our own survival and destroy Gren-del at all costs before he can gain a firm foothold here on the American continents and double his area of influence and his power. This is our world, our turf. No one knows it better than us. We must enact a guerrilla blitzkrieg now before he has time to react. And when I say now, I mean now. My fellows and I will plan an attack once we finish getting this word out to you." She found she stared at the camera, entranced, rather than at Butterfly, and the realization made her pause and look down at her notes.

"As Winston Churchill said, 'We shall fight on the seas and oceans, we shall fight with growing confidence and growing strength in the air ... whatever the cost may be, we shall fight on the beaches, we shall fight on the landing grounds, we shall fight in the fields and in the streets, we shall fight in the hills; we shall never surrender.'" She laid down the paper, wishing Winston Churchill were here now.

"I am reminded of another quote," she said, looking back up

at the camera. "I sincerely hope everyone takes it to heart: 'a common enemy unites the oldest of foes.' I beg everyone to put aside their differences so they may not hinder us in our quest for liberty.

"In truth, I cannot guarantee we will have the liberties we enjoyed before the Alamgirian conquest. And in truth, I do not believe we should hope for it because countries will probably attack their neighbors in hopes of gaining more territory before we all regain our footing," she said, lacing her fingers together in front of her. "Thus, I sincerely hope and pray Xor-nalden still lives—he has expressed his desire to return power to the nations, but in a way that ensures security for all. If he is dead, then I hope we find another Alamgirian of like mind to put in his place until we can achieve that goal. In this way, we will not descend into war among ourselves.

"This is how it is, but I can assure you we will know nothing but fear and bloodshed with Gren-del as our overlord, something we cannot and will not stand for, and so we must band together and act immediately. Are you with us?"

She glanced up and nodded to Hawkney, who shut off the camera.

"Perfect. I couldn't have done better myself," he said, taking it off its stand.

"I thought you were good," Butterfly added.

"Beautiful," Betty sniffed, wiping an eye from where she sat on the couch.

"Hey, Xor-nalden might be alive!" Foxfire suddenly said, standing from where he leaned against the wall, looking at his phone.

Callista sprang from her chair and stood at his side in an instant, peering at the screen.

"Gren-del released a statement about Xor-nalden's capture and torture by Humans, that his wounds were so bad he's in ICU, that he might not make it, and Gren-del has taken command until further notice. Did you guys really mess him up *that* bad?" Foxfire asked.

"No, just ruined his good looks for a long while," Hawkney said, scratching at his chin nervously. "Not to mention he looked pretty good, all things considered, the other night."

"It's just an excuse," Niki said, moving the phone so she could see. "He's trying to make us the villains."

"You made yourselves the villains," Callista couldn't help but snap, and turned away from them. "No time to edit the video; we need to get it out now. Flood every outlet with it; there's no time to lose."

"Right. Jose, take care of it," Hawkney said, handing him the camera. "Betty, Butterfly, go back to the community and get our medical supplies and all the able-bodied volunteers you can round up, so we'll be ready. Loui, Niki, find out where Gren-del is. T'Chamba, go with Foxfire and get enough explosives to take down a skyscraper and anything else we need—I leave it up to your expert discretion."

"What about me?" Callista asked.

"I interviewed for a security firm that hires ex-military before I went underground," Hawkney said. "You and I will go recruiting over there, maybe even go to the VA. I want some people I know I can count on rather than a barista who's never held a gun before."

"Understandable," Callista said with a hint of sarcasm Hawkney chose to ignore.

"Best change out of that dress, honey," Morticia said in her smooth voice, gliding up to Callista with a bundle of clothes. Callista skirted into Mortica's private restroom with the bundle.

When she lifted the shirt off the stack, she was surprised and a little shocked to find a pair of dangerous-looking weapons lying on top of the pants. She carefully laid them aside and slipped on the black pants and the black, long-sleeved shirt. She put her old combat boots back on and pulled her hair up in a ponytail. She folded the red dress none too carefully and left it in a corner.

She carefully picked up the knives—or at least she guessed

they were; they reminded her of skewers. The thin blades as long as her forearm looked more for stabbing than slicing, and the cross guards curved in the same direction as the blade with a slight flare out at the end. The handles were wrapped in thin red leather.

"What are these?" she asked when she emerged, holding them with thumb and forefinger like she would a dirty diaper.

"Ah, Morticia's *sai*," Foxfire said. "Oh, the poetry she wrought with those. She could open a window latch with a deft flick of the wrist as if it were nothing."

"They are my gift to you," Morticia said. "You're going to need them more than me, I fear."

Foxfire gazed at her in surprise. "Does this mean you will not be with us?" he asked in dismay.

"I'm afraid my time being in the thick of it has passed," Morticia said, touching a place on her side in remembrance, and Foxfire's face softened.

"Your legend will live on in my memory, darling," Foxfire said, stepping up behind her and pulling her up against him.

She raised her hand and touched the side of his face. "Your feelings distort that memory, Foxy dear."

"Come on, let's go," Hawkney said, brushing Callista's arm with his finger. She stuck a *sai* in each of her boots, turned and followed him out onto the street, and shivered in the cold, clutching her arms. Hawkney stripped off his jacket a moment later while they walked along and helped her into it.

"How far is it?" Callista asked, worried he would catch cold instead of her.

Hawkney held up a pair of car keys. "Foxfire's loaned me one of his rides," he said with a grin. "I hope it's not too ostentatious. Wouldn't want the people we're seeking help from getting the wrong idea about us."

"Hawkney, what will we do if they agree to help us?"

Hawkney clicked the keys, and was rewarded with an answering beep from a black Porsche in one of the parallel parking spaces. "We'll plan an assault of the government building the

Alamies mostly operate out of. Sooner the better. We said we were coming in the video, so best to give them little time to prepare."

"To capture Gren-del?"

"Taking him alive is too dangerous. His men would tear the city apart and kill everyone in their path in retribution. But if he's gone and we capture his close followers, we might be able to hold out long enough that Xor-nalden can wrest control back."

"You believe he's alive then?" Callista asked, getting into the passenger seat.

"I pray he is. Because if he isn't, there's no other Alamy we know we can trust not to take our heads." Hawkney put the key in the ignition and smiled when the engine roared to life. "If he isn't alive, sweetheart, I'm afraid you'll find yourself empress of the world."

As he looked over at her, Callista felt the color drain from her face. She turned to stare out the window and envisioned the city in flames as chaos reigned, with mass genocide of Alamgirians and hundreds of Humans falling in the mad attempt. She saw old enemies ravaging each other while she sat powerless and impotent.

She closed her eyes to hold back the tears as they sped toward their destination, praying Negev still lived or God would raise up another benevolent Alamgirian ruler to take his place and give everyone justice.

CHAPTER THIRTY-EIGHT

Quiet was never so beautiful. Negev enjoyed every moment of solitude to the fullest. A few hours ago, Gren-del had completed his first stage of making Negev into "art." He cut intricate designs all over his chest, arms, and back, careful not to cut into the taught muscles beneath. Then he soaked Negev in pure alcohol. "We wouldn't want you to get an infection, now would we?" he said smoothly, watching blood trickle from Negev's lip from biting it so hard and mingling with the tears streaming from his face. But he didn't cry out. He gave no more than a gasp as the alcohol burned through him. He would not give him that satisfaction yet. The drugs meant to heal his previous wounds were still in his system and caused the newly formed cuts to scab over quickly with little loss of blood. Otherwise, he might have bled to death, and he counted himself lucky for this small foiling of Gren-del.

But then he realized Gren-del knew he had recently been in the medical bay. He knew the cuts, though numerous, would not be fatal. He had much, much more pain in store for him. So Negev enjoyed his aloneness now. The quiet. The stillness. The absence of fresh pain. The pain in his arms from letting his full

weight hang from the ceiling paled in comparison to what he had
gone through and what he would go through.

The door opened, and his heart sank. He was content to stay
this way for the rest of his life. He heard the tread of boots, a
lighter scuffling, and a woman's grunt, making Negev's heart leap
into his throat. He glanced up quickly with a jerk, panic filling his
whole body.

It wasn't her. It was Niki Nain being dragged in by his jailers.

Negev let out his breath and relaxed against the chains. He
studied her curiously. The jailers strung up another pair of chains
over the rafters in the ceiling and wrestled her into them. Once
they were sure she was secured, they left wearily. He glanced over
at her and found her staring after them.

"So, we meet again," he began cordially.

"Yup."

He stared at the door nervously and resisted the urge to ask
what happened outside. "Do not tell me what goes on," he said
instead, peering around. "There are probably a dozen listening
devices in here."

"Yup."

Negev glanced at her. She still stared at the door. "They are
going to torture you."

"Yup."

The door opened before Negev could say anything else, and
Gren-del stormed in, his face a mask of rage. He stopped in front
of Nain.

"So this is the insect that killed *six* of my best men and
wounded three more?"

Nain gave him a full grin, and in a flash, Gren-del tried to
knock some of her teeth out with a punch, causing her to swing
backward in the chains and sputter.

"I want to know everything within the hour," he said,
whirling to his men, who prepared chains to bind her legs to the
floor as Negev's were.

"With pleasure, sir. We will try our best to have it sooner," said

Red Eyes, and Negev guessed some of his close comrades were numbered in the casualty list from the look on his face.

Gren-del stormed out, and the two guards approached Nain. When Red Eyes neared her, she suddenly put a foot on his thigh and used the leverage to complete a backflip that sent her other foot into his jaw, knocking him backward with force. Violet Eyes cursed and rushed her. Nain bounced on her tiptoes in readiness and managed to make a money-shot in between his legs when he neared. He quickly slumped to his knees in front of her, and she jumped and wrapped her legs around his neck and started to squeeze.

Negev rattled in his own chains restlessly, unable to move his secured legs and arms. Red Eyes staggered to his feet, feeling his jaw, and pulled out an electrocutor, making Negev's heart sink. He did not know what downing the guards would have accomplished, but he did not want her efforts to be in vain. Nain caught sight of it and tried to wrench her body to break the neck of the one in her grasp, but the chains would not afford her enough leverage. Red Eyes jammed the electrocutor into her side. She jerkily released her prisoner and slumped in her chains.

"Bind her!" Red Eyes barked to Violet Eyes on the floor, who gasped for air. "And help me hook her up. We start at seventy-five."

Negev's guts cringed. They had maxed him out at eighty on the spiked electricity.

"Hook him up too. I do not like his face."

"And what if you damage the work Gren-del has labored over?" Negev asked casually, splaying his hands in his cuffs to indicate the dense network of incisions on his body. "I imagine he would be none too happy with you if you—"

"I will take responsibility because I do not believe he will care in the least," the guard replied smoothly, feeling his jaw again and smiling.

Negev took a shaky breath, trying to prepare himself. He gazed at Nain in pity, her head still lolling from the effect of the electrocutor, meant to be used for suppression rather than pain. He could not help but be thankful Callista was not in her place and prayed yet again that Andor had gotten her far away from New York and Gren-del.

CALLISTA SAT on the bench next to Hawkney, waiting for the CEO of the security firm to meet them in the small park near the office building.

"You don't *actually* have to be queen," Hawkney said, breaking their long silence. She looked over at him. "You'd just have to endorse someone you believe is right for the job. Like in an election."

"Who do you think I should endorse? You?" Callista asked.

Hawkney barked a laugh. "Definitely not me. No, there's this general I admire, though. I'll tell you about him later. He's down-to-earth and a great administrator. He might be able to handle something that big and have the guts to stand up and not back down."

"That's good."

"Yeah."

Callista turned away when the conversation died. A stooped figure in a black uniform caught her attention between two bushes. Pat-farfth shuffled across the path and slumped down on a bench beyond Callista's sight due to the curve of the path.

"Stay here," she told Hawkney. "I'm going to go talk to someone I know over there."

Hawkney craned his neck to try to see what she spoke of but, failing to see over the tall bushes, settled back and nodded in affirmation.

She hurried around the curve to find Pat-farfth slumped against the arm rest, his hands covering his face. His breaths were deep and shaky.

"Pat-farfth," Callista said, sitting down next to him and laying a hand on his shoulder. "What's wrong? What happened to Negev?"

"They are torturing him," he said hoarsely after he glanced over and recognized her. "I heard some of Gren-del's crooks talking about it with glee."

"Where? Where is he?"

"The main government building. They have a torture room there."

"How do we get in to rescue him?"

"It is heavily guarded. Swarming with Gren-del's men. And he is, I believe, on the sixteenth floor. It will not be easy at all."

Callista chewed on her lower lip for a moment. "Do Humans or Alamgirians clean the building?"

"Humans," Pat-farfth answered, looking up at her. "But they are usually all women. If several strong men showed up, there would be suspicion."

"Then I'll have to go with a few other girls."

"No! Not you," Pat-farfth said, suddenly grasping her arm. "Negev is strong. He will not easily break. He will die with honor and give Gren-del little to no satisfaction in the pain he inflicts on him. But if Gren-del gets you, Negev will do anything, *anything*, for you. Seeing you hurt would *break* him." Pat-farfth gasped for air, his grip tightening on her arm. "You must go far away. If he knows you are safe, he can withstand anything and die in peace."

"And how can I go on living, knowing I did nothing to try to save the man I love?" Callista asked softly.

Pat-farfth's violet eyes met hers for a long moment, and the sorrow in them deepened. "Be careful," he whispered, releasing her arm. "And may the power of the Celestial Realm go with you."

"Do the maids come in the morning or at night?" she asked.

"At night, after everyone has gone."

"Can you be there to let us in?"

"I will try. The south entrance, near the loading bay, is best. I will try to be there at eight, but Gren-del knows I am Negev's uncle, so he watches me carefully."

"Maybe sulk on the first floor for most of the day, so your presence there won't be suspicious after a while," Callista suggested. She turned her head when she heard Hawkney's voice from around the bend, talking to someone. Their contact must have arrived.

"How many of the Alamgirains in the city are loyal to Xor-nalden?" she asked.

"Many. I am fairly certain they currently outnumber Gren-del's men, but that will not last long. Gren-del is doing his best to keep them in the dark, keeping the few of us who know the truth close to him and away from them. He tricks them while he tries to fool Humanity. In a few months' time he will kill Negev, and our people will believe it was by Humans and will follow Gren-del blindly in any retribution he sees fit."

Hawkney laughed along with another man, and the gravel crunched as the two appeared around the corner. When they caught sight of Pat-farfth they both hesitated. Callista jerked her head, indicating they should come over.

"Hawkney, this is Xor-nalden's uncle," she said, ignoring the need for further introductions. "He's going to help us get in the building and get Xor-nalden out."

"You trust him?" Hawkney said, staring into her eyes.

She met his gaze. "Completely. He helped me slip away from Gren-del not long ago. We've already made arrangements," she said, standing. "I'll brief you later." She turned to Pat-farfth and laid a hand on his shoulder. "Until we meet again. Be strong."

Pat-farfth raised his head and gave her a weak smile, laying his hand atop hers and giving it a little squeeze before letting go and looking at his feet again. Callista, Hawkney, and their contact quickly walked away. She gave their new comrade a quick glance —he definitely looked military, with his high and tight haircut and the muscles bulging under his long-sleeved shirt.

"'United we stand ... ?'" Callista asked.

"'One nation, under God, indivisible,'" Hawkney said, quoting back, and smiled at her with a twinkle in his eye.

"Franklin," the man said, shaking hands with Callista. "I take it we have our first mission?"

"I suppose," Callista said, diverting off the path and stopping to lean up against a tree. "If we're going to succeed in preventing Gren-del from taking control, we need Xor-nalden, and even if we didn't, we need him to hold the world together rather than plunging into chaos and total war after the fact."

"Makes sense," Franklin said.

"Xor-nalden is held in the main Alamy government building on the sixteenth floor. The plan is to have a few women slip in at eight p.m. as maids and make our way to him and get him out. If things go south, we'll need an extraction team on the outside."

"Why not go in guns blazing?" Franklin asked.

"The place is swarming with Alamies. Casualties on both sides would be heavy, not to mention, there are Alamies on both sides in there. Most don't know Gren-del locked up Xor-nalden but believe he's in the hospital," Callista said. "Besides, once a firefight started, Gren-del might have Xor-nalden killed immediately, just in case."

"Makes sense," Franklin said, rubbing his chin.

"All right," Hawkney said. "Loui, T'Chamba, Niki, and I will go in, Franklin, you—"

"No, no men. It needs to be all women to avoid suspicion," she said.

Hawkney cursed.

"I have two women," Franklin offered. "I'm sure they could be persuaded."

"That makes four with myself, and Niki. Good," she said.

"You're definitely not going," Hawkney said, glaring at her.

Callista glared back, making Franklin shift his weight back and forth after the contest stretched on for a long moment.

"Fine," she finally said. She turned to Franklin. "You'll need to brief your ladies well on what Xor-nalden looks like since those features will undoubtedly be ... altered. Pat-farfth says they've been torturing him."

A little color came to Hawkney's face in embarrassment, and he wiped his palms on his pants, giving Callista a stab of pleasure.

"What equipment do you need, Franklin?" Hawkney asked, changing the subject. "We have a supplier for just about everything."

"Oh, I've kept a small supply of my own ever since the invasion," Franklin said with a grin. "But how can I contact you if I need anything?"

"Go to Morticia's nightclub and ask for Foxfire. Tell him you're with me, and he'll get you anything you need."

"Sounds good," Franklin said, saluting Hawkney. "Until tomorrow night, Captain." He walked away briskly.

"I thought you were a sergeant," Callista said.

"I think I just got a promotion," Hawkney said with a grin.

Callista smiled back before looking away and plotting how she would get on the extraction team without Hawkney having a say in it.

CHAPTER THIRTY-NINE

Callista took one look at Loui when they came back to Morticia's and knew something was wrong. He sat at a table with Foxfire, a bottle between them, both looking glum, Loui looking pale.

"What happened? Where's Niki?" Hawkney asked, apparently sensing it too.

"*Ils l'ont prise*," Loui muttered, taking another sip of his drink.

"They took her," Foxfire said. "They were spotted staring at the building and were chased down. Niki held them off while Loui got away."

Callista took a deep breath. "Well, if she's still alive, we'll get her along with Xor-nalden tomorrow night. We already have an inside man and a time set up, plus some extra troops."

"Right," Hawkney said, running his fingers through his spiky blond hair. "Right. Okay. What do you have for me, Loui?"

Loui wearily pulled out a folded piece of paper. Hawkney sat down at the table, and they began talking about his observations. Callista hung around for a moment before slipping off to Morticia's office. She found her smoking a cigarette from a long holder as she stood at a latticed window, looking down at the club and the three men huddled around the table. She resembled a ghost in her white dress in the darkness—the lights were off, the only illumination coming from the latticed window and the ones looking onto the street. Cigarette smoke hung around her like a cloud, giving her a mysterious air.

"We have a plan to infiltrate the Alamy government building as maids and get Xor-nalden and Niki out," Callista said.

"Good." Morticia stared down at the men and took a long drag from her cigarette.

"Hawkney doesn't want me on the team, but I don't care. I want in, especially now that Niki's out."

"Understandable."

Callista watched the cloud of cigarette smoke dissipate for a moment and stepped closer to Morticia. "Will you help me?"

Morticia slowly turned. Callista noticed for the first time the wrinkles around her eyes, the age, and wisdom in them.

"I wouldn't miss it," she said, a smile forming on her mouth.

"You retracting what you told Foxfire?" Callista asked with a smile of her own.

"Everything Foxy remembers is colored by drink," Morticia said, taking another drag from her cigarette. "I don't do all-out firefights. At least not anymore. But a little infiltration? That's my cup of tea. Always has been."

"You want your stabbers back?" Callista asked, thinking back on the *sai* Foxfire said Morticia used.

Morticia tilted her head toward the ceiling and blew out a cloud of smoke, reminding Callista of a fire-breather. A smile spread across Morticia's face.

"Most definitely."

EVERY ONE OF Negev's muscles sagged when the electricity finally turned off. How long had it gone on? He knew it was not really an eternity but probably only a few hours. He imagined the sun fading over the city and the lights coming on one by one.

He slumped there for a minute, gasping for air, before lolling his head and peering over at Niki Nain. She, too, slumped at her chains but unmoving. The guards came in from where they monitored them on the other side of the one-way glass and pulled Nain's head back.

"Where are your fellow insurgents?" Red Eyes demanded. Nain did not react in the least as though she were fully unconscious.

Violet Eyes slapped her. "Wake up! Where are they?"

Negev noted one of her fingers high above her twitch in reaction, but her face remained the same. An idea occurred to Negev. "I think," he whispered in English. "You have slit your own heels. It occurs to me that Humans use electricity to alter their mental states, even to achieve temporary amnesia."

Violet Eyes glanced back at her in alarm.

"Human physiology differs from ours, undoubtedly. You must take that into account with your next prisoner. As for this one," Negev said, raising his head. "She is now useless. Look at her. You may as well dump her into the sewer. She will be a vegetable for days if not weeks."

Violet Eyes sighed. "What do you think?" he asked Red Eyes, who narrowed his eyes at Negev.

"I think he used English for a reason," he said, and Violet Eyes' face hardened at the realization.

Negev cursed himself. Nain probably would have continued her act even if she did not know what he said. He perceived the corner of her lip twitch in a smile. Red Eyes punched her in the stomach, making her grunt.

"I asked you a question," he said. "Where are your compatriots?"

Nain looked up and grinned. "Go to hell."

"Hell," Red Eyes said, stepping back, a thoughtful look coming over his face. "I have heard that before. Where?"

"Is that not a region, somewhere?" Violet Eyes asked.

"I believe it is. We must send some troops there. Though I

doubt that is truly where they are," Red Eyes said, his eyes narrowing.

Negev snorted. "They have found you out, Human. Not so clever after all, are you?"

Niki chewed on her lower lip, avoiding the eyes of their captors. Her reaction gave Red Eyes confidence, and he straightened up and smiled.

"Yes, we will send a large force to comb the area." He turned to his compatriot. "Find out where this 'Hell' area is. We must move quickly," he said, shutting the door on their prisoners behind him.

Nain snickered when the door shut, and Negev could not help smiling.

"Poor people of Hell's Kitchen," she said.

"At least we bought some time," Negev said.

"For us or them?"

"Both," he said and let his head hang back as he closed his eyes.

"Listen," Nain said after a moment, breaking Negev's prized silence. "Sorry about, well, you know. You're all right."

"Apology accepted."

"Really?"

"Yes."

"Why?"

Negev took a deep breath. "Because I am, or was, the face of the people who wrested control of your homeland. As I have said before, that energy and emotion you prepared to expend in a fight never came to fruition. You found no other way to vent it except on the person, or persons, it was intended for. Thus, your actions and feelings are understandable, and since you now regret that decision, it is forgivable."

"It's not just about you," Nain said, squirming in her chains. "Gren-del says we messed you up good, and you might not make it. So when he finally kills you, he'll blame it on us and use it as a license to kill. That's what bothers me the most."

Negev did not answer because his heart sank. If Gren-del lied convincingly to the Alamgirians about Negev's current state and whereabouts, he could persuade Negev's men to follow him in retaliation for the death of their favorite admiral.

"So you see," Nain said, "the situation is dire, far beyond us."

"Yes," Negev whispered. "So it is." He closed his eyes, and the vision of the red hands reaching up toward him burst upon him. What if they were not reaching out in anguish but in warning of what would come?

CHAPTER FORTY

Callista and Morticia arrived early. They stood next to the back door, hoping Pat-farfth would let them in before Hawkney and the others came. Callista smoothed down her apron and nervously glanced around. Morticia reached over to straighten the collar of Callista's uniform.

"Thanks," Callista mumbled.

"No problem," Morticia said, taking another drag on her cigarette.

How Morticia managed to look good even in a maid's blue and white uniform, Callista didn't know. Perhaps it was the copious amount of eye shadow that gave her a mysterious look, or the way she stood and held the cigarette with fingers sporting fake red nails. Callista felt like a frumpy doll in her knee-length uniform. Possibly because it didn't fit her well.

Callista reached up again and pulled at her freshly cut bangs, making sure they hung as far over her face as they reasonably could. Her worst fear was being recognized. She wondered again if this was a mistake, if she shouldn't have come. But she remembered the way Negev looked in the tunnel, tied up and bloodied, and her imagination multiplied it, making her stomach turn. She couldn't leave him—she needed to make sure he was safe.

The door squeaked open, and Pat-farfth peeked out, quickly opening it to let them in.

"Only the two?" he asked as he shut the door behind them.

"No, two more, maybe three," Callista said. "I was ordered to stay away from this."

"Ah. I would have preferred you respected those orders," Pat-farfth said, his mouth indecisive between a grim smile and a frown.

"Where is the cleaning closet?" Morticia asked, and Pat-farfth pointed to a nearby door. Morticia opened it and began rummaging within, handing out a spray bottle and cleaning rag to Callista. Pat-farfth stood casually next to the door, glancing at his watch every few minutes.

Morticia pushed out a rolling bucket and mop. Pat-farfth opened the back door again to check and flung it open for the two women who waited without. He gestured toward Callista, and they walked over. Callista couldn't help but note the defined shape of the women's muscles and the way they walked like soldiers.

At their approach, the short blonde's eyes widened. "You, you're—"

"Yes. Don't tell Andor," Callista said, thinking to use Hawkney's last name.

"I thought it was just us," the taller brunette said, looking grumpy.

"Well, now you have backup," Morticia said, handing a duster to one and another spray bottle and rag to the other. "Leave the manhandling to us; you two make the bodyguard."

Callista couldn't help but give a little snicker despite the tense situation.

"I'm Haggart. This is Tomlin," the brunette said, gesturing to her companion, who gave Callista a shy little wave.

"Good to have you both," Callista said, smiling graciously.

"Sixteenth floor, right?" Morticia asked, starting down the hall, rolling the bucket with the mop before her.

"Yes," Callista said.

"Then we'll start on the fourteenth," Morticia said, pushing the elevator call button.

"I will meet you there in one hour if I can," Pat-farfth said and meandered away. The women waited in silence, the loud dinging of the elevator making Callista jump the first time.

The 14th floor was deserted, only the security lights on. Morticia found the switch and flooded the area with harsh light. They started randomly cleaning in case anyone on the security cameras was watching. Callista found several vacuum robots lined up against an unused wall and placed them around the space. The only sound was the whirring and clacking of the sweepers as they bumped into objects and altered direction and the squirting of the spray bottles. They stayed there for a while before moving on to the next floor.

All progressed as before until an Alamy guard came through. They tried to ignore him as he sauntered through, his hands casually clasped behind his back. He stopped behind Morticia, who leaned over, untangling a vacuum robot from the legs of a chair. He gazed at her a moment and ran a finger over her waist and bottom. Morticia stood up with a jerk and brushed her hands over where he touched her and glanced about, though Callista suspected she knew what happened. Morticia caught sight of the guard, who grinned at her, and she giggled, covering her mouth.

"La, you startled me, sir," she said, turning to him. "Oh my, what a uniform you have." She ran her fingers over the insignia on his breast.

"You like?" He caught her hand, his accent the thickest Callista ever heard.

Morticia giggled again like a little girl, earning her a deprecating look from Haggard, who was cleaning a window. "I can't resist a man in uniform," Morticia said, running her hands over his chest and down to his belt, turning the belt buckle to look at it. Callista could practically see the Alamy's heartbeat pick up. "I tell you what, soldier," Morticia said, looking down at her watch. "I'll be done in ... three hours, maybe a little less." She gave him a wink. "Meet me on the roof, yes? We can look out over the city together." She rubbed her hands back up his chest and put her arms around his neck.

"Mmm, two hours," he said, cocking his head slightly to the side and gazing down at Morticia's lips that were now close to his.

"Two hours," Morticia whispered, moving her mouth closer to his. He moved in for a kiss, but she broke away and danced out of reach, snatching up the duster and vigorously dusting the nearest desk, whether it needed it or not, half looking back over her shoulder at the guard, giggling coquettishly. The guard grinned, gave her a little salute, and sauntered away with a little more spring in his step. Morticia continued to watch him with the same shy, flirty look until the door closed, and then the regal, distant Morticia returned like a switch thrown.

Tomlin quietly clapped. "Masterfully done, encore, encore," she said softly.

Morticia inclined her head toward Tomlin without further acknowledgment. Callista couldn't stop herself from smiling.

They soon moved on to the 16th floor. Callista could sense the tension heighten between them as they casually began to move down the halls. Rather than an open space full of desks, this floor was composed of halls of offices which, they soon discovered, were locked.

They split into two teams. Haggart and Tomlin started down one hall, one using a manual vacuum while the other wiped off doorknobs—while trying them—and cleaned the occasional window. Morticia and Callista did the same in the other direction.

Callista sighed when yet another door proved locked, hoping Pat-farfth would show up soon to guide them to the right door, when she almost ran into Morticia who leaned over, looking at the floor.

"What?" Callista asked softly.

Morticia moved aside and pointed at the floor, her face looking grim. Callista bent down and peered toward where her finger pointed and narrowed her eyes and leaned even closer when a dark splotch on the cream carpet caught her eye.

Blood. Dried blood.

CHAPTER FORTY-ONE

Callista noted the blood on the carpet was darker than the brown hue human blood dried to. This trace looked like a purple, so dark it was almost black. Callista wondered what color Alamy blood was and feared the answer lay in front of her. She glanced up to see Morticia two paces down the hall, pointing again. Callista caught up to where she stood and saw another, slightly larger blotch.

She and Morticia kept going, the trail becoming too easy to follow. When they passed a crossway in the hall, she spotted Tomlin and motioned to her, jerking her head for them to come over, and she and Haggart abandoned their cleaning supplies and joined them. A few more paces down the hall and a splotch became discernably from a shoe, with a pattern like the tread of a boot.

Callista swallowed hard. Her stomach hardened into a tight ball and sank like a rock. For blood to pool enough that someone could step in it and track it this far ... . She didn't dare finish the thought.

There were two more prints leading to a door. Morticia gently tried the handle. Locked. Haggart bent down and examined it closely while Morticia glanced around for a security camera or someone burning the midnight oil.

"Tomlin, give me the screwdriver. If I take off the handle, I can probably—"

"Allow me," Morticia said, brushing Haggart aside, producing lock picks masquerading as hair pins. She inserted the picks into the standard office handle lock and deftly turned it.

The first thing to hit Callista when the door slowly swung open was the smell. The sickening reek of blood wafted out the door and introduced itself to her nostrils, with the salty after-scent of stale sweat making Callista want to retch. She was no stranger to the smell of blood but not to something as heavy as what assaulted her now.

Niki and Negev hung by their wrists from chains attached to exposed rafters, both looking like wrung-out towels. Callista's eyes were immediately drawn to the bloody designs on Negev's body, and a quick look at Niki showed burn marks laced over her body. But what worried Callista most was that while Niki deliriously hummed gospel tunes, Negev hung motionless and silent, his chin resting on his chest.

Haggart cursed and rushed to Niki's side. "Get under her, be ready to catch her," she said to Tomlin as she produced a pair of thick wire cutters and began work on Niki's chains.

Callista slowly walked to Negev. Despite the soft commotion to his right, he gave no sign of life. "N-Negev," Callista choked out softly, gently touching his bruised cheek. He twitched at her touch, and Callista let out a sigh of relief. He gave a soft groan, letting his head fall backward, his fingers moving stiffly.

"Negev," she said more insistently.

Haggart cut through the first chain, holding Niki's legs with a *plink*, and pulled it out of the loop bolted to the floor.

"Negev, wake up."

His eyes blinked open, and turned toward her as he raised his head. His eyes widened as he seemed to comprehend who stood before him.

"You, you c-c," he coughed hoarsely. "Cannot be here; he will find you."

"We're getting you out of here," Callista said, and the second chain holding Niki's arms *plinked* as it snapped. Tomlin struggled a bit when Niki's full weight collapsed onto her.

"What did they do to her?" Haggart snapped, turning toward Negev.

"Electrocution," he answered, distracted. "How did you get past the concealed hand scanner on the door?" Everyone froze and stared at him. He must have noted the blood draining from their faces. "You have no time; go, go without me," he said urgently, straightening up in his chains. "If he catches you, it is all over; go —run."

Haggart hoisted Niki over her shoulders in a fireman's carry and headed out the door.

"I can't just leave you!" Callista said, panic setting in. "You're the whole reason we came."

"You can, and you will leave me. You need a new martyr for your cause. 'Yesterday, Saint Petersburg. Today, Xor-nalden. Tomorrow, the world.'" He gave her a crooked smile. "Perhaps I am here for such a time as this, for this purpose—to save an entire people through my death since I could not save my own."

"But, but," Callista stuttered, a thousand thoughts and arguments swirling through her head.

"Go. Live for me, do not die for me," he said, looking earnestly at her. Callista's eyes filled with tears. She lunged forward, grabbing him by the back of the head and pressing her lips into his mutilated ones. He pulled back after a moment.

"I love you," she choked out.

"I never would have known," he said, a mischievous smile sliding up one corner of his mouth. "Go," he said again, giving her a little push with his knee.

Callista drew breath for another rebuttal when Morticia grabbed her arm and dragged her from the room.

Tomlin and Haggart, carrying Niki, disappeared into a

stairwell down the hall. Callista and Morticia ran at full tilt to catch up with them. They rushed down the stairs—miraculously unhindered—Tomlin snapping details of their flight on a cell phone to the extraction team. By the time they were at the bottom, a handgun replaced the cell phone. She held it at the ready, her face a determined mask.

Tomlin reached toward the handle to open the door, but it moved away from her, and the door opened from without. She suddenly found herself face-to-face with an Alamy soldier, whose face contorted into rage at the sight of her. She quickly grabbed him by the uniform and hauled him inside while shooting him in the chest.

Callista yelped at the sound of the gunshot and looked away briefly, squeezing her eyes shut, tears leaking out.

Tomlin grabbed the door, letting the Alamy fall, and slammed it shut to the sound of more Alamy voices. It was all Tomlin could do to hold the door shut against the other soldiers outside.

"How many?" Haggart asked.

"I don't know, didn't see," Tomlin said when the door almost yanked her off her feet, but with Callista's help, they managed to pull it shut again.

"May I?" Morticia asked, stepping up to the door. Callista sucked in her breath—Morticia held out a hand grenade. She pulled the pin while continuing to hold down the lever, and with the Alamy's next yank at the door, Tomlin and Callista allowed them to open it further so Morticia could toss it out before all three of them yanked it closed again.

The shock of the explosion rattled the door, making everyone jump and tense as their ears rang. The impact wasn't as forceful as Callista supposed it would be, though plenty loud. Perhaps she had overestimated its power, or maybe the building was reinforced. But what mattered was the quiet outside and that no one pulled on the door. Morticia and Callista backed away while Tomlin slowly opened the door, pistol at the ready, and glanced out.

"Clear," she said softly, and they moved out, hurrying along the wall to the corner of the building.

Just as they approached the corner, four Alamies rounded it and yelled at them to stop, and they halted dead in their tracks. Tomlin held out her gun to the side. The leader shouted at her to drop it but became distracted when the Alamy in the back jerked and fell. The rest soon followed, stone dead. Callista and the other women ran forward, careful not to trip over the bodies. An armored bank car screeched to a halt at the corner, and T'Chamba jumped out the back, Tommy Gun in hand, ready to shoot anything that moved while they piled into the back. He jumped in after them.

"Go!"

Loui floored it, and the car lumbered off, picking up speed at a surprising rate.

The car came screeching to a halt a few blocks away. Callista took a peek out the tiny back window and spied Hawkney, Ali, and Jose rappelling down the building in controlled falls, sniper rifles slung over their shoulders. Hawkney and Ali jumped in the back with them, squeezing in, while Jose jumped in the front and pulled out a Tommy Gun from beneath the seat, looking ready to thrust his slim body out the window for a drive-by shooting.

As they shot out into the main street again, Hawkney glanced at Callista, let out a disbelieving breath, and shook his head. Callista's shoulders slumped, glad he didn't yell at her. She had just stopped crying when the action started. He leaned over and, with Ali's help, untangled Niki from Haggart and pulled her limp body onto his lap, looking her over for injuries.

"What the hell did they do to her?" he said, gently touching her burns.

"Negev said they electrocuted her," Callista said softly. Hawkney swore in answer.

A phone rang in the front seat, and Loui answered. "They have eyes in the air!" he yelled back after a moment.

"Execute plan S!" Hawkney yelled back and received an acknowledgment.

"What's 'plan S?'" Callista asked.

"Subway," Hawkney answered shortly, too absorbed in assessing his partner to give her a detailed outline. Ali made a phone call, speaking in rapid Arabic while T'Chamba perused the subway train times on his phone and called up to Loui which station to make for.

Callista began wondering if the Alamies would shoot at them if one of their ships spotted them when Loui yelled to brace themselves. Hawkney clutched Niki to his chest, and the others braced themselves against the sides and roof, and Callista followed suit when the car suddenly plunged downward and shook violently. Callista glanced forward to see they were plummeting down the stairs into the subway. People who were removing some turnstiles scurried out of the way with the stiles in tow, and the car passed smoothly into the hole they made. She turned to look out the back window, to see them rushing to put the stiles back in place. She sent them warm thoughts.

Loui suddenly swerved the car, sending it up on two wheels, and Callista glimpsed people crushing themselves against the walls, perhaps alerted they were coming. The van suddenly dropped down, and Callista discerned they were now on the tracks. She swallowed hard at the image of what would happen if they met a train coming the other way, or if one of the tires blew out and they touched the third rail. She reminded herself to keep breathing. The subway tracks were paved around the edges so service vehicles could drive over them, making their flight down the tunnel fairly smooth.

After speeding along in the alternating dark and light for some minutes, she heard what she feared—a train horn coming from behind them. Loui answered with a honk on his horn, and before long she spied light on the wall from the bend in the tunnel they just completed, and the train sped along not far behind and caught up fast.

Callista guessed the train moved three times faster than they did, but the closer it came, the slower it progressed toward them. The train inched closer and closer, and she looked back to see Loui constantly glancing in the rearview mirror. Finally, with a crunch and a screech, the train pressed into the back of the car, and Loui threw the car into neutral. The train began to speed up again, indicated by how fast the lights on the tunnel walls passed.

"Where's this train headed?" she asked.

"Doesn't matter where it was going," T'Chamba replied. "Now, it goes to the stop closest to our new base, at the end of the line."

They rode along in silence, praying the tires wouldn't give out, that Loui wouldn't lose control on a curve, and that the Alamies wouldn't catch on to their ploy.

She tried not to ponder what would happen to Negev in retaliation for Niki's rescue. She pulled out her father's rosary which she wore around her neck for good luck. She fingered the smooth black and white beads and Christ's tortured effigy, trying to remember what her father said when he used the beads, filling in her own words when her memory failed her, which involved a lot of *Please God, please God, please God.*

CHAPTER FORTY-TWO

The base wasn't even in the city. When they reached the subway terminus, they turned off the tracks onto a vehicle service ramp, pulled out onto the street, and kept going. The base was nestled in some dense woods miles away from the city limits. They'd set up tents and tarps in a sprawling camp, and Callista felt like she lived in a refugee or military encampment, the latter especially when she noted how many people carried weapons.

Here, her own personal torture began—forcing herself to remain silent and do nothing, waiting, each day going by in a meaningless blur while they consolidated their position. Even if she wept and wailed and begged, they wouldn't try to rescue Negev again, and she couldn't blame them—it was far too risky. But it was even worse to force herself to stay there and do nothing about it personally, even though she knew she was powerless to help him. She had stood there, spoken to him, touched him, and left him to his fate. His suggestion he was meant to be a martyr haunted her to no end and gave her sleepless nights.

Niki, too, suffered her personal torture—she became a spectacle and a victim posterchild. She was interviewed, photographed, and filmed in all her agonized glory, and though she clearly played up how much she'd been abused, the sulking look on her face, when not documented, said otherwise. But the media loved it–so much so they called for war.

Callista scowled at a computer screen playing one of the talking heads. Callista sat stiffly, arms interwoven in her thin camouflage jacket and legs crossed tightly in jeans one size too big, trying to stay warm against the cold. She couldn't help but despise the talking heads a little—they weren't the ones who would be on the front lines, who would do the dying, but here they were, calling for blood like they knew best.

"Backseat generals. Gotta love 'em," Jose grumbled, echoing her thoughts from where he sat huddled beside her with a blanket wrapped around his body and draped over his head.

Hawkney came into the tent behind her, a machine gun slung over his shoulder. Callista craned her neck back to look behind her to see who the newcomer was before returning her gaze to the screen. "How's Niki?" she asked. She hadn't seen her in a few days.

"She used to say, 'Give me three days, and I'll be able to hold a gun. Give me a week, and look out world,' whenever she was wounded or hurt in any way," he said with a watered-down smile, taking off his black beanie and scratching his yellow thatch. "She'll be fine—she's doing a lot better now. Snapping at and sassing everyone who comes near her. She hates bedrest and the babying."

"I can imagine," Callista said with a soft snort. "So. What do we do with this?" She pointed to the screen with her chin.

"I've talked to the council," Hawkney began, moving over into her field of view beyond Jose, who crouched next to her. From his tone of voice, she knew she wasn't going to like it. "They've decided we have to fight," he continued. "And not just little strikes and protests here and there—we're talking open warfare. We can't live in hiding like this forever. If we can get reinforcements in sufficient numbers soon, we will fight. We're hoping Niki's testimony will help with that."

"And the news of Xor-nalden being treated worse than her? That he's on our side and being destroyed because of it?" Callista asked defensively, hoping the outrage would encourage another rescue attempt, if not by them, then by an angry mob they could take advantage of, terrible and callous as that was.

"They talk about it some, on TV," Jose jumped in. "But they love talking about Niki more. Guess she's more relatable. At least they finally have the bad guy right—instead of bashing Xor-nalden, they're name-calling Gren-del."

"Well, that's a start, I suppose," Callista said.

"There's more," Hawkney continued.

"Isn't there always?" she said.

"I put something of an ad out on the dark web, calling for soldiers, munitions, and provisions. We're pretty confident the Alamies don't know about the dark web—people have started using it for clandestine transactions and propaganda against them, and nothing has happened, so I also put our location. It's a risk, but hopefully, we won't be staying here long."

"When did you put the call out?" Callista asked.

"Yesterday."

Callista continued to stare at the computer screen. Hawkney shifted his weight uncomfortably.

"Franklin got in touch with Pat-farfth. He's sent the word out among his people of Gren-del's treachery the best he could without risking getting caught, and they'll be ready whenever we are. We even arranged to get them some of our uniforms so we won't shoot the good guys in the heat of battle."

"That's good," Callista said, her voice neutral.

Hawkney continued to shift from one leg to the other, and she took notice of his discomfort and silence and gazed at him with a cocked eyebrow.

"What?" she asked.

"Well, what do you think?"

"What do I think?"

"Yeah, you know."

"I think a lot of people will die one way or the other, and Xornalden the first of many," Callista said, crossing her arms and looking back at the screen.

"No, that's not what I meant—"

"I'm not a tactician, Hawkney," Callista said. "Go ask McCaffrey if you want advice go to some of your Army buddies if you want approval." She looked over at Jose. "No offense."

"None taken," he said, staring at the screen.

"But you're smart," Hawkney persisted.

"Smart can be just as dead as stupid," Callista answered shortly.

Jose snorted. "Amen," he said.

Hawkney pursed his lips, seeming to weigh his answer or if he should give one.

T'Chamba came in before Hawkney could decide. "There are truckloads of volunteers here. A bunch of them do not even know how to use a gun, but they said, 'Give us liberty, or give us death.'"

A smile flitted across Hawkney's face. "I like them already," he said, turning to T'Chamba.

"There's more," T'Chamba said. "They came with donations. Tractor trailers, filled with water and food."

Hawkney left the tent with T'Chamba and Jose on their heels.

Callista waited a moment before she moved to the tent flap and peeked out. Men and a few women jumped out of the trucks and vans, wearing factory uniforms and average clothes under their heavy jackets. One man who appeared to be in his late sixties stepped forward, his scraggly white beard making him look to Callista like a prophet.

Callista caught pieces of the man's explanation that T'Chamba had just repeated to them over the general noise of the people who came to ogle the newcomers. Hawkney gazed around at the people, strangers, and friends, and he put his fingers to his lips and gave a shrill whistle, getting everyone's attention. A hush fell over the crowd.

"If you join us in this war, I cannot guarantee the safety of the families you fight for, nor that you or they will receive any sort of remuneration for your service," he said, his voice carrying clearly over the crowd. "I cannot offer you good odds or hope for a better future without our oppressors, and I definitely cannot promise a reward in heaven for your sacrifice, nor that it is sanctioned by God." He looked around at the intent faces around him, both young and old.

"All I can offer you is a chance. The chance to take back what is ours, the chance to avenge the martyred and the oppressed. The chance to stand up to a dictator who thinks he is the law and can do what he pleases. The chance to seize the values you hold dear and to fight for them with everything you have." He gazed around at the people again, having let his voice reach a fever pitch. "I give you the chance," he continued softly, but strongly for all to hear, "to discover who you are, and what you're made of."

"We have a pretty good idea who we are," the old man replied in a strong voice. "We are the Sons and Daughters of Liberty!" he shouted over the crowd. "Liberty or Death!" and the forest trembled with the replying chant.

Callista collapsed in a folding chair, forcing air in and out of her lungs. It was happening. It was really happening. They were on the brink of war.

With or without her.

Tears came to her eyes while the chanting continued, making her thoughts spin. She remembered everyone looking to her for guidance for the first protest, how Hawkney kept seeking her approval, how Negev had believed her to be a leader in the organization, and thought she kept underselling herself.

Perhaps I am here for such a time as this. Negev's words, unwittingly referencing the Bible's book of Esther, came back to her like a cold slap.

Perhaps **you** *are here for such a time as this,* she thought to herself and glanced back out at the people whose chanting devolved into cheering. Hawkney had said this was a chance for them to discover who they were, and she fleetingly questioned if he aimed it at her before she dismissed the thought.

Resolve began to harden in her heart. Perhaps it wasn't about who they were but who they wanted—or needed—to be. Loui called her *Liberty von Menschen*—Liberty of the People—and the others also saw her as its personification. Perhaps it was her role in all this—Liberty leading the people. She stood up slowly, trying to swallow her tears. If Negev would die for them, she would make sure his sacrifice would not be in vain and it would not be forgotten. She slowly passed through the mosh-pit to the supply tent and found the yellow flag with the coiled rattlesnake leaning up against some supply crates where she remembered seeing it.

She started to reach for it but paused when a glint of red caught her eye. She brushed the yellow aside to find the star-spangled banner furled underneath it. She lifted the flag upright and caught up the fabric, pressing it to her mouth, inhaling its musky scent. She carried it over her shoulder and the Gadsden flag, its black "Don't Tread on Me" lettering bold against the yellow background, in her other hand back to the clearing, handing the yellow off to a bystander and waving the American flag above her head when she gained some room. As the people continued to cheer, tears streamed from her eyes afresh, patriotic love the likes of which she had never known before overflowing and colliding with sorrow for the loss to come.

After a few minutes, she caught sight of Hawkney, who wiped the jubilant grin off his face when he saw her looking back, replacing it with a simple smile, and gave her a nod of appreciation and recognition. Callista soberly nodded back. When the crowd started in on *The Star-Spangled Banner*, she waved the flag with renewed vigor. For better or worse, they were in this together, until death or victory.

O say, does that star-spangled banner yet wave
O'er the land of the free and the home of the brave?

CHAPTER FORTY-THREE

They came in droves. Not only Americans, but also people from all over the world. The camp grew exponentially until it consumed the entire forest. One tent at the center became the situation room, filled with maps and charts, lists of resources—breathing, and inanimate—as they came in. Communications officers, organizers, and generals by the score crowded around tables, their heads together, whispering to each other or to an interpreter who turned to whisper to another.

A team went back into the tunnels the Renegades had inhabited to disarm the alarm systems and booby traps that the new people wouldn't know how to avoid. The tunnels would be an integral part in moving their troops unseen into the city when they enacted their blitzkrieg and attempted to overthrow the Alamgirian government.

But in the meantime, Callista tired of fame. People of all ages and nationalities came up to her, hugged her, told her what an inspiration she was—whether she understood them or not—for standing up to the Alamies and giving them the metaphorical middle finger. She kept reminding them it wasn't like that, Xornalden was on their side, and it was Gren-del she hated, not Alamies in general.

She strolled through the camp, seeing food prepared, clothing mended, weapons cleaned, drills taught, and maneuvers practiced. The greasy smell of food, the sickening one of oil and gasoline, the acrid scent of gunpowder from fired blanks, and the slick reek of sweat swirled around her like an ever-changing mosaic while she walked, the chatter of a plethora of languages and accents creating an overlapping collage.

She stopped at the edge of a drill-space to watch for a moment.

Niki seemed to relish being a drill sergeant. She strolled in front of the lines in her Army uniform, a semi-straight tree branch in hand, poking and slapping individuals who didn't stand up straight enough, didn't keep their eyes front and center, or didn't have their feet together correctly. Callista could hear her shrill calls coming from the drill field throughout the day, and when she saw her at chow time, she beamed and gave anyone who would listen, an update on how her unit, her pride and joy, shaped up nicely— she'd have them battle-ready in no time.

And that's what Callista feared they had: no time. While the people clearing the tunnels were experts, even experts make mistakes. She kept expecting them to come flying down the road, screaming that mistakes were made—one of the traps went off, alerting the Alamies, or the like. The camp would be thrown into high alert while they uprooted hurriedly, maybe even getting attacked if they were followed. That would be the greatest disaster. Everyone was crowded close together with nowhere to run—soldiers and civilians alike. Many civilians had volunteered as medics, cooks, and launderers. Callista could imagine the pandemonium if the camp were attacked, and this put her on edge, making her restless, so she wandered about the camp uselessly.

Callista pursed her lips, watching Niki begin another round of drills. Hawkney caught her eye, and she began to meander through the jungle of humanity toward him.

Like Niki, Hawkney, too, was in his element. Callista noted a new fire in his eyes, a flush in his cheeks not put there by the cold. An energy pervaded him and made him seem light as a bird. When she wandered closer, she observed him trying to have a conversation with a Chinese soldier, both of them stumbling along in their words, trying to be understood. Yet they laughed all the while at their blunders, slapping each other on the back. They shook hands, coming to some agreement or friendship before the man went his own way, and Hawkney caught sight of her and approached.

"We'll be ready to move out once the tunnels are cleared," he said. "Please tell me you'll stay back and not be on the front lines or in any of it."

"I'll go wherever I'm needed, I suppose," she said with a shrug. "I admit I do not relish the idea of being in the thick of it, though. I'd probably be far more useful helping the wounded."

"Agreed," Hawkney said, crossing his arms and turning to look around at the camp. "Helping with the wounded would probably be the most effective—if you think you can handle it. It can get pretty grisly."

"I'm aware."

"They adore you, you know," he said, looking over at her with a smile tugging the corner of his mouth. "You're practically Marilyn Monroe."

"I know," she said, frowning.

"I'm sure you'd be a great encouragement to the wounded."

"I hope I don't get sick or something," she grumbled. "That would certainly be encouraging, wouldn't it? I'm not cut out for all this."

"Well, like I said, why don't you sit it out entirely and be Marilyn Monroe for the wounded once it's all over and done with and bandaged up?"

"I can't just sit and wait," Callista said, turning to face him. "It's killing me, waiting while Negev is out there dying. I won't sit on the sidelines when we'll be so close … , " She caught her breath, tears springing to her eyes and forcing her to look at the gray, bleak sky to try to keep them from spilling over.

"I get it," Hawkney said gently, putting a hand on her shoulder. "I felt the same way when I couldn't rush in there and get Niki out but had to wait outside. I get it."

She stared down and took the corner of her flannel scarf out of her jacket and wiped her eyes with it.

"Do what you can," he said. "If you need to step away, step away. No one will blame you."

She acknowledged with a nod, lowering her head in slight embarrassment.

"It's nothing to be ashamed of, Callista."

"Yeah, right. It's just ... if someone is hurt and calling for help while I'm puking in the corner ... ."

"You're stronger than that," he said, placing his other hand on her shoulder. "I have faith in you."

"Thanks, Hawkney," she forced out despite her still choked-up throat and gave him a small smile in appreciation, wiping her eyes with the back of her hand.

"Callista, Callista!" Butterfly called, crashing into Callista with a hug. "The Chinese nurses made you a blouse out of real silk. They want to show you and have you try it on to make sure it fits. It's so pretty, Callista. You'll like it."

Callista gave Hawkney a smile. "I'll see you later, Hawkney."

"Yeah, yeah ... , sure."

Callista walked away, arm in arm with Butterfly, feeling his gaze on her back.

Butterfly led her to the Chinese nurses' tent. They had come with a platoon's worth of troops from China, and some were apparently expert seamstresses. They pulled Callista into the tent, chattering excitedly, and presented her with a deep red, sleeveless silk blouse with black dragons embroidered on it and black borders on the shoulders, collar, and bottom edge of the shirt. Callista held it to her body with a smile, and in no time, they made her try it on top of her shirt, along with a pair of snug black pants.

"They say you can wear this into battle. The silk is strong and has underneath a special weave that will stop a knife. It has red, like your signature, but is not too bright to be a hazard, not to mention the lucky dragons," Butterfly explained.

Callista thanked them earnestly but informed them she hoped to be attached to the nurses to help as needed and bolster the confidence and morale of the wounded. They appeared a little disappointed she would not be leading the charge but not at all opposed to the idea of her staying with them. They showed her their medical supplies and how to use some of them. They also invited her to eat with them, which she heartily accepted, and learned how to make wontons right there.

That night, the bomb and alarm experts came back, declaring the tunnels safe and ready for use, having disarmed their own traps so they wouldn't take out the uninitiated. Command announced a portion of the troops and the medical units would move out first thing the next morning to set up the hospital stations in the tunnels throughout the city, and the attack would commence that afternoon. Callista and Butterfly decided to stick with the Chinese nurses, and they all slept in the same tent that night so they wouldn't get separated in the chaos of the morning.

Callista found a piece of paper and a pen and took a deep breath. She had left her phone in the hotel room the day she first met Negev, and was forbidden to contact her mother or anyone else ever since. But now that they were on the eve of battle, she felt it necessary to write her mother a note. She didn't have a postage stamp, but if someone started reading it, she was sure they'd have pity and deliver it anyway.

. . .

Dear Mom,

I know you're worried sick over what has become of me, and in truth, I do not know what will happen tomorrow. There will be a great battle; perhaps you have heard about it by now. I have been caught up with the revolution and help out the best I can. If we fail, you may never hear from me again since we will undoubtedly be in hiding for a long time. If we succeed, I hope to call you before this note ever reaches you. Please pray for me, but do not fear for me, as hard as that is for you. I am in God's hands. May He do with me as He wishes.

Love,
Callista

CALLISTA SIGHED TO HERSELF. It wasn't all she wanted to say, but it contained enough to inform her mother without getting overly sentimental or giving too gloomy an outlook on her chances of survival, which she didn't want to admit even to herself. She folded the note and put it into her pocket, hoping to find a letter drop somewhere in the city the next morning.

She settled down to sleep and watched the nurses pray to their ancestors, the Dao, or the Buddha, the burning incense perfuming the air, reminding her of the Catholic service she once attended, and she pulled out her father's rosary. She wished she remembered what prayers the beads represented—she was brought up non-denominational. She tried to make up prayers specific to her situation for each bead, and fell asleep doing so, more at peace than when she started.

CHAPTER FORTY-FOUR

Callista knelt on the ground, her head bowed. Everyone scrambled around, getting ready to move out in the frosty mist of the early morning. She would not let the frenzy get to her, though. It was just her, God, the cold burning her lungs and the frozen flower peeking out of the pine straw between her knees. She wanted to touch it but feared it would shatter if she did.

Butterfly came and put a hand on her shoulder. "Come on, we're about to go."

Callista nodded, and Butterfly turned away.

It occurred to Callista the flower would blacken and die when it thawed, the frost having killed it. She leaned forward and gently touched its petals. It didn't break but moved gently in response to her touch as if it was not frozen stiff.

Callista stood and clutched her oversized leather jacket around her and moved to stand amid the huddled Chinese nurses. They were finally at the front of the line of medical personnel and soon climbed into a tractor-trailer car along with their medical supplies, which were loaded by some of the volunteers. When the doors closed, they were in complete darkness. They swayed with the moving truck and tried not to lose balance and start a domino effect of falling. Callista began to wonder, her legs stiffened from standing in one place, if she could manage to find a way to sit down even though they were crammed together, when the truck finally slowed to a halt.

The doors flew open, and the nearest nurses jumped out, assisted by the troops who accompanied them in a minivan. Other nurses handed down their medical supplies to those who had disembarked. They removed a manhole cover a few feet from the truck and soon formed a line of people from the truck down through the hole. When the tractor-trailer was emptied, everything disappeared down the hole, and the truck and van returned for more, the whole disembarking taking around twenty minutes.

Callista found herself in a bricked tunnel with an arched roof and a light bulb fixed to the ceiling every few yards. She was told it was once the end of the line for the Long Island Railroad but had been bricked up and filled with dirt long ago. The Renegades had slowly emptied it out and used it, like the bootleggers long before them, to hide gear and people. Callista hoped the street above them wouldn't get hit by a mortar and cave the whole thing in.

After the supplies were dumped, the nurses started air purifiers and antiseptic diffusers in an attempt to sterilize the environment. Callista collapsed on a backpack and ate lunch with Butterfly and a few others while some of the other nurses puttered. Callista was thankful the fight would not begin for a few more hours.

"Need any extra hands?"

The chatter ceased, and all eyes turned to the newcomer gliding into the room, her long hair bound up in a ponytail, swaying behind her.

"Morticia? What are you doing here?" Callista asked.

"As I told Foxy, I'm not good for the front lines anymore," Morticia said, stopping beside Callista. She wore snug blue jeans, a black sweatshirt, and black leather boots, out of which Callista spied the handles of her *sai*. "But that doesn't mean I don't have hands to help. I can bandage and hold down a person as well as anyone."

Butterfly translated, and the Chinese women nodded and chattered, handing Morticia a bowl of their steamed rice.

"It's good to have you," Callista said. She found Morticia had a calming influence on her in these tense situations.

Morticia smiled sweetly. "It would kill me to miss it, and it would kill me to be on the front, literally, so I'm happy to be in the middle."

"Same," Callista said. "I also have the selfish hope that when —if—they find Negev still alive they'll bring him here where I can take care of him."

Morticia gave her a sidelong, teasing look. "Callista, are you a victim of the Florence Nightingale Effect?"

Callista laughed. "Maybe. A little. But I've known and admired him before, so it's different."

"Is it though?"

"Does it matter if the outcome is sound?"

"I suppose not," Morticia said with a smile, sipping the broth from the bowl.

After break time, the nurses set about organizing their supplies and making ready for the upcoming battle. They worked until the walkie-talkie at Callista's belt squawked, and the placid voice of the English general who oversaw communications gave the order for the troops to get into position—in code, of course. He sounded to Callista like a narrator on a nature documentary. All heads turned when the walkie-talkie came to life, and Butterfly translated what he said. Callista took it off her belt and handed it to Butterfly.

"Here, you're the translator. You keep it," she said.

Butterfly took it almost reverently.

Everyone quieted and tensed, waiting for the command for the assault to begin. The sound of a subway rolling by behind a wall at the end of the tunnel seemed loud in the stillness.

One by one, each unit began calling in, informing command of their status.

"Bravo team, ready for the tailgate."

"Foxtrot, barbecue's cookin'."

"Delta, have the flags out and ready to cheer the team on."

"Alpha, is … ah … well, ready," and so it went. When all had checked in, an eerie silence pervaded until the Englishman's voice came over the coms again.

"God's speed to you all, and may He protect and keep each of you. Hail Mary."

Then silence. Even though Butterfly forgot to translate, Callista could see by the nurses' faces they understood the essence of what was said. The head nurse stood and clapped her hands together twice. The nurses began double-checking everything—bandages, sutures, rubbing alcohol, tweezers, and the two little medical tents they set up within the tunnel as surgery rooms.

"Hot resistance at Objective One," came Hawkney's voice over the walkie a few minutes later, and Callista tensed.

"Roger that, Alpha team," came the Englishman's placid voice in reply. "Sending in team Juliet from the south to assist."

"Copy that," Hawkney replied, the sound of gunfire leaking in, and the coms went silent. Everyone shifted nervously.

"Objective One is the HQ building, isn't it?" Butterfly asked.

"Yes, but we expected the heaviest resistance there, which is why Juliet and a few others were held in reserve, to go wherever they are needed," Callista said.

"Oh, okay."

"Incoming wounded to medical bay C," Hawkney said over the coms, and Butterfly shouted the translation. That was their unit. Everyone started moving at once. Some of the nurses picked up stretchers and hurried to the ladder; others rushed about, checking everything. The two guards climbed partway up the ladder to the subway vent, heaving it open with a whine of hinges. One would lower the wounded down on a rope, the other ready to guide them down.

There were three wounded. The one who caught it in the gut they lowered first. His jaw clenched, and he kept squeezing his eyes shut. The other was hit in the arm. He looked plain grumpy more than anything and insisted he was going right back out there as soon as he was bandaged. The third needed to be led by the arm. He had one hand with a handkerchief pressed to the side of his face, his expression one of confusion and awe. Blood soaked through the handkerchief and trickled down his cheek, making Callista feel nauseous and sweat break out on her forehead. She realized he probably lost his eye and was in shock.

The first was whisked off to the surgery tent, the second set down on a pallet to have his arm cleaned and sewn up, and the third also placed on a pallet where two nurses did their best to stop the bleeding. More wounded came in steadily, in twos and threes, some severely wounded, others just needing a patch job before they scurried out to the front again.

Callista took off her jacket and helped support the weight of the man in shock, staggering with him over to a cot. She retrieved some gauze and gently pried the soaked handkerchief from his hand with thumb and forefinger, trying very hard not to look at the remains of his eye as she stuffed gauze over it and clamped his hand back down. More wounded were lowered down, and she hurried to ferry them to other cots, fetching more gauze and painkillers in a seemingly endless back and forth. Screams caught her attention, and she rushed over to a man thrashing. She gripped his hand, telling him it was going to be okay until her words trailed off as his eyes turned glassy and the light faded from them. She stumbled away, looking for someone else to help, to forget what she just witnessed, and fell heavily to her knees next to the cot of a girl in a fashion camouflage jacket. She was met with a wide-eyed, thousand-yard stare, the girl's face frozen in eternal terror. Callista stumbled away, hand over her mouth, and propped herself up against the brick wall as she took deep breaths and watched her shaking hands, willing them to be still.

Suddenly, the guard at the top of the ladder yelled, and

gunfire flashed above the access point. He fell through the hole a moment later, slowed by his fellow who perched on the ladder, and they both hit the floor hard. The second guard wrestled his machine gun out from under the first, who clutched a wound on his upper leg and fired up into the hole. An Alamgirian soldier fell through, dead before he hit the floor.

Callista gasped and backed a little farther away from the hole, her gaze tracking the rivulet of purple blood trickling away from the Alamy.

Two more Alamies jumped through after him, their boots clapping on the brick floor. The second guard shoved his comrade off him and jumped up to grab one of the Alamy's weapons. The first guard kicked the other alien in the shin, eliciting a grunt, and scrambled up to grab the weapon, keeping it pointed away from himself as the alien sought to regain control.

Callista glanced down to see Morticia crouching beside her, hands deep in a soldier's wound, digging out a piece of shrapnel while watching the struggle out of the corner of her eye.

One of the guards cried out in pain when an Alamy managed to produce a knife and stab him in the gut. Callista lunged forward, snatched the two *sai* out of Morticia's boots, and ran toward the fight at full tilt. The Alamy with the knife went to help his friend who was getting punched out by the guard on the floor. He kicked the guard in the head, knocking him down alongside his Alamy comrade, and pointed his weapon at the man's face.

Callista screamed as loud as she could, an animalistic howl that succeeded in distracting the Alamy. He looked up as she leapt over the unconscious Alamy's legs and plunged both *sai* down into his chest. He gasped and staggered back, his gun slipping from his fingers, his other hand feebly trying to push her away. Callista grasped one of the sai by the cross guard with her right hand, ripped it out of his chest and slashed him across the throat with another scream. Some of the spewing purple blood hit Callista in the face. She yanked the *sai* in her left hand out of his chest, and he slumped to the floor. She stood over him, blood dripping off her hands and weapons, watching the life trickle out of him.

Suddenly, she remembered to breathe, gasping raggedly, letting the *sai* in her right hand slip out of her hand and clatter to the floor. Her hand moved to touch her lips, horror at what she had done washing over her, and, glancing down, saw blood covering her hands. She choked on a sob, and nausea hit her. A hand touched her shoulder, and she jerked and spun her head, subconsciously clutching and raising the *sai* in her left hand, ready to strike. It was the soldier who had nearly been shot in the head.

"Hey," he said gently. "You're my hero, champ. You saved my life."

Tears blurred her sight and Callista took flight, running down the tunnel to where they'd knocked through the wall into the subway line. She stumbled in a zig-zag pattern through the dark tunnel, frantically for a way out, up to clear air, not damp and claustrophobic—anywhere away from there. A tiny shaft of light caught her attention and led her to a ladder and access. Choking on tears, she climbed up and heaved up on the cover. She burst onto the street, scrambling out of the hole as fast as she could.

She took a deep, gasping breath and choked on smoke. She crawled on her hands and knees away from the hole, trying to stop coughing, and when she did, she glanced up to see a Human soldier lying a few feet in front of her. He appeared to be Indian and wore a bright shirt with a busy pattern under a gray jacket. But the thousand-yard stare in his brown eyes, looking to the sky, caught her attention. He was dead. She gazed beyond him. He was not the only one. She stood slowly and saw more and more Humans of all colors and nationalities stretching out before her.

She blinked rapidly and shook her head, hearing the bang and shriek of gunshots and laser pistols nearby. As she stood in the road a few Humans charged across the street a block away from her toward where some Alamgirians were taking cover. One at the front paused when he caught sight of her—Hawkney.

"Callista!"

An energy bolt slammed into his chest and knocked him to the ground.

"No!" Callista screamed and stumbled toward him, drawing in ragged breaths of the acrid air. She had to get to him, had to pull him to safety, had to make sure he wasn't—

Something slammed into the back of her head, and everything went black before she hit the pavement.

CHAPTER FORTY-FIVE

Callista woke up to a slap across the face. Everything came slowly back into focus, the bright light making her squint. Her wrists were in cuffs suspended from the ceiling, against which her weight hung. She scuffled to get her footing when she fully came back to consciousness. Someone grabbed her by the jaw and lifted her face. She slowly opened her eyes to see a black patch and a red eye staring back at her. Gren-del grinned maliciously.

"Tell me," he said in a menacing, quiet way. "How demoralized will your people be when I tell them I have their leader? Their 'Lady Liberty,' as they call you?"

Callista said nothing, realizing Negev hadn't been the only one keeping an eye on her, and he let go of her jaw, moving to run his finger gently down the line of dried blood that was not her own on her face. Callista squeezed her eyes closed, becoming aware of the crusty reminder.

"I see you have killed at least one of my men," he said in the same gentle tone. "Well, he will certainly be happy to know I will make you pay for every drop of his blood you spilled and then some."

Callista kept her eyes squeezed shut, and he struck her across the face again.

"Look at me when I speak to you," he roared in her face, and Callista burst into tears, keeping her head down, not heeding his demand. He grabbed her by the hair and jerked her head back. She opened her eyes to stare at his red one, still crying.

"Grotesque," he said. "Why Xor-nalden would have even the slightest interest in a sniveling worm like you is beyond my comprehension. No matter. You will be together in the Abyss soon enough."

He let go, and her head fell again, but she raised it a bit to watch him casually walk up to a nearby table and pick up the *sai* she had clutched. He strolled back over to her, turning the weapon this way and that, feeling its weight and balance.

"This weapon, what do you call it?"

It took Callista a moment to find her voice, and after she cleared her voice, she quietly responded, "It's a *sai*. They're usually used in pairs."

"Then where is the other one?"

"I dropped it. They're not mine. I grabbed them from my friend when some of your men attacked the medical camp."

"And you killed them."

"Just one," Callista mumbled.

"And how did you manage to drop your weapon?"

"I've never killed anyone before or done anything so violent." Callista sniffed back her tears, wondering why he was so interested. "I was terrified."

"Pathetic," he said, stepping close to her. With a curious look on his face, he flicked his wrist with the *sai* in his hand so fast Callista almost didn't see it slice her cheek. She hissed and jerked back as blood welled up and dribbled down her face.

"There. That's the right color I want to see on you," Gren-del said, turning her face roughly to better see the cut running from the bottom of her right jaw to her cheekbone. "I rather like this," he said, holding up the *sai* at an angle. "It cuts nicely. I also admire the puncturing, stabbing quality of it, the precision it affords, and these curved cross guards make for excellent finger holds." He took a step back and gave her a long look. She quaked under his penetrating gaze.

"You know, I am toying with your friends outside. Except for you, no one has yet to even kill one of my soldiers, only wounding a few with lucky shots." He leaned close to her and lowered his voice even further, barely a murmur.

"I could have them all dead within a matter of seconds," he snapped his fingers in her face, "with a single order, and fire would rain down from the sky and consume them. But let them waste themselves on an unyielding rock. It will make their defeat all the more demoralizing and crushing to the greater public. And then I will ... what is the word you use? Ah, yes, I will crucify you for all to see, and it will be glorious. It is my hobby, you see."

Callista said nothing. Though she held his gaze, tears streamed down her cheeks unchecked by her willpower.

He straightened with a malicious grin on his face and spoke to the two guards in their own tongue, turning and tossing the *sai* back on the table as he moved to the door.

"See you soon, darling," he said, pausing at the door. "Maybe some of your friends and your beloved Admiral will join you soon, but I will make sure you will see them later, in the Beyond, after I make an example of you," he said quietly, his red eye glittering as he grinned at her before leaving.

Callista squeezed her eyes shut and tried to make herself stop crying. It was hard to stop until the emotion ran its course, but now she needed to banish her tears and regain her cool head. Especially if she was going to get out of there and be any help to anyone.

Far easier said than done.

She twisted her wrists around in the cuffs, gulping air. Her wrists were slim but apparently not slim enough to slip through the cuffs, which felt like they were clamped over her bones, ignoring the flesh in between. Someone would have to release her.

One of the two guards sidled up to her a few minutes after Gren-del left, noticing her struggling in her restraints. Callista remembered Morticia's performance with the night guard and pondered if she could replicate it and get them to release her without getting hurt in the process. The guard grabbed her by the face and used his fingers to pry at the cut, making the skin pull apart and bleed afresh. Now in no mood to be flirty, she also discerned the act would be too suspicious, given the circumstances. She remembered her feet were free and kicked the guard with all her might in the stomach. He gasped and collapsed in a heap. The other guard dissolved in laughter. The first guard yelled at him and gesticulated at her, but the second just laughed and shook his head, wiping tears from his eyes. After regaining his breath for a moment, the kicked guard stood with a new fury in his eyes and punched Callista in the face. She coughed and spat out some blood and was punched again and again and again.

She desperately hoped Gren-del lied or was over-confident, and Hawkney and the rest were making more progress than he realized. Maybe they sent another group to breach the building a different way, and she'd be rescued soon, or they'd put a bullet in Gren-del's brain.

She spat out more blood after another blow caused her to bite her tongue too hard, but grinned when a sudden realization hit her. Pat-farfth and his loyalists had yet to join the fight. She giggled in anticipation despite herself and the situation, or perhaps because of it. In fury at her apparent response to his cruelty, the Alamy hit her especially hard, and she lost consciousness.

NEGEV CRACKED open the door and peered down the long hallway. Empty. He opened it further and motioned his three men through. They dashed in and spread out to the sides, weapons held at the ready. He followed them, closing the door behind him.

They walked down the hall cautiously, ready for everything. Negev glanced out the bank of windows. The flash and smoke of battle could clearly be seen, as could his men dressed in US Army uniforms to alert the Humans to their intentions. They were filing up several streets toward the fighting and would join it within moments, changing the tide of the battle.

"Unit three approaching target floor from north stairwell," the report whispered in his ear from his com earpiece.

"Unit two in south stairwell, approaching target floor," whispered another report.

Negev took a shaky breath to steady himself, his whole focus on the door to his office. They were a dozen feet away when it abruptly jerked open and two of Gren-del's men walked out, stiffening when they saw him, hands instinctively drifting to their holstered weapons.

"Stop," Negev said softly, and they froze.

Gren-del came out between them, stopped abruptly outside the door, and gave Negev a crooked smile.

"Human uniforms. Clever."

"You are under arrest for high treason, murder, terrorism, and I am sure I can find a dozen other charges," Negev said. "Lay your weapons on the ground. Slowly."

"I think it is *you* who will put them down," Gren-del said and lunged, jerking Pat-farfth out of the office and placing his weapon against Pat-farfth's temple as he held him tightly before him. "Are you willing to sacrifice your only kin to stop me?"

Negev pursed his lips, meeting his uncle's terrified stare.

Running feet sounded down the hall and the other two units who had come up the stairwells filed in.

"Drop the weapon!" one of them shouted.

"I should also mention I have your little girlfriend in my playroom. What do you think will happen to her if my men learn of my capture?" Gren-del grinned, never taking his gaze off Negev. "Well, what do you choose?" he said in that calm, smooth, unnerving voice.

"I think," Negev said softly, "you leave me no choice." He looked past Gren-del to his men and jerked his chin. Gren-del's grin widened, his eye gleaming in triumph. Negev moved his weapon to the side and started to slowly crouch, his men around him, standing down as well.

"Negev," Pat-farfth said, pain filling his voice.

Negev looked at his uncle, giving him a slight smile. He dropped to his knees, brought his weapon up with a jerk, and shot Gren-del in the head. Pandemonium erupted as Gren-del's men spun away and tried to get their weapons out, but Negev's men shot them down in a hail of gunfire before they could raise them. Pat-farfth stood stiffly in the middle, his eyes screwed shut.

Negev hurried up to him, stepping over a corpse, and laid his hand on Pat-farfth's shoulder. His uncle opened his eyes and stared into Negev's for a long moment. They hugged fiercely then as if they would never let go.

It was finished.

CHAPTER FORTY-SIX

Callista started to come to with the distinct sensation of falling backward. She jerked upright with a gasp and grabbed at the nearest thing, which happened to be a neck. Her eyes burst open, and she found herself staring into a pair of heterochromatic ones.

"Hello, my love, glad to see you are conscious," Negev said gently, smiling. Callista couldn't believe how good he looked compared to when she last saw him. The bruises on his face were almost dissolved and the cuts well scabbed over, as though they had been healing for weeks. She burst into tears again and buried her head in his neck and shoulder in relief. He kissed the side of her head and walked with her in his arms.

"My men are sweeping the building and arresting Gren-del's men as we speak, and the fighting in the streets is put down. It will all be over soon."

"Put down?" Callista asked, her head jerking up to look at him, a shot of fear stabbing through her gut.

"'Resolved' is perhaps a better word," he said, a smile tugging at the corner of his mouth. "You need not fear for your friends; we are firmly on the same side, see?" he said, nodding to his US Army uniform.

Callista heaved a sigh of relief and gazed around. "Where are we going?" she asked through her sniffs.

"To the medical bay to have you checked out. You have some nasty bruises and an equally painful-looking cut on your face."

Callista let her head fall heavily back on his shoulder, right on the cut Gren-del gave her, making her give a squeak and flinch as the pain rippled through her face.

"Easy, my dear," he murmured, stepping into the elevator with two Alamy guards who also wore US Army uniforms.

As they quietly rode down the elevator, Callista reached up to gently touch his lips, now almost healed compared to the split and bleeding specimens she had kissed not so long ago. He turned his head at her touch and smiled. "I am fine, truly, as you can see. The healing drugs from after my first ... misfortune were still in my system, in addition to a new dose I recently received. We will have your face patched up, too, in no time. He did not hurt you ... anywhere else, did he?" His words held a twinge of urgency, fear glinting in his eyes.

"No, he didn't stay long."

"Good," Negev said, relief permeating his voice.

"Where is he?" Callista asked after a moment.

"You need not worry about him anymore. He will never hurt you again."

The doors opened, and Negev walked to the nearby medical wing and set her on one of the beds. He sat next to her. One of the Alamgirian medics came over and gave her a cursory examination before pulling out some antiseptic solution and a few cloths. Handing them to Negev, he left to attend to someone else. Callista discerned most of the other patients were Human.

Negev began to gently wipe and rub at the open cut on her face, and it surprised her it did not sting. She stared at him while he worked, marking the slight color changes over the surface of his lavender and scarlet eyes respectively, as light hit them from different angles, the curve of his eyebrows, the lines of his nose and mouth. It was the first time she had ever truly looked at him.

When she was cleaned up to his satisfaction, Negev laid the supplies aside and smiled at her. "If your lip wasn't split right now, I would kiss you," he said.

Callista felt heat coming to her cheeks, and she couldn't contain a grimace. "Doesn't seem to be the right time or place," she said. "But I suppose a split lip didn't stop me last time when yours were considerably more torn up."

"Yes, but it was my split lip rather than yours. How do you say? The shoe is on the other foot this time?"

Callista gave a little laugh and rolled her eyes, making him grin.

"About that day, though," he said, scratching nervously at his chin and chewing the corner of his lip.

She gazed at him more sharply, but before he could continue, the medic returned with a handheld machine and began patching her cut and diffusing the bruises with its assistance. After he finished, he said a few words to Negev in their own tongue and left them.

"He has given you a clean bill of health. You are free to go if you wish," he said, standing. "I would have you stay here, though, until I am certain it is all over."

Callista opened her mouth to ask him to continue with what he was going to say but snapped her mouth shut and looked away. This wasn't the time—he was needed elsewhere. He hesitated at her response and sat back down, cocking his head in silent question when she glanced back at him.

"It's fine, go... I was going to ask what you were going to say a minute ago," she asked after a moment's hesitation, debating whether to brush it off until later or probe him now.

"Oh," he said, his gaze flitting around, everywhere but at her, and rubbed his palms on his pants. "Well, I lied to you."

"When?"

"When you came to rescue your friend, Niki. There was no hand scanner. I simply wanted you to go and leave me."

"Why?" she asked in disbelief.

"Once your friend was held with me, I expected you or some of your people to come. Pat-farfth had waited for an opportunity to rescue me ever since my arrest. We expected such an eventuality —Gren-del arresting me—but it would be rather beneficial to our cause if I did not stop it before it happened, making myself something of a martyr, like I mentioned to you.

"I anticipated, at some point, the Humans would make an attempt to either assassinate Gren-del or fight him in some manner, which would offer the perfect distraction for Pat-farfth to come and rescue me. Miss Nain's capture opened the perfect opportunity, and since Pat-farfth informed you of how to get into the building, he knew what to expect. He watched on the security cameras to see when you neared the room we were held in, and so came and released me moments after you left with your friends. We then slipped out the east side of the building while you escaped out the west, and we slipped back to one of my own loyal units, where we amassed a force to execute our own countercoup."

"How did you know my escape would succeed? Seems like a risky assumption."

"I did not know—it was an enormous risk, which is why I sought to return quickly in force, in case he held you. But since he did not immediately taunt me to encourage a rash mistake or demoralize me, I became a bit more confident you indeed escaped." He rubbed his upper lip pensively for a moment.

"I must admit, your people's attempt *en masse* on Gren-del so quickly was unforeseen, and perhaps a bit unfortunate on their part—I expected to lose many of my people in overtaking him, but have lost few, because his forces were spread thin fighting yours, and we arrived a bit late. I suppose I should be grateful, but I suppose more life was lost than should have been."

"I suppose so," Callista said, and took a deep breath. It wasn't such a bad lie, after all.

"You are not upset with me?"

"A little disappointed, perhaps. You seemed much more

heroic and self-sacrificing at the time, and I was worried sick I'd never see you again. But I'm not angry. I think."

"That is a relief," he said, standing. "I must go now. Stay here, yes?"

Callista nodded.

After he left, she gazed around at the people in the medical bay and regretted she had agreed to stay. Most were in rough condition: bloodstained, grimy, some missing limbs, most with red-stained bandages in various places, all looking exhausted or shell-shocked.

Two medics carried in a Human on a stretcher and laid him on a cot two down from Callista. She realized, with a gasp, it was Hawkney. He lay unconscious and wore a sizable bandage over his ribcage on the right side. His right arm was strapped to his body beneath the wound, and one of the medics lifted down a breathing mask from above him and placed it over his face. Callista sighed, relieved to see him alive and breathing. She watched his bare chest move up and down slowly, rhythmically, for a while before she glanced around again.

Her gaze fell on the bloodstained cloths Negev used to wipe her face, stained with both her own and the dark purple of dried Alamgirian blood. The memories of her violent encounter and the wounded, dead, and dying in the Chinese medical camp washed over her, and her encounter with Gren-del right on its heels. She curled up on the cot and wept until she dozed off and became barely conscious of the voices and movement around her, like a host of shades moving about in the mist.

CALLISTA WOKE up to someone stroking her hair. Her eyes fluttered open to find the lights dimmed and the atmosphere much quieter than before. She glanced up blearily to find Negev's eyes glimmering down at her. He smiled and tugged gently at her arm. She stood slowly and followed him out of the room, his hand still on her arm for support. He turned to look at her when they stood in the elevator.

"It is over. Everything and everyone is secure. The reign of tyranny is finished," he said, wiping the salt residue on her face. "They said you cried for a long time. What is wrong?"

Callista stared at her feet, twisting and tugging at her shirt. The doors opened before she could muster anything to say, and he led her down the hall and opened the door to a room, stepping aside for her to go in. It was compact, with a queen-sized bed, desk, couch, TV, and an adjacent bathroom—not much different from a hotel room. She remembered hearing that some of the guards and government personnel, like Negev, not only worked but also lived in the building. Hawkney chalked it up to fear of ambush or harassment by humans if they commuted, but perhaps it was more dedication than fear.

He followed her in, closed the door behind him, and turned her toward him.

"Talk to me," he said softly, putting his arms around her and kneading her back.

She took a few deep breaths while he quietly waited. "I killed one of your people," she finally murmured.

"One of Gren-del's men?"

"Yes," she said, taking a shaky breath as her airways tightened again. "I've never purposefully injured someone before, much less killed them." She sniffed, the tears returning. "It was like I suddenly became an animal. I never thought I could do something like that—it wasn't shooting, Negev, I—I stabbed him and sliced his throat!" She coughed as she lost control, burying her face in her hands and the whole bundle in his chest.

"I also killed someone today," he said softly into her ear after he let her cry it out for a few moments. "My people have been at peace with each other for centuries, and I never personally bore arms against your people in the takeover. It was my first lethal act of violence against someone too." He sighed before he continued. "I rather hoped I would not relish it, that I would be equally disturbed, but I cannot say that. I dreamed about killing him for days, ever since he threatened you, and it was a little sweet when I finally put an energy bolt between his eye and patch."

"You killed Gren-del?" Callista asked, raising her head to look at him.

"Oh, yes. We went to arrest him, but he would not go quietly, as I expected, and I was forced to kill him. His face will probably always haunt me, though."

Callista nodded and shivered in his embrace.

"Will you be all right?" he asked. "Shall I stay the night with you?"

Under normal circumstances, she would have given a definite "no," but the events of the day still haunted and upset her, and she wasn't sure she wanted to be alone. He sensed her hesitation.

"No crossing boundaries, I promise."

Still, she hesitated, nuzzling his shirt in thought.

"Here is what we will do," he said, pulling her away a bit so he could look her in the face. "I have some more things to oversee and attend to; I will not be able to sleep for a few more hours. I will come by when I am finished and see how you are doing. If you are asleep, I will leave. If you are awake and need my presence, I will stay. Yes?"

She considered it for a moment and nodded her head.

"Very well," he said and gently laid his hands on the sides of her face, careful of her stitches, and kissed her forehead.

"Sleep well, my love," he said and left.

She took a badly needed shower, scrubbing hard at her skin, trying to get rid of the sweat, smoke, grime, and blood of the day, though, like Macbeth's queen, couldn't seem to fully wash it all off. She finally gave up and slipped into the clean, cool sheets, hoping sleep would diffuse the memories and emotions and give her a few hours of sweet nothingness. But first, she needed to stop thinking about it all. She clutched her bathrobe around her and tried to focus on what Negev told her: how he escaped, how everything was fine now, how Gren-del was defeated and could hurt no one else again, trying to comfort herself.

Negev cracked the door open and heard Callista groan within. He stepped inside and heard the rustling of sheets and another groan. He pursed his lips and slipped his boots off, leaving them at the door. He lay on the bed, careful not to wake her, and rubbed her arm, whispered reassurances in her ear, and kissed her hair, cheek, and shoulder. She relaxed and quieted, heaving a sigh. Negev sighed, too. He shifted so he fit perfectly up against her and closed his eyes, hoping that he would not be plagued by nightmares as well. He took a deep breath, inhaling her musky scent, and smiled to himself. No, there would be no nightmares tonight.

CHAPTER FORTY-SEVEN

S he awoke in the morning to find the sunlight cheerfully streaming onto the floor, Negev's arm slung over her waist, and his face snuggled in between her shoulder blades. Though the weight of his body on top of the covers made it harder for her to snuggle closer, she managed to fit her body closer into his and pulled his arm more tightly around her like a blanket. He stirred when she began to move, and she could sense his smile before he kissed her neck and hugged her.

They lay in perfect peace until he raised his head with an effort and squinted at the clock on the bedside table beyond Callista. She followed his gaze: 9:12. He groaned and let his head fall back onto the pillow. After a moment, he struggled up onto his elbow and leaned over her to kiss her cheek.

"I need a shower, and then I have to go," he said.

"Okay," she said, giving him a sweet smile. He glanced down at the bathrobe she wore, and his mouth twitched in a frown.

"I will have some clothes sent up to you when I go."

"That would be nice, thanks."

Negev cleared his throat and ran his fingers through his hair, as if uncertain of what more to do or say, before turning and unbuttoning his outer blouse on his way to the bathroom.

Callista heaved a contented sigh, snuggled back into the pillow, and dozed off to the sound of the shower running.

Her clothes were delivered after Negev finished showering, and he laid them on the bed for her before taking his leave. She put on the clean underclothes, jeans, and white shirt emblazoned with the "I Love New York" slogan she rolled her eyes at.

She hurried down to the medical wing, hoping Hawkney was still there so she could check on him. People recognized and called out to her. She found herself visiting with the patients, and an hour later, she finally came to where she saw Hawkney.

She wasn't sure if she should feel lucky or unlucky when she found him not only there but awake. Even though he still wore a breathing mask and lay there with his eyes closed, his fingers drummed on the bed. She walked over to him and laid the palm of her hand on top of his restless fingers. He opened his eyes at her touch.

"Hi," she said softly and perched on the edge of the bed next to him.

"Where's Niki? And Loui? And ... everyone?" he asked in a hoarse voice.

"I don't know—shall I go find out?" Callista said, rising from the bed. He quickly reached out and snatched her hand, the sudden intake of breath under the breathing mask making him sound like a scuba diver.

"No, just ... stay for a minute before you do," he said, his eyes darting away and down in embarrassment.

"Okay," she said, sitting down again. "Maybe they'll be in to see you soon anyway."

"If they're alive," he said almost inaudibly.

"Yes," she said. "I think it's my fault you were almost killed, Hawkney."

"Not at all," he said shortly, not meeting her gaze.

"But if you hadn't seen me and frozen—"

"I still would have gotten shot."

"I doubt—"

"I still would have gotten shot."

"Okay," Callista said, letting it go and wanting to curl in on herself. She picked at her jeans, hoping he still wasn't looking at her. She couldn't resist glancing back up after a long moment of silence and found him staring at her.

"What happened?" he asked, untangling his hand from hers and reaching up to brush the bottom of her jaw near her new scar.

"It, it's nothing. Long story," she said.

His eyes narrowed. "What happened?"

"Really, it's nothing, I'm fine," she said, swallowing and looking at the other patients. She thought about going to talk to some of them. Hawkney must have read her mind and grabbed her hand again in a vice-like grip.

"What. Happened."

Callista swallowed hard and took a few deep breaths, trying to prevent herself from crying all over him because she would have to start at the beginning. "I killed an Alamy. In the medical camp." She paused to let it sink in.

"Good for you," he finally said and gestured to her face. "He do that?"

"No."

"Who did? The person who clocked you in the head?"

"No."

"Well?"

"Gren-del," she finally squeaked, hoping this wouldn't upset Hawkney and cause him to aggravate his wound.

His grip tightened on her arm, and he took a few deep breaths with his eyes closed. "And those faint bruises, too?" he asked after a moment.

"No, his henchman made those. But he's dead now, Gren-del," she continued on hurriedly. "Negev killed him himself."

"Who told you that?" he asked, looking back at her.

"Negev."

"And you believe him?"

"Oh yes," Callista said, remembering how emotional Negev

had become. Her tone of voice must have convinced Hawkney, because he relaxed back again.

"Where is he now?"

"Negev?"

"Yeah."

"Don't know. We parted not long ago. I imagine he has loose ends to attend to."

Hawkney narrowed his eyes. "So you ran into him this morning … ,"

"No, well, you see, what happened was … ," Callista felt the heat in her cheeks at the difficulty of explaining the situation without giving the wrong idea but saw it was too late when Hawkney rolled his eyes and leaned his head back and heaved a sigh. "It wasn't like that, Hawkney; he was concerned about me, so he just … stayed. That was all."

"Would that be all if the circumstances were different?" he asked, studying her.

"Absolutely," Callista said, crossing her arms. "I firmly believe in waiting for marriage."

Hawkney gave her a long, sad stare before looking up at the ceiling. "So I guess there's no chance for us, then," he said after a moment.

"You're like my big, protective brother, Hawkney," she said gently.

Hawkney sighed heavily and continued to stare at the ceiling.

An Alamy medic came over and used a hand scanner to check on Hawkney. He appeared pleased—he murmured to himself in his language and kept nodding his head and took Hawkney's mask off. Hawkney sighed and rubbed his face where the mask had been. He tried to sit up but the medic laid a hand on his shoulder, shaking his head. Hawkney nodded in understanding and laid back, remaining flat.

"So … , what exactly was damaged?" Callista asked.

"I think a lung was punctured. I lay there gasping like a fish out of water and drowning in my own blood until they came and fetched me."

The medic touched her shoulder and turned the screen of the medical scanner to her. She leaned forward to see the x-ray of Hawkney's ribcage, along with the bright metal replacement of a small section of one of his ribs and a chunk out of another. She exclaimed in surprise and turned it to show Hawkney, who raised his head up and squinted at the screen before groaning and letting his head fall back. The medic patted his shoulder, chattering and nodding his head before he moved on to the next bed.

Callista pondered whether she should go in search of Loui and Niki. Her eyes roved over the medical bay and landed on McCaffrey, sitting in a chair in the corner with a brooding look as he stared into space. She noted the bandaged arm.

"He was in the fight?" she said, gesturing to him with her chin.

Hawkney turned his head and squinted. "Yeah, was a sniper, because of his bad leg."

"You suppose he'll ever trust any Alamy?" she asked after a moment, noting the way McCaffrey stiffened when one of the medics passed close by him.

"Probably not," Hawkney said with a yawn.

"Will you?" she asked.

Hawkney gave a wan smile. "You're slowly convincing me, but I have a ways to go. What happens now, whether Admiral-Supreme-Commander keeps his promises, will largely determine that."

"Fair enough," Callista said. She wondered whether to keep talking to Hawkney or let him rest when a hand landed on the back of her neck and rubbed it gently. She quickly glanced behind her to find Negev standing there in his black Alamgirian uniform.

"Hi," Callista said. "You changed clothes. And back so soon?"

"Unfortunately, your Army green and tan does not complement my pallor," he said with a smile and touched his dusty, royal blue cheek. "And all is far better than I could have hoped. Admiral Tert-chon arrived late last night with a similar idea as ours—and an army—and cleaned up overnight."

"'Cleaned up?'" Hawkney asked.

"Yes. He made sure the wounded were cared for, the dead identified and prepared for burial, the guilty put in custody, and so forth."

Callista flicked Hawkney's hand, trying to get him to leave Negev alone. He gave her a quick glance before riveting his eyes on Negev again.

"What about the other admirals?" she asked.

"That is, indeed, the question still," Negev said, rubbing his forehead. "Those who are Gren-del loyalists—Can-let and Nunt-sir—will divide his territory among themselves, probably. Loc-mun is still a question. The first two are of the old guard and firm Gren-del supporters, while Loc-mun has always waffled between the sides on different issues. I purposefully gave Tert-chon the southern American continent in case it came to this. I did not want my only true loyalist far from me where we could not protect one another."

"Makes sense," Callista said. "So there still might be a war, despite Gren-del's demise."

"Indeed, I am afraid so."

Callista sighed and glanced back at Hawkney for a moment before turning her gaze back up at Negev. "What now?" she asked.

"Now, we inform the world of what has transpired and how this will affect life going forward. For example, I will have to promote someone to take Gren-del's place as regent, though I doubt the other two will allow it, as I said. I also hope to go on with my plans of integrating Humanity into the government on schedule, but if the war drags on, it must continue to be delayed," Negev said, running his fingers through his short-cropped black hair.

"If my opinion means anything despite my ignorance," Callista said slowly. "You should tell everyone what you have told us, that the admirals might squabble over the territory and continue what Gren-del started. You need them on your side now more than ever."

"You are right. You are absolutely right," Negev said, reaching down and taking her hand. "Which means I should ask the spokesperson of the heroes of this little uprising to stand by my side and support what I say."

"Gladly," Callista said, rising from her seat. She turned back to Hawkney and laid a hand on his.

"If I see any of the others, I'll ... ," she trailed off when she saw Hawkney wasn't paying attention to her but staring at something behind her. She turned her head to see Loui standing at the foot of the bed, holding a drooping dandelion with a doleful look on his face.

"All the florists were closed, *mon capitaine*," he said, gazing down at the limp weed. "But I did the best I could." He proffered the yellow puff ball toward Hawkney, unable to keep a smile from sneaking up the corner of his mouth.

"How touching," Hawkney said. "Did you think to bring me what I really want?"

"Only Morticia's best," Loui said with a grin, bringing out a bottle of booze from behind his back. "With her compliments. Foxy got hit in the leg, and works his way through her stock now."

"Where's Niki?"

"Tending to her beloved little brigade, last I checked," Loui said. "A few were hit, but most are just a little dazed and confused. But I've never seen a prouder mother."

"I bet," Hawkney said, sliding up so he wasn't exactly sitting but better for drinking alcohol.

"You're not supposed to be sitting up," Callista said.

"I'm not, I'm ... inclining," he said. "Give a man a break and let him have a drink."

"*Oui*, that's the truth," Loui said, sitting down next to him. "Hold this." He handed Hawkney the dandelion.

"What am I supposed to do with this?"

"Well, once you get drunk you can entertain yourself with 'she loves me, she loves me not,' despite the small petals."

"She loves me not," Hawkney grumbled, tossing the flower against Loui.

"I know," he said, working the cork out of the bottle with a grimace.

"What do you mean you know?"

"I've seen the signs and talked to Foxfire," he said, finally getting the cork out with a pop and gave Callista a wink.

She rolled her eyes and shook her head. "You're all gossiping old women," she muttered.

Negev put a hand on her arm. "Shall we go and prepare our statements for the press?"

"Of course," Callista said. "I'll catch you guys later."

The drinking duo acknowledged her but were more focused on the bottle.

She followed Negev up two flights of stairs and into a conference room. "So, am I just going to stand next to you, nod, and look pretty, or do you want me to do a little more than that?" she asked as Negev closed the door behind them.

He sighed, stepped over to her, and took her hands in his. "Though we are optimistic, I fear there will indeed be a war. How long it will be, how fierce and costly it will be, I cannot say. There is the distinct possibility this city will be leveled tomorrow, or a sniper's bullet may take my life—the future is full of unknowns, and I fear putting you in the middle of it."

"But there's no other place I'd rather be than by your side," she said, leaning toward him a bit more. "And whether I like it or not, I have become a symbol people look up to. I can't abandon them."

Negev nodded. "I am glad you feel that way because I would like to give you something of a promotion."

Callista raised her eyebrows and cocked her head, encouraging him to go on.

"I should like to make you my chief adviser or a sort of

diplomatic liaison. Not exactly my second in command—you would have no power over the military or to give any sort of orders—but I should like to consult you through most of my decision-making. Giving you an official title and a place at my side may grant you a measure of respect in the eyes of my people and yours."

Callista took a deep breath, weighing her options. She could either return home and get out of the whole mess now, which she knew her mother would prefer, or she could help a lot of people, like Butterfly and the other Renegades and so many more, by accepting his offer. She found she had no choice—her heart was in one place. "I accept," she said. "I just hope I am worthy of it and do not lead you astray."

"Well, if the office does not fit you, perhaps you will take another kind of role in future if all goes well?" he said, cocking his head, his eyes twinkling as a smile spread across his mouth. "My uncle does appear to have a gift of foresight."

"I suppose a man's wife does fulfill a similar role," she said, rolling her eyes at him. "But let's not get ahead of ourselves."

"No, of course not," he said, clearing his throat. "Relationships take time and should not be rushed into hastily. So," he said, changing the subject as he pulled out a chair for her to sit in before sitting himself. "I will briefly go over what has happened and acknowledge the continuation of hostilities. I want you to describe how our sides have united against Gren-del's tyranny and invite everyone all over the globe to join us."

"I can do that," she said. "Should we also announce my new status as your adviser?"

"Yes, I believe we should, to reinforce we have truly united our causes," he said, scratching his chin with the previous day's stubble upon it. "Your friend, Butterfly, is her name?" he asked, a smile tugging at his mouth and coming into his eyes.

"Yes, what about her?" she asked, realizing she should not be concerned because his manner was not one of the bearer of bad news.

"She brought the red dress for which you've become so famous. She said if you made any public statements you would need it because people might not recognize you otherwise."

Callista rolled her eyes, making Negev chuckle.

"It is in your room," he said, rising from the table. "We will set up the cameras in here, so come back when you are ready."

Callista stood with him and hurried out while he started rearranging the furniture. She passed through a lounge area adjacent to the bedrooms, and a chess set on the low coffee table caught her eye. She stepped over to it.

The black king sat in a corner with the white king next to it, preventing it from moving diagonally deeper into the board. The white queen sat next to the white king, preventing the black king from moving to one side. A white castle stood off to one edge, finishing the job. Callista smiled and continued to her room.

Checkmate.

EPILOGUE

He made it, and none too soon. Negev became instantly alert the moment he heard the first rustle, having not been asleep to begin with, and deftly slid out from under the covers without disturbing his wife, and reached the baby and soothed her before she could disturb her mother.

He glanced back at Callista, who still slept like a rock. Good. She needed all the rest she could get, between all she did to help him, care for their four-month-old daughter, and do so much more for so many others. He'd need to have yet another stern talk with her about saying no to people.

He stepped out of the bedroom and gently closed the door behind him, took the baby to the kitchen, pulled her bottle out of the refrigerator, and microwaved it for exactly eighteen seconds. She contentedly sucked on the bottle, watching him while he walked over to the floor-to-ceiling window of their penthouse apartment. He marveled at her eyes again. Unlike his solid-colored eyes, hers were like her mother's, with defined pupil and iris, but the irises were a deep purple, reminiscent of one of his own eye colors, complementing the pale blue dusting of her skin.

He felt warmth on his forehead and glanced up to see the sun beginning to peek through the forest of skyscrapers. It shone bloody red on the horizon. His old nightmare began to creep up on the edge of his memory, and he quickly gazed down at his beautiful daughter again.

She still stared at him. She paused in sucking on her bottle and moved it away from her face to better gaze at him with a soft but penetrating look.

Negev caught his breath. He stared into the eyes of his mother —it was as though he suddenly recognized her spirit in his daughter. Tears ambushed him and fell down his cheeks, and he remembered to breathe, a wave of longing washing over him. The baby blinked at him and reached up toward the glistening tears on his face, her hand catching the light of the morning sun as it flopped toward him, turning it red. She touched his cheek gently and moved it back and forth jerkily, wiping away his tears.

Then he realized. The red hands in his dream reached out not in anguish or for help, nor were they trying to signal a warning of disaster to come. They were reaching out in farewell and blessing.

He kissed his daughter on the head gently before laying the bridge of his nose and forehead against hers, his heart filled with more love and peace than he had ever known.

ACKNOWLEDGMENTS

Without the support and encouragement of my parents, this book, in all likelihood, would never have come to fruition. They can now think of themselves as patrons of the arts.

Without the honest, constructive feedback of my dearest friends Brittany Holbrooks and Cassie Zimmerman, I never would have believed in my capabilities enough to be brave enough to publish. Special thanks to Brittany for snatching it out of the digital trash bin at one point.

Thanks to my editors, Janet Lynn Eriksson and Janet Silburn, of Publish Authority, for their patience and dedication in editing this massive text. Thanks as well to the whole Publish Authority Team for their diligent and excellent work. Their expertise is greatly appreciated.

ABOUT THE AUTHOR

Though *The Red Days* is her debut novel, Katherine Ascalon has been making characters from different franchises work together to fend off robots and monsters from a young age. Characters she'd never met before introduced themselves to her and demanded she write about them during her pursuit of a BA in Creative Writing from Young Harris College, which was when *The Red Days* was first conceived. She has since received Honorable Mention for a story submitted to *Writers and Illustrators of the Future*, L. Ron Hubbard's Science Fiction and Fantasy contest.

Katherine lives in northern Georgia, where she works in customer support and enjoys making jewelry and playing video games. That is, when she's not wrangling dinosaurs, searching for dragon eggs in the desert, or figuring out cybernetic wings with new characters who sit themselves on the edge of her desk and say, "Hello."

For more about the author, visit her website at
KatherineAscalon.com

SCAN ME

THANK YOU FOR READING

If you enjoyed *The Red Days*, we invite you to leave a review online and share your thoughts and reactions with friends and family.

Publish Authority

Printed in the USA
CPSIA information can be obtained
at www.ICGtesting.com
LVHW011239071124
795952LV00013B/620